Ellen Rogers

JAMES T. FARRELL

Ellen Rogers

THE VANGUARD PRESS · NEW YORK

MANUFACTURED IN THE U. S. A. BY H. WOLFF, NEW YORK

TO
MARY AND ARTHUR PINCUS

Quelle âme est sans défauts!

from "Bonheur" by ARTHUR RIMBAUD

SECTION ONE

Chapter One

After dinner Ellen sat in the parlor with her father and her aunt, Mrs. Millen. Both of them seemed to her to be old and dead.

Ellen Rogers was nineteen, but often she could pass for twenty-five or twenty-six. Her figure was slim and well formed, and her bobbed blonde hair was luxurious. Her eyes were pale blue and expressive, often giving a suggestion of depth and intelligence. Her mouth was sensuous. She would twist it curiously sometimes when she smiled.

Ellen glanced around the room. She and her father had lived in this apartment on East Sixty-seventh Street for the last two years. But she was bored by it. Near her was the baby grand piano; her father had bought it, hoping that a new piano would induce her to go on with her music lessons. But she had abandoned them in second year at Saint Paul's. Practicing had been too much like work. Father had been disappointed, but he had adjusted himself to that. He always got used to whatever she decided to do. The furniture was new and practically without a scratch, but the room was not attractive. She could do almost anything she wanted to make her home more beautiful or attractive. What was the use? She didn't care to take the trouble.

Father was happy now, contentedly smoking a cigar after a good meal. He was sitting at her left. Her Aunt Alice was on the sofa, at Ellen's right. Mrs. Millen was a gaunt woman, who wore her thin brown hair plainly. She had a bad complexion, and her face was beginning to crack with small wrinkles; Ellen could see streaks of gray in her hair. Ellen thought Aunt Alice was very common.

3

Conversation had been casual, about nothing. Aunt Alice
was bossy with Father, always trying to push him and make
him do things. Father was easygoing. He did not want to know
too much about her because he was afraid. After all, she was
mature and developed now. Father should know about her! He
really did not know how much worry he saved himself by
leaving so much unsaid. Father was getting old. He was over
fifty, fat, with a shock of gray hair, a ruddy face, thick jowls,
and bags under his wistful blue eyes. There was something very
sad in Father's life. She didn't know just what it was. It was
something about her mother, who had died when she was an
infant.

"It's very nice and comfortable here. Tom, I'm sorry I have
to be going back home," Mrs. Millen said.

Ellen did not share her aunt's feeling. Aunt Alice had been
visiting them for two months. She had wanted the entire house
rearranged. She had not gotten on well with Mary, the maid.
She had wanted to know too much about Ellen's dates and
friends. Ellen was certain that her aunt knew what she really
thought of her. Usually when Aunt Alice had tried to talk
seriously with her, she had closed up like a shell.

"Jim needs me back home. That is my first duty, and I must
heed it."

Ellen felt sorry for poor Uncle Jim having had to live with
this woman for years.

"Alice, I'm sorry you have to leave us. It's been nice seeing
you, having you with us for so long," Mr. Rogers said.

Ellen kept looking around the room. She wanted time to
pass. She had stayed in tonight because it was Aunt Alice's
last night. If she'd made a date, her aunt might have raised
too much of a fuss. It was better to stay home and get her off
to Indianapolis.

"It's a shame Jim isn't located in Chicago. Then I could take
care of you two as well as Jim."

Thank God! Ellen told herself.

"Jim has never had enough gumption in him, not enough
get-up-and-go. Of course, he does well back home, but if he

had had more get-up-and-go to him when he was younger, he could have located here and done well." She sighed. "But that's too late now."

Ellen told herself that she really ought to make an effort to be pleasant to Aunt Alice. But she didn't feel like it. What a relief it would be in the morning to put her aunt on the train and watch it pull out of the station.

"I could be so helpful to you two if I lived here." Again Aunt Alice sighed. "But I suppose it is tempting God to complain. Still, when I'm back home I often worry about you two."

"You don't have to do that. Ellen and I are happy." Mr. Rogers turned a tender gaze upon his daughter. "Aren't we, Ellen?"

Assuming the insincere manner she often adopted toward her father, Ellen smiled in agreement.

"I don't deny that, Tom. But Ellen has reached the age where she needs someone."

Now it was coming. Ellen was not sure she would be able to control her temper, but she felt that she ought to. It was just too much effort to argue with Aunt Alice on the last night. If she lost her temper, Aunt Alice might become spiteful and suspicious and think it was her duty to stay on and guard over her niece's purity. Uncle Jim didn't really need her back home in Indianapolis. Why, he was probably glad to have her away.

"We three must have a serious talk." Aunt Alice paused. "I have been thinking a great deal about you and Ellen. I'm your closest relative, Tom, your only sister. I feel almost like a mother to Ellen. We must have a serious talk now before I go."

Ellen suppressed a yawn.

"The world has changed since we were Ellen's age. In this day and age a girl like Ellen needs guidance, a mother's guidance."

Father never talked much about her mother. When things like this were said, he didn't even seem to become sad. Hadn't he loved her mother?

"Tom, I don't at all mean that you haven't been a good father to her."

"I've tried to be."

"You have been, Tom. No one can gainsay that. But a young girl like Ellen needs the guiding hand and confidence of a mother, an experienced older woman."

"Oh, Aunt Alice, I can take care of myself."

"Of course she can, Alice. Ellen is a sensible girl."

"I trust her, too. But I don't trust the world. The world is full of pitfalls for a girl like Ellen."

If Aunt Alice only knew how boring it all was.

"Tom, I don't want to seem criticizing. I speak only for Ellen's own good. Since I have been here I have been observant. The world is different from what it was when I was a girl."

Could this homely old busybody have once been a young girl like herself? Ellen suddenly wondered how Aunt Alice had acted on the night when she had made the noble offering of her virginity.

"A girl was more guarded and protected in my day. And she had more to do. Girls nowadays don't sew, don't cook, don't do many of the things we used to do."

"I could sew and cook if I had to," Ellen cut in.

"Well, I tell you, Alice, I want to give Ellen the best I can give her. I don't think that at her age she ought to go and ruin her hands in a kitchen."

"Tom, I think that you are spoiling Ellen."

Ellen was not even listening to her aunt.

"Alice, I wouldn't say that. Ellen is a good dependable girl. She's not spoiled."

"I beg to differ with you, Ellen," the aunt said, focusing her eyes on her niece, "Ellen. some day you will thank me for doing this."

"Yes, Aunt Alice," Ellen said, almost in a manner of simpering innocence.

"Tom, suppose something should happen to you. You know, none of us knows the day, the hour, the minute."

"God willing, it won't. I've never felt in better health in years. I'm fit as a fiddle, Alice, even if I am a little bit overweight."

If anything did happen to Father, there was one thing that Ellen was certain about: she would not go to Indianapolis and live with her aunt. And she couldn't be forced to. She had reached the age where she was her own boss.

"I pray God that we will all have a long life. But one never knows."

Suppose one did die? What of it? Most people were dead on their feet anyway.

"If anything happened to you, what would Ellen do?"

"Of course, I would leave her provided for. I have some pretty heavy insurance, and then my business goes along pretty good. Yes, it's in good shape."

"Even so, life is more than a matter of money. Is Ellen prepared for the future? In this day and age a girl has to be educated, prepared. Ellen graduated from high school last June. What has she done since?"

"I think she'll go to college in the fall, and the year out hasn't hurt her. Ellen is still young."

"Yes, young lady, what have you done since you graduated from high school?" Aunt Alice asked Ellen.

"Nothing," Ellen answered, her casualness of tone almost insolent.

"Are you proud of that?"

"Now, Alice, Ellen is going to go to the University in the fall," Mr. Rogers said quickly.

Should she have it out with her aunt once and for all? Or should she let this pass? She was no child. She was more of a woman than her faded old crone of an aunt.

"She shouldn't go to the University. It's not the place for Ellen. It's not Catholic."

"Alice, that stuff won't twist Ellen's mind. She has too good a head on her shoulders."

"Tom, when you say that, you prove the very words I have just spoken. You are spoiling Ellen."

"Oh, Aunt Alice, I can take care of myself," Ellen interrupted.

"Of course she can," her father added promptly.

"Ellen, you are still a young girl."

"I can take care of myself," Ellen repeated.

"I hope to God you can. Why, even back home in Indian-apolis it's a fright what some young people are doing. Those college boys and girls with their wild parties, their drinking and cigarette-smoking—the newspapers call it flaming youth, the jazz age. Of course now, I'm not suspicious, but, Tom, do you know who the young fellows are who go out on dates with Ellen?"

"I know some of them. Fine young fellows. Take that Bill Northrup; you met him, Alice. He's all right. Serious lad, works steadily; he seems to me like a clean, decent young fellow."

Dad should only know. Dad would want to kill him. Bill didn't know himself yet. Well, he would. And if Aunt Alice knew of her condition the roof would come down and she'd faint. Aunt Alice was talking too late. Why wasn't she more worried? Well, she was sometimes. But Aunt Alice almost made her scream and shout out this news in defiance. And they were treating her as if she were a child.

"Of course, Alice, there is something in what you say." Mr. Rogers paused and grew moody. "And a girl does need a mother. But I did the best I could. And I'm proud of Ellen. Nothing is going to happen to her."

Her father turned to Ellen wistfully and bestowed a smile on her.

Sometimes she felt sorry for Father. She did now.

"Ellen, don't misunderstand me. I'm not old-fashioned. I approve of many modern things. I approve of giving girls a good education. But I think that young folks must know, must have ground into them, the simple old-fashioned truth that right is right and wrong is wrong."

"Aunt Alice, I know."

"Ellen, I am a frank person. I am worried about you. I don't like your wasting your time doing nothing. Why do we hear so much about flaming youth? Because so many young people have nothing to do."

"I'm going to college next fall," Ellen said.

Suppose there should be a scandal because of her condition? But there wouldn't be. If necessary, she would know what to do to get away from the scandal. And tomorrow, after going to the train with Aunt Alice, she'd walk miles and miles and miles. And tomorrow night she'd dance. Walking and dancing might have some effect.

"Tom, I wouldn't let her go to the University. It is in such places that young people are led astray. Why, you should have heard Father Shannon talk at our mission last fall about what is taught young people in some of these universities. There are good Catholic schools you can send her to."

"I've always heard that the University has good standing. Never having gone to college myself, of course, I'm not a hand for judging. But if Ellen wants to go there, I'll let her. She's too smart and sensible to fall for any of this atheistic stuff."

If she went to school, she'd go there. No more nuns for her. But what would happen by fall? This was only March. How would she look in the fall?

Her father and her aunt should only know!

"I'm warning you, Tom, don't let her."

Aunt Alice just blithely took it for granted that she herself should have no voice in determining what she did. If her mother had lived, would she have been like this? The mothers of most of her girl friends were pretty awful, or at least dumb. And this was all so boring.

She ought to tell her aunt to go to hell. But it was just as well to let her go on and have peace in the house. She was languid tonight. She didn't want to go to all the trouble of getting excited and yelling at Aunt Alice.

"There's lots of time to decide, Alice."

"You might as well decide now as later." She turned to Ellen. "Do you really mean it when you say you are going to college?"

"Yes," Ellen answered with utter lack of interest.

"You don't say so with enthusiasm."

"Oh, Aunt Alice, answering a question like that doesn't really call for me to get up and sing and dance, does it?"

"Ellen, you are really such a child, such a little girl," her aunt began.

Listen to what is talking, Ellen reflected.

"You must learn that life is serious, Ellen. You must begin to prepare yourself. And you must not be idle. Idleness breeds all sorts of mischievous things."

"Alice, she isn't going to be idle. To be sure, I don't want her to have to work like some girls do. But she's going to school, and she'll learn."

Ellen moved restlessly in her chair. Was this going to go on all night?

"Tom, you mark what I said. But now I have to go about my packing," Mrs. Millen said, rising.

Ellen realized that she should offer to help her aunt, but she decided not to.

"Alice, do you want Ellen to help you?" Mr. Rogers asked.

"No, no, I need no help," Mrs. Millen said, leaving the room.

"Ellen, your aunt means well, and what she says is right, but she worries too much."

Ellen nodded. She and her father did not speak for a while.

"Are you going out tonight?" he asked when Ellen got up.

"No, I think I'll read a book or do something."

Ellen went to her bedroom.

Mr. Rogers sat in the parlor playing solitaire from habit. He thought of Ellen. She was such a fine girl, and often when he looked at her he would become surprised because she was so beautiful. What his sister Alice had said was all well and good, but not necessary. Ellen was young and blooming, and he wanted her to make the most of her youth, without, of course, stepping over the line. But Ellen took after him, not after her mother, and he wanted her to be happier than he'd been when he was young.

Shuffling the cards and setting them out for a new game of solitaire, he remembered his own youth with bitterness. He had been young when he married Ellen's mother. He had never told Ellen about her mother, never told the girl that her mother had been such a bad and unfaithful wife. All those lies, deceits, subterfuges she had used in pulling the wool over his eyes.

Ellen had been only a baby when she died. He had not been sorry at her funeral. But that was all long ago. He scarcely ever thought about his dead wife any more. It was all so long ago, and now Ellen was grown into a stunning young lady.

He put a red jack on a black queen and went on playing.

Chapter Two

I

Ellen coldly resented Bill Northrup's manner toward her. Sitting opposite him, she took him in with a glance. He was a pretty boy, conceited, vain, empty. He was well built, neat, and he had curly light hair—just a pretty boy and nothing else. Why had she ever let herself get mixed up with him? She knew why. Boredom, and a couple of drinks at a party, and the feeling that, after all, what difference did it make? Yes, more than once she had gotten mixed up with someone, thinking the very same words—what difference did it make?

"Come over here and let me kiss your pretty face, Ellen," Bill said possessively.

"So, I'm a pretty face," she answered, smiling ironically.

"Well, is there anything wrong in my telling you that you're pretty?"

"No, but I wouldn't accuse you of being subtle in the way you reveal your intentions."

"Ellen, I didn't mean any offense. What's biting you tonight?"

"Nothing is precisely biting me," she said in a way to silence him.

He whistled the tune of a popular song.

"Like that song?" he asked as she continued unresponsive.

"Passing," she said.

"Not much to make you enthusiastic tonight?"

"No, tonight isn't one of my enthusiastic nights."

He went to Ellen and pulled her to her feet.

"Come on, Ellen, let's snap out of it," he said. He bent forward to kiss her.

Ellen pushed him away and looked at him in unmistakable disgust. Bill pouted with a defensive expression of anger.

"Sit down, Bill, I've got something to say."

He sat down. She faced him, cool and tense. He was nettled by the way she had just repulsed him.

"Say, what is this, a game?"

Ellen did not answer him.

"I suppose you're going to put on some weeping female act," he said with thick sarcasm. "Well, if that's on your mind, skip it."

Ellen again refrained from speaking.

"Well," Bill said with false bravado, not knowing really what to say.

"Thank you. Thank you for revealing yourself to me in your true colors. Now I see the *real* you," she said with noticeable restraint.

"Ellen, if there's something wrong, let's try and talk about it sensibly. Let's not fight."

"I suppose you look upon me as an easy mark," Ellen said, ignoring what he had just said.

"Well, not exactly."

"No, *not exactly*." She paused. "You couldn't have uttered more revealing words." Ellen's tone changed and she said, "Here, give me a cigarette."

Bill handed her cigarettes and matches. She lit one and returned them to him. With a cigarette in her mouth, she nervously paced back and forth, confident she was confusing him and putting him on the defensive. He watched her, disquieted. She continued walking up and down. She was satisfied with the way in which she had reduced this egotistical young man. She remembered how, at a party, Patricia Murray had made a splurge for him, talking in that boring way of hers, and how he had practically told her to shut up because all that came out of her mouth was drivel. He would never get away with treating her that way. No, he wouldn't!

"Ellen darling, tell me, is there anything the matter? Is there something I did? If there is, I'm sorry."

"Yes, it's something you did," she answered pointedly.

"Tell me, perhaps it can be—rectified."

She laughed sardonically, almost in hysteria. She sat down beside him, looking intently into his eyes. He turned away.

"I'll tell you," she finally said.

He gazed at her still bewildered.

"I'm going to have a baby, and you'll be its father."

He was speechless. His surprise changed to fear. He turned pale. Perspiration broke upon his forehead. He clenched and unclenched his fists.

"Well, don't you want to congratulate me?"

Still unable to speak, he became suddenly suspicious. He remembered stories he had heard of girls pulling fast ones over on fellows with this gag. He recalled a story that was supposed to have happened out in West Pullman, where a girl had tried to ring in some guy and he had gotten fifteen of his friends to testify in court that they'd laid her.

"What are you going to do about it, Ellen?" he asked anxiously.

She shrugged her shoulders. Trying to act calmly, he made much of lighting a cigarette.

"Well, isn't there something you can do?"

"I can have the baby."

"That would be a lot of trouble and dangerous. Why . . ."

"We'd have to get married, and you wouldn't like that—would you?"

"That isn't it, Ellen. We're still young, and I'm not making the kind of money that would—well, that would permit me to support you the way your father does."

She was deliberately quiet in order to do nothing to put him at ease.

"Or maybe I can get some medicine. A friend of mine . . . got a girl in trouble and he got this medicine from a drugstore. It fixed things up jake."

"I won't take any drugs. Before I do that, I'll commit suicide."

"Ellen, you wouldn't do that!"

The drama and splendor of a gesture of suicide suddenly appealed to her.

"Wouldn't I?"

"Ellen, we're in too much trouble for you to be talking nonsense."

"So I'm talking nonsense, am I?"

Ellen walked to the window slowly and deliberately. She turned and faced him.

"So I'm talking nonsense?"

Ellen stood by the French window opening onto the porch. Bill had watched her movements like one who has been mesmerized. Suddenly he leaped after her. Ellen was climbing onto the railing which extended around the porch. He grabbed her around the waist and pulled her down. She allowed him to lead her back to the parlor.

Bill closed the French windows and stood by them as if he were on guard. He breathed rapidly. While he had been rushing after her and holding her, he had been too excited to be fearful. Now a feeling of terror gripped him like a vise. He trembled, realizing that she had almost killed herself, thinking of how terrible it would have been, imagining how it might have caused a scandal.

Ellen stood a few paces from Bill, assuming what she conceived to be the manner of a caged tigress. Her heart was palpitating. The scene that had just occurred seemed unreal. She felt as if she were a spectator who had watched it. Suddenly a glow of satisfaction suffused her. She had carried through her gesture magnificently.

"Ellen?"

"Bill, don't ever try taunting me again. Don't dare me. I'm not afraid to takes dares."

"But, Ellen, I didn't mean to dare you," he said, struggling for words when he didn't know what he really wanted to say or what he ought to say.

Ellen sat down on the sofa. Bill sat beside her and held her wrist gently.

"You don't need to do that," she said, jerking her arm away.

"I'm not doing it for any reason you might expect," he said, confused.

She didn't answer.

"Ellen, I know you're a sensible girl. You were just excited."

"No, I was not excited. I was calm, much calmer than you were. Look, your hand is still shaking."

He flushed, looking at his right hand. He dropped it at his side. Ellen watched him, twisting her lips into a disconcerting smile.

"Ellen," he finally said. "Ellen, please let's talk this matter over. I'll be willing to do anything you want. If you want me to marry you, we'll go to Crown Point." He paused. Then he went on, a sudden note of resignation coming into his voice. "If you want, we'll go to Crown Point this minute." Again he halted a moment. "Or—if you want to try that medicine, I'll get it. Or I'll try and raise every cent I can if you'll have something done."

"Never mind. I'll take care of myself. I merely wanted to let you know, that's all."

Bill was unable to conceal his feeling of relief.

Ellen nervously jumped to her feet.

"Come on, let's go see a movie," she suggested.

II

"What a sappy movie," Ellen said.

They had walked most of the way from the theater at Sixty-seventh and Stony Island in silence. Now they were approaching Ellen's home.

"I liked it," Bill said as if he were mildly asserting his rights.

"What did you think it was, romance?"

"It was pretty good," he answered defensively.

He threw away his cigarette butt; a streetcar rumbled by.

"What did you like in it?" she challenged.

"Ellen, you know, I don't understand you."

"What's that got to do with why you liked the movie?"

"Well, it has."

"How? Pray tell me—*how*?"

Bill glanced across the street at Jackson Park. The foliage was dark, in shadow. It was a fine, clear night.

"Ellen, let's take a walk in the park."

"Is that suggestion a product of the movie? Couldn't we walk in the park like the lovers in the picture and be romantic?" she said curtly.

"Ellen, you're different from other girls. You're different from other people."

"Yes?"

"Now, I'll bet there wasn't another person at the whole show who didn't like the picture."

"And what does that make me?"

"Different. You're different."

She yawned.

"Ellen, let's take a walk in the park. It's such a swell night."

"The dew is out and it's damp. You might catch cold."

"You don't have any poetic feeling in you, do you, Ellen?"

"No, I suppose not."

Ellen turned and went up the small step before the entrance to her building. Bill followed her.

"Well, thank you for a very lovely time. Good night," Ellen said, holding out a limp hand to him.

"Ellen, I don't know why you're so sore at me."

"Why, Bill! I was saying good night and thanking you for a very lovely and pleasant evening."

"You don't have to be sarcastic."

"I'm not sarcastic."

"I can't make you out," he said, looking at her, puzzled.

"Well, good night."

Ellen left him. Bill followed her into the lower hall.

"Ellen, aren't you going to kiss me good night?"

"Oh!" Ellen exclaimed, as if she had been unaware that he had followed her.

She came closer to him, stood on tiptoe, and extended her left cheek. He embraced and kissed her on the mouth. She was unresisting, but cold and limp. She remained indifferent while he strove to rouse her.

"What's the matter, Ellen?"

She said nothing.

He released her, but searched her eyes vainly in search of an explanation of her conduct.

"Good night," she said again.

He put his arms around her, but she remained unresponsive. Dropping his arms to his side, he scowled.

"Why, you goddamn . . ."

"Go ahead, say the rest."

"I ought to sock your damn face in."

She stuck out her chin and met him with a determined and taunting gaze.

"You haven't the guts to hit me."

"Why . . ."

"Go ahead! You haven't the guts."

He unclenched his fists. She sneered.

"What a frost you turned out to be," he said feebly, in a weak effort to salvage his pride.

"Again, good night, Bill, and thank you for everything. You treated me like a gentleman."

She turned her back on him.

Bill left the hallway and strode along Sixty-seventh Street. He told himself that Ellen was nothing but a goddamn whore. Who was she to be putting on airs? Why, damn her soul, you'd think she had a right to act that way! The nerve she had, too, after he'd laid her. And he hadn't been the first, either.

And now she said she was knocked up! Would she make trouble for him? He swelled with pride. You had to be virile to knock up a girl. He forgot how she had just insulted his vanity. The situation he was in was dramatic. Look at what happened in her parlor. It would be quite a dramatic episode in his life, something to talk about boastfully after it was over.

But he was disappointed. He'd come to see her tonight hoping to get something, and she had practically slapped him in the face. Well, he'd pay her back for this with compound interest.

He tilted his hat at a rakish slant. He walked rapidly, taking decisive steps. Yes, if he could only pay her back and get out of this business. It was experience. It was living.

He stuck a cigarette in the corner of his mouth.

Chapter Three

I

Ellen came out of the park at Fifty-first Street and Grand Boulevard. She had walked all the way from home, going through Jackson Park and along the Midway, and then traversing the length of Washington Park. Would this exercise do any good? She was afraid not. Last Friday, after seeing her Aunt Alice off on the train, she had walked for miles. And that night she'd gone to a dance with Frank Dolan and she'd danced herself into weariness. But it had done no good. Again today she was walking miles, tiring herself out. Oh, if something would only happen. She didn't want to have a baby. What a mess it would be! Why, it might even ruin her figure for life. And think of it, having a baby whose father would be Bill Northrup. The very idea was too ridiculous for words. It couldn't happen. It must not happen! And yet it would happen unless something were done.

She felt so helpless. It was a warm and sunny day, lovely weather. But for her, it was the bluest of blue Mondays.

She wanted to ride back home, bathe, sleep, forget all about her problem, forget about it at least until tomorrow. But she couldn't go on forgetting about it every day. It was revolting that this should happen to her.

Ellen looked absently at the statue of George Washington on horseback guarding the entrance to the park while automobiles flowed steadily by it. Horseback riding might be good for her condition. She had started to go in for horseback riding, but learning was too much like work, and she had given it up. She had given up all sorts of things because they were too much trouble. She told herself that she did not have perseverance. And

20

what difference did it make? She answered herself with a careless shrug of the shoulders.

A man whistled at her. It wasn't flattering to have any man on the street try to pick her up. She turned her back on him and returned to the park, determined that she would walk home just in case this exercise might produce results. Pursued by the man's whistle, she walked rapidly, although she was almost exhausted. Aching muscles in her thighs rebelled against her movement. Her ankles were tiring, and she felt pains in them. Her eyes were heavy-lidded. Her mind was in a fog. She felt dusty, dirty. She got gravel in her slippers. Oh, God, why should she be in such a condition? Why should she have to be doing this? If this were happening to one of her classmates from St. Paul's, it would seem like a joke. But no, it wasn't a joke.

Ellen found a deserted bench in the shade and sat down. All around her she heard the birds as some vague and distant chorus. She took off her slippers and emptied them of gravel. She rubbed her ankles and the soles of her feet. She yawned. If she didn't look so awful, if she weren't so dirty and tired from her long walk, she'd go across the park and visit Saint Paul's, see the girls she had known, and talk with the nuns. It would be humorous for her to go back to Saint Paul's today in her condition. She could see Sister Michael. She could act sweet and innocent. But she was sure Michael didn't think she was innocent. Michael had always been nosey concerning her and her dates. Ellen laughed, recalling how Sister Michael had once searched her pocketbook and found rouge and powder. Sister Michael had acted horrified. How horrified she would be if she knew of her condition. Well, unless something happened, Sister Michael would know in time. It was disgusting to be a female and to have such things happen to one. She was not the first girl who found herself in this way. What comfort was that? None, none whatsoever.

She looked off at the green grass. It was all senseless. Life was senseless. Having to walk for miles like this was stupid. And all because she just didn't give a damn and hadn't said no to Bill Northrup at a party.

She walked on, fighting with her growing exhaustion. Coming to the duck pond just inside the park at Fifty-third Street by South Park Avenue, she stopped.

Suppose she had her baby? Would she some day be a mother coming to a place like this? How horrible it would be. She couldn't fancy herself doing that. What a life it would be for her. And then to go home and cook supper for Bill. Yes, what a boring prospect. What a dull scene. Think of her, a little mother, as contented as a cow, sitting here while her child played.

She turned away and walked as fast as she could. She was too fagged out to think, even to complain to herself. Her mind wandered, floated through a vague series of memories, impressions, hopes, and she was scarcely aware of what she was thinking or of what images were passing through her consciousness.

If this walk would only bring her around. If it did, Bill would be happy. That would be the one thing to spoil her pleasure. She didn't want to see him released from worry. He was such a prig, such a ninny. At times she almost wanted to have the child just to cause him embarrassment. She had contempt for boys like Bill. And yet she had not repulsed him. Oh, was she a fool!

She had to slow down. Her legs were almost refusing to carry her. Dogged, determined, she continued on her way.

II

"Bill, this is Ellen," she said, speaking into the phone, her voice sounding wan because of her physical condition.

"Oh . . . oh, hello."

"Bill, I have to see you."

He hesitated before answering her. Ellen grimaced with pain.

"I'm lined up pretty much this week."

"I have to see you. Come over and see me tonight," she said, speaking in a voice that was tired but insistent.

"Ellen, I have a date," Bill said apologetically.

"You have to come. It's important."

"How important?"

"I can't discuss it over the telephone. Isn't it enough for me to tell you it's important?"

Ellen waited, and there was no immediate response. Her cramps had gone, but she was very tired. She smiled, thinking that, yes, she was going to give him the kind of buggy ride he deserved.

"Bill, I must see you tonight. Come at eight-thirty."

"But, Ellen, tell me . . ."

"I can't discuss it over the telephone. Are you coming tonight or not?"

"I was just thinking, Ellen . . . couldn't . . ."

"Bill, I take it you don't want to see me. All right, I'm warning you—you come tonight!"

Ellen hung up while Bill stuttered. She remained seated by the telephone in the hall, pleased, a smile on her haggard face.

The telephone rang.

"Mary! Mary!"

Mary came down the hall as the ringing continued.

"If that's for me, say that I can't come to the phone. If it's Mr. Northrup, say that I expect him here at eight-thirty tonight."

"Yes, Miss Ellen."

While Mary answered the call, Ellen walked away slowly. She heard the maid carrying out her instructions.

Ellen dropped onto her bed. She lay there, listless. Suddenly her hands went to her abdomen. She was gripped with severe cramps. She relaxed after they had passed. Perhaps it was the long walk she had taken yesterday. She was so happy that her worry was over.

"It was Mr. Northrup, and I told him what you said. He'll be here tonight."

"Thank you, Mary."

"Miss Ellen, can I make you a cup of tea?"

"No, Mary, I'll be all right. I'll lie here and try to sleep."

Mary left.

Ellen closed her eyes, hoping to sleep. When Bill came tonight she wanted to feel fresher than she did at this moment.

If Bill had not acted like such a coward, she wouldn't do what she was planning.

Her face suddenly contorted with pain. She clenched her fists. Then she lay relaxed and quiet.

III

Ellen felt more rested. She was no longer in any pain. She had dressed and fixed herself up carefully. She wanted to look as beautiful as possible, and she was wearing her new dark-green chiffon dress; it brought out her figure, and she knew she looked appealing.

The doorbell rang. She gave her hair a final pat and looked at herself in the mirror. She had circles under her eyes, but with make-up they weren't so noticeable.

"Mr. Northrup, Miss Ellen," Mary said at the door.

"Tell him I'll be right in."

Ellen sat on the bed. She was ready, but she would let him sit alone and wait for about ten minutes. It would make him nervous. She calmly thought of how she would play cat-and-mouse with Bill Northrup.

IV

Ellen stood at the parlor entrance; she frowned. Unaware of her, Bill was looking out the window. He heard her as she stepped forward and he wheeled around.

Ellen spotted at a glance that he was distraught and worried.

"Oh, hello, Ellen."

She smiled.

"Gee, I never saw you looking so beautiful."

She shrugged her shoulders and sat down on the sofa, smoothing out her dress.

Bill was at a loss for words. He lit a cigarette.

"Sit down. You're nervous," she said calmly.

"No, I'm not. Me, nervous? No, not at all," he answered, dropping into a chair opposite Ellen; he crossed his legs, took a puff on his cigarette, and tried to appear at ease.

"I'm glad you're not nervous. I don't have any good news for you."

He leaned forward, his face drawn and tense.

"What's the matter?" he asked anxiously.

"You know what's the matter."

"Nothing's happened?"

She shook her head from side to side.

"What do you think we ought to do?" he asked, speaking slowly.

Ellen did not answer. She sat as if she were deep in thought. Bill leaned forward, resting his elbows on his knees and sinking his chin in cupped hands.

"Give me a cigarette," Ellen said casually.

He dug in his coat pocket for his pack.

Ellen saw that he was waiting for her to talk. She puffed on her cigarette and watched the smoke drift to the ceiling.

"Don't you think that something should be done?"

"What do you think?" Ellen asked.

"Well, I tell you what I did. I bought this medicine," he said, handing her a small bottle that was wrapped in white paper.

"Suppose it doesn't work?"

"But it might. If it does, then everything is settled."

"How do I know but what it will harm me? It might be dangerous to me physically."

"It couldn't do anything worse to you than having a baby would. And it might save your reputation."

"What do you mean—my reputation? What's wrong with my reputation?"

"I didn't mean to criticize you, Ellen."

"I don't know if I'll take this medicine. It might hurt me."

"Well, you have to take something. You've got to do something, don't you?"

"Why?"

"Well, you do. You can't just sit and wish yourself out of this . . . this trouble."

"I can have the baby."

"But it will be a scandal."

"Suppose it is. Who will be most affected, you or me?"

"But, Ellen, I can't stand by doing nothing and let this happen to you. Think of what it'll mean."

Ellen got up and walked back and forth across the room.

"Suppose I take this medicine and become terribly ill? Suppose I have to go to the hospital?"

He turned pale.

"Maybe you won't," he said feebly.

"Suppose I go to a doctor and I get killed?"

"We don't have to think of such things, do we, Ellen?"

"Why?"

"They might not happen."

"And they might."

He didn't say a word.

"You don't have much to contribute to this discussion, do you, Bill?"

"Ellen, I'll do anything you say."

"What do you mean, *anything*?"

"Why, anything to get us out of this trouble."

Ellen stood over him.

"The only thing you can do is marry me."

Bill was taken aback. He looked up at her, puzzled, but he could not meet her eyes. He glanced aside.

"All right, Ellen—if you say so," he muttered.

"You say that with boundless enthusiasm."

He hesitated before answering her:

"Well, it took me by surprise."

"And after recovering from your surprise, I must say that you welcomed the idea with open arms."

"I do. I'm ready. If you say so, I'm ready. Only . . ."

"Only what?" she asked, dropping down beside him on the sofa and fixing critical eyes upon him.

"I thought you might take this medicine first."

"And if it doesn't work successfully?"

"If everything else fails, then . . . then we get married."

"Now, isn't that a romantic proposal?"

He leaned forward, his hands in his lap, his eyes fixed vacantly on the opposite wall.

Ellen jumped to her feet.

"I don't know what to do," she said broodingly as she again paced up and down the room. She watched him out of the corner of her eye and noted that he was anxiously following her movements. She sank into a chair and sighed.

"Bill, what do you really advise me to do?" she asked, her tone becoming almost childlike.

"Well, now, let's see," Bill replied slowly and seriously.

"You're going into a huddle with yourself, aren't you?"

"No, not exactly."

"Then what are you doing?"

"Ellen, I'm thinking."

"That's interesting. Go ahead."

"Ellen, this is serious."

She waited for him to go on. Confused, he did not know what to say.

"Bill, you aren't acting decently toward me."

"How come? You know that isn't so."

"You hem and haw. After all, you're responsible for my condition and you won't accept your responsibility.

"Have I said that I wouldn't?"

"Not in so many words. But you've made it plain in other ways."

He stood up.

"All right, Ellen, I accept my responsibility."

"Bill," she said.

She went to him and kissed him.

v

Ellen sat beside Bill on the sofa. Her hair was mussed.

"Please, Ellen."

"Father might come in and catch us."

"Can't we hear him in time if he does?"

Ellen slid off the couch and straightened her dress. She shook her hair back. She looked at Bill, who was watching her, his eyes lit with desire for her.

"No, Bill, not now. I can't."

He stared at her, disappointed.

Ellen left the parlor. When she returned, her hair was combed and there was fresh make-up on her face. Bill's manner was sheepish.

"Bill, I'm very tired. Will you call me in the morning? We'll see each other tomorrow night and arrange when we'll get married."

Nodding, Bill got to his feet slowly. They walked to the front door and stood facing each other. Bill acted as if he wanted to tell her something.

"Bill, you're not sorry you decided to marry me, are you?"

He gulped.

"No," he said.

"You'll like the baby?"

"I guess so."

"You only guess so?"

"Well, I haven't had it yet."

"You haven't had it?"

"I didn't mean that exactly."

"Good night, Bill."

She kissed him good night and closed the door.

Ellen went to the parlor window beside the front porch, opened it, and leaned out to watch him depart. He emerged downstairs. He seemed to be walking with his shoulders slightly hunched. He lit a cigarette and disappeared from sight.

What a poor goof, Ellen thought.

She closed the window and went to the sofa, curling up on it comfortably. If Bill knew what she was doing to him, he'd punch her. If a man punched her, she'd tear his eyes out if she could, even kill him. But she couldn't say that Bill was a man. He was a conceited cad, and she was going to take the starch out of him. She was going to teach him the kind of lesson he needed.

Ellen yawned. She was very tired. She went sleepily to her bedroom.

Chapter Four

I

Idling over a cup of coffee at breakfast, Ellen wondered how soon Bill would phone her. He had better call soon if he knew what was good for him.

It was really a fascinating game she was playing with him. She had him under her thumb. She gained a sense of power in herself by what she was able to do to Bill. It was going to be fun. Yes, without knowing it, Bill was going to relieve the ennui of the days immediately before her. Life did get dull sometimes, and some means had to be found to escape that dullness.

Maybe she ought to go to the University in the fall. But every time she seemed to be coming to this decision, she would decide that perhaps she wouldn't go. Well, she had plenty of time in which to make up her mind.

Bill had his nerve taking so long to telephone. She didn't feel like waiting in all morning just for him to call her.

She left the table.

II

"Ellen, you don't show. Nobody would even guess about your condition just from looking at you," Bill said.

They were settled in Ellen's parlor. She watched Bill studiously. He was a poor goof.

"Yes, I can say absolutely that you don't show," Bill said as if this statement were a genuine source of hope and encouragement to both of them.

"I'm wearing a girdle. And anyway, it's still too soon for me to show."

"Yeah, I understand that. I was only remarking on the fact that to date you don't give your condition away."

"In due time I'll be showing."

"Did you take the medicine I left with you?" he asked.

"I'm not going to take a chance with it."

He assumed an injured air and was momentarily silent. Ellen fixed her eyes on him. He avoided her gaze.

"Bill, suppose I should take that medicine and suppose it should ruin me for life. I can't take a chance like that."

"I understand how you feel. But I do know that there are cases where girls took it, and it had its effect and didn't seem to do them any real harm."

"Even where it seems to do no harm, it might still, but you might not learn about it until years later," she said.

He had no answer. She lit a cigarette and puffed on it.

"Anyway, we have settled the whole issue."

"What did you say, Ellen?"

"I said that we settled it all. We have, haven't we?"

"What's that? Settled what?"

"Our problem."

"You mean . . . ?"

"We have to make plans. That's what we have to do, isn't it, Bill?"

"That's why you said you had to see me tonight?"

"We can't delay too long. If we do, people will count how many months we've been married when our child is born."

"They would, wouldn't they?"

"Of course, we can say we've been secretly married for several months. We'll just say we went to Crown Point."

"Yes, we could do that, couldn't we?"

She heard the key turning in the lock. She quickly handed him her cigarette. He puffed on it.

"Hello, Father," Ellen called.

"Hello! Hello, Ellen, are you alone?" Mr. Rogers asked, entering the room.

"Bill's here, Father."

Bill rose, grinning, a smile that seemed almost to have been pasted onto his face. His manner became formal.

"Hello, Bill, how are you?"

"Fine, thank you, Mr. Rogers."

They shook hands. Bill's grip was firm, calculated to impress Mr. Rogers.

"Anything new, Ellen?"

"Nothing, Father."

"Well, I won't interfere with you young people."

"Father, stay with us. You're not interfering."

Mr. Rogers sat down.

"Bill came over and asked me to go to a movie with him. He didn't have anything to do tonight," Ellen said.

"Well, why don't you go, Ellen?"

"Oh, I don't know. I've seen a lot of movies of late and I just didn't feel like it. So we were just sitting here, talking about nothing in particular," Ellen said, watching Bill from the corner of her eye; he seemed to wince for an instant.

"We still have time to make a movie," Bill said.

"No, we haven't."

Mr. Rogers looked at his watch.

"Hm, I doubt it. You might just have time to catch the last show, and then again you mightn't," he said.

"No, we couldn't make it now, Father."

"Well, I wouldn't be so sure. You might just catch the last show."

"Oh, we'd have to rush too much," she said.

"Yes, you would have to rush," Mr. Rogers said.

All three of them lapsed into a short silence.

"Are you still working for the Poynton Coal Company?" Mr. Rogers asked.

Bill nodded.

"There a future in it for you?"

"Oh, yes, yes, I think so," Bill said.

"Good. What a young man ought to do nowadays is to find a job with a future in it, and when he's found such a job, he ought to stick to it, plug away at it as hard as he can. I wish I was a young man in this day and age. Of course, I've no complaints, and I think I went into the right thing when I went into real estate. But there's no comparison between the oppor-

Chapter Five

I

Ellen was waiting for Bill.

She had been nervous all day. Eating alone because her father had not come home this evening, she had quickly bolted her food and left the supper table at seven-fifteen. Since she had told Bill to come at nine o'clock, that meant she had faced the prospect of passing an hour and forty minutes with nothing much to do. She had decided not to dress immediately after supper, because if she did, then she would have had to sit and watch the minutes pass and almost listen to the seconds ticking away. Nothing made her more restless than to be alone and have to sit and wait for time to pass. And she knew that restlessness was the curse of her life. That was why her actions were often unpredictable, unpredictable even to herself.

She had played the victrola without listening to the music. She had idled at the piano, starting one tune, changing to another, and then abandoning that. She had drifted out onto the front porch and stood looking at the Jackson Park golf course opposite. Then she had gone to her bedroom and had nervously smoked two cigarettes, throwing each of them away half-smoked. She had undressed, put on a bathrobe and gone to bathe. With her body comfortably immersed in a tub of luke-warm water, she had been able to relax. Her mind had become lost in revery, and she had seemed to be neither asleep nor awake. From moment to moment she had been unaware of the thoughts and images that had just slipped through her consciousness. She had gotten out of the bathtub like a person awakening after a restful sleep. Humming, she had dried herself with a thick towel and had felt warm, cozy, lassitudinous, sensuous. Returning to her room, she suddenly had discovered that it was only five minutes to eight, and that she still had to wait more than an hour.

Sitting on the bed, Ellen had suddenly pondered the question—did others see through a person? She saw through so many people. She saw through boys when they tried to impress her with little tricks, dodges, innuendoes, indirect remarks. If she could see through them, then couldn't they see through her? She had wondered about this question. Was she as clever as she sometimes thought herself to be? She had told herself that perhaps she wasn't. Perhaps boys caught on to little tricks of hers. But they didn't act as if they had. She had decided that men were usually not very smart in dealing with women.

She had begun to get ready, first combing her hair carefully and slowly. And she had thought that if she were the daughter of a millionaire, she would have all sorts of help in dressing and she would have been getting ready to spend an evening with somebody other than Bill Northrup. And then she had reflected that she didn't have to be a millionaire's daughter to be having dates with persons better than Bill. It was this particular business with Bill. She had thought about this matter, sitting before her dresser, combing her hair and applying make-up to her face. How long would she allow it to continue? Should it be kept going much longer? Should she tell him this evening? If so, how? Should she say to him that she'd simply been making a fool out of him in order to teach him a lesson? Or should she spare his feelings and say that she'd come around since seeing him yesterday? But why treat him so lightly?

Suddenly she had dropped her hands to her side and looked in the mirror to ask herself whether or not she couldn't find better things to do with her time than to toy with Bill this way.

And she had answered her own question with a shrug of the shoulders. She had continued getting ready, polishing her nails after putting on make-up and penciling her eyebrows. And then she had selected a print dress which fell loosely and softly, giving her figure a free and easy grace. And she had thought that she was going to all this trouble merely for an evening in the parlor with Bill.

And now she was ready. She sat in the parlor, waiting for him to arrive.

Yes, was her game worth the effort?

Ellen waited for Bill.

II

"Tell me, Ellen, how do you feel?" Bill asked.

"Oh, I'm all right," she answered carelessly, glancing aside.

"I mean, how do you feel?"

"But I told you. I feel all right."

"What does that mean?"

She pretended not to understand him.

"How do you feel?" she suddenly asked.

"Oh, all right."

"What does that mean?" she asked sarcastically.

"I'm sorry, I didn't mean it that way. You didn't understand me, Ellen."

"No, I'm sure I didn't."

"Don't be sore. It wasn't your fault you didn't understand me."

"I'm sure of that."

"What I mean is, did anything happen?"

"Oh, that!"

She became pensive. Perceiving the change in her, Bill's face took on an anxious, brooding expression. Neither of them spoke.

"My God, this is a morgue!" Ellen said, jumping to her feet and pacing about the room.

Bill was disturbed by her restless movements.

"We can't delay any longer," Ellen said energetically.

"No, we can't," Bill answered, almost as if he were in a trance.

"Tomorrow we've got to do something. Can you get off work tomorrow?" Ellen asked, sitting down beside him.

"Maybe . . . that is, perhaps I can if it's absolutely necessary."

"It is absolutely necessary."

"Yes?" he asked, anxious, leaning forward.

"Tomorrow. . . ." She paused and let her eyes wander wistfully about the room, "It's going to be funny."

"What?"

"Oh, leaving this house and Father. Living with you. Having a baby. Being a mother as well as a wife."

He was uncomfortable. Not knowing what to do, he lit a cigarette.

"It makes me sad. I suppose all girls are sad on the night before they become brides," she said, speaking as though to herself.

"I don't know much about it," he said, puffing nervously on his cigarette.

"We have so much to do," she said.

"Huh?"

"We have to find a place to live in."

"Do we have to do it right away?"

"If we don't, it is going to look even more odd when I have a baby."

"When will you begin to show?"

"What?" she asked, pretending not to have heard him because of absorption in her own thoughts.

"When will it be noticeable?"

"Oh, I was thinking. Forgive me. I think it will be showing very soon." She paused. "But, Bill, you're not afraid, are you?"

"Me? No."

"If we're not afraid, we'll manage . . . somehow."

"Sure we will! Certainly! It's going to be a little bit tough, but then others have done it, and . . ."

He stopped talking. He looked at the smoke trailing off the cigarette in his hand.

"Bill, how much money do you make?"

He glanced at her, rather shamefaced.

"I'll have to know if I'm going to be a housekeeper."

"Twenty-five a week."

"We'll have to be thrifty, won't we?"

"I suppose so."

"But we will. You watch. I'll learn to cook, and I'll cook you wonderful meals when I learn how."

"When are we going to let your father know? And my folks?"

"We can't let them know until after we get married tomorrow. Then we'll tell them." Her manner changed. She appeared to be almost frightened. "Bill, I'm afraid to tell Father. You'll have to do it. . . . Poor Father, I don't know how he'll take it."

She seemed to be very pensive. Her mood conveyed itself to Bill. He was glum.

"Anyway, we will make it fun."

"What?"

"We'll make everything fun. Bill, have you ever looked for an apartment?"

"No, I never did. I've always lived with my folks, and my mother, she always tended to such matters. I never bothered."

"Bill, now you're going to be a man on your own, with responsibilities and a family. You'll have to do things. And one of the first tasks will be to find a place. . . ."

Bill nodded his head in agreement, like a man forced to acquiesce in the inevitable.

"We'll begin looking right after we get married," Ellen said.

"Where are we going to go?"

"Why not Crown Point?"

"All right."

"We'll have to get a ring."

"How much will it cost?"

"I don't know. But you wouldn't want me to have a cheap wedding ring, would you?"

"I hadn't thought about that."

"You wouldn't, though, would you?"

"No. When do we have to get it?"

"We ought to have it for the ceremony tomorrow."

"Where do we go to get it?"

"A jewelry store, where do you suppose you'd get one?"

"What I meant is, what store?"

"We'll find one."

"Well, we don't want to spend too much. After all, we've got to have some capital to get started on, don't we?"

"Yes, we do. And I don't have any money. We can't count on a cent from Father. He's not doing too well, and even if he were, he wouldn't give us a penny, considering the circumstances under which we are being married."

Bill sat watching her, hopeless, his shoulders sagging. All of his spirit was gone.

"I have a little money in the bank," he said lifelessly.

"How much?"

"Not so much. A little."

"You had better tell me. I have a right to know, haven't I?"

He gazed at her, puzzled, as if he were trying to think his way through a difficult and perplexing problem.

"I suppose so. Yes, I've got a hundred and forty dollars saved up. I was saving it to buy a car, or else, next winter, to take a couple of weeks off and go to Florida."

"You aren't sorry, are you?"

"No. No, of course not."

"We have to do so much, get so much. We have to get dishes, silverware, furniture, things for the baby," she said.

"Well, we'll have to do it, I guess. I never thought that so many things were involved in all this."

"How do you think people set up a home? It takes a lot of trouble. It's just like a man not even to realize what is involved."

"Well, of course, Mother always managed those matters and I never thought of them."

"You never thought?"

"Well, it's natural that I never thought."

She did not answer him. He waited for her to speak.

"We are like two people at a funeral. It's a fine way to spend our wedding eve," she said.

Bill didn't answer.

Chapter Six

I

Bill waited in front of the drugstore at Sixty-third Street and Stony Island Avenue. It was a quarter to ten, exactly the time he and Ellen had arranged to meet, and she ought to be along any minute. He had gotten to the bank just as it had opened and he'd drawn out all his money except one dollar. He had never walked around with so much money of his own in his pocket as he had this very minute. To be exact, there was one hundred and forty-four dollars and forty-eight cents in his pocket. But considering his present circumstances, this was damned little money. When he dug his hand into his pocket and felt the thick wad and thought that he was rich, he knew that he was only kidding himself.

Bill casually observed the people who were passing on the corner. Three girls, bound for Park High down the street, walked by within two feet of him. They were so young, just the age when a girl begins to bloom. He looked after them nostalgically, wishing he was in high school again. He thought of how free he had really been in those days. But those days were gone. He watched the girls crossing Sixty-third Street. One of them was blonde and especially attractive. She had very neat legs, and he took one final glance at them. Yes, those days were gone forever. Why, even the life he had been living of late, that, too, was now in the past. No more irresponsibility, no more playing around, no more dates on successive nights with different girls.

He peered down Stony Island Avenue to see if Ellen were coming. In a few minutes she would join him. Then they would look for a jewelry store and buy a wedding ring. After that, they'd take the train to Crown Point. It was difficult for him to realize and believe that he was actually going to be married. It seemed too strange for him to accept. He felt as though he were dreaming. But the noise and clatter of the street cars and automobiles on the street and of the elevated trains overhead convinced him that he was awake. Decidedly, it was all real.

Why didn't he just blow? He had enough money with which to strike out by himself. He could live carefully and look for a job. He would be able to make a new start, to begin an entirely fresh life. It would be adventurous. And he would be free. Or he could join the Navy. He might be sent to Hawaii, China, Cuba. It would be hard in the Navy, but think of the fun landing in strange cities, finding girls, Chinese, Filipino, Hawaiian. Wouldn't that be better than what he was facing here? Yes, why didn't he just blow? But if he were going to, he would have to do so in a hurry. It was after ten now, and she wouldn't be delayed much longer. Should he blow? Walk away, out of her life, out of Chicago? It was tempting. All he had to do was turn to his left, walk around the corner, and straight on down Sixty-third Street. She might never catch up with him. Why, she wouldn't even know where to begin looking for him. He could go to New York, Washington, Boston, Cleveland, San Francisco, New Orleans, Texas. He could go somewhere. But then, going away might not be all milk and honey. He mightn't land a job. He might go broke without landing anything, and then where would he be? Or he might get a job where he had to give references, and she might locate him in that way! It wasn't easy to go to a strange town and land something that promised a future.

He looked at his watch. She was already half an hour late. How soon would she come?

He'd thought that her old man was well heeled. That, at least, would have been a cushion for them. But he'd learned last night that this wasn't so. What a break he was getting! She was damaged goods. And she wasn't rich. Even if her father did have money, he wouldn't want to get married. Twenty-one was no age for wedding bells.

He looked southward along Stony Island Avenue. She wasn't in sight. He wondered whether or not she would be coming by streetcar. He watched an approaching car crawl along. It stopped directly across from him. Through the platform windows he could see passengers getting off at both ends. He wasn't sure that she was among them. He waited for the car to go on and then he saw that she hadn't been on it. Perhaps she would be on the next car.

He wondered if something had happened to her. But immediately he told himself that would be too good to be true. He lit a cigarette and stood with his hands in his pockets, imagining that she had come around and that all his troubles were over.

Suddenly he began to pace nervously back and forth from the drugstore to the Greek restaurant a few doors from the corner. He halted abruptly. Strangers would notice him unless he acted very casual. They would wonder what he was doing. Why was he waiting this way? They might even laugh to themselves and think he was waiting for a girl who was standing him up on a street corner.

He slowly drifted back and forth between the restaurant and the corner, trying to appear nonchalant. Without realizing it, he again lengthened his stride and began to pace nervously. He tossed away his cigarette, but promptly lit another one.

A northbound street car stopped on the other side of the street. He halted, waiting to see if she were on it. She wasn't.

Why was she late? How did she expect them to get to Crown Point today if she met him so late?

This could have happened to so many fellows he knew. Why did it have to happen to him? And to make it worse, he wasn't the only one who had ever made her. God, he had to marry a girl he didn't love, a gal that perhaps many a lad had made.

II

He just had been told over the telephone that Ellen had left home at nine-fifteen. And it was now ten-thirty. He peered down Stony Island Avenue. He watched another streetcar come and go. Where was she? What should he do? Why had

she done this to him? Wasn't he treating her right? He knew
many others who wouldn't treat her as he was. Yes, he knew
fellows who would walk out on her, leave her cold. Instead of
doing this, he was acting so fair to her. But look at the way she
was treating him.

Where could she be? Where? Last night she had warned him
more than once that he must not be late. And now, look at her,
already so late. Here he was standing up to his responsibilities
like a man. And what was he getting for it?

He stopped, tense, and like a person who has been shocked
by an unexpected fear. Why, he wasn't even certain that it
was his responsibility. Judging from the ease with which he
had made her, he had real grounds for suspicion.

He saw that the newspaper dealer was eyeing him. He
dropped into a nonchalant manner and strolled back and forth.
The newspaper dealer was a dark, swarthy, tough-looking little
man. Bill felt like walking up and punching him in the nose. Let
the Dago mind his own business.

It was such a sunny morning. Spring was in the air. And
look at what spring was bringing him.

Once again fright choked him, almost paralyzing his legs.
Perhaps she had done it. Hadn't she threatened to jump off her
front porch?

He waited anxiously for another streetcar to come and go.
She wasn't on it. He peered down the street in vain.

She wouldn't have done it. No, she wouldn't.

She might have had some errand to run this morning, something to do. She might have gone to the bank. True, she'd said
that she had no money, but she might have done that in order
to surprise him. She might show up late and flash a roll of bills,
telling him that the money was for their coming treasury.

Ellen was proud and vain. She always wanted to look her
best. Couldn't it be that on her wedding day she wanted to
look particularly well? She might be at a beauty parlor getting
all trimmed up, a permanent wave and whatever else a girl had
done to her at a beauty parlor.

But suppose she had committed suicide? Her body might be floating in Lake Michigan this very minute.

If she had killed herself, that would relieve him of all responsibility. But she might have left a note behind, naming him. It might be in the newspapers. That would mean his disgrace. How could he expect to hold his job? Or face his folks?

A pretty dark-haired girl passed. He looked after her, wistfully, longingly.

Ellen Rogers might be dead at this very minute. Even if she had not left a note mentioning his name, her suicide might be traced to him. He'd left his name with her maid over the telephone a little while ago. He'd laid off work this morning without telling his mother and he'd drawn his money out of the bank. How could he explain these actions if he were cross-examined?

She was ruining his life.

He noticed that his hands were shaking. He must pull himself together and not look like a holy show on the street.

He couldn't be so sure that she had committed suicide. She might be at a beauty parlor. She might come along any minute. Then they would go off, and he would marry her. He would marry—damaged goods.

Why, the goddamned dirty little bitch! She was driving him nuts, absolutely nuts.

It was eleven-twenty. He would wait only for one more streetcar. No, three. If Ellen Rogers did not show up on the next five streetcars that passed, then he was washing his hands of her. With his jaw set, he stepped over to the curb and spat. He frowned and waited for a streetcar to nose itself along Stony Island Avenue.

Chapter Seven

I

At twelve-thirty Bill saw Ellen strolling toward him, taking her time as if she had all day. Seeing him, she waved gaily.

Cursing angrily to himself, Bill ran to meet her. She smiled sweetly. He glared at her, momentarily speechless.

"Say, what's the idea?" he finally asked.

"I'm so sorry. I had no way of reaching you and I just couldn't help it."

"Couldn't help it? Say, what do you take me for?"

"Now, don't be so angry."

"Who do you think you are? I got a good mind to let you go to the devil and face the music. This is no way to treat me. Why, this is supposed to be our wedding day."

"Bill, please control yourself. I have to talk with you."

"That's a fine way to meet me, almost three hours late."

"I tell you I couldn't help it."

"Couldn't help it? What were you doing?"

"Don't talk to me as if you owned me. Let me tell you why I'm late," she answered.

"Don't talk to me!" he shouted.

He thought he ought to sock her square in the jaw, and right here in the street.

"Bill, stop shouting at me. Let's go and sit in the park," she said.

"We haven't got all day," he answered.

"Bill, I want to talk to you."

She started across the street. He tagged at her side, neglecting to take her arm. They found a deserted bench inside the park. He sat beside her, sulky.

45

"It's a glorious day, Bill."

"Is it?"

"Well, don't you think so?"

"Of course."

"It makes you enthusiastic, doesn't it? It makes you romantic, too," she said, gazing off, watching a brood of chattering sparrows.

Bill lit a cigarette. He couldn't comprehend what her strange smile meant. It was upsetting.

"Bill, I have something to tell you."

"What?" he asked disconsolately; he felt like a washed-out rag and now had neither curiosity nor spirit.

"I came round. I got the curse."

His shoulders sagged. He was too happy, too relieved, to show his feeling. He mustered up a smile.

"So you are saved from me," she said.

"That's no way to look at it," Bill said, his pretense feeble.

"How?"

"Considering my being saved. I'm no kid, you know. It was only not advisable. I mean for you. You're too young, too pretty, and you have too much of a future to be tied down with babies and all those responsibilities right now."

"How about you? You were worried for me and for my future?"

"Well, more than for myself. After all, I'm a man."

She fixed her eye on him.

"What's the matter?" he asked.

"Why, I feel sad. After all, I'm losing the opportunity to marry a man."

"Well, not necessarily," he said, perplexed.

"You mean?"

"Well, I don't mean anything particular. I mean that, well, we could let things ride now, and a little later on, see how we feel."

"Bill, there's no need for your pretending anything."

"I'm not pretending."

"Of course not. Forget it."

They sat there. Bill smoked, physically tired from the strain.
"Let's do something," he said.
"What?"
"Anything. Go to a show. Have a drink. Walk, anything."
"I don't feel like it. After all, Bill, you know this was more of a strain on me than it was on you."
"I don't deny that."
He sat up. He took out his money and started fingering it.
"You're rich, aren't you?"
"It depends on how you look at it. Yes and no."
He put the money back in his pocket.
"Maybe we ought to do something," she said.
"I don't know. I feel awful tired. I think I'll go home and sleep and take it easy since I'm not working today."
"Yes, that might be good for you."
He stood up.
"Well," he said, obviously talking to make conversation when he didn't know what to say.
"After this, keep out of trouble," she told him.
"When am I going to see you?" he asked.
"Call me up. But, Bill, you don't really want to see me any more, do you?"
"Ellen, why do you say things like that?"
"Because I know they're true."
She got up.
"That's not so, kid."
He took her face in his hands.
"Aren't you going to kiss me good-bye now?"
"Please don't. Don't get sentimental now."
He withdrew his hands.
"Bill, boys like you like to talk."
"What do you mean?"
"You know what I mean."
"Huh?"
"If you ever talk about this affair between us, and I hear of it . . . well, I'm warning you, that's all," she said.
"Why do you let such ideas fill your pretty head?"

"Never mind why. Just remember what I've said."

"But, Ellen, I'm your friend. You talk as if I was a heel."

"I've warned you."

She turned and walked away.

"Good-bye, Ellen," he called after her, not knowing what to make of her.

She walked on without acknowledging his farewell.

SECTION TWO

Chapter Eight

I

Frank Dolan drove the shiny five-passenger Ford through Jackson Park, going slowly because of the newness of the machine. Ellen sat beside him in the front seat. She thought that Frank was like so many others his age. She had even come to think that Frank, Bill Northrup, and most other boys all looked alike. It was not really so. Bill was better looking than Frank. Frank was thin, bony, and he had ugly thick lips. Bill hadn't called her up since the day she had left him in the park. Bill should only know what she had done to him. Frank was not as bad as Bill and he was less conceited. She had given him a date tonight because there had been nothing else lined up and she had thought, what difference did it make?

"I'm glad I found you in," Frank said.

"You've been neglectful of late, Frank."

"I know it, and I'm sorry. To tell you the truth, I've been busy."

"You have?"

"Business is good. That means I've been tied up nights with customers."

"That's good news. But does it mean that I'm a substitute for a customer?"

He glanced at her, puzzled.

"Why, no, I wouldn't say that—not at all. No, not at all. I don't like to have to spend my nights trying to sell cars. But then sometimes I got to. You know, I get a prospect, and so I have to see him, give him a sales talk, explain things to him, give him a demonstration. And then, since I'm trying to sell him a car, after all, if he says he wants our appointment at night, I'm not going to say no, am I?"

Ellen had been paying no attention to him. As the car swept along parallel to the lake, she had kept her eyes on the calm waters upon which the moon poured a dazzling light.

Receiving no response, Frank glanced at Ellen.

"Say, it's nice, isn't it?"

"What, Frank?"

"The lake."

"Frank, tell me—what do you think of the lake?"

"What do I think of the lake? It's pretty. It makes you feel all sorts of things, you know."

"You mean it provides a romantic setting, don't you, Frank?"

He slipped his right arm around her, holding the steering wheel with his left.

"Please, Frank."

"What's the matter, Ellen? Don't you know that I really go for you? Honest I do."

"Hadn't you better drive with two hands?"

Frank removed his arm. They drove on for a stretch without speaking.

"Frank, why do you boys always want to neck with girls?"

He was grateful that the darkness hid his face, for he was sure he would have revealed his embarrassment.

"Huh?" he asked, sparring for time.

"I asked why fellows always want to neck with girls. Can't a boy and a girl just be friends?"

"Sure, of course they can."

"But it doesn't seem so."

"It all depends."

"Depends on what?"

"I don't know. It depends. It depends on the fellow and the girl, I guess."

"Frank, why did you put your arm around me?"

"I like you," he answered rather shyly.

"Is that the only manifestation of liking me?"

"If you like a girl, you want to show it, I guess."

"Can't we be friends without having to neck every time we go out on a date?"

"Of course. I'm not like a lot of fellows. I don't think that way. I just sort of put my arm around you as if I was a . . . well, a friend. Because I like you, Ellen, and want to be your friend. Ellen, if you ever need a friend, I want you to know that you can always rely on me."

"Frank, I don't know what to say. Except that I appreciate what you said to me just now. I appreciate your sentiments deeply."

"I understand how it is, Ellen."

He drove north, out of Jackson Park.

"Say, Ellen, how do you like the way she runs?"

"You mean the car?"

"Uh uh! Doesn't it run like a dream?"

"Yes, yes, it's a very good car. I'm impressed."

"I'm going to sell a lot of these cars," he remarked, looking straight ahead.

II

"Frank, can't you ask them to join us after the dance?" Ellen asked, taking his arm.

He didn't answer. They drifted lazily off the dance floor of the main ballroom of the Shrifton Hotel, part of a large crowd of young couples.

"Why can't we have a little party after the dance instead of going some place alone?"

"What did you say, Ellen? I didn't hear you."

"Why can't we ask him and Catherine Anne Freer to come with us after the dance?"

"They might be going some place themselves."

"But you don't know. Ask them and find out. Don't you like double dates sometimes? Often a foursome is more fun than two."

"It isn't that important. I don't have any objections except . . ."

"What?" she interrupted, her eyes twinkling.

"What I mean to say is that I'm not sure you'll like him. He's pretty wild. And he belongs to that fraternity you once poked fun at. You know, the one that Marty Mulligan, Ike Dugan, Hugh McNeill, Danny O'Neill, and that bunch belong to. They used to be quite a gang of souses. I guess they still are."

"I've heard of Edmond Lanson. But you don't have to be worried. He won't overpower me."

"He's always brawling and fighting. He doesn't know how to behave with nice girls."

"He's with Catherine Anne. She's a nice girl. And surely, if we go out with them tonight, you and he won't fight?"

"No, not unless he starts it."

"There he is."

Frank frowned at the sudden lift in her voice. She nodded in the direction of Edmond Lanson and Catherine Anne Freer, who stood talking just outside the ballroom. She led Frank toward them.

"Hello, Catherine Anne," Ellen said cordially, paying no attention to Edmond Lanson, who stood at ease, his hands in his pockets.

"Ellen Rogers, I haven't seen you in a dog's age. What have you been doing with yourself?" Catherine Anne replied, while Frank and Lanson nodded to one another. "Ellen Rogers, this is Edmond Lanson."

"How do you do," Edmond Lanson said.

Ellen curtly acknowledged the introduction.

"Catherine Anne, you know Frank Dolan," Ellen said.

"Yes, hello," Catherine Anne said.

"How do you do," Frank said.

Catherine Anne seemed like a simple, friendly girl. She was plain, with long brown hair, a round face, and attractive gray eyes.

"I'm not doing much of anything. A little of this, a little of that," Ellen said in answer to Catherine Anne.

"You're not going to school?" Catherine Anne asked.

"Father wants me to, but I haven't made up my mind."

"You don't want to go to school, Miss Rogers?" Edmond Lanson said.

His voice was deep but soft, and it immediately attracted her. She imagined a person with such a voice must be gentle. She turned to face him. Close up, his appearance impressed and excited her even more than it had from a distance. She singled out his hazel eyes as his most distinctive feature. She told herself she had never before seen such fine eyes in a young man. He was tall, broad-shouldered, well built, and he exuded radiant health. His nose was straight but prominent, and his lips were long and thin, constituting the weakest of his features. She thought his swarthy, almost bronzed, skin was lovely and that his dark-brown curly hair added to his attractiveness.

While she had been sizing up Lanson, Ellen had not spoken. She feared that he, and the others also, would sense and interpret her delay in replying to him. She shifted her eyes from him and said in a flat tone:

"I'd be so bored with school. I'm sure that I would."

"I only went to the eighth grade and look at me," Lanson said, introducing a slight note of self-deprecation in his tone.

"I don't think I would be sorry if I had more education. No, I wouldn't. But then, I'm getting along better than a lot of fellows who have had much more education than I got," Frank said, and in contrast to those of Lanson, his very words seemed dead.

"You and me, Dolan," Lanson said.

"Your first name is Edmond?" Ellen remarked.

"Don't be so formal. Call me Ed."

"Well, Ed, Frank was thinking that if you two aren't planning to do anything definite after the dance, the four of us might go some place together."

"I don't believe in plans. That is, except when we formulate them in order to disregard them. But ask Catherine Anne."

"Of course, but I have to be home a little early tonight. I promised my folks I wouldn't be out too late."

Ellen suppressed an impulse to express contempt for Catherine Anne for such a statement.

"I'll get you home early. After midnight it gets early immediately," Ed said, turning to Catherine Anne.

Ellen laughed.

"We'll go some place and have some chop suey," Ed said.

They heard the music for the next dance.

"Frank, how about changing dances?" Ed asked.

Flustered, Frank nodded. Ed moved toward the dance floor with Ellen beside him.

III

Lanson did not dance as well as Frank. Frank was smooth and graceful. Lanson took short, choppy steps, the style of dancing that usually disconcerted Ellen. But she knew she would rather dance once with him than all night with Frank. Moving about the dance floor in Ed's arms, she was titillated. Yes, he was magnetic. He seemed so interesting, so much more mature than clods like Frank or Bill.

But what was the matter with her? Was she falling? No, she wasn't, not in the least. She was merely appreciating a personality which, even on sight, she could perceive to be interesting, alive, unusual.

"Oh, pardon me," he said after stepping on her toe.

"My fault."

"That's kind of you."

"Not at all. A girl should be a good dancer. That means she should be able to follow anybody."

"I presume, then, that I belong in the category of anybody."

"Oh, I wouldn't say that. I hardly know you."

"If you did, you'd know something," he said, smiling down at her.

"Yes," she responded, meeting his gaze challengingly.

"I mean *yes*."

"And what would I know?

"That Lanson isn't anybody. He's Lanson."

"Well, now, that's profound."

"Damn tootin', kid."

"You're a fast worker."

"No, I'm not. Not at all. I'm not a worker at all."

"What do you mean?"

"I don't have to work."

"No?"

He laughed, a friendly open smile, revealing perfect white teeth.

"I'm a strange animal."

"I suppose you're so strange that I couldn't even find you in the zoo?"

"You'd find me there."

"Under what species?"

"A Lanson."

She laughed. The orchestra stopped. They waited for the next number.

"What are the characteristics of a Lanson?"

"A very rare category of misogynist."

"You're clever."

"Clever," he repeated, laughing ironically.

"Aren't you?"

"Not in the least."

"I'm sorry to hear that."

"Why?"

"Because I'd like you if you were clever."

"Perhaps you could teach me."

"You don't really think you need to be taught."

"Well, perhaps yes—and perhaps the converse."

"I'm not a teacher."

"New experience is always exciting. Perhaps you might experiment and become a teacher."

"That would be too much."

The orchestra began again. He took her in his arms, pressed her closely to him, and danced her toward a corner.

"I don't feel too much at home in this joint."

"Why?"

"Not swell enough for me. I like a dive that's swell," he said.

"A man of definite likes and dislikes. Is that one of the characteristics of the rare species of . . . Lanson?"

"You said it, sister."

"Tell me more about yourself."

"Where shall I begin?"

"The best place to begin a story is at the beginning, I would presume."

"The beginning? That's long ago, on a dark night. There was a beautiful woman, dark and handsome."

"Yes."

"She was young. And there was a man, also dark and handsome."

"Who were they?"

"My mother and father."

"Go on."

"Well, now we skip a space, because otherwise I would be offending your ears with what I said they did."

She laughed.

"So to go on, after the story begins at the beginning, with a tall, dark, handsome man and a beautiful woman, there is a succession of asterisks. You wouldn't, of course, know what the asterisks mean. But they mean something. So the next event to be recounted is the joyful tidings of my birth."

"You have a line, haven't you?"

"Frankly, I have no line. But to go on, when I was born a prophecy was made about me."

"The plot thickens."

"The prophecy foretold that the day would come when Mr. and Mrs. Lanson's son, Edmond, would meet a girl."

"A girl?"

"Yes, a girl, a lovely creature about five foot four. She was described as slender and sylphlike. With blue eyes, blue eyes deeper than pools of moonlight in the merry month of May."

"What else? This is strange and interesting."

"She was to have a fine, pert chin and a pert adventurous disposition. And—let me see your ears." He stopped dancing, gently turned her head to the left, examined her ear. "Yes, small, exquisitely shaped and involuted ears."

He took her in his arms to continue dancing.

"And she was to have finely sculptured hands. And lips as red as cherries."

"The prophet was exceedingly vivid in his description."

"Yes, it was predicted that I would meet such a person. In fact, the prophecy foretold that she would be gorgeous."

"And then what would happen?"

"It was then foretold that I would master her."

"So that's the prophecy?"

"Yes. What do you think of it?"

"Not very much."

"You might change your mind."

"Do you think so?"

"I *know* so."

"Tell me some more about yourself."

"A space of some years intervened between that birth and the fulfillment of the prophecy. In that interim Mr. and Mrs. Lanson's son Edmond did a number of things, most of them insane."

"Perhaps that is a good recommendation."

"With whom?"

"Oh, a blonde."

"No, she's too sensible to like some of the things I did."

"If I were that blonde, I would have to know what they were."

"Well, jumping in the Washington Park Lagoon with my new and only suit on."

"Why did you do that?"

"Because somebody dared me to."

"Do you ever refuse to take a dare?"

"Never."

"How am I to believe that?"

"Try me."

"Be careful or I might."

"Nothing is stopping you."

"What kind of dares do you like?"

"Any kind."

"Can't you be more specific?"

"Of course I can. I like gorgeous blondes to dare me."

"Now, if I were such a person I would dare you."

"Well, you are."

"I might dare you to kiss me on the floor here."

He kissed her on the lips.

"What will Catherine Anne say to that?"

"Need we talk about unimportant matters?"

"Don't you like Catherine Anne?"

"Of course I do."

"What are you—a trifler?"

"I am a victim of fate."

"How, fate?"

"Fate, precisely as it was foretold in the prophecy."

"And so you have met your fate?"

"No, my fate has met me."

He squeezed her.

"What else does the prophecy foretell?"

"Asterisks."

The music stopped. They walked slowly off the floor. Ellen saw Frank Dolan frowning at her and Ed.

IV

The morning sun penetrated the bedroom window and seemed almost to create living yellow patterns on the floor near the sill. Ellen lay in bed, a rising tide of excitement surging within her. How glorious to lie in bed this morning, thinking, dreaming, looking at the sun so full of the promises of the newly arrived spring. What a wonderful state she was in, knowing that it had been such a long time since she had felt about anyone the way she felt about Edmond Lanson. Since she had met him two nights ago she had not been restless, nervous, anxious, bored. Just to think about Ed had been sufficient to calm her.

She wondered whether or not he would call her up. He'd said that he would. But would he? Had she worked too fast with him? She remembered how he had kissed her on the dance floor of the Shrifton Hotel. She smiled at the memory. Here was one more story to be spread about Ellen Rogers. And it could be spread far and wide without her caring the least bit.

She remembered how he had kissed her. She had dared him to do it, and without hesitation he had bent down and accepted her dare. Was it an illusion that his lips had tasted so sweet, that his kiss had seemed so different from other kisses? She tried to recapture the sensation of his lips meeting hers, and at the same time she tried to recapture exactly how it had felt to have his body so close to hers when they danced. This was something she usually did not do. But it brought her such contentment. It was as if a glow had spread through her entire body. How many times had Patricia Murray and other girl friends told her that all she needed was to fall in love? And what fools, what children they had appeared to be, talking in that vein. Now she knew that in their innocence they had stumbled on the most important truth in life. And she knew positively, absolutely, with no possibility of doubt, that she was truly in love.

But this knowledge should be a warning to her. She had to play her cards carefully. There must be no mistakes. Even in love it was necessary to play your cards. Suppose you demonstrated too clearly to the person you loved that you really cared for him. That might very easily cause him not to care for you. Was it actually possible for two people to care deeply for one another, to be in love, and for that love to run smoothly? There were no happy endings in life as there were in moving pictures. She feared that such love as she wanted for herself and Ed was not possible. She would have to feign a certain indifference to him.

Suppose all this turned out to be mere dreaming? Suppose he didn't telephone her again? Would he call today? Tomorrow? When? Ever? How silly a girl she was! He was practically a stranger to her. And still she felt this way about him. She was convinced, as she had never been convinced in her whole life, that she was not being a silly girl. She knew for a certainty that he would call her.

She had flirted recklessly with him. After the dance the four of them had gone to Fraternity Row, to eat, talk, and dance.

Poor Frank Dolan, he had been so unhappy, so displeased. And
Catherine Anne hadn't been any too pleased. But Catherine
Anne had been a good sport and she had masked her feelings
much better than Frank had his. Frank was a ninny, a nincom-
poop. She had realized how much so when she saw him beside
Ed. Her one meeting with Ed had more than satisfied her that
she had never met any human being like him. Why, here she
had gone on, wasting herself on this or that Tom, Dick, or
Harry, even on Bill Northrup, and all the while Ed Lanson had
been living in the world, going out with girls with whom she
had gone to school, knowing many persons she knew.

Ellen stretched out comfortably in bed, relaxed. She strove to
recall a vivid image of him. His curly hair made him look so
boyish. How she had wanted to run her hand through that hair
the other night! And his hazel eyes. She had not been sure of
the color because of the light, and she had asked him about it.
Yes, such hazel eyes. They were so soft, so deep, so full of innuendoes, emotions, so much a mirror of his personality. When
he had danced with her, he had clasped her firmly. There were
so many things about him to remember. Yes, what babies other
boys were beside him!

If he didn't call her up, what would she do in order to see
him again soon? She could learn of his address and sooner or
later could find a way. If necessary she would cultivate Catherine Anne, manage to see him through her. There would be
means. And life promised so much. Walks, dates, dancing,
going to the beach, love. He had not been unimpressed by her.
He would call her.

But no matter what happened, she must not allow herself to
lose him. She must not make a fool of herself over him. And
she wouldn't.

She rolled over. She hummed a tune and thought of Edmond
Lanson.

Chapter Nine

I

Their first date. What they had done was so ordinary, and yet at the same time it was so extraordinary. They had seen a movie, and now here they were in an almost deserted restaurant run by a Greek, and it seemed to her as if she were living in a world entirely new, entirely fresh.

"I'm going to have pancakes.."

"Aren't they too heavy for this time of night?" Ellen asked.

"That's precisely why I'm going to order them."

"And that's why I'm going to do the same thing."

Ed smiled at her boyishly. She adored his smile. And it revealed such fine teeth. But if she told him how boyish he looked this very minute, she was sure that he wouldn't like it.

"Two nights ago I told you about a prophecy."

"Oh, that's right. A prophecy. And how is the prophecy working out?" she asked playfully.

"Perfectly."

"That frightens me," she said.

"You shouldn't be frightened—not yet."

"Why—not yet?"

"Asterisks."

They both laughed.

"Here's the waiter. Order me pancakes," she said.

"Two orders of pancakes and coffee."

"Tell me more about yourself."

"No, you tell me about yourself."

"There's nothing for me to tell. I've never had anything interesting happen to me."

"You've never been thrown off a freight car by a gang of dumb Irish with strong backs and weak minds, have you?"

"Do I look as if I had?"

"Do I? But I have been."

"That sounds horrible. When did it happen."

"Oh, a couple of years ago. When I was young and foolish."

"And now you are—"

"Older and more foolish," he interrupted. "But that's probably what's wrong with me."

"I hope that didn't do anything to you."

"It did. It made me what I am today."

"If that's really so, I'd like to have you throw me off a freight car," she teased.

"Your slightest wish is my command."

"You're funny."

"Yes, just a clown. But here's the chow."

The waiter served them.

"Last year I went to a Citizens' Military Training Camp. Do you know what I did the minute I got off the train?"

"I'm sure it was something unusual."

"I yelled: when do I eat? My picture got in the paper because of that, and as a consequence my mother learned of my whereabouts."

"Would you like to be a soldier?"

"I wouldn't mind. That is, if I could be a general. But I'd prefer the Navy or the Merchant Marine."

"That would be frightful."

"Oh, not at all. Think of being at sea, alone with the elements. You feel such a release, such a release and escape from man's little world. You are face to face with the stars, the moon, the elements."

"I can think of other things to do that are more interesting. But of course, that would be more exciting for a man. A girl wouldn't be permitted to do that. If girls were, maybe I'd do it."

"Why don't we both go? You could dress as a boy."

"I couldn't get away with it."

"You could go as my kid brother."

"What would happen to me if I were found out?"

"Probably nothing—at least nothing unpleasant."

"Is that another prophecy?"

"I'd protect you."

"How heroic."

"Tell me about yourself," he said.

"I'm just a little girl. What should I say?"

"You're too coy. Why do you have to be so coy?"

"Am I coy?"

"That might be one reason why I might like you."

"So you like coyness?"

"What use is a girl if she isn't coy?"

"Is Catherine Anne?"

"If she were, I'd be out with her instead of you tonight."

"Why?"

"I broke a date with her. I told her I had to stay home because my mother was sick. Of course, that was foretold, too."

"In the prophecy?"

"Yes, in the prophecy."

"What hasn't been foretold?"

"You should know."

He had broken a date with Catherine Anne in order to take her out. She felt triumphant.

II

"I feel rare tonight," Ed said.

"Uh huh!" she muttered, her voice soft.

They strolled along a quiet and shadowy path inside of Jackson Park. They could hear the noise of automobiles outside the park on Stony Island and on Sixty-seventh Street.

"I wonder," he muttered.

"Yes?"

"I wonder exactly how many couples have walked in this park before us on nights like this."

"What a thought."

"And think of all the couples that have walked in other parks on nights like this."

"Why think of them?"

"And think of all the couples in the history of the world who have walked in the moonlight and shadows on nights like this."

"But why should I?"

"Do you realize what happened to most of them?"

"What?"

"They're dead."

"That's a romantic thought."

"They were young lovers, pulsating with life, happy, heedless of the morrow. They thought only of the moment, of themselves, of their dreams. Ah, the dreams of lovers. To each pair of lovers the old, old dreams seem so new, so fresh, as if those dreams had never been dreamed before." He laughed ironically, "Ah, where are the snows of yesteryear?"

"Melted."

"I'm in a philosophical mood tonight," he said.

"Perhaps the occasion warrants it."

"Doesn't it?"

She shrugged her shoulders.

"After all, it's being a little different, isn't it, you and I walking along in the night here and talking philosophy."

"I would guess so."

"Let us sit down," he said with sudden and elaborate politeness.

They dropped on a bench, shadowed by a large leafy tree. He put his arm around her. She rested her head on his shoulder.

"Just think of it. Two days ago neither of us knew that the other existed. And now here we are, thanks to—fate."

"I suppose you can call it fate," she said, just to be making conversation.

"I suppose you think I'm foolish," he said.

"Why should I?"

"Because I am foolish. Now if I weren't foolish, would I be sitting here with you—philosophizing?"

"I don't really know. Perhaps you're right."

> *A fool there was and he made his prayer*
> *(Even as you and I!)*
> *To a rag and a bone and a hank of hair*
> *(We called her the woman who did not care)*
> *But the fool he called her his lady fair—*
> *(Even as you and I!)*

"That's Kipling," he said.

"Yes, I know it is."

"But here's a better poem of Kipling's. Let me recite it to you. Catherine Anne taught it to me."

He recited in a melodious voice:

> *I've taken my fun where I've found it;*
>   *I've rogued an' I've ranged in my time;*
> *I've 'ad my pickin' o' sweethearts,*
>   *An' four o' the lot was prime.*
> *One was an 'arf-caste widow,*
>   *One was a woman at Prome,*
> *One was the wife of a* jemadar-sais
>   *An' one is a girl at 'ome.*
>
>   .   .   .   .   .
>
> *I was a young un at 'Oogli,*
>   *Shy as a girl to begin;*
> *Aggie de Castrer she made me,*
>   *An' Aggie was clever as sin;*
> *Older than me, but my first 'un—*
>   *More like a mother she were—*
> *Showed me the way to promotion an' pay,*
>   *An' I learned about women from 'er!*

"How do you like that?" he asked, turning to her and smiling broadly and charmingly.

"I like it. I never heard that one before."

"You like Kipling?"

"Yes, but I don't read much any more. At one time in high school I did."

"Why don't you?"

"Oh, I don't know. I just don't."

"Some day, do you know what I might do?"

"What?"

"I might write. I have a friend and fraternity brother who sometimes talks as if he wants to write. Do you know him, Danny O'Neill?"

"I've heard of him. In fact, I think I met him once at the Carberrys'."

"He wants to write. But I don't know what he could write about. He's never had any experience."

"Isn't he a chump?"

"No, he's just serious. He should have been a priest."

"Tell me about your fraternity."

"Oh, it seems to have disintegrated. After I was initiated I became president of my chapter. Then I became grand president. It seems to have fallen apart. I haven't seen many of the bunch of late. I don't know what they're doing or are up to these days. I guess they're drinking their share of the world's liquor."

"What will you write about?" she asked pensively.

"I want to write about the unattainable dreams of men."

"What dreams are unattainable?"

"All dreams. That is, all dreams that are worth dreaming."

"For instance?"

"Love. Love is unattainable. That is why I like Kipling's poem, *The Vampire*. Man—'a fool there was.' "

"I see you have a high opinion of women."

"*The female of the species, more deadly than the male.*"

"I should be angry with you for that."

"Why aren't you?"

"Oh, what's the use?"

"Do you want to know what might be said about all our puny little strivings on this earth? Ellen, look up," he said, pointing to the sky.

Ellen was bewildered. Obeying him automatically, she looked at the sky. It was a deep blue. It had never seemed so vast to Ellen. At first she did not notice the stars. Then she saw myriads of them, silver, twinkling, like a cosmic Christmas decoration.

She was overawed. A sense of wonder and mystery rendered her thoughts vague. She was stirred by longings, longings she could not describe to herself. She felt that she and Ed were alone in the world. And the world had, in an unsuspecting moment, become frightening. Yes, human beings were so little, so small. What did it all mean?

She asked herself what difference it made, no matter what it meant.

It made no difference, so a person might just as well have a fling. She and Ed ought to have their fling.

"Does not the spectacle of the heavens convince you how unimportant men are—how unimportant even a pert, coy, beautiful girl is?"

"Oh, I guess so."

What was he driving at?

"It should signify to us how unattainable everything worth while is, everything that we strive for. But—what is important? I ask. Say, do you know what?"

"What?" she answered, anxious, hopeful.

"Because I was thinking of all this today, I did something."

"Was it interesting?"

"Highly interesting. I quit my job."

"Will you be able to get another one?"

"Sooner or later, if I want to. But it's spring. There is something incompatible in the moods of spring and working in a department store. They are like oil and water."

"What will you do with yourself all day?"

"The best thing a man can do with himself in the spring. I shall do nothing."

"I've been doing that for a long time."

"Does it satisfy you?"

"It gets boring. My father and aunt want me to go to school. I don't want to, but sometimes I think I might as well. It will be a way of passing the time."

"Loafing is an art. Perhaps, if you will permit me to, I will teach you the art of loafing."

"Do you think you can?" she asked, her voice soft, gentle, inviting.

"I know I can."

"When do you begin? Right now?"

He looked at her, an enigmatic smile on his lips. He kissed her tenderly and he softly stroked her hair.

III

They strolled toward the southern end of the park. Ed was now strangely silent. Ellen was puzzled. How unusual their first date had been. A movie, pancakes, then the park. Was he afraid to go further than he had? He didn't act like a shy boy. He gave her the impression that he had had loads of experience. But still, why had he kissed her almost as if she were his sister or a little child? What was there about him? He was so fascinating. Even though he had not really made love to her, it had been a divine evening. She wished it would never end.

He was so different. Think of it, taking her to the park on a night made for love, and what does he do? Spouting the way he did, talking as she had never heard anyone talk. But he was so charming. Whatever he said was charming. If anyone else talked that way, it would sound too silly for words.

They left the park and sauntered east on Sixty-seventh Street. She was anxious to get to her hallway, hoping that there he would take her in his arms. She had never wanted to be held, kissed, petted as ardently as she did now. She walked more rapidly.

"What's the hurry?" he asked.

"Nothing."

"I frown on haste, particularly when it's a night like this and I'm with a girl like you."

"Oh!"

"Do you know what I'll do when I leave you?"

"I haven't the slightest idea."

"Would you like to know?"

"Yes."

"Then you shall not remain in ignorance. After leaving you I shall go home and think of you."

"But how? Critically? Will you go home and think of me as just another rag, a bone, and a hank of hair?"

"Not at all. Those words apply to the mere female of the species."

"But am I not that? Do I look like a man?"

"I except you from that category."

"But why?"

"Because you're you."

He sang:

> *Just because you're you,*
> *That's why I love you.*

She turned to look at him, bewildered but thrilled, moved by his voice. An unexpected warning came to her. She must watch her step because she knew she would fall hard and heavy for him. She must play her cards, and play them well. He didn't act as if he cared too much for her. He showed a kind of indifference which was inexplicable. And, yes, annoying.

"Am I supposed to believe you?"

"Do you think that Edmond Lanson would lie?"

"I don't know him well enough to say."

"Do you think I'm impertinent?" he asked.

"Why should I think that? Why do you ask me?"

"A test of your insight. Am I?"

"Why, no, not in the least."

"But I am impertinent. When I was born my first action was one of impertinence."

"What was it?"

"I sassed the doctor. And when I was baptized I drank all the holy water."

She laughed gaily.

"Listen, do I bore you? If I do, just say the word and I'll padlock my tongue."

"Bore me? You amuse me."

"That's me. Just a clown. Lanson is merely a clown. He

amuses charming young girls, takes them out when they have nothing better to do. He says foolish things, and that evokes their prim and sedate smiles. Yes, just a clown. What a mission in life!"

"Now you feel sorry for yourself."

"No, I feel sorry for the human race."

"I wouldn't say that you're exclusive in your sympathies."

"Why don't you ask me why I feel sorry for the human race?"

"Tell me why."

"Because it has to put up with Lanson."

She laughed.

"You're a funny fellow."

"Well, here we are home."

She faced him.

"It has been delightful to see you," he said.

"It was a pleasure for me, Ed."

"No, it was mine."

He held out his hand. She looked at him, her expression inviting.

He kissed her on the forehead.

"I'll call you up."

"When?" she said, asking the question against her own determination not to.

"Soon."

"How soon?" she asked, the question again coming against her will.

"Do you want it very soon?"

"What do you think?"

"That depends on whether or not you are in the mood for finding substitutes for a circus."

"Now, why don't you stop that, Ed? Call me up . . . soon."

"What is the definition of soon?"

"What would you say it is?"

"Well, that's a relative question. Do you know anything about the theory of relativity?"

"Do I look as if I do?"

"Well, I don't either."

She laughed.

"Good night, Ellen. I'll call you up *soon*."

"Good night, Ed."

She watched him saunter away. He broke into song. She put her hands to her lips and then waved a kiss after him. Disappointed, she turned to go upstairs.

Chapter Ten

I

"Ellen, your friend Bill hasn't been around to see you or take you out in a couple of weeks, has he?" Mr. Rogers asked at the dinner table.

"He hasn't called me up lately."

"He hasn't let you down, has he?" he asked playfully.

"Not at all. He never received much encouragement."

"I guess you're not too much interested in any particular young man," her father said, smiling.

She shook her head in a negative gesture, wondering at the same time what her father would think of Ed.

"It's good to be that way. There's safety in numbers."

"Father, I'm able to take care of myself."

"I'm certain of that."

"What did Aunt Alice say in her letter?"

"I'll get it and show it to you."

"Don't bother now while we're eating."

"She asked if you were going to school this fall."

Ellen did not suppress her boredom.

"She made it a point of asking if you were registered yet."

"She must have lots to do."

"You have to understand your aunt. She's right in her way, even if she doesn't know just how she should put things."

"She's too concerned in my business for my taste."

"That's because she hasn't any children of her own."

What dreary conversations she had with her poor father.

"I hear that they are pretty crowded at the University. If you don't hurry up, you mightn't get in this fall. They're supposed to be a bit strict. Of course, if you want to go away to college. . . ."

"No, I don't, Father."

He beamed at her gratefully.

"Your aunt doesn't approve of it, as you know."

"Oh, please, Father, she doesn't know anything about it."

"I don't see any harm in going there. It seems to me that we have to meet many people on the other side of the fence in this world. If our faith is strong, we can do it."

If our faith is strong! Ed spoke once about baptism. He must be a Catholic. Suppose she told him that she was just an infidel. But if he didn't like her to be an infidel she wouldn't talk about it.

"This is a new age we live in, the age of education. It means something these days to be a college graduate. And it helps out socially. I see more and more college men coming into the real-estate business."

Ed had told her that he had only a grammar-school education.

"What did you do today, Ellen?"

"Oh, not much. I was going to fix up some of my clothes, but it was such a nice day. I read a little—and I don't know. I believe I must have spring fever."

"I was kind of lazy myself. I had to go around and look at some apartments on Crandon. They're being redecorated. I didn't feel much like doing it, but I had to. Yes, I guess I had a touch of spring fever myself."

She wished dinner would be over.

"I'd like to have you come with me to look at the decorating. Can you come tomorrow?"

"I'd love to, but I have to go downtown tomorrow."

"Well, the day after maybe," he said, disappointed.

They went on eating.

II

Ellen handed the box of chocolates to Gertrude Dorgan. Gertrude took a piece of candy. Ellen thought that poor Gertrude was generally a bore. She walked with a limp, and she was not homely but merely plain, with coarse features. But Gertrude's complexion was a little better now than it used to be. At Saint Paul's Gertrude used to break out with pimples.

"What's new?" Gertrude asked.

"Nothing much."

"Seen any of the kids lately?" Ellen asked.

"I saw Loretta Lonigan the other day. She's not doing anything now. And I saw Catherine Anne. She goes out with a new fellow, and you should hear the way she talks about him. She doesn't tell you so much, but it's easy to see that she's simply crazy about him," Gertrude said in a dreaming manner.

"Is she? What's his name?"

"His name's Edmond Lanson. She calls him Edmond and never says Ed."

"Oh, I know him. I had a date with him two nights ago."

"Why, Rogers! Are you still the same? Same old Ellen Rogers."

"What do you mean?"

"Attracting other girls' fellows and then dumping them. Getting them and then throwing them away like old shoes." Gertrude giggled. "Well, some day I bet you're going to fall."

"I met him at a dance, and then he called me up and asked me for a date. So I went out with him."

"What do you think of him?"

"He's all right," Ellen said casually.

"What's he like? Is he really good looking?"

"Yes, he's good looking. Except for his nose," Ellen answered casually.

"What's the matter with it?"

"Oh, it's a little too big."

Gertrude reached for another chocolate.

"What else does Catherine Anne say about him?" Ellen asked.

"Oh, I don't know. She just raves."

"Does he go out with her often?"

"You ought to know that better than I, Ellen, since you went out with him."

"We didn't talk about Catherine Anne."

Gertrude reached for another chocolate.

"It's funny," Gertrude said. She giggled. "He mustn't be as crazy about her as she is about him. If he was, he wouldn't be having other dates."

"I don't think he's the type that falls easily for any girl," Ellen said.

The telephone rang.

III

"Gertrude, guess who that was?" Ellen said, returning to the parlor, smiling. "It was Ed Lanson. He's coming over."

"Maybe I better go. Three's a crowd."

"No, we're all going out. He's bringing another fellow along and we're going on a double date."

"But, gee, Ellen, I'm not dressed up or anything. I can't go out looking like this."

"Yes, you can. They'll be over in a half an hour, and we're going out some place to dance. Come on, we'll fix up."

"All right, but I don't look dressed up. Who's the fellow?"

"Frank Dolan."

"Him?"

"He's not so bad."

"But the things you said about him, Ellen."

"We'll have a good time."

"All right, if you say so."

Gertrude got up and limped out of the parlor after Ellen.

IV

After the introductions, Frank Dolan looked at Gertrude, crestfallen. She sat primly in a chair, eyeing Ed Lanson.

"I just had the idea on the spur of the moment, so I called you up, Ellen. Frank and I were cruising around with nothing particular to do, and I thought we might as well call you up," Ed said.

"I'm glad you did. Except that it's not very complimentary to us to think of us just as a substitute for boredom," she answered.

"But why think that?"

"That's what you said, isn't it?"

"Not at all. We had the stars to look at. The stars are magnificent tonight. We were admiring the stars, and I said I know a girl who's even more magnificent. And look at this," he added. He pulled a little notebook out of his pocket. "This is full of telephone numbers. But from among them all, we chose you."

Still crestfallen, Frank sat slumped in his chair. Gertrude giggled.

"What a line!"

"Line? Not at all. You do me a terrible injustice," Ed said.

"Is it the first injustice that was ever done you?" Ellen asked.

"If it is, it'll be the last."

"Well, let's go, anyway," Ellen said.

They left the apartment.

v

"How did you and Frank become such fast friends overnight?" Ellen asked, leaning across the table toward Ed.

He raised his brows, and there was a twinkle in his eyes, but he didn't speak.

While Frank and Gertrude danced, Ed and Ellen sat alone near the large dance floor of the Palm Tree, a spacious dine-and-dance chop-suey establishment on Sixty-third Street. The orchestra was playing *Valencia*, and the midweek crowd only half filled the place.

Ellen glanced toward the dance floor and she saw Frank struggling to dance with Gertrude. Because of her limp, she danced very badly. He had a bored expression on his face. Nevertheless Frank was shimmying with her. Poor Gertrude, she thought. The girl was dying for a man and she couldn't control herself when she got a chance to dance.

"It puzzles me, your sudden intimacy with Frank," she said, turning back to Ed, who was puffing on a cigarette.

"Every Don Quixote has his Sancho Panza."

"Which means?"

"To every man, his chump. Rubber tires are better than shoe leather," Ed said, laughing.

"He hasn't sold you a Ford, has he?"

"No, he loans me one, and he drives it."

She smiled knowingly.

"I've thought of you ever since I met you," Ed said.

"Yes, and what else? Finish it."

"You don't seem to believe me."

"Of course I do," she said.

"I have. But then, what good does it do? I suppose that the only reason you are out with me tonight is because there was no one better available."

"Isn't that what you more or less told me?" she asked.

"Dreams! Puffy little wisps of nothingness."

"Is it that bad?"

"Don't make light of a man's heart."

"Don't make light of a woman's heart then."

"How could I do that?"

"Couldn't you?"

"Not yours."

"Oh, just someone else's."

"Until I saw you I was a thwarted romantic."

"And now what else? They lived happily ever after?"

"There is only one way that I can live happily ever after."

"Yes?"

"Yes, only one way."

The music had stopped without their being aware of it. Frank and Gertrude came back to the table, interrupting them.

VI

"Well, what about it?" Ed asked, holding Ellen tightly as they danced.

"What about what?" she asked.

"What about it? Are we engaged to be married or aren't we?"

She looked up at him, bewildered.

"Silence gives non-consent," he said.

"Or consent."

"Which means we're engaged. We must buy the ring to-morrow."

"What is this—a game?" she asked.

"If it's a game, it's the most fascinating one I have ever played."

"You're trying to tease me."

"You have banished all other thoughts from my mind ever since I met you."

"Ed, are you being serious?"

"I adore you. I can't live without you. I mean it."

Ellen felt as if she were dancing on air.

"Kiss me."

He kissed her. As they both looked up, they noticed that Frank and Gertrude were dancing near them and had seen them kiss.

"Shall I tell them?" Ellen asked.

"Wait until we sit down. Let me tell them."

She nodded her head obediently.

"My Sweet," he said.

"What will Catherine Anne say when she hears the news?"

"Poor Catherine Anne."

"Why poor Catherine Anne?" she asked.

"She's a nice girl."

"And?"

"My Sweet is divine."

She had never thought that such words would make her ready to swoon.

VII

Joining Ed and Ellen at the table, Frank and Gertrude almost smirked. Their peculiar stares seemed to say that they had seen the kiss. No one talked for a moment. Ellen beamed, her eyes fixed on Ed. He sat smiling, poised, and self-possessed.

"Well, well, well, well," Ed said, breaking the silence.

"What is this?" Frank asked.

"Ed, you're so amusing," Gertrude said.

"Ellen and I have some news. We're engaged."

"You take my breath away. When did all this happen?" Gertrude asked.

"Just now."

"Congratulations to both of you," Frank said rather dispiritedly.

"I'm so excited, I can hardly catch my breath," Gertrude said.

"I take credit for this," Frank said.

"Dear old Frank," Ellen said.

"Frank is going to be our best man, aren't you?" Ed asked.

Ellen checked herself just in time before suggesting that Gertrude should be a bridesmaid.

"And Gertrude is going to be a bridesmaid," Ed added.

Gertrude grinned. Excited, she kept gazing at Ellen. Frank was silent, unenthusiastic.

It suddenly seemed to Ellen to be a wonderful idea to have Gertrude as bridesmaid. She would have a big, a lavish, wedding, and she'd invite almost her entire graduating class from Saint Paul's. And they would see that among them all she had picked Gertrude Dorgan. But what would her father say? She didn't really care. This was not the time to ask herself such questions.

"When are you going to get married?" Gertrude asked.

"As soon as I can borrow the money for the ring and license."

"But how can you live?" Gertrude asked.

"I always live." Ed turned toward Ellen. "Sweet, I forgot to tell you when I proposed that I am a pauper."

"That's wonderful," Ellen said in elation.

"You're both so brave," Gertrude said.

Frank quickly smiled to mask the look of contempt he had cast at both of them.

The music began again.

"Sweet, we must dance," Ed suggested.

They got up to dance, and Frank and Gertrude sat at the table, silent.

Chapter Eleven

I

Catherine Anne hurried across the campus. It was such a lovely day. The sun was shining. The campus was so green this morning. She was going to meet Edmond.

She had thought that her nine o'clock in English Lit. would never end. She couldn't remember one word that Miss Murtle, the instructor, had said about Robert Browning, and she had not taken one note. Ed had telephoned her just before she had left home for classes, saying that he wasn't working today and that he had to see her. She was to meet him now in front of the Coffee Shop in the Reynolds Club at the other end of the campus. She was concerned lest Edmond be in trouble. And at the same time she was excited, expectant. Maybe it was good news he had to tell her. Perhaps she would be the first one to hear it. In class she had sat like a lovesick girl in a story book. And what hadn't she dreamed? She had thought of Ed proposing to her, of Ed and her being married and going on their honeymoon to Paris. Of course it was all impossible, but still she had imagined it while her instructor had droned on about poetry.

She passed through the corridor and waited in front of the building, looking eastward along Fifty-seventh Street. The spring morning thrilled her. Edmond was often late, and she was used to it, but she wished he would come soon. It might be that he was attracted to her because she never complained if he were late or if he neglected her now and then and she didn't hear from him. He seemed to care for her, and once he'd told her that he valued her too highly to treat her as a plaything.

82

He praised her for her intelligence, her seriousness. She was serious, but she didn't think she was particularly smart. But he was. He was clever and he had so much more intelligence than many of the students she knew at the University.

She saw him sauntering along. Wanting to run to him, she stood waiting primly and quietly. He joined her and they went inside to the Coffee Shop, a small, pleasant little room with tables on the side near the windows and a fountain on the opposite side. It was almost deserted. They ordered coffee and toast.

"I quit my job," Ed said.

"What happened?"

"I couldn't stomach one of the floorwalkers. When he got snotty with me and tried ordering me around, I told him to shut up before I teed off on him. He reported me to Miss Staller, the assistant buyer. What a hag she is! She tried to lay down the law to me, but I interrupted her." Ed showed how much he was enjoying this anecdote. "I said that I had a very good idea for improving business. She changed in a trice, because she does think that I'm a good salesman and have good ideas for selling. She asked me what my idea was. With a dead face, I answered her: 'Miss Staller, we could make a pretty penny if we used your face for Hallowe'en masks.' Then I announced that I was quitting."

"How terrible!" Catherine Anne remarked, laughing.

Ed became suddenly glum.

"You're so funny," she said, feigning laughter.

"What's funny?"

"What you said to the assistant buyer, even if it was so cruel."

A girl brought their order. Ed lit a cigarette. He extended his pack to her.

"Oh, forgive me. I forgot that you don't smoke," he said, drawing the pack back.

Catherine Anne idly put sugar and cream into her coffee and stirred it.

"It's a magnificent day. It's just the kind of a day on which to loaf instead of being held a prisoner selling fabrics in a department store."

"Edmond, you're so much better than your job. You should have a much better one."

"I've had good jobs. I can always get one if I make the effort. When I was seventeen I was earning fifty dollars a week. One day I had a whim and tossed it over." He paused. "I was born in the wrong age."

"Why do you say that?"

"The present century hasn't the glamor of the middle ages. Think of the contrast between being a medieval knight and a slave in a department store! I should have been a knight. And you should have been my lady fair, waiting for me in a castle, waiting in a Gothic tower like those towers on the campus here."

"And what would have happened?"

"I would have come riding to your rescue."

"On a white steed?"

"But I should not have rescued you in the standardized manner. I should have conceived a special and unique method. It would have been cleverer than any of the tricks pulled by Mark Twain's Connecticut Yankee. Do you know that book?"

"No, I don't."

"Read it some time. It's amusing."

"I will. But I don't doubt that your rescue would have been something special."

"Old Hellfire."

"What is the meaning of that?"

"Didn't I ever tell you?—that's one of my nicknames."

She shook her head to indicate that she hadn't known this.

"What am I doing? Indulging myself in talk, idle talk."

"Edmond, what are you going to do now?"

"I haven't decided. Yesterday I didn't even bother to collect my pay."

"You'll be able to get it."

"Yes, but not today." He paused. "I did something foolish last night, something that reflects no credit on my perspicacity."

"What was it?"

"I was shooting craps. I ran two dollars up to thirty, and then lost it all. I borrowed some money and lost that, too. I had to sign an I.O.U. promising to pay it back by twelve noon today."

"What will happen if you don't pay it back on time?"

"Catherine Anne, most females don't understand what honor is. But you do."

She was silent, giving him her full attention.

"Perhaps I'm a damned fool to place so much store in a word." He waited a moment and added ironically, "Honor!"

"Don't speak so cynically. I know you don't mean it," she said, looking at him tenderly.

He poured another cup of coffee for himself. He gazed past her, as if he were lost in complete and subjective absorption.

"Edmond, please don't get angry at what I'm going to say."

He turned back to face her. She thought that he had such lovely eyes.

"Catherine Anne, how could I be angry with you?"

"I can go to the bank right now. In fact, I have to go there today anyway, and I can lend you the money."

"I hate to think of doing that."

"But after all, if you gave your word you ought to keep it. And it's just a loan."

"I know it. But rather than borrow your money I'd pull off a stick-up job."

"Edmond Lanson, you don't mean what you're saying!"

His manner changed. He spoke to her as if she were a little child.

"You mustn't force me into a position, you know, where I have to accept a dare."

"But if you mean what you just said to me—why, you could ruin your life over a trifle!"

"Trifles! What else is there worth ruining your life for?"

He sat silent. She watched him.

"It rubs against the grain for me to accept a loan from you."

"Edmond, be sensible. We're good friends, aren't we?"

"I wish I could say that I was worthy of being your friend."

"Please don't talk that way. You know that I have confidence in you and that I am your friend. I will always be your friend if I can."

"Catherine Anne, I will always treasure those words of yours. Remember that I will. No matter what happens to me, remember that I will always treasure your words."

"I can't understand why you talk that way. You have the world before you. A person with your brains, your presence—there's no limit to what you can't do or accomplish if you will only let yourself. You can do anything that you want to in this world. Edmond, I believe that. I believe in you."

"It's a shame that you have such misplaced faith in me."

"Stop saying that. You know it isn't true."

"I make a mess of everything."

"Edmond, come on now. I'll go to the bank."

"I don't like to do it."

"After all, this is merely a loan. After you pay your debt you can go downtown and collect your pay, and then give the money back to me."

He seemed lost in thought.

"Edmond, you have a lot of sense. Now, just look at this matter sensibly. I'm doing nothing extraordinary. Isn't it silly of us to hold to foolish boy-and-girl ideas? This is just a favor that one good friend is doing for another."

He smiled at her, whimsically, boyishly.

"I'm more than glad to do such a small favor for you."

He reluctantly picked up their check, and they left the Coffee Shop, Ed paying at the door.

II

"Catherine Anne, I don't want to debase my feelings of gratitude to you by uttering commonplace words which have been rendered banal by conventional usage," Ed said, guiding her toward Fifty-fifth Street.

She smiled at him, a smile full of love and tenderness.

"I'll never forget this favor."

"It's really such a small one."

"And I'll pay you back as soon as I collect my pay."

"If you need more than twenty-five, why don't you take the amount of your salary and then give it back to me?"

"No, I can't do that."

"Come, tell me how much you need."

"Well, it would be convenient. But no . . ."

"Edmond, you have nothing to be ashamed of."

"It's the idea of the thing."

"We're not children exactly."

"Well, if I did, I could get Mother a present. Today is her birthday, and it would save me rushing to the store."

"Tell me how much you need."

"I'll just take my salary, because I am sure I can give you that back tomorrow."

"How much is it?"

"Forty dollars."

"I can draw that just as easily."

"I wonder what I'll buy Mother."

"Do you want me to help you pick it out? I can cut my two o'clock class."

"Would you?"

"Why, it would be such fun."

"But no, I can't. Do you know why?"

She waited.

"Sentiment. Every year I make it a rule to go all by myself and pick out Mother's present. It's a ritual, and I hate to break it because Mother knows about this little ritual. It would be so much fun, but . . . no, I can't break this ritual. That's the kind of a damned fool I am, Catherine Anne, always permitting sentiment to interfere in my life."

"You're not a damned fool. I understand. It's because of those things in your nature that . . . well, that so many people find you so attractive, and so worthy of respect."

They turned onto Fifty-fifth Street, Catherine Anne walking happily at his side.

III

She came out of the bank and handed him an envelope containing forty dollars.

"Catherine Anne, you're a darling," he said, pocketing the envelope.

She smiled at him in gratitude.

"I'm going to do something."

She waited, watching him.

"I'm going to kiss you on the street."

He kissed her.

"I have to hurry to pay back this I.O.U. in time."

"Of course. You go, and call me up."

"Yes, I'll call you up . . . let's see. Tonight is Mother's birthday. Tomorrow? I'm going to look for a new job tomorrow. I'll call you at suppertime tomorrow."

"All right. Now get something lovely for your mother."

"It'll be lovely . . . and original."

"I'm sure of that. If Hellfire gets the present, it'll be original."

He patted her cheek.

"Good-bye. You're a wonderful girl, Catherine Anne. No one ever had a finer friend than you."

"Why, Edmond, you'll give me a swelled head."

"A girl with your qualities has more than earned the right to have a swelled head."

He sauntered off, whistling a gay tune. Her eyes followed him, filled with devotion.

Chapter Twelve

I

After leaving Catherine Anne, Ed walked rapidly over to Sixty-third and Stony Island Avenue to meet Ellen.

"You're late," she said, meeting him in front of the drugstore.

"Sweet, you must take my word for it, I couldn't help it." He kissed her.

"I don't imagine you'd be late because of seeing another girl this early in the morning," she teased.

"Never fear. Never fear. This is the first morning that I didn't have to report for work at nine o'clock. I merely overslept. But you were in my dreams. As a matter of fact, I was dreaming of you and that is why I did not awaken sooner."

"I hope this is not a foretaste of things to come."

"What does that mean?"

"Am I always going to be kept waiting on corners while you dream of me?"

"No, not at all. Not when you have a date with Old Hellfire."

"Old what?"

"Old Hellfire. That's my nickname."

"I like it."

He took her arm.

"What are we going to do?"

"First of all, we're going to have lunch. Then we are going to buy a ring."

"Yes?" she asked, surprised.

"Do you think that I'm getting engaged to an angel like you and that I'm not going to buy you a ring?"

"But, Ed, remember what you said last night?"

"That's not today."

"No, I guess it isn't."

He led her to the elevated steps.

Ellen recalled that Catherine Anne went to the University. If they had lunch around there, perhaps they just might happen to meet her.

"Ed, let's have lunch some place around the University. It's pleasant over there."

"I'd prefer to eat downtown."

"But if I asked especially?"

"I want to eat in the Loop. Come now, Sweet."

"Please, Ed."

"Papa is the boss," he said, holding her firmly by the arm and guiding her up the steps of the Jackson Park elevated station.

She did not resist him. She could have her hour of triumph over Catherine Anne another day, and if she managed it properly it would be under more dramatic circumstances.

II

Ed and Ellen sat in the crowded restaurant of the Sheriff and Forest Department Store.

"Imagine it. I used to be a serf here."

"You're not getting lonesome, are you—Hellfire?" she asked playfully.

"I, lonesome? I've never been lonesome in my life. And before I met you I had come to the conclusion that the best company I could find in the world was my own."

"And now?"

"The best company is you and Hellfire together.

She gazed at him softly.

He laughed as a prelude to a comment, and then said:

"I was just thinking. You can never eat here on the salaries they pay you selling their fabrics."

"I wouldn't know that. But I do know that you're too good for such work."

"It's in the past. Tomorrow I go out for a real job. I can make plenty of money if I set my mind to it. All I ever needed was a genuine incentive. Now I have that."

"You put everything so charmingly."

"If so, it's because my stimulus is so charming."

She smiled.

"Ed, you've had all kinds of jobs, haven't you?"

"I've had a number of them. But I've always been whimsical. The better a job I've had, the more quickly I've become whimsical and quit. But now I'm going to get something good, selling. As soon as I get going I'll go in business for myself."

"And this ceremony?" she asked.

"Any time."

"Even today?"

"Why not? After lunch we can go to City Hall."

A waitress served them their coffee and dessert.

"Of course it will have to be a secret marriage since I am, what shall I say, pecuniarily unstable at the moment."

"It will make it so much more romantic."

"Yes, it will."

She observed a sudden change in him.

"Ed, what's the matter? Don't you really want to?"

"I am tempted. Yes. But it would make our love and our marriage a lie. Why should we have to hide it from the world? I would detest it if we had to live a deceit, as we would if we were to be secretly married."

Ellen's disappointment was eased by her admiration for Ed. She felt that she should not press the point.

"Yes, if you agree with me, it would be better to wait until we could be married openly. And when we are married, my adorable, I want it to be with a bang. As soon as I get on my feet, we'll have a real wedding."

"Where?"

"In a Negro church."

"That would almost kill poor Father. But . . ."

She smiled at him.

"Do you object to the future Mrs. Lanson smoking in public?" she asked when he lit a cigarette.

"Not at all. I should be pleased," he answered, handing her the cigarettes.

As she smoked, several women sitting near by looked at her with sternly disapproving faces.

"I haven't told Father about our engagement. It came so suddenly last night that it's still hard to believe."

"Not for me. I was singing in my sleep last night."

"I wonder how Father will take it."

"Should I break the news?"

"No, Ed darling, let me. First, though, I want you to meet him."

"I presume that he will disapprove of me." He smiled gaily. "Parents usually do."

"He'll approve. He approves of everything I do."

"Everything?"

"Everything he knows about. Poor Father, he's so lonesome."

"Tell me about your mother."

"I don't even remember her. Father never speaks of her. He mustn't have loved her."

"Some day we'll have children. They'll speak of us as we do of our parents," Ed said.

"How gruesome a thought!"

"Are you afraid to die?"

"No. Not if I die with you."

"Sweet, you not only fascinate me because you are beautiful—you are also intelligent."

"Do you really think so?"

"Do you know how I got the money for our ring and for the splurge we plan today?"

"I never even gave it a thought."

"I won it in a crap game. Does that disturb you?"

"Disturb me? It's wonderful. I've been waiting to meet someone like you. Most boys are such cads and prigs, so conventional—oh, such bores."

"You mean Frank Dolan?"

"Yes, and Bill Northrup, and others."

"Who's he, an old flame?"

"He wanted to marry me."

"And he didn't."

"Thank God!"

"Even though there be none?"

"Ed, you don't believe in God?"

"Does that shock you?"

"No. I don't, either."

"You're a gorgeous, glorious nymph."

She blew him a kiss.

"Sometimes I jot down notes, oh, random little reflections and epigrams. They'll be useful when I really write. The night before I met you I jotted down an epigram. It may interest you: 'If mankind had no God, it would have to invent one.' "

"I like that," she said, and he smiled boyishly.

III

"Some day I'll be rich and I'll buy you real diamonds," Ed said as they walked happily along Michigan Boulevard opposite Grant Park.

Ellen looked at the sparkling imitation diamond engagement ring he had just bought her.

"Ed, this ring is enough for me. It's the spirit of it that's important."

"Of course, neither of us is the kind of person who is impressed by baubles. But I don't like any kind of imitation. I regret that it is the best I can do. Soon I'll do much better."

"Ed, I'll always treasure this ring."

"Accept it as a symbol."

Could there be a happier girl on Michigan Boulevard this minute? Ellen was certain there wasn't. And she thought that she and Ed made such a fine-looking couple. She wanted every passerby to notice them.

"What are we going to do now?" Ed asked.

"Anything you say."

"There are endless possibilities."

"What is that?"

"The case of what happens when an irresistible force meets an immovable object."

"And what will be the result?"

He half rose, clasped her, gently but firmly pushed her into a reclining position, and kissed her passionately.

"Hey! Hey, kiss me again, Sweet Patootie!"

Ed turned around and looked up. About ten feet away he saw a broad-shouldered, beefy man.

"Be careful, lad, or somebody will turn in a four-alarm fire because of you," the man said in a sneering tone of voice; he laughed a belly laugh in appreciation of his own humor.

"What did you say?" Ed asked, jumping up and coming face-to-face with the stranger.

"I'm too busy laughing to say anything, kid."

"Ed! Ed!" Ellen called, upset and fearful.

She got to her feet, grabbed Ed's coat, and rushed after him, heedless of her appearance.

"What's so funny, you loud-mouthed peeping Tom?" Ed asked in blazing anger.

"Take your time there, boy. Instead of inviting a clout in the puss, wipe the lipstick off your funny face."

The man laughed again.

"Listen! Freeze your mouth and give your tongue a sleigh ride!"

"Why, you dime-store Romeo . . ."

"Speak with your fists!" Ed said, and at the same moment he snapped his left out with such speed that the man did not even see a blow coming. Ed's left landed between the man's eyes, rocking him to his heels. He stared in stupid surprise. Ed crowded him, and his left shot out again like lightning.

Ellen screamed.

A third left, and the man was on the ground, groggy, bewildered, his eyes glazed, his face already swelling and bleeding.

"Ed, let's go," Ellen said, still frightened.

Ed stood over the man, poised for further action.

"Do you have anything more to say?" Ed said, still angry.

"You didn't need to lose your temper, lad. I was only kidding."

"So was I. I have a wonderful sense of humor in my left here."

The man continued to wipe his face.

"Now, get up and apologize to this girl."

The man didn't answer.

"Are there any obstructions in your ears?" Ed asked.

The man stared at Ed. His bleeding nose seemed to have been smashed, and the lids of both eyes were swelling rapidly. Around the swelling his face was red and bruised.

"You heard me!"

The man slowly got to his feet. Ed watched him intently. The man's hand went to his pocket. Ed threw another left at the man, catching him on the jaw. The man was felled. He lay on the grass, cold.

"Ed, you've killed him," Ellen cried out.

"No, I merely knocked the bastard out."

Ed bent down and felt in the man's back pocket.

"He was going to pull a knife on me," he said.

"What'll we do?" Ellen asked.

The man came to and stared at Ed dully.

"He'll be all right," Ed said.

Ed took his coat from Ellen and they sauntered off.

"I was so frightened," she said as they found a path and followed it.

"It was just a little fracas."

"But you were wonderful," she exclaimed.

"I needed a fight. I hadn't had one in some time."

"How long?"

"Oh, two weeks. But that wasn't a fight. I just hit a guy a few times."

"What for?"

"Oh, he was a louse. I went into a drugstore at Fifty-eighth and Calumet. I used to live around there. A snotty clerk was bullying a little kid. The kid had stolen a bar of candy. The clerk was twisting the kid's arm. I told him to let the kid alone.

He got snotty and said he'd knock my block off. So I just let him have two lefts. His face looked about as bad as that guy's face back there is going to look. He swore out a warrant against me for assault and battery. But I managed to avoid that complication."

"So the police are looking for you?"

"Not too diligently."

"Am I going to go though life watching you get into fights? I hope not. I couldn't stand it if I had to see you beaten up. You don't know how frightened I was a few minutes ago. . . . But, Ed, darling, you were so wonderful."

Ed examined the knuckles on his left hand.

"I didn't hurt my hand."

"I couldn't bear to have anything happen to you."

"You don't have to. I take care of myself pretty efficiently. All I need is a chance to throw my left at some bozo, and it usually settles issues."

"My goodness," she exclaimed, looking into a pocket mirror. "I look like a cyclone."

She stopped on the path, combed her hair, and made up.

"You have lipstick on your face," she said, noticing him.

She wiped it off. They walked on.

"Let's go some place and dance."

He put his arm around her; they ambled on.

v

The five musicians at the Blue Elephant set their instruments down. Ed and Ellen walked off the small, polished square of dance floor and found their table.

The Blue Elephant was an inexpensive cabaret on Clark Street in the Loop. Dim lights turned its constricted space into a world of shadows. Adding to the dimness were walls of deep blue, on which were painted white elephants of various sizes. At the tables there were a few scattered couples who talked in low, almost hushed, voices, each couple seeming oblivious of the others.

Ed idly took Ellen's hand. He turned gentle eyes on her

and examined her studiously. She waited for him to speak. This afternoon time seemed to have halted. There were no minutes, no hours, this afternoon. The world itself appeared to have receded into a background of stage setting for her and Ed. She observed nothing which did not relate itself directly to him and to herself.

"I was just thinking." He laughed. "It's a card."

"What, Ed?"

"Here are you and I, idle. Life is passing. Time is fleeting. Outside of this place in a little while the sun will begin to sink and another day will be gone. And in this city millions toil and moil. Millions of the spiritual dwarfs in the multitude are accomplishing something. They are adding up columns of figures. They are selling pots and pans, Fords, real estate, fabrics. They are grubbing for pennies, nickels, dollars, with greasy hands. They are doing something of value in this world. They are pushing each other in the face in order to climb the rungs of the ladder of success. But Ed Lanson and Ellen Rogers, they are like the lilies of the field. They are neither toiling nor spinning." He laughed quietly. "They are merely—*living*."

"Ed, you are eloquent."

"Ellen, do you like graveyards?" he asked.

She raised her eyebrows. At the oddest moments he would ask the most unexpected questions. She loved him for it. It was one of his most charming traits. He was so full of surprises. You never knew what to expect from him.

"You do not answer me. I take it that you don't like cemeteries."

"I never give them a thought."

"I sometimes find them enchanting. When I am alone at night, one of my favorite preoccupations is to stroll around a graveyard. On a moonlight night they have a weird and eerie beauty. They are strange, fascinating. I spin fancies, ponder the mystery of life, mull over questions. Often, I sit on a tombstone and I wonder about the corpse below me. What was he like? I try to visualize him when he was alive. I ask myself questions. Was he another one of the units, the ciphers in the common multitude? Or was he a superior being? How did he pass his little days? Did he fritter away his days climbing the stupid ladder of success? Or did he live? Whom did he love? And then I wonder—will some Don Quixote of the future sit on my tombstone? Will he try to imagine what I was like? Will he try to reconstruct a sense of my life, my personality?"

"I don't want to think about such things now. I don't want to think of you dead."

"Falling in love, when one has the capacity to feel, tends to make a person cogitate about such questions."

It was disgusting to think that some day she and he would have to die. She wanted them to be always young.

"What is love?" he asked, as if the question were addressed as much to himself as to her.

She did not answer. She fingered the engagement ring on her left hand. She loved that ring, even if it were merely an imitation.

"I mean it, what is love?"

"What do you mean?" she asked.

"Is love purely physical? Or is it something finer?"

His moods and his conversation were so bewildering. A moment ago she had been dancing in his arms, feeling his body close to hers. That was part of their love. It was a promise of the future fullness of their love. Tonight they would answer his question, but not with mere words. Now she did not speak. She would be cautious, because she wanted to agree with him and she wanted to say whatever he would like to hear. Before meeting him, she had been cynical about the very word love. It had seemed silly to her. Now she was too happy to express her feelings to herself or to concern herself with the effort of trying to analyze them. Love, at this very minute, was whatever he wanted it to be, whatever he wanted her to do. Every minute she spent with him he became more fascinating. She was attracted to him more strongly. Tonight he and she would know love. That was more important than talking about it, even when one talked as he did.

"Do you think that I am foolish in asking you such a question?"

"Ed, you know I don't."

"If love is purely physical, what's the use? Then it is merely a matter of a few moments of sensation, and that is all."

She had an impulse to tell him that that was what she had thought of love so often when she had been with men. But she didn't say it. It might be dangerous to let him know that she had let herself be an easy mark.

"Ellen, I am a romantic."

Her face melted with affection.

"What are you thinking about, Ellen?"

"I was thinking—I am a romantic, too."

"Do you think that I would be in love with you if I didn't know that you were a romantic?"

"I've always been romantic," she said thoughtfully. Then she spoke more rapidly. "That's why I've always been so restless, so unhappy. Ed, before I met you, I wasn't happy. I was bored most of the time. I didn't know why. Now I do. I was searching. I was searching, but I didn't know what I was looking for."

"It was the Unattainable," he said profoundly.

She nodded, her eyes lighting with agreement and recognition.

"The essential characteristic of the romantic is that he seeks the Unattainable along the highways and byways of the world. He is always traveling toward the mirage on the far horizon. He is embarked on an endless quest, and for what? The most important object of desire in life. The beauty of the will-o'-the-wisp. But he is doomed never to find that." He paused before changing to a lighter tone. "But, Sweet, you and I have come very close to finding the Unattainable."

"Of course, I don't express myself as well as you. But I feel the same way you do. You have given me the words that describe what life means to me, Ed, darling. Since I met you, I feel that I've become a different person. I feel so differently—about everything. I don't feel restless, empty now, the way I used to. I don't go around saying to myself all day that life is so stupid. That's the way I used to feel."

"I am glad to hear this. But at the same time you must be careful. The kind of contentment you describe can be double-edged. It can be a warning signal."

"Why?" she asked apprehensively.

Ed lit a cigarette. Calmly, he delayed his answer in a telling pause. She waited, anxious.

"The moment we lose our desire for the Unattainable, that moment we lose our soul. It is because we are imbued with this desire, because we love the beautiful will-o'-the-wisp, that our souls are filled with rebellion against the drab, the paltry, the stupidities of the common herd. If we allow ourselves to become contented we sink back into the sloughs of common humanity." He became stern. "Do you want that to happen?"

"I'll never let it happen to me. Why, I'd even kill myself before it did."

"Ellen, we're kindred spirits."

She showered a smile of gratitude on him and allowed her knees to touch his under the table. She glanced toward the orchestra, anxious for more music so that she could lose herself in his arms, in motion with him, in common sensations. But the orchestra had not returned.

"And, Ellen," he went on. "We are going to make our life together into a poem, a poem that is strong, beautiful, sad."

"But why must it be sad?"

"Without sadness there is no depth to love. If love is to be mere joy and ecstasy, then it must remain childish. We don't want our love to be childish."

"Of course not. We're not children. . . . Ed, I'm not a child," she said, speaking softly, slowly, striving to tell him with her words, her eyes, the very tone of her voice, that with her he need not be shy or hesitant.

She stirred in her chair.

"There is something exceptional about you. Of course, you are beautiful. You have fine eyes. You have exceptional qualities. But I have in mind something special about you that strikes me."

"Ed, darling, you make me out to be so much more than I really am. But I'll try, I'll try to live up to your opinion of me. I'll try!"

"You need not try. I do not idealize the female of the species. I know better than to do that."

Every so often he dropped remarks which seemed like hints, frightening warnings. She was already convinced that he possessed remarkable insight and was sharply observant. She was almost frightened because of this conviction.

Ellen squashed the half-smoked cigarette in an ash tray. She patted her hair.

"Yes, I am amazed to find you so different from what one would expect from a girl of your background. I've met a number of them, St. Paul girls and others. You don't seem to come from their world. You come from a world of strangeness. Why, to meet you is like coming face-to-face with a girl I have read about in an exquisite poem. To look at you in the flesh is to look at a girl I have seen painted in a fine picture. My Sweet, you are like meeting a girl of far-flung dreams."

"Ed, you say such wonderful things."

"Don't you believe that I mean them?" he asked, a slightly harsh note creeping into his voice.

She reached across the table, took his hand, squeezed it tightly.

"Ed, when you talk to me, I realize so many things about myself. You know, I never felt close to the girls at school. I never felt that I was like them. When I would hear their silly talk about dates, dances, their sororities that I always refused to join, their boys, I always felt that they were so childish, so young."

"You are different. I've known a number of girls, so many that before I met you I had become a misogynist."

It was unbearable to think that he had known other girls, talked to them, kissed them, petted them. She hated all the unknown girls of his past.

She glanced again toward the orchestra dais. The musicians were returning.

"Ed, let's dance."

"I would prefer to sit this dance out and to talk to you."

"We can talk while we dance."

"No, let us sit here. I do not want to disturb our mood."

She said nothing. He calmly lit a cigarette. She lit one, and again she puffed rapidly.

"Ed, tell me about the girls you've known."

"Why speak of such trivialities? It is all so inconsequential. Why even bore oneself with insignificant episodes from the past? All that does not matter, because now I know you."

Had Catherine Anne slept with him? She doubted it. But had she?

"Yes, now I know you."

"Ed, darling, we've still hardly begun to know each other. Ed, we have so much more to know of each other," she said as the musicians tuned up.

"And when we discover each other, my Sweet, it will be like reading a great poem in which there is fresh beauty and insight on every page. And we mustn't be banal. Do you know what is the plague, the scourge, of love? It is banality. The banality of the common herd. The mob wallows in banality." As he spoke, the orchestra began softly to play a piece, *Seventeen*. They were able to talk while it was played. Ellen kept time by tapping her feet on the floor. "Yes, the mob wallows in the pig troughs of banality. Ciphers from the mob fall in love, after their greedy fashion, and of course they make their love disgusting because of the dreariest sentimentality. They say to one another that they will love forever. As if they had the capacity to love truly for a day, let alone for an eternity, when they will return to the mud some day, the mud that they merit. How disgusting these human zeros are! When I think of these flesh-and-blood minus signs, I could retch." He paused for effect. "Our love is not going to be like that."

She continued to tap her feet on the floor. From the corner

of her eye she saw a few couples pass before her as they glided around the floor.

"Of course our love won't be like that," she said.

"I have a philosophy of love. The girl I love must share it."

"Yes," she said demurely, effacingly.

"To love is not merely to take; it is also to give. In love we give what is called the soul as well as the body. But don't think I'm inconsistent. Don't think that I place any supernatural connotations on the soul. To believe in a supernatural soul is to be weak, cowardly, to need crutches. By the soul I mean the *I*, the *Me*, the *Ego*, all that which is *You*, that makes you distinguishable from all other human beings alive, from all others who have ever lived, or who ever will live."

She fingered her engagement ring and began to twist uncomfortably in her chair. She played with her dress.

The saxophone broke through the rhythmic pattern of the music, its notes wailing, brassy, like a cry of desires which knew no words. Ellen felt almost as if the very notes of the saxophone were entering her body, were lodging themselves in her spine, were creeping up and down it to thrill her to the point of discomfort. Her head was light. The saxophone faded out of the music. She felt momentarily weak, as if she had been drained temporarily of her personality. She smiled at Ed, almost apologetically.

"Yes, my Sweet," he went on. He seemed so calm, so poised, so fully in possession of himself. "I said that love is to give as well as to take. In the primordial society in which we live, the savages believe that the man takes and that the woman gives. The man gives, too. The man gives the woman his body just as much as she gives him hers. And the man gives his Ego, too. Sweet, when you and I are prepared for the consummation of our love, each of us will give. We will give our beautiful bodies. For it is not conceit but merely a recognition of realities to say that we both have beautiful bodies."

The saxophone again dominated the music, making her more restless. She was unable to sit still. She hastily lit another cigarette. She tapped the table with her fingers.

Ed watched her closely. She blew him a kiss.

"Ellen, don't think that I am sentimental because I say that love can be beautiful. It can, it can if it is like the soaring of two eagles over the mountains where they are far, far above the valleys of the commonplace. That is a figure of speech of mine to describe how I conceive of the emotional aspects of love—our love."

The orchestra paused between pieces. She was aware of the absence of music. Absent-mindedly she kept turning her engagement ring around and around on her finger.

"But before our love is consummated, we must be ready for one another. We must feel that each of us is making a gift to the other. We must know beforehand that each of us is exposing our nature to the other. That is not something that can be done lightly, if it is to have meaning, meaning other than the meaning of a mere sensation. Until we are fully prepared we must not do this."

She strained in her chair, and at the same time a puzzled expression came over her face. The orchestra played a soft, a mawkishly sentimental tune which she couldn't remember ever having heard before. The lights faded out and a blue spotlight played across the floor.

"Ed, I love you," she said breathlessly.

She squashed her cigarette.

"When I feel that I am ready, and you feel that you are ready, we will consummate our love like free spirits. We will be pagans. But the time must come, and it will. Until then we must not do anything to spoil our love. We must not, my Sweet. I tell you, I disdain all the clumsy fumbling, the devious trickery, the lascivious inching of most chaps when they try to make a girl. Sweet, I disdain that. And, Ellen, I am not trying to make you. But we must understand what we are doing fully so that it will be beautiful."

Again she beat time to the music. She let her hands drop under the table, and monotonously she rubbed them together. She sat on the edge of the chair.

"Ed, please, let's dance."

He stood up.

"Yes, let us dance."

She strained herself to him. The lights went on. The music stopped. The musicians set down their instruments and rose for an intermission.

Ellen glanced toward them, disappointed. Ed walked over to the orchestra while she waited. She saw him talking to them, noticing his broad shoulders.

Suddenly she heard him raising his voice.

"Don't talk to me that way!"

The few couples present turned to watch and listen. Waiters and the managers scurried forward to surround Ed, and at the same moment Ellen ran across the small dance floor.

"You'll have to leave, sir," the manager said to Ed; he was a plump little fellow with a small black mustache and beady eyes.

"I'll leave with pleasure. And take your hands off me if you know what's healthy for you," Ed shouted to the manager who had begun to push him gently.

A burly waiter, huskier than Ed, drew up by the manager's side.

"Come on, you, get the hell out of here!" he said.

Ellen stiffened. Her features were distorted because of her fright.

The manager turned from Ed and took the burly waiter's sleeve.

"Stop it, Joe!" the manager said.

He stood between Ed and the waiter. Ed's fists were clenched, and his left was cocked. He looked lean, catlike.

"Please leave my establishment, quietly. I can't have this here. This is a respectable place," the manager said.

"Ed, let's go," Ellen said persuasively; for the first time she noticed that the few customers had formed a circle around them on the dance floor.

"If any of you bozos will step up to me, come on!" Ed said.

"Why, say, you . . ."

The manager turned to the burly waiter.

"Go way, Joe! I tell you to go!" the manager said.

Sulkily, the waiter moved off, but he stood glowering from a distance.

"Will you go now, or will I have to call the police?" the manager asked.

"You'd have to call the cops, wouldn't you?" Ed retorted.

"Joe, call the police," the manager said.

Ellen tugged at his sleeve. Ed sneered and turned to go back to his table. His waiter followed with the bill. Ed paid, and didn't give any tip. He walked with Ellen to the door. He turned around by the hat-check stand.

"Anybody want to come downstairs?" he called.

No one answered him.

He got his hat and they walked downstairs. Outside, it was sunny. The sidewalk was crowded.

"I'm going back there. They refused to play an encore and then they insulted me," Ed said.

"Oh, forget it, Ed."

His mood changed. He laughed heartily.

"Ellen, you have had quite a bit of excitement today."

"Too much. I was shaking up there. I was afraid they would all jump on you."

"I could have taken care of myself."

She slipped her hand in his arm.

"Now, what will we do?" she asked.

"Your slightest wish is my command," he said.

They wandered off.

Chapter Thirteen

I

Ellen went to her room again and looked at the clock on her disarranged dresser. Only eleven-thirty. Ed was looking for a job today and he wouldn't come to see her until eight-thirty tonight. She had the rest of the day to get through. Gertrude Dorgan was coming over for lunch and that would help pass the time. But she didn't really need any help in passing the time. She had her thoughts now. Yesterday had been like a dream, the happiest day of her whole life. The feeling of yesterday persisted in her. Her pleasure from all that she and Ed had said and done continued. It now seemed as if it had been such a long day. When she had gone to bed last night, it had seemed as if it had been so short. Because of Ed, it seemed to her as if the dividing line of day and night, the divisions of time, had been erased. She had a curious sense, as though something from yesterday continued to exist in her, and in all of the world.

She went to the parlor and stood by the window, looking across at the golfers moving about on the green in Jackson Park. They seemed small, strange little creatures inhabiting a world different from hers. And they did. She and Ed lived in a world all by themselves. No one could possibly understand how this was. Were any of these people playing golf in love? If they were, it was not like her and Ed. It couldn't be.

She turned from the window and sat on the sofa. Her father wouldn't be home tonight. She and Ed would be all alone. She counted the hours which she must wait on her fingers, starting with the right hand. Then she counted the hours starting with her left hand. Even though she wished he was already arriving, it was still pleasant to wait for him. Now everything was pleasant.

Last night Ed had petted her and kissed her good night. She had been so shy. He was so delicate in his feelings, in his conduct toward her. She smiled. He was more delicate than he needed to be. After their conversation in the Blue Elephant yesterday afternoon, she had imagined that he would make love to her. Why did he say that they had to wait until they were both ready? Could it be that he did not love her as much as she loved him? But he said that he did. She was positive that he did. Of course, the way he talked about love was strange to her. But he spoke with so much conviction, he seemed to be so sincere when he talked, that he must believe what he said. And in a way what he said was true. She felt so much more than she used to feel. Being in love had aroused so many feelings. That was what he must mean. What he said were figures of speech to tell her what these new feelings all were like.

Oh, she adored him!

And just think, at this moment the poor boy had to go tramping around looking for a job. That was wrong. He shouldn't have to work—now. He should be able to live without working, to live for her, to spend these glorious spring days with her, spend them the way he and she had spent yesterday.

Tonight when he came to see her, what would he talk about? What would they do?

She stretched out, closed her eyes, and tried to imagine him as he would look when she met him at the door tonight. She jumped up impulsively and went to her room. She dug into her dresser drawer where she had hidden the engagement ring. She looked at it. She cared more for it than if it were a real diamond, the most expensive diamond in the world.

II

"You say that you saw Catherine Anne?" Ellen asked Gertrude while the two girls sat having lunch at Ellen's. A large salad bowl was on the table between them.

"I went over to see her yesterday afternoon."

Just at the time she and Ed were talking and dancing at the Blue Elephant!

"And what happened?" Ellen asked.

"She turned white. I felt sorry for her."

"What did she say?" Ellen asked eagerly.

"At first when I told her, she didn't say a word. She sat so still. And she turned so pale. She sat like a statue. I said to her: 'Catherine Anne, I was out on a date with Ellen Rogers and two boys last night. We went out on a double date with Edmond Lanson and Frank Dolan. And guess what? Edmond Lanson and Ellen Rogers got engaged to be married dancing on the floor at the Palm Tree.' She turned pale."

"What did she say about me?"

"Nothing."

"Gertrude, we're such good friends that you mustn't hide anything from me," Ellen said, seeking to hypnotize Gertrude with a steady gaze; Ed did that to her sometimes.

"Honest, Ellen, she didn't say anything against you. In fact, she was dazed by the news. I could see that it phased her. Before she recovered herself, she was just petrified—petrified. Then she tried to be brave, and she smiled. She asked me twice was it the night before? I said yes. That seemed to hit her harder. Why, it almost hit her like a thunderbolt. Ed must have had a date with her and not kept it. I can't think why she should have become so petrified unless it was that he became engaged to you on a night when he had two-timed her."

"Here, have some more salad," Ellen said, passing the bowl to Gertrude.

Gertrude helped herself.

"I feel sorry for her. But she's not the first person in the world who cared for someone and lost," Ellen said.

"Ellen, I want to ask you a question."

Ellen nodded majestically.

"Have you ever loved and lost?"

"No," Ellen answered emphatically.

"Then maybe you don't understand how Catherine Anne must have felt. I was sorry for her. Honest I was."

"Perhaps she's crying over spilt milk."

When she was so happy, why should she be jealous of Catherine Anne for having gone out to dances with Ed?

"Ellen, would you cry over spilt milk?"

"Look at me, Gertrude! You know me. Do you think I would?"

"No, I don't," Gertrude said with noticeable admiration. She thought for a moment. "But you'll never have to. You'll always get everything you want in life. You're just that kind of a person. I don't think Catherine Anne is."

"Catherine Anne has no wings. She's prosaic."

Gertrude looked puzzled.

"She hasn't any wings. She doesn't try to fly."

"I never thought of her that way."

"She's not Ed's type."

"I always thought of her as a kid who's awfully sweet and is never catty or back-biting."

Ellen pushed aside her plate, rose, and paced back and forth by the table.

"What if she is? I'm fed up hearing everyone say that Catherine Anne is so sweet. She's sweet. She's decent. What about it? Is nobody else? You'd think she was a saint. I never cared too much for saints, anyway."

"Ellen, you don't really mean what you said."

"I don't?" Ellen said, halting in her tracks.

"I mean you don't mean it about real saints. Like Saint Theresa."

"What do I care about saints?" Ellen said, sitting down, speaking with ennui.

"I wouldn't talk like that," Gertrude said, hurt.

"What else did Catherine Anne have to say?"

"Oh, not much. She wished that you and Ed would be happy."

Ellen didn't reply. Why should she resent Catherine Anne? She was the victor. She should at least not show any resentment and gain credit for being magnanimous. Ed said that magnanimity was a sign of weakness. He was the first person she'd ever met who said what he thought. That was why they'd fallen in love. He had told her that they were kindred spirits.

"Do you think Catherine Anne meant what she said?"

"Yes, I do. I could tell. She wasn't just putting on an act. She was terribly hurt. But she meant it."

How would she act if she ever lost Ed? She wouldn't lose him. She wouldn't!

"You're different from most of us girls, Ellen. You're strong. But everybody isn't like you."

"Do you know what's going to happen to Catherine Anne? She'll end up an old maid, going to everyone's wedding and everyone's funeral. And everybody will go on saying that Catherine Anne is so sweet . . . so sweet you can't eat her. Christ, put her in a glass case. I never could stand girls like her. Another girl in our class that I think the same of is Natalie O'Reedy," Ellen said.

Gertrude looked wistfully at Ellen. Ellen was immediately sorry that she had said this. She shouldn't have. She should forget that Ed had taken Catherine Anne out.

"Gee, Ellen, I wish I was like you," Gertrude said sadly.

Ellen's mood changed inexplicably. She smiled graciously at Gertrude. She thought that it was spring, the most gorgeous spring that had ever come into the world. And the world was like a flower opening its petals, opening them to Ellen Rogers. And poor Gertrude here, she couldn't know this joy. She never could. She couldn't help feeling sorry for Gertrude. Even for Catherine Anne.

Again Gertrude looked wistfully at Ellen, then she smiled sadly.

Ellen was going to speak kindly to Gertrude, but the telephone rang. She dashed to answer it. Gertrude listened intently, trying to hear every word Ellen was saying to Ed on the phone in the hallway.

Chapter Fourteen

I

"I'm sorry that Father isn't home. I wanted you to meet him," Ellen said.

"I'll get plenty of opportunities to meet him."

She nodded thoughtfully.

"What did you do today?"

"I talked to you on the telephone. Gertrude Dorgan was here for lunch. I read."

"What did you read?"

"A book. With letters on the pages."

"How remarkable."

They smiled at each other.

"It was poetry."

"What poetry? Edgar Guest?"

"Who's he?"

"I was being sarcastic. He writes about home sweet home in the newspapers."

"I read Kipling poems because you talked of them."

"What else did you do?"

"Waited until I would see you," she said demurely.

"I'll bet you did."

"And you'll win your bet."

"Impossible."

"Why?"

"I never win bets. That's the secret of my failure."

"I'll bring you good luck. From now on you'll win your bets."

"You must seal that promise with a kiss," he said.

She kissed him passionately.

"Do you know what I'm doing?" he said, holding her at arm's length.

She didn't speak. Her expression itself was a question mark.

"I'm adoring you."

She moved to embrace him, but he held her firmly.

"Yes, I'm adoring you. You're like nothing else in the world."

"Darling, I'm . . . oh . . . I love you," she told him helplessly.

"You're so adorable that there are no words to describe how adorable you are."

She was anxious and, also, grateful.

"No, words are inadequate. Were I not so realistic, I should compare you with the beauties of nature. I would say that your eyes are a cosmos containing all the stars of the heavens. But the stars are cold and distant planets, with a temperature so low that human habitation on them is impossible." He laughed ironically. "I would say that your hair is like the sun, but then, I'm realistic. Therefore I do not say that your hair is like a crown of sunlight. The sun is huge, ungainly, and it is not possible to fondle the sun as one can fondle your hair, run one's hands through it. And should I compare your lips to wine? Wine makes men babble. Your lips don't. They are made for kisses, for passion. And is your body that of a nymph? It is not. A nymph is unreal. You are real, terribly real, beautifully real."

He caressed her.

"But why should we bother now with words. My Sweet, I am now ready."

SECTION THREE

Chapter Fifteen

I

Ed frowned when he came out of the Owl Drugstore at State and Quincy. He walked briskly toward Randolph Street and let loose a flood of curses. But why should he curse Catherine Anne? He had just telephoned her and had been prepared to give her a cock-and-bull story about the money he'd borrowed and an explanation for not having telephoned her as he had promised he would. But she had interrupted him to wish him good luck and happiness. She hadn't uttered one word of recrimination against him. That made him sore. He couldn't stand people like that. She was trying to shame him with her nobility. Nobility! Saintliness! It was enough to make him puke. That kind of nobility in women, that characteristic of the female, was the most difficult trait a man must cope with. Women wanted to make you feel guilty. That was why Catherine Anne had been so sweet to him on the phone, so noble, so Christian. She had said not one bitter word. He liked bitterness. When you stepped on someone and she acted like a saint, how could you respect her? The answer was that he couldn't. Bitterness was one of the necessary ingredients of strength and character. But Catherine Anne was without a touch of bitterness.

He paused in his meditation and turned to look after a cute flapper. Not bad quail, he thought. He remembered how he used to go over to Washington Park with the boys from Fifty-eighth Street a few summers ago looking for girls. They used to call it gash hunting. He had come a long way since then. He had come a very long way since he had been a boy graduating from Conception school on Grand Boulevard.

He walked on.

There was more than meets the eye when a girl acted like Catherine Anne. There was calculation. If there were a God, and he were praying to that God, he would ask that he be delivered from weeping, noble Penelopes. Lord deliver him from all good, calculating women. Save him from their machinations.

When he came to State and Randolph Streets he stopped and began to laugh. He was out looking for a job. That was part of the joke. He was looking for a job in order to get some money. Then he would get married. Ellen last night had been lovely. He had found her so lovely that he had spent all of the morning remembering her. The after-effects of pleasure, the memories of it were as delicious as was the pleasure itself. And he had played his cards with her so perfectly. Never had his technique worked better. He had worked her up just properly for the moment, stimulated her, prepared her for passion. What exquisite pleasure she promised now for the future. Yes, his workmanship on Ellen was admirable. No, this wasn't a conceited thought. He was merely describing the evidence of his own senses. When he had allowed it to happen, he had already impressed on her that it was he who was really giving, not she. He had transvalued all value, he told himself with a laugh.

But this wasn't finding a job. Lanson, you're job-hunting for the steenth time in your short life. Yes, his life had been short so far, but how full a life.

He crossed State Street. What a sunny day it was, a hell of a day on which to go job-hunting. Look at the sun! Man was not made to work in the springtime. After he and Ellen were married, there would be plenty of time for work. But perhaps he might wangle her father into taking care of that peccadillo. Why not? The old man was well off and he ought to take care of a son-in-law.

He turned back on State Street to go to a Thompson Restaurant for a cup of coffee. Finding the restaurant, he entered,

got a ham sandwich and a cup of coffee and sat down at a chair
with a marble-topped arm.

He ate, thinking that last night he had attained the Unattainable. Perfect and delightful happiness. Would it last? He
had never had a love experience to match last night's. And she
had been so lovely. She had thought that he was so tender,
so delicate, so gentle, so tactful and considerate. It was technique that he could be justly proud of. Too bad she hadn't been
a virgin. But that was not important. He was no moralist. Yes,
with his technique a beautiful girl was like clay in the potter's
hand. He was the potter, she the clay, and he was fashioning
her into an image of heart's desire. Catherine Anne could never
be the companion that Ellen was and would be. Catherine Anne
was moral, saintly to the core. And Ellen, like himself, was an
immoralist. What a future they could look forward to. Yes,
what a future—if they only had money. But then, what was
money to deter Hellfire Lanson? Money was easy to get in this
world, particularly if you didn't place an inordinate value upon
it, and if you were smart. It was a means, not an end. But right
now he could use a little of that means. He wanted to get a new
suit as a kind of celebration of his new role. He wanted to take
her around. She was so beautiful that he wanted to show her
off, take her to swank places where they would both be the
cynosure of all eyes. He wanted people who saw them to know
that she was his woman. To be able to say *my woman*, to feel
the exhilaration of possessing her, that gave you a sense of
dignity you attained in no other way. Egotist that he was, he
was forced, in the name of truth, to make this admission to
himself. However, he would never admit it to anyone else.

If he wanted a job, he could go back with John Devormer.
John would be delighted to have him back. Their misunderstanding could easily be patched up. All that had happened
was that John had tried to press him to work harder. But no,
he wouldn't go back. That would be eating crow. Lanson would
go to his grave without ever having eaten crow.

On that resolution he lit a cigarette.

A new idea lit up his face. He had a plan for a job. It would mean a little confinement, a week, and that would net him thirty-five bucks. He might even borrow some money on the basis of his job, and that would be so much extra cash to the good. Borrow money. He took out a little notebook from his coat pocket. Every cent that he had borrowed in the last three years, every penny he had gotten by gypping someone, was listed in this book. Some day, in the coming period of his affluence, he would pay back all this money. He opened the book and saw the list, written in a neat hand. There it all was, the names and the amounts even down to the games of pool he had played at the expense of the Greek poolroom owner on Fifty-eighth Street. What a model of scrupulous accounting it was. All the sums listed and added up. The last figure was $40, and beside it was the name *Catherine Anne*. This ran up the total to $1,419.50.

Not bad, considering that he was only twenty-one. Ah, this was a card.

Some day he would be rich, and then it would be a considerable pleasure for him to pay back this money. It would be a good gesture. In the case of some of the sonsofbitches he owed money to, he would throw the money back at them, throw it in their faces. For girls like Catherine Anne who were so goddamned noble, he would enclose a check and some holy pictures, or some other sacred and priestly object. Ah, he would buy a copy of *The Lives of the Saints* and send it along with the check to Catherine Anne. That would be a subtle gesture. No further comment needed.

He got another cup of coffee and sat down to drink it and tend to his plan concerning this displeasing little matter of work.

II

"Congratulate me. I've got a job," Ed said, leaving the building with Ellen and beginning to walk along Sixty-seventh Street toward Stony Island Avenue.

"Tell me about it."

"I'm in the real estate business."

"Wait until I tell Father."

"Don't; I'd rather you didn't."

"But he might be able to help you."

"I don't need help. I shall only be occupied in this business for one week."

"For a week?"

"For one week Hellfire will be associated with Batten, Fish, O'Doul, and Schwartzfield, Inc."

"What are you going to do?"

"I'm supposed to spend a week in training, learning to sell suburban lots. For one week you study inside and get thirty-five dollars. Then you go out and sell lots on commission. So I'm taking the cash and letting the credit go."

He laughed.

"I don't understand you. Darling, you often speak in riddles."

"This is no riddle. I talked myself into the job. I am a good boy for a week beginning next Monday. I get paid a week from Saturday. Then I'll look for a better connection."

"But how can you get away with it?"

"Hellfire can outwit the universe," he said, following his statement with an ironic laugh. He added, in a self-deprecatory tone, "I suppose you think that I'm conceited when I say that."

"Why, how could I, darling?" she answered, breaking into a happy laugh.

"But what do you think of such conduct—morally?"

"What?"

"Do you approve? Or do you disapprove?"

"I love you."

"Well, then, in order to grasp your answer, it will be necessary to analyze love."

"Let's not analyze love. Making love is much more fun than analyzing it."

"Is it really?"

"Isn't it?"

"Yes and no."

"What did you say, Ed?" she asked, her tone suddenly sharp.

"Just a minute. I said yes and no. Take your friend Gertrude Dorgan. I would rather analyze love with her than make love to her. But with you I would rather do the converse."

"But suppose Gertrude were a beautiful girl?"

"Tempt me not. How could she or anyone possibly be more beautiful, more attractive than you?"

"You say such flattering things."

"Truth is stranger than fiction. But what's on the agenda?" he said.

"Let's do things. Let's have some excitement. I want to dance. I want people to see us."

"So do I."

"Where'll we go?"

"We can't. Batten, Fish, O'Doul, and Schwartzfield, Inc. don't pay me until next week."

"Darling, I have some money."

She dug into her pocketbook and pulled out a small roll of bills.

"But, darling, what's the matter?" she asked, seeing that he was scowling at her.

He didn't answer. She watched him questioningly.

"Put that money away," he ordered peremptorily.

She obeyed him, startled.

"What's the matter, Ed? Please don't look at me that way."

"What do you think I am, a gigolo?"

"Oh, Ed, I didn't mean anything. Ed, I'm yours. Everything I am and own is yours. Ours."

"Don't think I'm a gigolo."

"But I don't."

As they walked along he didn't speak. She waited for him to say something.

"Well, how long is this going on?" she asked, suddenly becoming sharp.

"I don't answer questions addressed to me in that tone of voice."

"You don't? Well, you don't have to act toward me the way you are."

"I wouldn't, if you hadn't insulted me. I'm made in such a way that I don't take insults."

"But I wasn't insulting you."

"That makes it worse."

"What are we going to do now, play riddles?"

"You didn't mean it as an insult. You just took it for granted."

"No, I didn't. I was just happy. After last night I was so happy, and I wanted to go out and dance and be happy, that's all. I didn't even think of it. After all, the way we have talked together, I thought we were above . . . above conventions."

"I don't care about conventions. But what do you think I am?"

"Ed, let's forget it."

He unbent into a charming smile.

"I don't need crowds, music, noise. Let's take a walk in the park."

They crossed the street, entered the park through a path in the bushes, hugged, kissed, and came out on the damp grass of the golf course. He put his arm around her.

"Ed, we don't have to have misunderstandings."

"I know it. But I have a beastly temper. And I'm proud. I take great pride in my pride, Ellen."

"And I take great pride in my Ed."

He idly took her right hand and squeezed it tenderly.

"Did you think about me today?" she asked.

"Ask me if I think two times two equals four," he answered.

"Do you love me more now than you did before last night?"

"Ask me the same question over. Does two times two equal four?"

"I hope so."

"It does. That's the answer. Give me a kiss."

He embraced her. They strolled on arm-in-arm in the park. It was a fine spring night.

Chapter Sixteen

I

"Mr. Lanson, my daughter has talked a lot about you. I'm mighty glad to meet you," Mr. Rogers said, seated at the dinner table between Ed and Ellen.

"Thank you, sir," Ed said deferentially.

"Yes, I am always glad to meet Ellen's friends."

"Father, they couldn't help but be glad to meet you."

"I am sure, Mr. Rogers, that you will not consider me presumptuous when I say that Ellen expresses my feelings."

"Not at all. Not at all, Ed."

"That's right, Father, you call Ed by his first name. Mr. Lanson is too formal."

"Well, I'm not the type of man, Ed, to stand on formalities."

They went on eating.

"You go to college . . . Ed?"

"No, I don't, Mr. Rogers. I work."

"What line are you in, Ed?"

"My real business is in advertising. But temporarily I've been considering a connection with Batten, Fish, O'Doul, and Schwartzfield, Inc."

"Who's that?"

"Batten, Fish, O'Doul, and Schwartzfield. They're in real estate."

"Of course. I've heard of them. They deal in subdivisions. I've never handled any of that myself."

"The real estate business can be promising for a young man if he plugs at it, I'm sure. But my heart is in advertising."

"I suppose you have to plug just about as hard in any line, Ed."

"That just about sums it up properly, Mr. Rogers. What I'm interested in is direct-by-mail advertising. I have a lot of promising ideas about it. I'm planning to work with the ultimate object of establishing my own business."

"Have you had experience in that game?"

"A great deal of it. I've sold advertising. I was on the road for John Devormer. He has a big agency and handles sizeable accounts. And I've sold advertising for other agencies here in the city, direct-by-mail, various promotion ideas. I know the game pretty well and I have a number of contacts now as a result of my experience."

"How old are you, Ed?"

"Twenty-one."

"You talk as if you had a great deal of experience, considering your age."

"I don't want to overstate how much experience I've had. But considering my age, I have had fairly wide experience in selling, particularly in advertising."

"How did you happen to show an interest in real estate?"

"I was considering it as something temporary."

"That's good. It never pays to be idle. Something is always better than nothing. But I don't think that outfit you mentioned as connecting with is too honest. I hear that they sell a lot of worthless subdivisions."

"I feared that. So I've been hesitant about connecting with them. I have another proposition now to consider, one in my own line."

Watching and listening, Ellen believed Ed was making a good impression on her Father. But he should. He was so smart. He was going to be a great man. And he would be her husband.

She would tell Father about their engagement soon. But first she would let Ed make an impression.

"You said you were with a good firm, wasn't the name you mentioned Devormer?"

"Yes, John Devormer."

"How did you happen to leave him?"

"I wanted to locate in Chicago rather than stay on the road

for John Devormer. And, besides, he wasn't giving me enough."

"Did you sell well on the road?"

"I think he was more than satisfied."

"Why didn't he want to pay you more? Did he say?"

"He gave me a song and dance. He likes to squeeze his pennies. I wanted him to branch out and expand the business, too, but he couldn't see it because he won't take chances. We didn't have a falling out, and parted friends, but we did disagree, so I decided that I'm young still and I can take a chance of locating with a firm that promises me a better future. Then, too, John runs his own business. I couldn't have gone much higher with him. I want to attain a higher status than that of traveling salesman, not that I deprecate that, of course. I'm ambitious, though. And I thought that if I came back to Chicago I could locate here and work toward establishing myself."

"Sounds sensible. Of course, you're young, Ed, but you talk in a mature manner. And maybe you're right in your ideas. Let's hope so, anyway."

"Thank you, Mr. Rogers."

The maid removed the dishes and served them cake, ice cream, and coffee.

"But while we've been talking business, Mr. Rogers, I fear that we've ignored Ellen. Perhaps she doesn't care to hear so much conversation of a business character."

"Don't mind me," Ellen said gaily.

"Yes, Ed, Ellen told me a lot about you, and I'm mighty glad she brought you around tonight. You must always know that you're welcome here. Come and see us often. And some time when Ellen isn't around, you come and we'll go into your ideas about advertising. You know, I'm inclined to believe in the motto 'it pays to advertise.' There's a big future in that game. Years ago I read a good book, a novel, *It Pays to Advertise*. Ever hear of it?"

"No, I didn't. Who wrote it?"

"Golly, I don't remember. I'll look around and see if it's on the shelf here and let you take it. Do you read much?"

"Ed reads a lot, Father."

"You do. What kind of books do you read?"

"I read all kinds of books, poetry, philosophy, all kinds."

"Deep stuff, huh? Does reading philosophy, Ed, help you in your line?"

"No, I wouldn't say it does. I wouldn't say that Herbert Spencer would make me a better salesman. Philosophy is about the general problems of the world, the nature of the world. I enjoy it. I like to speculate."

"How far did you go in school, Ed?"

"I only went to eighth grade, and then I went to work."

"Only eighth grade? You sound like an educated man. You must be a hard worker."

"I must say I'm not afraid of work. And then, also, I've tried to educate myself."

Ellen smiled.

"Well, that's the spirit. With an attitude like yours you have a fine chance of getting ahead. And, of course, nowadays the world belongs to youth. There's a premium on youth. Yes, the world is a new world, different from what it used to be. Great times are ahead for youth in this country, Ed. I wish I was a young man again myself."

Ellen believed that Ed was saying just the right things. It was all so funny, but she had to keep a straight face. But still, what Ed said was not just lying. Ed had a wonderful future. Ed was a wonderful person, and he was hers.

Mrs. Ellen Lanson!

Mrs. Edmond Lanson!

"Smoke?"

"Yes, I do."

"Well, here, have a cigar with me."

Mr. Rogers handed Ed a cigar. They lit and puffed. Mr. Rogers leaned back in his chair comfortably.

"Well, Ellen, it's been a nice supper, and I had a nice little visit with Ed here."

"Father, I knew you'd like Ed."

II

"Ed, did you mean what you said to Father tonight?" Ellen asked, alone with him in the front of the apartment.

"Of course. If I had my own business, I'd really buckle down. What I can't stand is to be working for someone else, to be hired by some cluck and to have him as my boss."

"Well, Father fell for you like a ton of bricks. I could tell."

"You think so?"

"Did you like him?"

"Why shouldn't I? Of course I did."

"I sort of take him for granted. It's hard for me to see him clearly."

"After this real estate venture of mine is over, I'm going to look around seriously."

"You asked me not to mention it to Father. And then you spoke of it yourself."

"Did I? It's not important. I'm going to find something worth while next week."

"You don't think it would be worth your while to stay with this real estate firm?"

"What? I should sell on commission?"

"I wouldn't know if it's good or not. But I do know that my darling can be a success at anything he wants."

"Are you trying to convince me that I should get ahead in the world?"

"What do you mean?"

"Since you are going to be Mrs. Lanson, you are going to see to it that Mr. Lanson amounts to something."

"I wasn't thinking of that. I was thinking of it for you, for your own sake."

"And that's just what I want you to do. I need someone to push me, to help me find myself. You know, you and I want to get somewhere. We want to live a beautiful life, and I'll have to earn the money that will permit us to do just that."

"Ed, you know, you're so intelligent."

"Am I?"

"I don't have to tell you how smart you are."

"You mean I'm conceited?"

"Not at all. A person as smart as you must know that he's smart."

"I *am* conceited. I believe in conceit and pride. What the hell is a man without them? Ellen, are you proud of being so beautiful?"

"Am I so beautiful?"

"Don't you know that you are?"

"That's a question to ask me."

"I'm going to teach you to be conceited about your beauty. I want you to be proud and conceited under all circumstances— except one."

"What is that?"

"That your pride and conceit doesn't conflict with my own."

"You're such a darling. You're so sweet," she said, kissing him.

"You say I'm sweet? No one else in the world could get away with an insult like that, no one but Ellen," he teased.

"I have a favored position."

"You're my favored nation," he said, smiling.

"Ed, when we get married, what am I going to do about cooking? I don't think I can even boil an egg properly."

"I'm not marrying you because you can or cannot boil an egg."

"Thank God for that."

"If there be such a God."

"Thank God for that if there be a God."

"And to continue, I'll teach you to cook."

"You know how to cook, too?"

"Of course I do."

"You can do everything."

"Not quite."

"What can't you do?"

"Oh, for instance, I couldn't fall in love with an ugly girl."

"Not even if she were me?"

"You couldn't be ugly."

"Suppose I was. Suppose I should be injured in an automobile accident and have my face disfigured?"

"I'd sue the guilty rascal. Then I'd knock his block off. And then—I'd take you to Paris. You know, my ancestors were French. I want to go to Paris. As a matter of fact, I think that I'd fare better in Paris than any place else in the world. My oldest brother's been in Paris."

"You haven't talked much of your family."

"My brothers and my sister happen to be away. My sister is in California, married. My kid brother's got some job up at Madison, and my oldest brother's at sea. He's traveled around the world."

"I'd love to travel with you, Ed."

"We will. Everything will come to us in time. Everything always comes to me."

"And I'd adore being in Paris with you."

"That settles that—some day we'll go to Paris."

She kissed him.

"Ed, I've got to decide on how I'll break the news to Father."

"Is it a problem?"

"Yes, in a way."

"Then I'll solve it."

"How?"

"Whenever you want a problem solved come to me and allow me two minutes to think about it."

"I adore the way you express yourself."

"Keep quiet. I'm solving problems."

She laughed and waited. He sat perfectly still, his face blank.

"All right," he said after a few moments of silence. "Here's what you do. You prepare your father first for the revelation. You sound him out in order to find out his impression of me. If he thinks I'm intelligent, you stress that when you talk about me. If it's ambition, ditto. And then for two or three days, in an unobtrusive way, keep bringing the subject of conversation around to me. Prepare him that way to accept me. Tell him, also, that you go out only with me. That will further help him to get used to the idea. He will begin to see that you care for me. Finally, after such preparation, you will tell him. However, you must also let him know that you care for him and that you are his devoted daughter. Your only wish is to make him happy. You know that he would wish for you to be happy." Ed smiled. "You see, if you put him in the position where he is on the defensive, it will be harder for him to refuse giving his permission. Put him on the spot so that if he refuses to sanction our engagement he will seem unfair, even in his own eyes. That's the way to handle him."

"Mightn't it be better just to tell him straight out?"

"No, it wouldn't."

"Why? It might."

"But if he doesn't approve, then he can act as if he were the injured one. If you blurt it straight out, you cast aside the chance of manipulating him. The key to getting what you want in this world is found in the knowledge and ability to manipulate people."

"Do you like to manipulate people?"

"Of course I do."

"I just wanted to know," she said, smiling enigmatically.

He returned her smile.

"I know what entered your little brain," he said jocularly.

"What?"

"The seeds of doubt. The poison of doubt. The snake of doubt."

"About what?"

"Hellfire."

"Oh, Ed, don't be silly."

"Silly? That is one thing I would never let myself be. Silliness is incompatible with pride."

"I'll tell Father. I'll do it just the way you want me to do it."

"I couldn't manipulate you, even assuming that I wanted to."

"No?"

"I love you. And, besides, you're no innocent little lamb coming to the slaughter. You're a girl with experience. Tell me something personal."

"What?"

"Tell me, I know I'm not the first man in your life. How many were there before me?"

"Does that make any difference?"

"No, not fundamentally. I was just curious."

"There were not many."

"How many?"

"Two."

"Who were they?"

"Bill Northrup was one. He was terrible. I was such a fool. The other was a friend of Father's when I was only fourteen."

"Who was he?"

"His name is Stevens. You don't know him."

"Maybe I will some day. And Northrup, who's he?"

"He's a cad. I thought I was in trouble. And when I told him, oh, he acted like a cad."

"I'll arrange to meet him."

"Don't, please don't, Ed."

"Why not? You say he's a cad."

"He isn't worth beating up."

"If he is a bounder, that is precisely what he deserves. When I see him I'll decide on this question."

"I didn't know much—about life. It was just one of those things that happened. And then, when I found myself in trouble, he tried to get out of it and leave me to take care of myself. Oh, he disgusted me. You don't know what it did to me, to my feelings. Until I met you, I was cynical. I hated everybody. And it was largely his doing. He made me cynical."

"What kind of a bozo is he?"

"Oh, he's just another boy. He's not interesting."

"And weren't there any others?"

"No. That's all."

"Are you telling me the truth?"

"Ed. I couldn't lie to you."

"We'll never lie to one another, will we, my Sweet?"

"We won't. I couldn't lie to you."

"And neither could I."

"Ed, what I told you doesn't make any difference, does it?"

He took her in his arms, kissed her, caressed her gently.

"My Sweetheart, why should it? We are above such matters. Ellen, you and I are beyond good and evil."

Chapter Seventeen

I

"Say, Ellen, what do you think of your friend, Ed Lanson?"

"I like him. He is very charming and intelligent, and he's ambitious," Ellen said; wearing a bathrobe, she sat having breakfast with her father.

"Well, he seems to be, I grant that."

"Judging from the way you talked with him, I thought you were impressed by him."

"Well, I can't say that I disliked him. When I was talking to him, I thought he was a fine lad. However, I started thinking about him after I left here last night. He seems to talk so damned well. Somehow or other I'm always suspicious of glib talkers."

"He's not glib."

"At times he seems mighty glib. I don't say there's any harm in your going out with him to dances and parties. But, Ellen, I wouldn't let myself get serious with that fellow."

"Don't call him that fellow."

Mr. Rogers raised his bushy eyebrows and looked at his daughter, surprised, anxious, uncertain.

"Ellen, are you serious about him?"

"I had planned to tell you this morning. We're engaged. We're going to be married."

Mr. Rogers did not react instantly to Ellen's announcement, and she waited, defiant. The words seemed to sink slowly into his consciousness like water being soaked up by a sponge. As if he were making a discovery, he realized the meaning of her words several seconds after she had spoken. He was stunned.

Ellen, watching the change that had come upon her father's face, remembered Ed's advice to her about the way she should break this news. Ed had been right. Well, it was too late now to follow Ed's advice.

"Ellen, have you given this serious thought?" her father asked, a note of alarm in his voice.

"I love Ed. Father, I wouldn't want to do anything you didn't approve of, but in this I have to decide for myself. Don't try to change my mind because you can't, you can't."

She had spoken rapidly, without any premeditation.

"Ellen, you know—you're still young."

"I'm old enough to get married—if I'm in love."

"Can he take care of you?"

"I'd marry him even if he couldn't."

"Ellen, Ellen, you mustn't become so excited. Don't lose your temper that way."

"I'm not losing my temper. But, Father . . . it's embarrassing to have to talk about this—I'm in love."

Ellen became calm. With the return of her equanimity, she regretted her outburst and decided to win over her father. She metamorphosed herself into a totally different person, a young girl who was shy, demure.

"Father, I know you don't mean to cast aspersions on him after only meeting him once."

"Of course, I don't. I admit that I'm thinking of you, not of him. My girl, you're taking a very serious and important step. You can't be rash about marriage without paying a price for your rashness. You can do something here that can embitter your entire life. If you marry the wrong person your entire life can be poisoned."

"Father, I know it, I know it. Ed isn't the wrong person."

"Well, it takes a little serious thought. If I was convinced that he was the right one for you, why, you could have my approval in two shakes of a lamb's tail."

"You will be when you really get to know him."

"Ellen, you're not going to rush . . . this marriage?"

"We haven't made any plans. I wanted to talk with you before we even considered making plans."

Ellen observed how, due to this statement, her father's shoulders had sagged in a physical revelation of his relief. Almost simultaneously she grasped what she was certain was a plan forming in his mind. He would try to wean her away by proposing a long engagement. She was more than prepared for anything like that.

"Ellen, I want you to give me one promise. I want you to promise me that you won't be precipitate."

"What do you mean?"

"You won't run off in flightiness and marry secretly, and you won't . . . you won't do anything that's not right. You know what I mean."

Poor, foolish old thing!

"Promise me, Ellen."

"Father, you know I couldn't do anything like that."

She went and sat on his lap and kissed his forehead. He smiled wanly.

"Father, you'll change your mind about Ed. And Ed likes you. He thought you were wonderful."

"Why didn't both of you tell me last night?"

"He wanted to, but I wouldn't let him. I wanted to tell you when we were alone."

"Is he Catholic?"

"Yes."

"What about his people?"

"His parents are well off. He comes from a good home. You mustn't worry about that."

Mr. Rogers said nothing.

She kissed him. She dropped off his lap and returned to her place.

"I wonder what your aunt will say. I'd better write her."

"I'll write her, too."

"It would be nice if you did. She complains that she seldom hears from you."

He glanced at his watch and gobbled his cup of coffee.

"I'm due at my office now. Ellen, I'll talk to you tonight. You'll be home, won't you?"

"I'm sorry. I'll be out."

"With him? . . . Ed, I mean?"

"No, I arranged to have supper with Gertrude Dorgan downtown. You know Gertrude. She'd be disappointed if I broke our appointment."

Ellen had not intended to tell him this lie. Nevertheless, she had told it; she was so used to lying to her father.

He smiled feebly, kissed her on the forehead, and left the room to put on his coat and go to his office.

II

The day was raw, cold, more like a day in March than in May. They walked aimlessly in Jackson Park under a sky that was heavy and dull. The green of the grass and the trees was deepened by the absence of sunlight. The wind was strong and steady as it battered through the trees and shrubbery.

"So, your father said that I'm glib," Ed said, clutching Ellen's arm.

Ed's strange laugh puzzled Ellen, disconcerted her.

"Ed, don't be angry. I'll bring my father around."

"Why should I be angry? Your father's comments on me, his distrust of me, is merely a self-portrait. He described himself when he talked to you about me this morning."

"Ed, just what do you mean?"

"I mean that now I know how to classify him."

"You're not going to quarrel with Father? That would spoil everything."

He stopped, half-turned, and fastened a look of accusation on her.

"What will it spoil? Do you think I should go to your father, with my hat in my hand, begging his approval?"

"You know I don't mean that. What I mean is that, if we have Father on our side, it will be a great help to us. Just consider—a place to live—Father could arrange that for us for nothing."

"I don't need help. I don't want charity. I don't require any crutches, financial or spiritual."

"Ed, dear, please don't jump down my throat. I didn't mean crutches. You don't have to call it a crutch."

"A rose by any other name is just as sweet."

"Ed, you're angry."

"I *am* angry. But not because of your father. He doesn't phase me. I don't like the mien and aspect of things today."

"What things?"

"I don't like this goddam weather. Just look at that lousy sky!" he said, stopping and pointing upward with his left arm.

He shook his fist at the sky and exclaimed simultaneously:

"Goddamn you!"

Too bewildered to speak, concerned, fearful that she might become the object of Ed's anger, she stared at him. He stood in the center of a gravel path, continuing to shake his fist at the sky and to goddam it. She was frightened. He was inclined to such unexpected and curious moods of temper. He was so moody and so changeable. With a person like that she could never be sure of herself.

Ed ceased to berate the sky. He took off his hat and stood scowling as the wind mussed his hair.

Ellen remembered how he had lost his temper and beaten up the man in Lincoln Park. He had been magnificent then. Now his anger had another meaning. It was disturbing. She wished he would snap out of this mood of his. If she didn't know him and love him, she'd think that he was mad.

"Ed, we can't help it because of the sky and the weather."

"That's why I'm so angry. That's precisely what gripes me. We can't help it. I can't do anything about it. My wishes are disregarded by the forces of nature. I can't tell the goddamned sun to come out and make it obey me. I can't force the dirty, filthy wind to calm down and transform itself into wafting zephyrs."

"But, Ed, darling, what's the use of getting angry at something that's beyond our control?"

"That's why I should become angry." He glanced off at a deserted, dark green patch of the golf course. "Master of all he surveys," he said in self-lacerating irony. He gritted his teeth and scowled theatrically. "Master of all he surveys," he repeated.

Ellen had an impulse to laugh, but she did not obey it. This was fantastic. Ed was a true puzzle to her. He was so full of moods, so changing, so unpredictable. She watched him as he again shook his fist at the elements.

"I suppose you think I'm crazy?" he asked, turning a challenging frown upon her.

"Ed, you know I don't. Please don't talk that way to me, and please don't wrinkle up your brows and scowl at me."

"I'm not angry with you. My displeasure is not connected with any action of yours."

"Well, Ed, why are you angry? I'm sorry I told you about Father if this is the way it is going to affect you. You mustn't worry about his attitude."

"Oh, I don't give a good goddamn about your old man. I'm marrying you, not your father, and I ask no man's consent or permission for what I do or plan."

"Then, Ed, please, please tell me why are you in such a mood? What's the matter?"

"Life."

Not knowing what to say, she didn't answer. This was such an entirely new mood in him, and it was showing her a side of his character she had never even imagined or suspected. How could she, how should she cope with him? She was tense, anxious, unable to prevent her worry from writing itself upon her face, but she did not speak.

"Life is the cause of my mood. Life disgusts me. Look at what a lousy day it is, and I wanted today to be warm, rich with sunshine. Why in the name of Dionysius is such a day necessary? Who ordered it? Who wished for it? Why shouldn't I be out of sorts on such a day? But you still have a puzzled, quizzical expression in your eyes."

She shook her head as if to tell him that his statement wasn't so. But he continued speaking.

"Do you know why I'm angry? I'll tell you. I am annoyed.
Do you know what annoys me?"

"What?" she interrupted.

"The wind. I disapprove of it. The sun. I want it to shine in
the sky. It isn't heeding my wishes. It isn't even visible today.
I don't want this beastly wind cutting into my bones. But all
the same, it cuts and slashes like a knife."

"Let's get out of the wind. We can go some place and have
tea."

"That would be surrender on my part. I won't run away from
something that gripes me."

His eyes wandered from her. Vaguely, he gazed at the deep
green grass. He snarled, then turned back to Ellen.

"Do you like the weather?"

"Of course not. I don't like it cold, ever."

"Do you know what happens to me when I don't like something? A fire blazes inside of me. A fire blazes in me and wants
to down every goddamn thing."

"But, Ed, when it's the weather and you can't control it,
what's the use?"

"I disapprove of the weather," he said with a tone of finality,
as if to end any further discussion.

She waited meekly for him to continue or to walk on. And she
wished that they were alone somewhere, in a room where she
could cuddle against him, pet and kiss all of the anger out of
him. She thought of how, when she and Ed were in each other's
arms, and she was kissing him, loving him, she was able to
change him into a tired, spent, and charming little boy who
would fall asleep with his head on her shoulder. When this happened, she experienced so calm, so lovely, so charming, so sweet
a moment. Remembering how she had already had such delicious experiences with Ed in the immediate past, knowing that
she would have them with him many more times, she felt a sense
of power in her own body, a power which enabled her to make
Ed calm, sweet, tractable. How she had misunderstood so much,
so much about sex. She had used to laugh scornfully at men because, with the sexual power of her body, she could make them

spend themselves and become weak and even wearied. It had seemed like a power in her, a power enabling her to be superior to them. Now she had such a different attitude, such wholly opposite feelings. Her body gave her the power to make Ed love her, to make him seem like her little boy. At such moments Ed was all hers. Yes, she could make of him a boyish lad whose head drooped sleepily on her shoulders.

"What are you thinking about?" Ed asked suspiciously.

"How much I love you."

"But are you laughing at me?"

"Ed, you know I couldn't."

"Are you with me or against me? Are you on my side, or are you on the side of the world?"

"I'm on your side, my darling."

"You are not on the side of that goddamn muddy sky. The sky is like a garbage dump today. I don't approve of it. The wind is insulting me. Are you for me or are you for the wind?"

"Why, Ed!" she exclaimed, puzzled.

"I want to know. Does it give you any pleasure to witness the obscene spectacle of the cosmos insulting me, telling me, in effect, that I am just a puny mortal and that it doesn't give a good goddamn about my dreams and wishes?"

Again Ellen wanted to laugh. But she was so in awe of him that she didn't dare to.

"Ah, I wish that there were gods so that I might fight them. That is why the very cosmos is so insulting. There are no gods. There is nothing but blindness, nothing but forces telling us that we are insignificant little mortals. What are we alleged men but the helpless victims of iron laws and disgusting forces?" He paused and then went on, with flourishing gestures. "The forces of the world are a mighty army, full of clash and clangor, and they march forward to destroy man. The wind riding across Jackson Park on invisible cosmic horses shouts at men in contempt. Puny, paltry, insignificant race of men! And I am a man. Ah, how I hate man! Man is weak. I want to be strong. How can I be strong in the face of the wind? How can I smash a left hook into the eyes of the cosmos?"

"Ed, darling, one can't hit one's head against stone walls."

"But if I do, I can then rest my battered head on your shoulder."

"You're so darling."

"No, I'm not. I'm just a weak mortal, a victim of the powers that blindly shape the world and destroy the dreams of man. There is no Poictesme. And I am Manuel and I follow my own bent. I am Lanson. And what is Lanson?"

"He is everything in the world to me."

"And to the world—he is nothing."

"Ed, who is Manuel? What do you mean?"

"You don't know who James Branch Cabell is?"

"No, I don't. I'm so ignorant. I used to think I was smart until I met you."

"James Branch Cabell is one of the greatest living writers. Poictesme is a land of make-believe about which he writes, and Manuel is one of his characters."

"I must read his books."

"That is obligatory. I command it."

"I want to read him."

"Cabell reveals with beautiful irony, and in a beautiful style, how the dreams of man are unattainable. Poictesme is the other side of the sky. It is the world of men's dreams. The Dorothys of Poictesme are the dreams of woman harbored in the heads of men. Cabell writes of the only goal in life worth striving for—the Unattainable."

"You said that you had attained the Unattainable."

"I was speaking metaphorically. But not only women have feet of clay. So have men. I have feet of clay, too. You will learn that some day."

"No, I won't."

"That is the most profound illusion under which the human race labors. But what is life without illusions? That is why I am so annoyed today. The wind—goddamn it—it tells me that illusions are scattered in the cold frosty glare of reality. Dull, drab reality. Look at us. We are walking in the park, and our heads are filled with illusions and dreams."

"I could go on forever like that."

"But life won't allow us to. We have illusions and dreams, and we know not whither we go in this life, the only life we will ever know. I walk in the park today and I think of you, more lovely than a Dorothy in Poictesme. And the wind, the dull sky, duller than iron, the cold, everything tells me—illusions, illusions. We walk through the land of the Unattainable and our clayey feet weigh down every step of our passage."

"Ed, you know, in a way I agree with you. That's one reason why I love you. You won't give in. Well, neither will I. Ed, darling, I'll fight the wind with you as long as we have breath, and then we'll die together."

He smiled at her patronizingly.

"We'll burn the candle at both ends, even though it doesn't last the night," he said.

"No, we'll turn it into an electric bulb. That's brighter."

"Come on, Ellen, let's get out of this goddamn park."

III

"This has been a strange day," Ellen said, sitting opposite Ed in a prim little tea room close to the University.

There was a pot of tea, Melba toast, and marmalade on the table.

He leaned forward with a twinkle in his eye.

"So your father thinks I'm glib?"

"Oh, Ed, I thought we had agreed on that."

"The Babbitts of this world can't stand me."

"Ed, do you think my father is a Babbitt?"

"Isn't he? Aren't all his values the same as Babbitt's? What does he consider the good life to be? Getting ahead, making money. What you and I did today would be inexplicable to him. I wasn't up and doing."

"But, Ed, Father belongs to an older generation."

"I have declared eternal war on the Babbitts. Would they climb the stairway of illusions? So I'm glib? No, I merely speak another language."

"Ed, let's forget poor Father—he doesn't know any better."

"My old man is the same. My old gaffer can't understand why I quit selling fabrics in a department store."

"When am I going to meet your family?"

"I told you that my brothers and sister are out of town. And I can't manage about Father and Mother now. I left home. I have to find a place to stay myself tonight."

"Why did you do that?"

"I'm fed up living at home. I got my pay from Batten, Fish, O'Doul and Schwartzfield, Inc. So I'm leaving home."

"Where are you going to live?"

"I'll find a place."

"I'll help you."

"But some day I'll take you to see my mother and father."

"Will they like me?"

"That is incidental."

"Ed, I used to think I was hard. But you're so much harder."

"Do you disapprove of my hardness?"

"I adore it. I want to be as hard as you."

"I can't allow that."

"Why?"

"If you're as hard as me, then I shall have to surpass myself. And if you're too hard, you won't be the pert and lovely girl I have found you to be."

She sipped tea and took a bite of the Melba toast, telling herself that he was too smart.

Two couples, students from the University, entered the tea room and took a table at the side opposite Ed and Ellen. Ed's back was to the group. Ellen didn't look at them, but suddenly she recognized a voice.

"Why, Ed, I hear Catherine Anne," she said.

"Yes, I hear her. She's with some college boys."

Ellen looked over at the group until she caught Catherine Anne's eye, and then she waved.

"Ellen," Ed said in a low but stern voice.

She lowered her eyes and leaned forward.

"I can't stand college boys. Let's get out of here. They'll make me burst a blood vessel," he said.

"Ed, it's so pleasant here."

"It was pleasant—when we were alone."

Ellen wondered whether or not he was afraid to meet Catherine Anne. Did the prospect of such a meeting embarrass him? Had he loved Catherine Anne? Ellen asked herself these questions. His reaction was unexpected, and she was uneasy.

Ed sensed a change in Ellen and decided that he had to do something. He turned around and casually nodded to Catherine Anne. She smiled at him.

"I suppose that I'll have to go over and say hello to her just for the sake of form," he said, as if this were a disagreeable necessity which couldn't be avoided.

"Ed, let's go over and join them, just to annoy them. I don't like college boys either. We'll gripe them, just for the fun of it," she said, still leaning forward, speaking almost in a whisper, anxious that Catherine Anne see her and Ed talking in such an intimate manner.

"You can, if you want to. I don't want to. I haven't anything to say to half-educated ignoramuses."

"Ed, dear, it might be fun."

"I wanted to be with you alone. I wanted to talk to you, and not to the neighborhood. But if you insist." His tone changed to one of mockery. "Your slightest wish is my command."

"Let's," she said, ignoring his sarcasm.

"All right."

Ellen glanced over at the group, again catching Catherine Anne's eye.

"Can we come over and join you?" she called.

Catherine Anne's face became expressionless, but she nodded affirmatively.

"Come on, Ed," Ellen said.

Ed nodded, and got up after her. Calm, detached, he reflected that this was a ticklish situation. But he would dominate it. Lanson would always carry himself off well.

IV

When Catherine Anne had introduced Ed and Ellen to her friends, she had seemed cordial. Ed had perceived no sign of anger or embarrassment in her. She was a good sport and she was playing her cards admirably, he observed. Yet he did notice that she avoided meeting his eyes directly, or Ellen's. In a sense he admired her for her conduct, and yet resented it. He told himself that he believed in a one-way categorical imperative, and he admired his epigram. But then, most of the human race actually believed in that, only they wouldn't admit it. He felt that he was more honest with himself. There were a few people like his mother who were selfless. Perhaps Catherine Anne was really of this type. But it was the one type that was most dangerous to a man who was walking his own road in his own way.

He had tentatively sized up Catherine Anne's friends. The thin chap on her left was named John Delafield and seemed to be a serious and decent lad. Ed assumed that Delafield was interested in Catherine Anne. He had heard of the other chap at the table, Mike Mooney. Mooney had been a star football player in the Catholic high school league, and when Catherine Anne had been at Saint Paul's he had paged her seriously. But that had broken up, apparently because Mooney was a dumb Irishman. And Mooney looked the part. Sandy-haired, broad-shouldered, he had a freckled stupid face. The girl with Mooney, Patricia Smith, was just innocent, plump, virginal feminine fluff, a little flapper—amusing if there were no better attractions in sight, but that was all. She sat holding a teacup as if the world owed her homage. And she didn't really know the difference between Mike Mooney and the world.

He was tempted to throw a bombshell into the group. But he wouldn't. He would sit back, relax, observe.

"Are you on campus, Mr. Lanson?" John Delafield asked.

"No, I never got beyond the eighth grade," he said.

Patricia Smith raised her eyebrows.

"Ed doesn't need to go to college," Ellen said.

She kept her gaze unobtrusively on Catherine Anne. Did

Catherine Anne really care for Ed? If so, she did a good job of hiding her feelings. It might be that Catherine Anne was proud. Ellen could not quiet a sudden feeling of admiration for Catherine Anne. But, no, the girl was taking a defeat too easily. Ellen would never do that. She would fight tooth and nail for Ed. But she didn't have to. She glanced at Patricia Smith. Just a child. She felt sorry for both Catherine Anne and Patricia Smith. And think of the difference between Ed and these two boys. Oh, what a lucky girl she was!

"I try to educate myself when the fancy takes me. I read. I dabble in this and that, mainly in philosophy," Ed said.

"Say, I got in a lot of trouble because of philosophy," Mike said.

"Ideas can cause trouble," Ed said dryly.

"Last year I let my dean talk me into signing up for a course in philosophy. I flunked in it. It was too deep for me. And that's why I wasn't eligible to play on the football team last fall. I planned to go to a lumber camp this summer and get in condition, harden myself. Instead, I have to take courses to make up my grades or I won't be eligible for football this fall. It's all because I took that philosophy course. It dragged me down in my grades."

"It's all so foolish. Who cares about philosophy?" Patricia Smith said.

"I do," Ed said quietly.

"Oh!" she exclaimed.

Ellen glared at her, but Ed nudged Ellen under the table.

"All I say is that the course I took was a tough break for me."

Ed saw that John Delafield looked at Mooney as if he were a child.

"I just dabble in philosophy, a little here, a little there." He turned to Patricia. "Have you ever read Lucretius?"

She returned a blank stare.

"Lucretius has written eloquently. I have imbibed his contempt for ignorance, and with it, I would say, some tolerance for the ignorant person."

"I took a course in the Stoics. I'm majoring in philosophy," John Delafield said.

"Yes, I used to be intolerant of ignorance and conceit. Lucretius taught me to take an aloof attitude toward it. Human ignorance is so abysmal that I've got to respect it," Ed said.

Catherine Anne was apprehensive. Ellen grinned. Her Ed was so brilliant, and he knew how to put people in their place.

"What do you do, Mr. Lanson? Do you work?" Patricia Smith asked, flustered.

"No, Miss Smith. Did you ever hear of what is called a home girl?" he asked.

"Why, of course."

"I'm a home boy. Except there are differences in the occupation of being a home girl and a home boy. A home girl has a limited sphere, a house, an apartment for her activities. A home boy has the universe. The universe is my home," Ed said.

Everyone but Catherine Anne and Ellen looked at Ed, puzzled.

"I don't understand you," Patricia Smith said.

"We'll forgive that," Ed said.

He drew out a package of cigarettes.

"Ed, give me a cigarette," Ellen said.

He handed her the pack, and then lit her cigarette. Patricia Smith and Mike Mooney frowned at her. She was pleased that she had annoyed or shocked them.

Ed held the package to Patricia. She shook her head with negative emphasis.

"You don't smoke, Catherine Anne?" he said, and Catherine Anne also shook her head.

"A cigarette, Mr. Mooney?" Ed asked.

"I couldn't smoke. We're having spring practice now and I have to keep in trim. If I smoked and my coach, Mr. Jackson, heard about it, he'd feel that I had let him down."

Delafield took one of Ed's cigarettes and thanked him.

"You seem to like Lucretius, Mr. Lanson," he said.

"He's not my favorite philosopher. Nietzsche is. But I admire Lucretius. There is one passage in Lucretius which has always struck my fancy. You might remember it. He talks about how sweet it is to stand aloof, on the edge of the world, as it were, watching the little troubled world of human vanities and hopes, the little world of despairs. I don't remember how the passage goes exactly, but he says something of how pleasant it is to stand as on a darkling plain looking at the distresses of others, not that one necessarily enjoys the suffering of others, but that one is not suffering oneself—one is bulwarked against the distresses of others. And then he remarks about the miserable minds of men. What blinded beasts!"

"Mr. Lanson, you must be blasé," Patricia Smith said.

"I don't like that talk. Of course I'm a Catholic. I don't think man is a beast," Mike Mooney said.

"Edmond likes a good dispute," Catherine Anne said.

"Oh no, not at all. I wouldn't try to convince any man," Ed said.

"Say, I have to go or I'll be late for spring practice," Mike said.

He got up, and Patricia rose after him.

v

"Mr. Delafield, I've mulled this question over and over many times. When I first read about it, I was skeptical, as skeptical as you are. At sight it seemed fantastic. But I've thought about it. I weighed it, tested it, and I tried to formulate objections to it. Finally I was forced by logic itself to accept this idea. I became convinced that Nietzsche's idea of eternal recurrence is irrefutable," Ed said modestly, his voice seeming to ring with sincerity.

For a moment Ed shifted his head so that Ellen, and then Catherine Anne, could see him in profile. He faced John Delafield again.

"Even if what you say were correct, that would not prove the absolute validity of this doctrine as a prediction concerning the future of the universe," John Delafield said.

Ed didn't understand what he meant. Puzzled, he delayed speaking, and to hide his hesitancy he idly lit a cigarette.

"Why? I don't follow you," he said.

"I mean merely this. An idea can be logically irrefutable, and nevertheless not necessarily certain in . . . in an existential sense. By that I mean that an idea can be logical and yet not be a warranted truth."

"But it has to be. If it is logical, it is so."

"Can't a man argue from false premises?" John Delafield asked, smiling graciously.

"As a matter of fact, I often like to do that," Ed said, returning the smile.

Ellen felt that she must look, act, talk intelligently. She was interested in the discussion, but mainly because Ed was involved in it. Even though these new ideas did not catch her fancy, she knew she could have gone on in her life without ever having heard of them, and withal, not feeling any loss or deficiency in herself.

Had she not felt so before, now she knew that she would be convinced that Ed was brilliant. And just think, he had only gone as far as the eighth grade. Despite his lack of schooling, he could not only hold his own with college students; why, he could even mop the floor with them. She had thought that this college boy, John Delafield, was nice but naive. Now she was beginning to resent him for daring to disagree so firmly and consistently with Ed. And she kept watching Catherine Anne. Ellen could tell from her expression that Catherine Anne was following the discussion, although sometimes Catherine Anne would seem puzzled. She knew that she had to match Catherine Anne, comment for comment, question for question. In every way, in Ed's presence, she had to be superior to Catherine Anne. She had won Ed, but she had to hold him.

Would a person as brilliant as Ed tire of her? Compared with him, she knew so little. Sometimes this fear was really frightening. But she wouldn't let him tire of her. Ed was not just brains. He was human, natural, boyish, contradictory. Even so, she had to appear smart and she had to show an interest in his ideas. He seemed to take them so seriously.

Catherine Anne was sad, very sad. But she was determined

not to show it. Ellen's presence caused her to feel self-conscious. What had a person like Edmond seen in such a girl? Ellen Rogers was attractive, but she was not at all serious. Ellen Rogers had never played fair with other persons. But neither had Edmond. Look at what he had done to her. Why had he done it? She knew in her heart that it had not been the real Edmond who had played such a trick on her. It was just a superficial Edmond, an Edmond who felt that he had to act according to this philosophy. He would change. He would settle down and he would go back to the Church. She was sure of it. But she had lost him. Sometimes she hoped that he would come back to her. But now he was engaged to Ellen. They would probably be married, and it was all over between her and Edmond. A girl like Ellen Rogers might well ruin his life. And there was nothing she could do. She was sad and she was not going to show that she was, especially to a girl like Ellen.

The discussion was very interesting, but it worried and concerned her. John Delafield had never been a Catholic, and he didn't believe in God. She would like it so much better if Edmond were doing what she felt he ought to do, defending his religion. She wanted to do it, but in the face of these boys she felt so stupid and she didn't know what to say. They had so many answers for everything she said, and all she could do was to fall back on her faith. John was a nice boy, very smart and quick, but she didn't think that he was as brilliant as Edmond.

She had lost Edmond. What was it in her that was deficient? Was it because other girls were loose, free-and-easy? But Edmond had never tried to take liberties with her. Why? At times, although she didn't want him to go too far, she could probably not have resisted him. What was deficient in her?

Ellen Rogers kept watching her. Ellen could do that from now until doomsday and she would not show one sign of disappointment. Ellen had joined them, bringing Edmond along, just to humiliate her. But her humiliation would be kept deep within her. No one would know of it.

Interesting as the discussion was, she wished she had never

come here today. She would rather not have seen Edmond and Ellen together. And yet, it was nice to see him under any circumstances. There was something so refreshing about him. And the real Edmond was so misunderstood. She knew the real Edmond. He was worlds apart from the one who had lied to her, deceived her, tricked her out of that forty dollars. And the real Edmond was guilty because the superficial Edmond had done this.

She felt that she had to ask questions to show that she was listening and that she wasn't a complete dunce. Just as she opened her mouth to speak, Ellen beat her to it.

"Ed, what does this mean? Eternal recurrence, what is it?"

"It's nothing like the transmigration of souls, is it?" Catherine Anne asked.

Ed smiled condescendingly before answering.

"No, it isn't. That's weak-kneed religiosity. The lunatic fringe of religion believes in nonsense like that. Nietzsche was not a God-creating philosopher; he was a God-destroying one."

"I don't understand why you accept such an utterly fantastic idea," John Delafield said.

"It's not fantastic. I confessed that I thought so when I first met with it. But it isn't. I can show you that it isn't," Ed said.

"But, Edmond, what is it?" Catherine Anne asked.

"First let me explain what this idea means for the girls, if you don't object, Mr. Delafield," Ed said.

John Delafield shrugged his shoulders a bit impatiently. He puffed nervously on a cigarette.

"According to what Nietzsche wrote on this subject, and I accept it, everything that happens in the world will happen not once, but many times. Everything that happens must happen again. Every manifestation of energy must be repeated."

"Everything?" Ellen asked.

"Yes. That means that once again the four of us will be seated here in this same tea room, having precisely the same argument. And see that dust spot on the table?" Ed pointed with his left hand. "Even that will re-occur. It will be the same dust spot and I will again point it out to you precisely as I am doing now. And when I do, we will all think that it is May, 1925. We shan't remember that we have all had this same discussion, not once, but many times before."

"In other words, history is nothing but a phonograph record. It seems to me that the record ought at least to get scratched," John said.

"What a promise that is," Ellen said, turning toward Catherine Anne.

She thought that if what Ed had said were so, it would mean that she would know all the joy of meeting him all over again, of loving him for the first time. In a sense, her love and Ed's would go on forever.

"It's not a doctrine of hope and optimism. It's the most pessimistic philosophy ever developed."

"Nietzsche wasn't quite systematic enough to have really formulated a philosophy," John Delafield interrupted.

"Why systems? I abhor systems, systems and God-builders. But first let me go on. When Nietzsche tells us that there will be eternal recurrence, what does he tell us? Not only that we will live through our joys again, but also that we will live through our sorrows. He tells us that man, miserable, puny, little man will go on forever in his paltry fight for gain, for pleasure, in order to pursue his transparent little games of vanity. His bitter day must be lived over again, not once, not twice, but endlessly, forever. And it isn't only a pessimistic philosophy. It is a brave one. For it says this—that no matter how hard life is, the Superman will face it again, many times, and forever, and the Superman will always say—'Yea'."

"Nietzsche's idea of the Superman was the idealization of a physically weak man, influenced strongly by the example of Napoleon Bonaparte. But Bonaparte wasn't such a Superman, either. Did you ever read Tolstoy's portrait of him in *War and Peace?*"

Ed nodded to John Delafield's remark, but quickly went on lest he be tripped up on details of *War and Peace*.

"John, let's dispense with formalities. Call me Ed. But to continue, you say that this is fantastic. Is it more fantastic than the systems of the philosophers who created their God's, the philosophers who created *as if* fictions of synthetic faculties, pretending to be truth-tellers when they were spreading a poisonous lie in the world—the lie of a God?"

"That is irrelevant," John said.

Catherine Anne smiled mechanically. Ellen fastened her eyes proudly on Ed. He was now in such extraordinary form. What a day it had been. Being in love with Ed was a succession of endless surprises.

"I'll prove eternal recurrence to you now," Ed went on.

"That's a big order, Ed," John Delafield said.

"I don't claim any originality in proving it. What I say is Nietzsche, not me. I'm only a humble seeker and I found the object of my search in his vineyard, if I may indulge in a figure. We know about the law of the conservation of energy."

"It doesn't prove eternal recurrence."

"Please, let me make my point, and then I'll listen to your refutation. I am anxious to hear it, but first, let me make my point."

Ellen was impressed by Ed's politeness and modesty. When he discussed ideas he was so different from what he was when he got into a fight.

"According to the law of the conservation of energy, no energy is lost." He turned to Ellen. "That means that when we die, the energy that constitutes us is not lost. It changes. In the case of beautiful girls like you and Catherine Anne, that energy probably becomes flowers, flowers that the lovers of a future May will pick."

Watching Ellen, Ed did not see Catherine Anne wince and then try to hide her feeling with a pathetic smile. John Delafield looked at him, impatient.

"But persons like myself, their energy will probably turn into onions."

"But what does that prove?" John Delafield asked.

"Just a humorous digression," Ed said genially.

"I don't believe that. I am a Catholic," Catherine Anne said.

"I'm not," Ellen said emphatically.

"But let's not get into a religious discussion," Catherine Anne quickly added.

"I shan't permit myself any more humorous and figurative digressions. Energy never dies. But the sum total of energy in the universe is limited."

"We really don't know, and we can't know, if it is or if it isn't. We can't form a total picture of the universe," John Delafield said.

"Then you deny the law of the conservation of energy. If you do that, you say that the world is infinite. If it is infinite, there must be a God. Of course, if you argue from such a standpoint, I can understand your views, although I think I've made it clear that I have no sympathy with them."

"No, not at all. All I say is that we can't talk about the total universe as you do."

"Will you accept the law of the conservation of energy as a hypothesis for the sake of argument?" Ed asked.

"Obviously. I don't say that energy is destroyed. I merely pointed out that what you are doing is reducing the world to a kind of monism which padlocks the universe. That is what is wrong with your argument."

"Then you do believe in spirit? You divide the world into matter and spirit?"

Ellen had grown bored. But she suddenly sat up and feigned interest. Ed turned to her.

"Does this bore you?" he asked Ellen.

"Ed, how can you ask that question?" she replied.

"I wouldn't be guilty of being a bore. I just wanted to make sure." He turned to Catherine Anne. "Does this bore you?"

She shook her head that it didn't.

"You say, John, that you accept the law of the conservation of energy but you deny eternal recurrence."

"Certainly. There are fields of energy. There are recurrent patterns in the manifestations of energy, the permutations, and the development or happening of events."

"Do you deny the law of cause and effect?"

"What do you mean by cause and effect?"

Ed leaned forward and met John's eyes. This chap was insistent, and he couldn't really fathom his mind. He had a definite suspicion that John would pull God out of the bag sooner or later. And he was concerned. He couldn't let John make a fool out of him, but he couldn't quit the field. He had to win this argument.

"What do I mean by cause and effect? Merely this, that every effect means that it must have a cause. Since the world spins on in terms of cause and effect, it means that either there was one first cause that set it all going, and that is God, or that it has gone on forever. Since there is no way of proving that there is a God, we must assume that the law of cause and effect has been at work forever. That means that time is infinite. Since time is infinite, and since the law of cause and effect holds, and since energy is conserved and is not infinite, that leads irrevocably to the acceptance of eternal recurrence."

"But you simplify everything. All that we mean by cause is that if an event occurs, it is related to the conditions surrounding its occurrence."

"That means it has a cause."

"No, it means that an event has a past. This view of eternal recurrence is based on nineteenth-century physics."

"Well, what if it is?" Ed asked, sparring for time.

"Nineteenth-century physics, that is, the Newtonian universe, holds for relatively low velocities. But it doesn't hold for high velocities. We know today that there is uncertainty in our knowledge. Briefly, we can't be in two places at one time, and therefore we have an irrevocable indeterminacy in our knowledge. Our laws of science are only statistical statements."

Why did this college boy bore her so? Ed didn't. Ed talked so that she could understand him. But this boy didn't.

"This is all beyond me," Catherine Anne said.

"I fear we are boring the girls," Ed said.

John frowned, displeased. He lit another cigarette.

"As I was saying, if I may go on without boring the girls in a long discussion of abstruse problems . . ." Ed waited for them to speak.

"Oh, Ed, don't pay any attention to me. I'm learning something," Ellen said.

"Since time is infinite, and since with nineteenth-century physics or any other physics energy is always changing, that means that unless energy is infinite also, there are only so many possible combinations of energy. No matter how large that number is, it is limited. With the constant change of manifestations of energy, sooner or later every possible combination of energy must take place. The world goes on forever, and so everything must happen again. For energy keeps combining in different ways, and nothing remains static," Ed went on.

"You don't believe that energy can run down and be stabilized?"

"If that is possible, it must already have happened, and then we couldn't be here."

"How do you know that?" John asked.

"I have just explained how I know it."

Catherine Anne stirred restlessly.

"We can't say with the certainty that you seem to hold that there will be no new permutations, radical permutations and novel events in the world. We don't know. The likelihood is that there will be."

"Nothing is new under the sun," Ed said oracularly.

"Every minute something is new. Every minute the world recreates itself," John said.

Did this college chap think she was interested in hearing him tell her what some professor told him? Ellen asked herself.

"Your argument, Ed, reminds me of this. If monkeys were taught how to typewrite and put to work twenty-four hours a day for eternity, then they would eventually produce all the works that are to be found in the University library."

"Isn't that silly?" Ellen asked.

Catherine Anne was bewildered. She gazed off, seeing nothing.

"If time is infinite, that is possible," Ed said.

"Can't there be repetition of the same combinations? Can't certain concatenations reappear over and over again? If monkeys were taught to typewrite, it is probable that in six eternities they would never produce one book that made sense. The number of possible combinations in the letters, numbers, and punctuation marks of the typewriter is very large. It would be unlikely that they would ever hit out many words."

"The law of averages would favor the monkeys," Ed said.

"No, it wouldn't."

"But in the long run it would. Because in the long run they would make all the mistakes, and hit upon the gibberish, and exhaust the possibilities of gibberish."

"You're wrong. Then they would be likely to produce more gibberish."

"I don't see why," Ed said.

"Ed, I think we ought to go," Ellen said possessively.

Ed didn't miss the possessive note in Ellen's voice. But he didn't feel like taking umbrage at it now. In time, if it continued, he would set a stop to it. And he was fed up with this argument. The Delafield boy was smart, but why carry on such an argument?

"I have to go, too," Catherine Anne said.

Did he really believe in eternal recurrence? Sometimes he did. He didn't care about it. It was just an excuse for discussion and thinking.

Catherine Anne and John rose.

"Sometime when we won't be boring the ladies, I should like to continue this discussion. It is an interesting problem," Ed said.

"My telephone number is Wentworth 4418," John said.

Ed copied it down in his notebook. Catherine Anne and John turned to go. A tear slid down Catherine Anne's cheek, and she glanced aside. She blew her nose. Ellen had caught her action and suddenly she felt sorry for Catherine Anne. She knew what Catherine Anne had lost. She had thought that she would feel so happy in her triumph. But when she had thought this, she hadn't really known what love was, what it meant. Now she did. Now she didn't care about such triumphs over other girls.

Having gained her composure, Catherine Anne smiled good-bye to both of them. Ed and John shook hands, and John and Catherine Anne departed.

VI

"Ed, isn't it wonderful!"

"What?"

"To think that in millions of years you and I will again be the same and we'll be in love all over again. Think of it, we'll have asterisks for the first time all over again."

"Yes, but suppose that you will have to hear me gab all over again, saying the same things so many times."

"I'll love it," she said enthusiastically.

"I wonder," he replied.

He ran his hand idly through his hair.

"What's the matter, Ed?"

"I was thinking of some poetry."

"Please recite it for me."

He leaned forward. Placing his head close to hers, he recited in a low but resonant voice.

> *What ails us to fear overmeasure,*
> *To praise thee with timorous breath,*
> *O mistress and mother of pleasure,*
> *The one thing as certain as death?*
> *We shall change as the things that we cherish,*
> *Shall fade as they faded before,*
> *As foam upon water shall perish,*
> *As sand upon shore.*

"That's lovely, Ed—when you recite it. But what are you trying to tell me?"

"You will change—perhaps."

"No, I won't."

"You don't know. You might find somebody better than me, more attractive, more scintillating—somebody like John Dela-field."

"Ed, you were brilliant today. You were so much more brilliant than he was."

"He really believes in God."

"He doesn't interest me. Ed, why do you tell me I'll change?"

"Because people change. Because I don't want you to. Because I don't want it to happen. Listen again, Ellen."

Again he recited.

> *I said "she must be swift and white*
> *And subtly warm, and half perverse*
> *And sweet like soft sharp fruit to bite,*
> *And like a snake's love lithe and fierce."*

He paused, held her in his gaze, and then, as if throwing away the last line of the verse, he continued:

> *Men have guessed worse.*

"Who wrote that?" she asked.

"Charles Algernon Swinburne. He was not a respectable character. I'm going to get a copy of his poems and read them to you in the park on the next sunny day."

"Let's."

"But in the meantime another day is gone, and I must find me a domicile."

"Can I go with you?"

"Yes—if you'll be like a snake's love, lithe and fierce."

She squeezed his hand.

He picked up the check, and they left. Outside, it was almost dark. The wind had abated.

"Ed, were you in love with Catherine Anne?" Ellen asked, taking his arm.

"No. She was just a light occupation. She's too noble. She's the martyr type. But I sent her a letter this morning. She'll get it in the mail tomorrow."

"What was it?" she asked, concerned.

"You shouldn't ask me."

"All right," she said, jealous.

"You shouldn't ask me so that I can tell you without having

been asked. I sent her a stanza from Swinburne's poem, *Félise.*"
He halted. "Here is how it goes."

> *Live and let live, as I will do,*
> *Love and let love, and so will I.*
> *But, sweet, for me no more with you:*
> *Not while I live, not though I die.*
> *Good-night, good-bye.*

"But if you didn't love her, why bother?"

"I'll tell you why—gesture."

Ellen remembered seeing that tear on Catherine Anne's cheek
a little while ago. She vowed that she would never let herself
be placed in Catherine Anne's position with Ed. But hers was
so different. Even though she would have to watch so that she
wouldn't be placed in that position, she and Ed really were
kindred spirits. She felt so good. So often of late she had felt
this way—as if it were the very first day of the world.

"When will I receive a poem like that in the mail?" she asked,
her gaiety contradicting her words.

"Never!"

She gazed at him enigmatically.

"Ellen, all my life has been a preparation, it seems, a preparation for the day when I would meet you. And that has come to
pass. Thus spake, not Zarathustra, but Lanson. But now let us
not be standing on the sidewalk in the twilight. Let us be up
and doing, finding Lanson a domicile. I left my grips at the
I.C. station at Sixty-third Street, and we must get them."

They walked on.

"What an exciting day it's been," Ellen said.

"For us life will always be exciting. And we will live dangerously."

"Is that one of your sayings?"

"No, it's Nietzsche's, but it's my motto. However, our
philosophical friend doesn't appreciate it, I fear. What's his
name again? Oh, yes, Delafield. How could he understand what
Nietzsche meant? Imagine him living dangerously."

He laughed, and broke into song.

The girl of my dreams is the sweetest girl . . .

He didn't go on singing.
"That's too sentimental. But do you know what?"
"What now?"
"You trust to me and we'll do everything we want to in our life. We'll obey even our slightest whims."
"Yes, we will."
"And I have one this moment."
"And what is this one?"
"Kiss me."
She kissed him.
They strode on briskly toward Sixty-third street.

Chapter Eighteen

I

Ed and Ellen sat in the rear of Frank Dolan's Ford. Frank drove slowly along Sixty-seventh Street, toward Stony Island Avenue. A plain-looking girl named Elsie Smithers sat beside Frank.

"Ed, what are you doing with that?" Ellen asked when Ed took a powder puff and mirror out of his pocket.

"What's Hellfire up to now?" Frank asked without turning around.

"Ed, why have you got a powder puff and mirror?" Ellen asked.

"I'm practicing."

"Sounds to me like a new one from the book of Lanson," Frank said.

"Funny, awfully funny," Elsie said.

"Ed, what are you going to do?" Ellen asked.

"You wait and see. I guarantee that it will be exciting."

"What's he planning, Ellen?" Frank asked.

"I don't know."

"Oh, just a little game to drive away the tedium, don't you know," Ed said.

"Why do they call him Hellfire?" Elsie asked.

"Because the name fits me."

"Oh, I see that you blow your own bugle," Elsie said.

"Yes, and loudly," Ed said.

"I bet Ed just likes to shock people. He likes to be unconventional," Elsie said.

"I'd rather be unconventional than conventional," Ellen said, looking sharply at the back of Elsie's head.

"I wouldn't," Elsie said.

"Each to his own choosing," Ed remarked.

"I like people to be ladies and gentlemen," Elsie said.

"Do you know, Elsie, I actually have missed my calling," Ed told her.

"What was that?" Frank asked.

"To be a gentleman."

"I don't like to make fun of things like that. It's nice to meet gentlemen," Elsie said, looking out the window of the moving car.

"What do they do, bow and kiss your hand?" Ed asked.

"And talk like foreign princes in a moving picture?" Ellen added.

"Anybody can be . . . crude," Elsie said.

Ed exchanged a knowing glance with Ellen.

"Milady," Ed said to Ellen.

"Sir," Ellen answered.

"Methinks we are descending tonight to mingle with the canaille," Ed said.

"But will it be amusing, Sir Hellfire?" Ellen asked.

"Lady Ellen, take caution, pray take caution, and do not allow the hoi polloi to tread upon thy skirts. And above all, pray take guard lest it not breathe foul breaths into thy fair face, corrupting thy noble nostrils. And now, milady, pray pardon me because methinks that I must give my nose a loud and noble lordly sneeze."

He burlesqued a sneeze and blew his nose dramatically.

"Milady, I like to see a man blow his nose with gusto," Ed said.

Ellen laughed.

"Say, is this a game?" Frank asked, driving on.

"No, just a lot of plain unadulterated crap," Ed said.

Elsie swung around and tried to sting Ed and Ellen with a glance. She turned back, not speaking. Ellen put her hand in Ed's as they both smiled.

II

"Elsie, I have a suspicion," Ed said.

"What?" she asked.

They occupied a table by the dance floor at the Palm Tree Inn. The orchestra was opposite them. There was a fair-sized midweek crowd.

"I have a suspicion that you do not approve of me."

"Ed, of course she does," Frank chirped in promptly and in a conciliatory voice."

"Why do you say that? You talk awful funny," Elsie told him.

"Funny. Yes, that's the right word. That's me, just a clown," Ed said.

"I don't think that. Not at all."

"Of course you think."

"Doesn't everybody think?" Elsie asked.

"I don't. And do you know why?"

"That's funny. Why?"

"Because everybody else does. Just catch me doing what everybody else does."

"I never met anybody else like you," Elsie said, beginning to thaw.

Ed laid his powder puff and mirror on the table.

"What's that for?" Elsie asked.

"Yes, let us in on the plot," Frank said.

"After the next dance I shall walk off the floor powdering my nose and prancing like a fairy."

"What do you want to do that for?" Elsie asked.

"It's an experiment."

"What do you mean?" Frank asked.

"I want to find out if any so-and-so in this place doesn't like what I do."

"Suppose you find out, Ed?" Frank asked.

"If a female objects to my conduct, then I shall do nothing. Disapproval is the privilege of the fair sex. But if a male disap-

proves and let's out one bat, I shall walk up to him nonchalantly, don't you know, and merely tee off on him."

"Ed, just for a change, let's not have any fights tonight,"
Ellen urged.

"Ed, what's the use of doing it? It isn't worth it. But, of
course, if you do get into a fight, I'm your pal. We're buddies
and I'll stick by you. You know that. But I don't see any use
of starting one," Frank said.

"I don't propose to start any fights. All that I shall do is to
stroll casually off the dance floor, powdering my nose. When I
was a boy, I was told that this is a free country. But I'm from
Missouri. I want to find out, put it to a test to see if this is or is
not a free country. Am I allowed to powder my nose in public
and to comport myself as if I belonged to the neuter gender?"

"What's that mean?" Elsie asked.

Frank showed his embarrassment.

"You don't know what a fairy is, Elsie?" Ed asked.

"No, I don't know what you're talking about."

"Did you ever hear of a man being in love with another
man? That's what a fairy is," Ellen said.

"That's something terrible," Elsie said.

"The Greeks and Romans liked it," Ed said.

"Ed, listen to me. What's the use of pulling off a stunt like
this. We're having a good time as it is, aren't we? You know
if you do, I'm with you to the end, but I don't see the use of
doing it," Frank argued.

"Frank, look around this place. Notice the people here, playing at having a good time. Right on a line from me at that table
there, I spy a false face in a gray suit, and with him a fluffy
and vacuous head in an organdy dress. Observe them closely.
Look at the smirk on his face. Look at the superior expression
and manner of his broad. Are they having a good time? The
answer is no. But if I do something to give them a little fun,
pep up the evening for them, why, I'm being their benefactor."

"How do you know they aren't having a good time?" Elsie
said.

"Looks are not deceiving, not in this instance," Ed told her.

"Judging from the looks of that particular person, Ed, darling, I'd guess that no one could have a good time with him. If you ask me, he looks like wood dressed up in an installment-plan suit," Ellen said.

"Ed, I still don't think you ought to do it. You and Ellen are engaged, and if you get in fights over such matters, you'll both get a bad name. It won't reflect right on either of you," Frank argued.

"That doesn't worry me. But, Ed, dear, I'll be afraid if you get into a fight. I don't want you to be injured."

"That's no cause for worry."

The orchestra began playing. To Frank's dismay, Ed led Ellen onto the dance floor.

III

"Have you noticed my pal, Frank," Ed asked, dancing with Ellen.

"What in particular?"

"He's giving us a wide berth on the dance floor. In case any trouble starts, he's going to be on the other side of the floor, too far away to come to my aid. My pal, Frank, oozes bravery."

"Darling. I don't like him."

"Everything has its uses, my dear."

"Ed, I'm afraid. What you plan to do is amusing, clever. But I don't want you getting into fights where you can be hurt."

"Do you think that the puny sticks miscalled men in this establishment could hurt me? Do you think that the specimens of flaming youth on this dance floor could injure me? Where is your sense of humor, Sweet?"

"Ed, darling, I love you. I can't even stand the idea of your being hurt, the thought that anything could happen to you."

"I give you my word of honor that I shan't be hurt. I value my word and don't give it lightly. But I give it. That settles the question. Now I can't be hurt."

He accidentally stepped on her toe.

"Oh, I'm sorry."

"It's nothing."

"I'm a lousy dancer."

"Ed, it's not so."

"It is. I dance too jerkily. But I'm going to learn to dance better. However, a good dancer is a sign of a misspent youth."

"Who said that?"

"Lanson."

"Lanson says so much. I could listen to what he says forever."

"Lanson is merely glib."

"Ed, please don't rag me because of my father. I'm not responsible for him."

"Hasn't it dawned on you that he might be right? Perhaps I am just glib."

"Stop that," she said, lightly tapping his back.

"I still observe that Frank is busy keeping clear of my traces."

"Ed, you notice everything, don't you?"

"Everything that I shouldn't, and nothing that I should."

"Ed, please don't get in a fight tonight."

He smiled at her. He began singing loudly on the dance floor.

Oh, they called her frivolous Sal, a peculiar sort of a gal.

IV

Following the last encore, the dancing couples drifted off the floor.

"Come on, Ed," Ellen said, stepping ahead of him.

Ed did not follow her. He drew out his powder puff and mirror and nonchalantly dabbed at his nose and cheeks.

Ellen looked back. Momentarily, she was frightened. Then she laughed. She stepped back to his side and glared right and left as if to cut and freeze anyone who cast a disapproving eye at Ed. The dancers continued drifting off the floor, heedless of Ed as he again dabbed his face with the powder puff. Those who did notice him passed on, unimpressed. No one laughed at Ed or paid any attention to his conduct.

Disturbed by his failure to attract attention, Ed burlesqued his actions. He powdered his nose again with elaborate and exaggerated gestures. Still dabbling his nose, he minced off the floor, swaying his hips and buttocks and making sounds with his lips. This gained no attention; even the Chinese waiters refused to notice him.

When they reached their table, they found Frank tense and nervous. Elsie was annoyed. Laughing uproariously, Ed and Ellen sat down. Persons at near-by tables stared, but when Ed looked about fiercely, no one met his eye.

"This is . . . Humoresque," he said, still laughing.

Elsie sat stiff, upright. She blushed. Frank's shoulders sagged, expressing how helpless he felt. Ellen and Ed continued to laugh, but he held his left fist cocked waiting for any stranger to make a remark about him. No one did.

v

Ed turned from the wash bowl in the men's room and dried his hands.

"Frank, are you holding?" he asked.

"Well, I got a little money."

"I just discovered before signaling for you to come here to the crapper with me that I left my dough back in the hotel. I haven't a sou on me. I don't know how I forgot my wallet. I laid it on my dresser when I cleaned up. I guess that in rushing out it just slipped my mind. Can you take care of the bill for me? I'll repay you as soon as I get back to the hotel and fetch my money."

"I'm glad to help you out."

"Frank, can you manage it this way? I don't want to look like a deadbeat in front of the girls. Can you let me take the money for my share and I'll pay it when the Chink gives us the bill?"

Frank drew out his wallet and looked in it.

"The smallest I've got is a five. Here, take it, and give me the change."

"Thanks, Frank. I appreciate it," Ed said, accepting the five-dollar bill.

VI

When they were leaving and received the bill from the Chinese waiter, Ed flung his five on the table. Frank did likewise.

"Get us change," Ed said.

The waiter returned with the change. Ed left fifty cents on the tray and pocketed the balance of the five dollars he'd just borrowed.

They left. By the hat-check stand at the stairway leading down to the street Ed nudged Frank. They allowed the girls to drift downstairs ahead of them.

"Frank, would you mind if Ellen and I walked home?"

"I can drive you just as easy."

"I know, but I want to talk to her. I have something to discuss alone with her."

"Marriage?"

"No, not that. Something personal. Not anything you might suspect. Ellen isn't that kind of a girl. But I want to talk to her, you understand, don't you?"

"Of course."

"Thanks, you're a real friend. I'll see you tomorrow. I'll give you a buzz at six, how's that?"

"All right, Ed."

They followed the girls downstairs.

VII

"I told Frank we preferred walking," Ed said, strolling along Sixty-third Street away from The Palm Tree Inn.

"Ed, you were such a scream walking off the dance floor," Ellen said, hanging onto his arm.

"I was waiting, ready to let go, too. And not one measly bastard had the guts to crack wise at me."

"If Elsie heard that, she'd disapprove."

Ed laughed heartily.

"What's the joke?" Ellen asked.

"I was just thinking—perhaps Frank is petting Elsie now." He laughed. "Imagine necking a cake of ice."

They both laughed.

"Ellen, you take this key and go up to my hotel room first. I'll follow you. You just skip by the desk quickly. No one will bother you."

"All right, darling."

"Oh, I almost forgot something."

He took out his notebook and stopped under a lighted window. With a stub of pencil he marked down Frank Dolan's name and, after it, five dollars. Then he added the amount to the total of his listed debts and smiled.

"A telephone number?" Ellen asked.

"No, just high finances. This is my account book."

"May I see it?"

"Little girls shouldn't trouble their little brains with high finances. It disturbs their looks. In this family I'm the financial wizard."

"Sometimes you talk in riddles."

"I'm a riddle. The riddle of the universe."

"If anybody else said that, it wouldn't be proper. If you say it, it's wonderful."

"The hell with riddles. Let us move on," he said, taking her arm.

He broke into song:

And when I told them how beautiful you were,
They wouldn't believe me, they wouldn't believe me.

Chapter Nineteen

I

Ed was in his BVD's. He sat on his unmade bed smoking a cigarette, his lips curled into a smile. He brushed back a curly lock.

It was an ordinary hotel room. On the dresser in a corner he had set up a Gideon Bible as his altar. It was flanked by two gin bottles, and before it he had placed a package of cigarettes and a tray full of butts and ashes. His altar amused him. It had amused Ellen, also.

His week in this room was up today, and that created a new problem. But problems were easily settled. This one was particularly simple. It offered two alternative solutions. He could pay his hotel bill. Or he could not pay it. What could be more simple? The first solution required money. He had no money. Therefore events forced him to adopt the second alternative. He went to the closet and got out his little notebook. Sitting at the desk, he wrote down the amount of the bill, $26.74, in his list of creditors, and added this sum to his total list of debts. His problem was settled. Now all he needed to do was to leave the hotel.

Ed dragged his suitcase out from under the bed. Every time he had left the room, he had locked it, and on one side he had pasted a thin strip of adhesive tape so that he could detect if the suitcase had been opened in his absence. He observed that the tape was in place. All was well for Lanson. He unlocked the grip. Inside, there were three shirts, an extra suit of BVD's, three ties, two pairs of dirty socks, three Chicago telephone directories and a stack of newspapers. The extra paper had given his suitcase weight, and when the bellhop had carried it upstairs to show him his room, it had seemed as if he had a grip full of clothes. That had saved him the inconvenience of being asked to pay his bill in advance. It was a card all right. And it proved that newspapers had at least one decent use in the world. They could be of help when you were defrauding a hotel. He smiled at this thought, and flicked ashes on the rug. He took his clothes out of the grip and laid them on the bed. He dressed, putting on two suits of underwear and four shirts. He stuck the extra ties and socks in his coat pockets. Then he carefully locked the suit-case, and shoved it under the bed. He pulled it out and, for the gesture, put another strip of tape on one side. He shoved it under the bed a second time.

Studying himself in the mirror, Ed was pleased with his husky appearance. And he didn't think that he would look suspicious, even though the extra shirts caused noticeable creases near his collar. A dumb hotel clerk wouldn't be observant enough to draw any deductions from these creases. He could idly drift out of the hotel, and then, for all eternity, it would never have further dealings with him—not until that day of eternal recurrence when he would be back where he was this minute, gypping the Tudor Hotel once again. Now, did he honestly believe in eternal recurrence? It was a fascinating speculation. It impressed most people when he explained it to them, even if it hadn't impressed Delafield. And it was more plausible to believe in and accept than God. But that was another department of human interest, and it was not on the order of the day.

He was all ready now, fully prepared to say good-bye, hail, farewell, *Ave atque Vale* to the Tudor Hotel. He had enjoyed its comforts and conveniences for a week, but one had to be on the move. New fields of exploration were always open. New hotels, new boarding houses awaited him.

He lit a fresh cigarette and left his room, slamming the door. He took the elevator down. Emerging from it, he told himself that what he ought to do was to walk right out, quickly, but without creating any suspicion. But he couldn't do that. Inas-much as he was never again going to return to this hotel, inas-much as he and this establishment were parting forever, he should not make his departure precipitous. He strolled to the desk. The clerk was busy sorting mail.

"Good morning, Mr. Devoe."

"Good morning," Ed answered the clerk.

"Here, I have a letter for you."

The clerk passed the letter to Ed. He had written it to himself, trying to disguise the handwriting. It made him seem more reliable if he received mail.

"Mr. Devoe, you've forgotten to settle your bill."

"Did I? I forgot to attend to it. I'm going out on a business appointment now, and then I'll cash a check. I'll be back at lunch time and I'll settle it then. I'm staying here another week. Business is pretty good."

"That's all right. I'm glad to hear that business is good, Mr. Devoe."

Ed turned away from the desk. He turned back, stuck his hand in his pocket, pulled out the key, and laid it on the desk. He sauntered off. He was starting to sweat because he was so well clad. He took out a handkerchief and mopped his face. He left the hotel and, turning the corner of Sixty-fourth Street, he strode on toward Sixty-third.

Now the problem was to find another room in which to stay for the coming week. However, it was not yet lunch time. Why concern oneself with such a question so early in the day?

Why concern oneself when the sun was shining, heralding the summer that would soon arrive, particularly when he had a girl like Ellen. She was wonderful, and all of the other adjectives. In his fashion, he truly loved her. He would never forget the Tudor Hotel, not merely because it was now on his creditor list. However, he'd have to keep this fact in mind now, and not walk past it lest he be seen by an employee. But there was a more important reason than that connected with filthy lucre why he would never forget the Tudor Hotel. Ellen had been lovely in that hotel with him.

He strolled along Sixty-third Street, smoking a cigarette, swinging his arms, sweating.

He got out a suitcase he'd checked at the Illinois Central station and lugged it to the lavatory. There he was alone. He undressed in a toilet booth and put on fresh underwear and a fresh shirt, which he took from the suitcase he had checked. He stuffed his spare clothing into this grip. He was now comfortable. He rechecked the grip and went outside. He walked on to a near-by Greek restaurant and sat down to eat ham and eggs, coffee and doughnuts.

After breakfast, his total capital would be twenty cents. That created another problem. Money. He couldn't touch Frank Dolan right off because of that five spot he'd borrowed from him at the Palm Tree Inn the other night. He'd explained it to Frank, though, telling him that he'd gotten into a crap game, run his dough up to fifty bucks, and then had a streak of bad luck. Frank was his chump. Frank believed him.

He could telephone Ellen and see her this morning. He was inclined to, but it wouldn't be the best strategy. Strategy and technique were as necessary in love as in war. So let her sit home and wait for him to call her. And let there be no call. Absence makes the heart grow fonder. Let her think of him. That wouldn't do her any harm.

He finished his breakfast in leisurely fashion. He signaled for a second cup of coffee. Suddenly he realized that he had forgotten something. He'd meant to steal the Gideon Bible at the hotel and he'd left the room without it. He must not be so careless the next time.

The waitress brought him his coffee. He put sugar and milk in the cup and stirred the coffee. He lit a cigarette. There was nothing like a hearty breakfast and a good cigarette on a spring morning when you were without a care in the world. He told himself that the gods could be no happier than he was at this moment.

II

After breakfast Ed stood in front of the restaurant, indecisive. But he recalled that there was a branch public library at Kimbark Avenue, so he ambled down to it. He hadn't been doing much reading of late, and he ought to spend more time in the library.

There was a reading room in the front of the library. Having found a copy of *Thus Spake Zarathustra*, Ed selected a chair at a table where he would be opposite a cute girl who was reading and making notes with a stack of books in front of her.

Ed took out a notebook and pencil and began thumbing through the book. He had read it once, and now he was skimming it, looking here and there for sentences, insights, thoughts that would refresh his memory. His attention was caught by a short paragraph in the first portion of the book. He read and reread it several times with mounting enthusiasm and decided to copy it down. He slowly transcribed the sentence in his notebook:

Behold the good and the just! Whom do they hate most? Him who breaketh up their tables of values, the breaker, the law-breaker:—he, however, is the creator.

He glanced at the ceiling reflectively. The noble law-breaker. What a mission to perform! After skimming through more pages, he copied down another sentence.

Ah, my brother, hast thou never seen a virtue backbite and stab itself?

He never ceased to marvel at Nietzsche's passion, insight, hard thinking.

. . . hast thou never seen a virtue backbite and stab itself?

Link this with Freud and think of young virgins from good homes. Think of religious people who prayed throughout their lives, did not their "virtue" backbite and stab itself, turning into hypocrisy, into pride and arrogance, into intolerance against the sinner and the unbeliever? This single sentence of Nietzsche's was like a door opening up whole avenues of insight and reference.

He thumbed on, thinking how he some day would write a book, one full of aphorisms, thoughts, mottoes, insights, a new

Nietzschean work. It wouldn't be systematic. And that meant that that fellow, Delafield, wouldn't consider it philosophy. Why be systematic? Nonsense. He didn't want his book to be systematic. It would be fragmentary, but full of darts and arrows, lightning flashes. He wasn't yet ready to write it. He had to think, concentrate, work hard, correlate thoughts and experiences. But good hard work of this kind would do him good. The only question was how he could support himself. But that was not the proper question to ask himself in a library. How would he support himself? This, properly speaking, was a cross-reference. It was a problem to be handed over to someone else. Ellen? Why not? Then, after he finished his book, he would get a job, marry her, and . . . Did he want to marry her? Did he really want to be tied down? His older brother, Pierre, had gone around the world. How could he surpass Pierre if he were tied down?

Where was Pierre now? Pierre had introduced him to Nietzsche. But he and Pierre never did get along. The rivalry between them was too intense. Pierre didn't like it because he usually took Pierre's girls away from him. Well, Pierre was somewhere east of Suez this very minute. Some day, to go to the East!

But he did love Ellen, after his fashion.

He thumbed through the book some more and, coming on the final paragraphs of the first part, there was a rising excitement within him. He remembered how he had been exalted, thrilled, emotionally energized when he had first read this section in the Chicago Public Library at Randolph and Michigan. He had compared that experience to sex and called it an intellectual orgasm, but it was not an apt comparison. His mind had been on its toes, just as he was on his toes when he was in a fight. And the words he had read had been a promise of the future. He had associated them with sunshine and he had vaguely imagined himself climbing yellow mountains of sunshine, climbing to heights where there were undefined experiences awaiting him, experiences laden with all sorts of promises and thrills.

He read again the words that had so stimulated him.

And it is the great noontide, when man is in the middle of his course between animal and Superman, and celebrateth his advance to the evening as his highest hope: for it is the advance to a new morning.

On rereading, these words had a diminished effect upon him. The cliffs of sunlight to be scaled seemed less vivid. The words were more like words, less like inexplicable sensations, inexplicable calls to self-realization. He was disappointed in them. He read the remaining two paragraphs on the page.

At such time will the down-goer bless himself, that he should be an over-goer; and the sun of his knowledge will be at noontide.
"Dead are all the Gods: now do we desire the Superman to live."—Let this be our final will at the great noontide!
Thus spake Zarathustra.

Now, these words which had once stirred him evoked a mood of nostalgia. Gone, perhaps gone forever, was the thrill he had known the first time he had read this same passage. He longed to recapture his sensation from that experience, his sense of elation that he used to be able to call forth from that same stimulus. But he could not do it. The words had less effect on him, his reaction was less intense, and his images had become less vivid. Often the words which stimulated a man played a role in his inner life, went through the same cycle as did a woman. Just as a woman lost her capacity to give him pleasure and amuse him, so did the same words, on being reread, lose their magic power to stimulate, ennoble, lift him upward to an inner plane of rare experience.

He glanced up from his book and noticed the girl opposite him. She was a cute little trick. There was something fresh about her. She was like the morning, or the noontide, he told himself. Catching her eye, he smiled charmingly. At first she acted as if she did not see him. Then her face changed, broke into a childlike smile.

"You're working hard," he said in a half-whisper.

"So are you."

A girl who worked in the library came by the table and shushed them. He took out his cigarettes and nodded in the direction of the door.

She followed him outside.

III

Ed walked toward Jackson Park with the girl, Betsy. He was gratified because of his characteristic good fortune. Just as he'd come away from the library, he had met Eddie Dill, a friend of Musty Mulligan and one of the boys who hung around Sixty-third and Stony Island, and he'd been able to bum two dollars off Eddie. He was going to while away the time until lunch, take Betsy to eat, and then he'd call Ellen and see her. Not that he loved Ellen less, but that it was good for her soul to be kept home waiting to hear from him. She was getting too possessive about him. He glanced at the girl by his side. Sweet and young —a virgin. A lovely flower to pluck and wear in your coat for a day or so. But he would leave this flower unplucked. He'd merely talk with her in order to while away the morning.

"I'm a bad influence," he said.

"Don't say that. I don't like to have to work so hard on my term paper," she said.

Ed thought that this girl had better watch out or her virtue would certainly backbite and stab itself in the back.

"I'm a bad influence nonetheless, taking you away from your work," he said.

"I'll go back to it. The air won't hurt me."

Seducing a virgin satisfied the ego more than it did the aesthetic sense. The world should be so organized that this task was departmentalized, and virgins went to professional de-flowerers just as children went to doctors to be vaccinated.

"I should be working, too," he said.

"It must be hard to write a book."

"I don't think so."

"Some people write books, and look at the time I have writing a term paper, and my old teacher, Mr. Weber, he'll probably give me a C if I'm lucky."

"How did you happen to come down to this library instead of going to one at the University?"

"Oh, I never get a thing done in Harper, that's the library at school. I always see some girl I know, and we get to talking, and first thing you know we're not studying, and maybe we're going to the Coffee Shop to get hot chocolate. But I have to write my term paper. I must pass in my courses. If I flunk out, my Daddy will be mad at me."

According to Zarathustra, woman was the most dangerous plaything of man. What—call Betsy dangerous? Even Ellen wasn't really a dangerous plaything, but she was a closer approach to danger than any other girl he'd ever loved.

"Tell me about yourself, Betsy," he said as they crossed Stony Island Avenue to go into Jackson Park.

IV

"I've never known a person named Algernon before," the girl said.

"It is an unusual name. It's an aloof name, lacking in the same friendliness as the human note of Elizabeth or Betsy. It doesn't have the same character to it as your name does," Ed told her.

They were near the Jackson Park lagoon and they heard the swish of oars as someone passed in a rowboat. Betsy sat prim and stiff, her legs together, her dress smoothed out neatly. Ed lay on the grass facing her, his coat carefully folded beside him.

"It's too bad," Betsy said sympathetically.

"It's nothing." His manner was cavalier. "It's nothing. Others before me have sacrificed more than I am giving up." He glanced at the lagoon where the sun created a dazzling and jewel-like surface on the calm water. He turned back to Betsy. "After all, what did I sacrifice?"

She listened intensely. He had impressed her, and he could perceive that she hung on his every word, believed what he was telling her. It was amusing. The female of the species was so credulous. Of course, Betsy was just a child. How could a girl remain so innocent in her sixteen, seventeen, eighteen years? But this was a charming little experience, something to pass the time while Ellen learned to care for him by the absent treatment.

"I don't think that I can even call it a sacrifice. My father wants me to work in his office, and to be a junior executive. But I loathe business. I will be an artist or nothing in this world."

"You mustn't lose confidence in yourself," she told him.

"It's kind of you to be so encouraging."

"I know you will be successful," she said.

He fixed his eyes on her. She lowered her head, and a blush came to her plump cheeks. She smoothed out her dress. He smiled, amused, sardonic.

"As I was saying, Betsy, I have sacrificed little. A job that I don't want. I could have money, but then I am an austere and frugal person and I have few needs. I could drive around in my own automobile, a sports roadster like many of the young wastrels in the city. My brothers do. But is that giving up anything? I wouldn't say so."

"But it is nice, isn't it, to have a car of your own . . . Algernon," she said, pronouncing the name self-consciously.

"I suppose it has its conveniences, but we do have two feet and we can walk on them. Many chaps my age have their own cars, just as my brothers do. Will they be remembered in thirty years because they had sports' roadsters? I might not be remembered and I know that. But I will give up everything to achieve my purposes. No, I can't say that my sacrifices to literature are really consequential."

"Yes, yes they are. What you are doing is very brave."

He lit a cigarette and gazed off at the silvery lagoon, morose, glum.

"You seem unhappy," she said, touched.

He faced her, smiling graciously, his mood changing instantaneously. "No, not at all. I was thinking of my work. You must forgive me. At the oddest moments, ideas, phrases, incidents occur to me."

"It must be very hard to be a writer. I know it is, because I know how much trouble I have to go through to write a term paper."

"It is, and it isn't. It is the only life worth living. At all events, that's what it means to me. That is why it seems to me that what I have given up is nothing, nothing of the slightest significance."

"Can't you explain it to your father so that he'll understand?" she asked.

"No, I don't think that I can. You see, my differences and misunderstandings with my father go back a number of years. When I was sixteen, I was in college."

She listened with awe.

"Yes, I was at Harvard at sixteen. But I saw nothing in that moth-eaten establishment that would help me in my career as a writer. I quit. I had a row with my father. But I wouldn't go back to college. Ever since, we have never gotten on, and he has never been sympathetic to my work."

"That's too bad."

"Oh, what can you expect from a businessman?"

"My Daddy is a businessman, but he's nice. He is, he's nice. And he reads, he reads all of the time," she said.

"Now, however, my battle is almost won. I am finishing my book. It is just about written."

"I know that it will make you famous, too. I just know it will."

"I don't seek fame and fortune. I seek, in my humble way, to discover truth, and to record it. But I want your help, if I may ask for it."

She was too flustered to answer him. There was a twinkle in his eyes.

"Betsy, tell me, do you think I should publish my book under my own name, or should I use a pseudonym?"

"I wouldn't know."

"What do you think of my name? Do you think it's a good name to be used by the author of a book?"

She thought for a moment. He watched her, giving the impression that he was anxiously waiting for her answer.

"I like it. Yes, I do. It's an unusual name. Algernon Stillwater. If I saw that name on a book, I think I would remember it."

"That settles my problem. I am grateful for your aid in solving it."

"But it's nothing," she said, girlish, shy.

The sun slanted across her round and vapid face. He observed her closely. She seemed to be out of something other than life. How could a girl be so dumb? But it would be a shame to change her. She should be put on display in a museum. She was too young to play around with. Seducing her would be like seducing an infant. For while she had a neat and developed body, her emotions, her mind, were years younger. And yet in a few years this girl would become scheming, crafty, bourgeois, and dull, unspeakably dull.

Why was he wasting his time telling her a cock-and-bull story? But why not? It suited his fancy.

"What is your book about?" she asked.

"It is difficult to say. You see, it is not a plot story, and it doesn't have a happy ending. It is a kind of chronicle, and it is a sort of philosophical novel. It seeks to depict the romance of reality, and the reality of romance," he said, and she was unable to mask her bewilderment. "It is set in a strange and imagined land which I call Fantasia. I place this land on the other side of the moon."

"You must have imagination to write a book like that."

"The main character is a young knight, and just as knights used to seek the holy grail, he is a seeker. He has a dream of fair women. But each fair damsel disappoints him, disillusions him. He seeks, but he doesn't find. With all the trappings of romance, I try to depict emotion realistically."

"I'll bet it will be interesting."

"This is not the kind of an age for such writing. This is an age where business counts. Success, sports roadsters, bank accounts, that's the thing."

"You're an idealist. You know, I am an idealist, too. I am."

"I believe you," he said solemnly.

She smiled a shy invitation.

Twelve o'clock whistles began to fill the air.

"Would you like to have lunch with me?" he asked.

She shook her head girlishly.

He rose and held out his hand to her. He pulled her up, embraced her, kissed her.

She blushed and turned her head away from him.

"You are very sweet, Betsy."

She didn't answer.

"Let us go and have lunch," he said.

Still flustered, she coyly took his arm. He guided her across the driveway and toward a park exit.

Betsy, he thought—Betsy, a droll little episode.

v

"Ed, why didn't you call me? I waited all morning for you to," Ellen said, angry.

He did not answer her promptly.

She let her eyes rove about her. It suddenly occurred to her that she and Bill Northrup had sat on this very same bench that morning she had kept him waiting so long, making him think that he had to marry her. What a coincidence! Then she had suffered from ennui. She had not even realized what happiness was around the corner. But from then to now, roles had been reversed. She had made Bill wait. Now she'd had to do the waiting. But it was not the same. And she didn't want to think such thoughts. They contained a possible prophecy she didn't want to face.

"Why didn't you call?" she asked.

"I can explain, but you shouldn't ask me in such a peremptory tone," he said quietly.

"I didn't mean it that way."

"I had you on my mind all morning. I wanted to telephone you, but I couldn't. I had to attend to important matters. I had to get out of the hotel and I didn't want to get caught."

"But after you got out, couldn't you have telephoned me?"

"Theoretically, yes. But I couldn't because I was distracted. I didn't want to call you in a distracted mood."

"Distracted?" she asked him.

He stared off at the blue sky, moody. He had to make his expressions match his words. But he thought of what had happened. This morning he had been with one girl at one spot in Jackson Park. This afternoon he was with another girl, in another spot of the same park.

"I waited all morning for you to call. You promised me you would."

"What do you think I was doing—flirting with somebody else so early in the day? Ellen, I can't stand jealousy. If you don't believe me and trust me, well, we might as well call it quits now."

"What is this, an invitation?"

"You know that it isn't. You know I worship you. If you deserted me, you cannot begin to imagine how distraught I should be. I would almost go out of my head."

He stopped speaking to kiss her. Holding her in his arms, he said:

"Ellen, you must trust me. And if you do, we'll conquer. But I can't buck the whole world and then feel that you disbelieve in me."

He withdrew from the embrace and dropped his arms in his lap. His shoulders drooped in dejection.

Ellen forgot that he had not given her any specific reasons to account for not having telephoned her. She was fearful, but her gaze was tender and loving.

"Ed, I'm sorry."

She kissed him affectionately.

"Ellen, I spent this morning pondering, ruminating over many matters. I'm fed up. I'm fed up with this idea of frittering away my time. I'm going to get some decent work done. And then I'm going to marry you."

"Ed, I knew you would come to this decision."

He looked at her strangely.

"But, darling, what's wrong?" she asked, observing the change in his expression.

He broke into a smile.

"Yes, I'm going to put my nose to the grindstone. And at the same time I'm going to write a book. I'm going to make enough money to keep you in style by fall, and then we'll do all of the things we want to. Why should I go on frittering away my time? It doesn't make sense."

"Ed, dear, I love you for yourself. But, my darling, we ought to think about what we're going to do. And I want you to show my father, too."

"Has he been talking against me again?"

"Not exactly. He just says that he's from Missouri."

"Goddam it! Damn him, trying to poison you against me."

"Please, Ed, don't get excited about it. You know Father. He's just what you said he is—a Babbitt."

"Listen, Ellen, before I cash my chips in I'll show plenty of people, plenty more people than him. Ellen, I have a plan."

"Yes, darling."

"Here, I'm disintegrating. I have to go away and get a new start. That's how I will have to make my mark. And when I do that, I'll send for you."

"But, Ed, you mean leaving Chicago, without me?"

"Do you trust me?"

"You know I do, you know it, darling."

"You believe in me?"

She squeezed his hand in answer.

"I'm going to New York. I'll get on my feet there. Wouldn't you rather live in New York?"

"Yes, if you are there with me."

"Ellen, I couldn't permit that—I couldn't allow you to go through the first stage with me, living in cheap rooms, eating bad food, suffering all the worries and frustrations that inevitably come to one when one sets out to crack a strange town."

"Ed, dear, why can't I go through it if you do? Why can't I? What kind of a person am I if I can't?"

"I'll have to consider it all further. But I'll settle everything in short order. And we'll be married and do what we want. Whim will be our God, and I'll enthrone it. Whim will be God, Whirl will be King, and Ellen will be Queen."

"You say such charming things," she said, but there was a touch of sadness in her voice.

He patted her cheek and kissed her.

"Darling, did you get a new room yet?" she asked.

"No, but I shall."

"Do you want to come home with me? This is Mary's afternoon off."

He stood up, pulled her after him, and with his arm around her, they walked toward Ellen's home.

Chapter Twenty

I

The pitch black night, like a piece of cardboard, was pasted against Ellen's bedroom window. The quiet was absolute, and she lay in bed remembering how, during the afternoon, she and Ed had been together in this same bed. Had she ever been more happy than this afternoon? Had it been the realization that he was going away, that they would part for a while, that had made their love more tender, and, at the same time, more passionate?

She loved Ed, and he was going away. A mood of sadness took possession of her. What would she do without him? Just a moment before, the darkness of the evening had been the background of memories of love. Now the melancholy that invaded her poured out of her being and spilled, like ink, over her room, over the world that stood beyond her opened window. The darkness of the night was the color of melancholy, the sadness of thoughts of parting.

Why couldn't he get on his feet here in Chicago and not have to leave her?

She could see clearly now that Ed was his own worst enemy. He was not easy to understand. So often he changed from one mood to another. Ed was such a boy, such a child—her child. She had to take care of him. But he was going away where she couldn't do this.

So many things could happen to him. Suppose that some girl in New York should cast her net for him? Could he resist? If he resisted, and the girl were smart, all she needed to do was to dare him. He wouldn't refuse a dare because he was such a boy. But if he wouldn't refuse a dare from a girl, didn't that mean Ed didn't really love her?

190

Sometimes she was not sure of his love. It was difficult at times to know when he meant what he said and when he didn't. Sometimes when he talked of his love and his affections there would be a mocking, ironic note in his voice. But he must be in love with her. This afternoon he couldn't have been so tender if he didn't love her.

Ellen turned onto her left side and curled up.

Even though he didn't meet with dangers, even though he didn't fall in love with any other girl, it would still be sad. She would not see him every day. She would be alone, without him. Life would be so empty while he was away from her. Why did he have to go away? What could she do to stop him? She couldn't tell him that she didn't want him to go, because he couldn't be handled that way. If he was commanded to do something, his spirit of contrariness flared up. Should she pretend that she was sick? Or should she tell him that she was going to have a baby? Could she succeed with Ed with such a trick? She didn't know what to do.

She thought of how she and Ed would cut a figure in New York. She had no clear idea of what it would be like. There were many skyscrapers there, and Riverside Drive was supposed to be quite nice. They would live on Riverside Drive. Then she would be so happy. But between such a time and now there was the intervening period when she would be separated from Ed. How would she be able to go on from minute to minute, from hour to hour, from day to day? It would be ghastly. This morning, when she had waited for him to telephone her, she had been the prey of so many fears; she had been so miserable. How much worse would it be with Ed in New York. He had grown into her life. She and Ed were part of each other.

And suppose their parting was to be forever. She couldn't bear such a thought. But need she entertain it? It wouldn't be forever. If necessary, she would follow him to New York.

Why did he have to go away?

She realized, in asking herself this question, that she had made mistakes with Ed. She had allowed him to gain the upper hand. But perhaps that was the nature of love, and to love meant to allow the one you loved to have the upper hand over you. If so, then she had to conclude that she loved Ed more than he loved her. He would then be able to bear their parting more easily, more lightly than she would. If he loved her, why did he want to leave now, so shortly after they had become engaged, had begun to know and to enjoy each other? The reasons he gave for leaving were not very forceful ones, particularly now when he was not present to urge them on her with all his persuasiveness. He knew people in Chicago. In New York, he was unknown. It should be easier for him to get ahead more rapidly in Chicago than in New York. She did not want to pursue this line of reasoning further. It would only cause her agony. She could see that the more she thought of his reasons, the weaker they seemed to be. She dreaded the conclusions that could be drawn from this observation.

It was not a lack of love for her that was driving him to New York, she argued with herself. It was his spirit of adventure, his dear, dangerous, adventurous spirit. This was what was so wonderful in him. This was why she loved him. And it was separating him from her. She didn't want to change him fundamentally. But couldn't she check that adventurous spirit in him just enough to keep him with her?

If she could only sleep. She could dream of Ed. Perhaps she would have happy dreams. She would dream that he was not leaving her, but then she would wake up in the morning and realize that it had only been a dream. Even so, she wanted it, wanted such comfort for the short space of the night. And she could not sleep.

She turned and sank her face in the pillow.

What should she do? She recalled how she had been so bored when boys tried to force their attentions on her. She had only been contemptuous of such boys. She must do nothing that would cause Ed to feel this way about her. What should she do? All is fair in love and war. But all is not good and wise, because some of the things you did might cause you to lose.

And where was her pride? What kind of a person was she that she had to let herself grow so dependent on another person

—even on Ed? But, oh, how silly, how ridiculous pride was when you were in love! She wanted Ed so much. She wanted him to be with her in her bed at this very moment. She wanted to have him with her every minute of her life. And he was going away.

She felt like crying. But she gritted her teeth, tautened her limbs, clenched her fists. She would be dry-eyed. She would not be weak.

But, oh, God, how could she prevent Ed from leaving?

She heard the rumble of a streetcar passing on Sixty-seventh Street. Its echo faded. All was quiet. She was alone. The silence, the loneliness, of the night seemed sad, poignant.

II

Ellen rose at dawn. She had slept badly during the night, but, yawning, she realized that she was not really tired. She was dull, half listless, but not actually sleepy. She dressed quietly and in haste. She wrote a note saying that she had gotten up at dawn to go out and take a walk in the park, so that her father need not worry if he discovered she wasn't in bed. She didn't want him to worry. She left the note by the telephone and tiptoed out of the apartment.

Ellen stepped out of her hallway into a scene half obscured by a thick gray mist. She stood in front of her building for a moment, breathing deeply of the clear, fresh, invigorating early-morning air. Off in the eastern wing of the sky she saw low, fleecy clouds lightly veined with pink. Soon the sun would rise. It would be glorious. While she stood looking opposite her at the trees and shrubbery outlined in the fog, she heard the echo of footsteps about a block away. They were a light tapping on the pavement, but it sounded strange, mysterious. She heard it die away. The world was so quiet. She heard nothing, and she was absorbed in her own thoughts and feelings.

She crossed the street, found a path through the dew-moistened bushes, and then strolled over the wet grass of the golf course.

The miracle of dawn was preparing for its unfoldment before

her eyes. She could see the fog lighten; white chunks of mist floated and faded away like clouds. While she had been finding her way into the park, the pink in the clouds had spread and deepened. A shadow swept across the dark grass like a frightened animal in flight. She strolled on, her feet beginning to get damp. The departing mist was turning from gray to white and silver. During the time required for her to walk a few yards, the color in the sky had again been transformed, and the clouds were stained with red.

How lovely, Ellen thought.

Ellen felt so young, so gay, so like a child. Not knowing why she did it, she broke into a run. Giggling and breathless, she stopped as suddenly as she had started. She walked on, tracing a zigzag course, walking as she used to when she was a little girl. Her manner of walking brought back her childhood to her. She was under the spell of an illusion, the illusion that years of time had been washed away and that she was a flat-chested little girl in grammar school. Just as the mist was vanishing before her eyes, so did her illusion disintegrate in her mind. She was not a little girl, and she was melancholy. She wanted to reach backward and restore the time when she was a small child. She thought of Ed, and her nostalgia faded. It was more fun to be with him than it would be to return to the past. Oh, what fun it would be to spend the night with him in love, to wake at dawn, spent, listless, satisfied, to rise and walk hand-in-hand with him toward the sunrise. Yes, if he were only with her, and they were now breathing in the fresh morning air, walking in the same wet grass, waiting together for the sun to burst upon the world.

She missed him so much now. When they were married, this is what they would sometimes do. When she saw him today she would tell him of what she was now doing. He would understand her feeling and he would approve of this adventure. He was capable of doing the same thing himself. Ed had a soul. She and Ed had similar souls. They were made for each other, if ever man and woman were.

In her absorption she had not heard the birds. Now she heard one, and then others took up the notes, and a chorus of singing and chirping unexpectedly burst upon her. She listened as if she were hearing birds sing for the first time in her life.

Though still hidden, the sun was burning through the fog, like an X ray. The world was growing lighter. The mist scattered. The sky was bright. The deep red which had stained it only a moment before was erased, and the sun hung over the eastern horizon, a rising ball of orange fire, gradually, subtly changing to gold and luminous yellow. It rose higher, a yellow disk, so brilliant that she could not focus her eyes upon it directly. It hung high in the sky, as if it were somewhere above the unseen blue of the invisible lake beyond Jackson Park. As the sun rose, the scene changed. Shadows swept the earth. Fields of grass turned into diffused and uncertain lagoons of color. Drops of dew were endowed with the glistening brilliance of diamonds. And the sun rose higher until it seemed to become fixed, anchored in the sky. A new dawn, like an act of creation, had burst upon the world.

Awed, enthralled, Ellen had watched this spectacle. Every object, every color, each movement, the grass, the trees, the singing birds, the blue sky, had appeared as if imbued with a life which matched that which throbbed within her own body. She wanted to penetrate to the heart of this life, to possess it, all of it, until it was absorbed into her own nature.

And, oh, she wished Ed were with her. She stood still and a strange sense of loneliness came upon her. The world borrowed from her her loneliness. It was a lonely world, one which only Ed could make friendly for her.

Somehow he seemed related to, connected with, and involved in everything she had just seen. The sun was part of Ed, and Ed was part of it. The drops of dew on the grass, they were suggestive of Ed. The world was a mystery, full of motions, saturated with a life all its own, and Ed was part of it, and it was part of Ed. Everything she saw, everything she thought, everything she felt, she was doing for Ed as well as for herself.

This was why she missed him so much. If he were only with her, they could talk of the dawn together. She would listen to him. He would describe the dawn for her. He would hold her, kiss her, and, holding hands, they would run over the wet grass like happy children, and they would laugh together. She was anxious for the time to arrive today when she would see him. Her Ed!

But he was going away, and she feared he would not come back to her.

Ellen strolled on, heedless of her soggy feet. She thought that six months ago, if anyone had predicted that she would be doing precisely what she was now doing, she would have laughed scornfully. How unpredictable life was. In the distance she saw a man and a dog, separated from her by such space that they appeared small, strange, as if they were figures from a world different from that in which she walked. A cloud hid the sun, breaking, distorting, blunting its warm rays. Shadows of this cloud stole across the grass, taking away the sparkle of the blades of grass it touched, painting these blades a deeper, darker green. But then the cloud was gone, and the motion of another shadow was traced on the same grass. How charming! How wonderful was life!

She began to sing a popular song which she knew was cheap. But it entwined its tune into the warp and woof of her emotions, and it moved her as she sang.

When you and I were seventeen, and life and love were new.

If Ed were with her, she would ask him to sing. He had such a rich voice. He was such a spirit, so poetic, so sensitive, so brave, so adventurous. Although he was not with her now, it was because of him that she loved this dawn, this world and everything in it.

The man and dog in the distance had disappeared from sight. She was alone, and she strolled aimlessly on.

III

Ellen quietly let herself in by the front door.

"Ellen!" her father called, his angry voice breaking into her mood. "Ellen, where are you?" he called from the dining room.

She found him standing by the table in his shirtsleeves, his hair tousled. He looked worried. Saying nothing, she faced him, impassive.

"What the hell's gotten into you?"

"You got my note, didn't you, Father?"

"Yes, but what the hell's the idea of scaring the life out of me, going out walking at this time of the morning? Why, what would people think? A decent girl shouldn't be out in the park at this hour of the morning. What would people think of her?"

"It was so lovely. I wanted to take a walk and see the sun rise."

"You never did this before . . . before you met that fellow. I suppose you were meeting him. What kind of monkey business is this?"

"No, I wasn't. And there's no kind of monkey business. I wanted to get up and see the sun come up. It was so lovely."

"You didn't even comb your hair. You look like a fright. I don't want my daughter carrying on this way."

"Carrying on? What's wrong with getting up early and going out for a walk in the park? Didn't you ever do it? Didn't anybody ever do it?"

"Ellen, you're acting queer and strange, not at all like yourself ever since you met this fellow."

"Don't call him this fellow. He's my future husband and your future son-in-law."

"Well, I don't think he's a good influence."

"Father, stop it!"

"You're my daughter, by God!"

"But I own myself. You can't change my mind. And you're making a mountain out of a molehill. All I did was to get up and take a walk in the park to see the sunrise, and because of that, you carry on like this."

"Me, carrying on?"

"Well, aren't you?"

"You look like a fright."

"Father, don't be so old-fashioned."

He sputtered. He didn't know what to say. His anger vanished, and he stood before her, a sad old man, his expression weak. She was touched. Although she was sympathetic to him, sorry for him, she believed she had to defeat him once and for all.

"Father, I shan't argue with you. I love Ed and I'm going to marry him," she said, speaking slowly, decisively.

Mr. Rogers said nothing. His shoulders slumped. His fat arms hung helplessly at his side. All firmness had left his body.

"My feet are wet. I want to change my shoes and stockings," she said.

"Risking catching your death of cold in the park!"

Without answering him she went out of the room. He stood at the doorway through which she had just passed, his face blank. His jowls were slack. His eyes were dull, surrounded by little bags of fatty tissue. His thick lips were relaxed. He dropped into a chair and thoughtfully drank his cup of cold coffee.

Chapter Twenty-one

I

Ed sat alone on a bench in the lockup of the Woodlawn police station. It was a large room with high barred windows on one side; the other three sides consisted of iron bars. A toilet was in one corner, hidden by a door; along the wall and on one other side were old benches. The lockup was well filled with males of varying ages, both black and white. They sat, alone or in groups, stood, moved idly about. Ed had talked with some of them and then had retired to sit by himself on a bench and observe. He decided that his companions in crime constituted a motley collection. He reflected for a moment, weighing the words *motley* and *nondescript,* and he concluded that *motley* was the more applicable one. There were Negroes arrested for an odd assortment of petty offenses, mostly robbing ice boxes; there were two high-school students, from the near-by Catholic high school of Mary Our Mother, arrested for fighting. That was the school Danny O'Neill and Marty Mulligan had gone to, only then it had been named Saint Stanislaus. There were drunks, some sobering up, others floundering around in alcoholic stupor, pedlars caught selling odds and ends of junk without licenses, a burglar trapped in an apartment, a poor sap of a fellow who was being jugged for non-payment of alimony, and some others. Yes, a motley collection of human animals, he reflected.

Ed was hoping he would get out of this jug in a hurry. The short time he had already spent here in the protective arms of the law had been enough to convince him that he didn't fancy it. The realization that he was being held forcibly, that he was enclosed by iron bars, that his movements, his privacy, were restricted, was irritating, aggravating; it was just goddamned lousy gripe. But suppose he shouldn't get out in a hurry? He enjoyed asking himself this question, especially because he was certain that his mother was on the way over to rescue him and that when she came and paid the bill he owed his landlady, he would be released. That fat slob of a landlady wasn't interested in getting him jailed. Her concern was the rent for her cramped little room. Even if she did want to press charges against him, it would only be a first offense, and at that, just a matter of a five-dollar bill for rent. He was in no danger. Therefore it was particularly attractive and amusing to think of being sent up the road.

He would be happier if he had a cigarette. But Mother would be along very soon, and everything would be taken care of.

He smiled ironically, thinking that once in his life Lanson hadn't been so smart. He'd thought that he was getting away with something, sneaking out dirty underwear every night. And the beefy, stupid-faced slob, Mrs. Brinn, hadn't been as dumb as she looked. Today when he was walking out she was waiting for him at the foot of the stairs, and who stepped out of the side room but a goddamned dick. Thus, here he was. So it was another episode, another little detail in his life. Some day he ought really to be able to write the true story of his life, and it should make quite a book.

The two high-school students sat down beside Ed.

"Hey, what do you think they'll do to us?" one of them asked.

"Nothing. Don't worry, bud," he answered.

"You sure?" the boy persisted; he was pimply faced, with light hair and blue eyes.

"Hell, nothing's going to happen to us. That is, unless we get canned from school," the other student said.

"What was you picked up for?" the pimply-faced student asked.

"Safe cracking," Ed said casually.

They looked at him, amazed. And then their amazement
turned to speechless admiration.

"Say, you'll go to Joliet, won't you?" the pimply-faced student said.

"I don't know. I think my pals will spring me. If not, I'll
have a long stretch to do. This is the third time the bulls
nabbed me."

A keeper stood by the bars near Ed, pointing at the students.

"Come on, you two," he said authoritatively.

Timid, frightened, they rose and went to meet the cop at
the gate of the lockup.

Ed watched the kids go, amused. He thought of Ellen. He
was late for a date with her. She didn't know what had happened to him, unless Mother had told her. When they'd let
him make one call, he'd phoned Mother and he'd asked her to
get in touch with Ellen. Mother probably had been too ashamed
to tell Ellen where he was, but she'd probably called and given
some other excuse. Well, that was the least of his worries right
now. Cigarettes were a bigger one. He got up and decided to
stroll about and see who would be most likely as a touch for a
fag from among the inmates.

He saw his mother standing by the gate with a cop. He
walked over to where she stood.

"Come on," the cop said.

The gate was opened, and Ed walked out of the lockup. His
mother hugged and kissed him.

"Why did you do it, Edmond?" she asked in a troubled
voice; she was a dark woman in her forties, but with no gray
hair. She was slight of build, with even features, a pleasing and
intelligent face, and hazel eyes that were like Ed's. Very fine
wrinkles were drawn around her eyes. Standing beside Ed, the
resemblance between mother and son was clearly discernible.

He followed his mother and the keeper into the front of the
station.

The keeper motioned for Ed to go to the window where a
red-faced, stout, gray-haired lieutenant sat.

"Please, Edmond, don't answer him back," Mrs. Lanson whispered to her son; she followed him to the window.

"We didn't book you—this time. But you can thank your stars we didn't. If you're brought back to us, fellow, you won't get off so easy. You ought to be ashamed of yourself. A lad like you with as fine a lady for a mother as you have, why do you do such things?"

Ed didn't answer.

"Officer, he won't again," Mrs. Lanson said.

"Let me handle him, lady. I'll put the fear of God in him for you," the officer said.

Ed controlled himself. But he felt like sounding off and also swinging on this fat slob of a cop.

"You ought to be ashamed of yourself, a big, strapping lad like yourself, playing dead beat instead of working."

How long would the slob go on? Ed wondered.

Just then two cops entered with a Negro. They shoved him across the room. One of the cops took a poke at the Negro.

"Come on," the other cop said, "come on get up to that window, you black . . ." He spied Mrs. Lanson and instead of swearing he shoved the Negro.

"All right, Lanson, you're released," the lieutenant said.

"Leave him alone. Because you've arrested somebody, you haven't the right to punch hell out of him," Ed said to the cop who'd just punched the Negro.

"Say, who are you?" the cop asked.

"Never mind who I am. You have no right to punch people around," Ed said.

"Edmond," Mrs. Lanson called.

"Oh, I haven't. Suppose I punch you around?"

"You won't be able to—not if you take your star off and step outside with me."

"Edmond, please!" Mrs. Lanson said.

"I won't, huh? I don't have to step outside. I'll take care of you inside. How do you like that?"

"Who is this guy?" the cop's companion asked.

The lieutenant who had released Ed, and had been booking

the Negro, heard the angry argumentative voices. He got to his feet and waddled out of his partitioned cage. He glared at Ed.

"What's up now?" the lieutenant asked.

"He's interferin', Lieutenant. He's interferin' with the law, and threatenin' an officer. We ought to book him," answered the cop with whom Ed had been having words.

"Son, please come on with me," Mrs. Lanson said, pulling on Ed's sleeve and cutting in on him just as he was going to retort to the cop.

"You're just one of those smart boys who don't know when you're well off," the lieutenant said.

"Officer, my son didn't do anything. He and I both saw this policeman," Mrs. Lanson pointed. "We saw him brutally punch a prisoner. The law doesn't give you police the right to beat people up. All my son did was protest, and this officer threatened my son. If anything happens, I'll take his star number, and yours, too, and if you dare touch my son, you'll pay for it. You have no right to break the law."

"Mother, I can take care of myself," Ed said.

"Say, lady, we been considerate of you, haven't we? We didn't book your son? What's the matter? Now, why don't both of you leave the station?" the lieutenant asked.

"Yes, we'll leave," Mrs. Lanson said.

The lieutenant turned to the cops.

"Take the shine back to the lock-up. And don't be punching him." He turned back to Ed and Mrs. Lanson. "Now, good day. You're released. Better leave the premises."

Without saying a word, Ed and his mother left the station.

"Edmond, what's the matter with you?" Mrs. Lanson said as they walked away from the station along a narrow street toward Sixty-third.

"Nothing, Mother. I'm not going to stand by and let a brutal cop beat up a helpless, defenseless dinge just because the cop has arrested him and the cop has the alleged authority on his side."

"Edmond, you were perfectly justified in standing up for that poor colored boy. I was proud of you. It was noble. But,

Edmond, why did you let yourself sink so low that you would be arrested as a dead beat? When you have a decent home to come to—why do you lie to Mother?"

"I'm sorry, Mother, I was proud."

"Your pride will lead you into trouble yet if you don't discipline it."

"Would you want me not proud?"

"Now, Edmond, Mother is on to your sophistries," she said. He smiled at her.

"Mother, did you telephone Ellen?"

"Yes, I did. I didn't tell her the truth, though. I said that you were doing an errand for me and would telephone as soon as you were free. She seemed to understand. Her voice is sweet. Edmond, for my sake, for your own, don't let Ellen know what happened to you."

"Of course I won't."

"You better telephone her. But, Edmond, after what you've gone through, your mother is taking you home tonight."

"I have to see Ellen."

"And then where are you going to sleep?"

"I'll come home."

"Promise me, Edmond?"

"Of course, Mother. But let's eat now. I'm hungry. And Mother, have you some money to buy me cigarettes. I'm dying for a smoke."

She dug into her pocketbook.

II

Ed sat with his mother, eating lustily. It was the same restaurant at which he'd had breakfast the morning when he had walked out of the Tudor Hotel.

"Edmond, what's the matter with you? Why won't you settle down?"

"Mother, I'm going to."

"Where have I heard that tune sung before?"

"You don't believe me?"

"Of course I do. I always believe my son. Why, like George Washington, he never told a lie."

"Don't rub it in. You know, Mother, that when there is anything serious, I never lie to you. Maybe I tell you a white lie to spare you worry, but I never tell you a lie if it's serious."

"Edmond, when are you going to settle down? Haven't we had enough of your escapades?" she asked.

Ed thawed his mother out with a boyish smile. She returned it.

"You're using technique on your mother," she said.

"Oh, no, not on her. She's too smart for me to get away with technique with her."

"Well, she understands her son better than anyone else does."

"Of course she does. Mother, what do you think of Ellen?"

"From talking to her I judged she must be a nice girl. She has a sweet voice."

"You must meet her."

"I invited her to come over and see us."

"But how did you know I'd be there?"

"I assumed it. After this experience, I assumed you'd rather have your mother as a landlady than someone else. One thing about me as your landlady—I shan't call the police on you. But, Edmond, with your two brothers away, we have so much room, it's foolish of you not to stay home with us. And after all, we are your parents. We have some interest in the future of a bright but foolish son."

"Now, Mother, you know me. You know that some day I'll settle down."

"But it's high time that you did, Edmond. I'm no goody-goody. I know a little about life—I'd have to, after raising three sons such as mine!"

"Mother, would you really be pleased if I were a boy scout?"

"Indeed I wouldn't. But, Edmond, you can't go on doing what you did today. It's unworthy of you. It demeans you."

"Mother, I live dangerously."

She laughed at him.

"You don't take me seriously," he said.

"Edmond, I have heard you sit at home and tell the darndest, the most implausible, stories to girls, and they believed you. But your mother is smarter than your girls. I don't know about Ellen. But some of the others believed you more than your mother does when you say such things. Edmond, you're too good to do such things as you did today and you know you are."

"Mother, you do have faith in your son, don't you?"

"Of course I do, but he does such terrible things to me. How do I feel, how do you think I feel, having to come to the police station and face that landlady, and those policemen, in order to get you out? How do you think I feel? It's the same as when that other thing happened to you, that sickness."

"Mother, that's over. And after all, you must know that I'm only human," he said, thinking that it was good that he had been cured of his dose.

"I'll not rake up the past. I'm interested in the future. How long are you going on being foolish?"

"Mother, I'm getting a job in New York."

"With whom?"

"Through John Devormer. He's giving me a letter of introduction, and I'll land a good connection. I see bigger game in New York than here. I'm going there to settle down, and then I'll send for Ellen as soon as I make my start."

She looked at him anxiously.

"Edmond, if you really have a chance, you know I won't stand in your way. But if this is another wild goose chase . . ."

"Mother, I need a fresh start, a change of scenery."

"Edmond, you'll break my heart yet."

"Mother, how did Father take the news about me?"

"He was very hurt. He didn't say a word except to tell me that I'd better straighten it out and bring you home. When will you be home?" she asked.

"Early. I have to see Ellen."

"Edmond, are you serious about going to New York?"

"Yes, Mother. But don't worry. This time I'm going to make good."

"You can make good in Chicago."

"I want to reach the real top of the pile. New York is the place for me."

"My son, don't go on in life being your own worst enemy."

"This time I'm not. This time, Mother, I'm serious. I'm going to make good in New York, and in a hurry."

"Have you seen Mr. Devormer?"

"Yes, I've talked to him. He believes it's a good idea for me to go to New York and thinks that I'll make good."

"Edmond, look me in the eye. Are you telling me the truth? Look me in the eye. I can tell." She fixed her gaze upon him. "Now, answer me, are you telling me the truth?"

"Yes, Mother."

"I believe you this time, Edmond," she said, smiling at him tenderly.

"Mother, if only Ellen, even Ellen, were as smart and as wonderful as you are."

"I'm not as wonderful as all that. But I do understand my strange son."

"Strange?"

"No, not really strange. Just seemingly so. Edmond, you are really just a wonderful little boy."

"You know, Mother, that you are idealizing. Every mother thinks that of her son."

"No, you are still a boy. I'm not idealizing, either. I know you."

Ed smiled at her, blew her a kiss. He finished his meal, and they got up. She paid the bill.

"Mother," he said on the sidewalk in front of the restaurant.

"Yes, Ed."

"I hate to ask you, but I need carfare."

"I forgot to give you some change. But, Edmond, don't be ashamed to ask me for money. I'm your mother."

He frowned.

She pulled out three single-dollar bills.

"I don't need that."

"Take it. You're going to see Ellen. You ought to have something to buy her a sandwich or something. You'll pay me back."

He accepted the money with seeming reluctance. He kissed his mother good-bye. She watched him stride off, her face sad.

Ed stopped in front of the drugstore at Sixty-third and Stony Island. He took out his notebook and jotted down the five dollars his mother had paid for his rent and the three dollars she had just given him. One more debt. He went inside to telephone Ellen. He came out, smoking a cigarette, and he looked about to see if any of the boys he knew were around the corner. But none showed up, and he started walking towards Ellen's.

Chapter Twenty-two

I

"Oh, I'm so glad you came . . . at last," Ellen said, meeting him at the door.

"I was forcibly detained from seeing you by nothing less than society itself," Ed told her after kissing her.

"What does that mean?"

"Oh, aren't my words clear enough? I should say they are clear and precise."

She led him into the parlor.

"Your mother telephoned me and said that you were on some errand for her. How is that being forcibly detained by society? Oh, so your mother is society. You had to do something unpleasant but necessary for your mother."

"No, that is not quite what happened."

"Then what did happen?"

"I'll tell you . . . sometime. Perhaps the walls have ears here."

Ellen looked around the parlor.

"Ed, tell me, did something happen . . . serious?" she asked, lowering her voice.

"I'll tell you later," he replied in a mysterious whisper.

He picked up her hand, and he noticed that she was wearing the ring he had given her.

"You don't think that I wouldn't be wearing your ring?"

"I was sure that you would. I merely wanted to look at it, that's all."

"I'm dying to know what you did today, what happened to you."

"And I'm in the same state about you. I wouldn't use the word dying. I would say I'm keen to know, very keen."

"I just stayed home."

"You didn't go wandering about at dawn in the park like Lady Macbeth."

"Who?"

"Lady Macbeth. She was a friend of Will Shakespeare, and as a matter of fact, she was quite a bimbo, if I may lapse into the vulgar." He thought for a moment, and then said, stressing his irony: "Come to think of it, I wouldn't want you to be like Lady Macbeth."

"I'm so dumb. We studied *Macbeth* in high school, but I don't remember anything about it."

Mr. Rogers entered the parlor.

"How do you do, Mr. Rogers," Ed said, rising.

"How do you do. How do you do," Mr. Rogers replied.

He sat down.

"It's nice weather we're having," Ed said, a twinkle in his eyes.

"Oh, yes, pretty nice. Spring's getting on. Before we know it, it's going to be summer."

"Time flies, doesn't it," Ed said.

"How are things going with you, Ed?"

"Didn't Ellen tell you? That I'm thinking of locating in New York? I can do better there than I can here."

"No, Ellen didn't say a word about it to me."

"Well, she must have forgotten to mention it."

"When are you going to New York?"

"I haven't decided the exact date, but I expect to locate there and get something pretty good."

"Do you plan to stay there permanently?" Mr. Rogers asked.

"Yes, I do."

"It's a risky step—to try and connect up in a strange town, especially New York. It's expensive, too, supporting a family in New York. Have you taken that into consideration?" Mr. Rogers asked.

"Oh, yes. But I expect to get on. I'll send for Ellen when I am settled and have landed something good."

"Can't you manage something here? Seems to me that Chicago is full of opportunities."

"Chicago isn't big enough for me."

"It's big enough for a number of pretty big men, Ed. You know, youth is often cocky and confident."

"I've weighed all the possibilities, I've weighed and considered them carefully. I'm not acting on the spur of the moment, but rather after careful consideration and forethought."

"What do you think about it, Ellen?"

"Well, Father, after Ed and I are married, I'll have to go where it's best for Ed."

"I know. But it's a question where it's best. There are plenty of opportunities here in Chicago. And the people in Chicago are better people, homier people, simpler. And all your friends are here. It might be hard, and lonesome, too, in New York. As far as I'm concerned, of course, I wouldn't consent to my daughter marrying and going to New York until you had made your mark there. You understand that, don't you, Ed?"

"I share and appreciate your feeling and attitude perfectly, Mr. Rogers. I wouldn't think of asking Ellen to come to New York and make sacrifices. I value her too highly. That's why I'm setting out alone."

"I'm glad to hear you say that. But I'd think it over before I acted. I'd think it over."

Ed lit a cigarette, leaned back on the sofa, crossed his legs.

"Well, I have some work to do, leases and things to look over. Good night," Mr. Rogers said, rising and leaving the room.

II

"Your father is concerned about me. He doesn't trust me," Ed said.

"Ed, tell me what happened this afternoon."

"Something trivial and sordid."

"But what?"

"Ellen, why do our parents find it necessary to lean on us as if we were crutches? It's weakness—the weakness of parents. It's the decrepitude of approaching old age. If the life of a parent has been bungled, or even if it is over, then the child must pay for that failure, justify it. That is what I mean when I say that parents want to use their children as crutches. But do parents honestly say this? Not at all. No, instead of telling us the truth, they invoke universal morality. Because God is supposed to exist in his ungodly Heaven, they would saddle us with duties. And then, to add insult to injury, they, father or mother, say that they are only interested in the good and the future happiness of their children. Ah, it makes me want to puke."

"Ed, I don't like that word."

"And I don't like the experience it connotes. But sometimes it is an inevitable, unpreventable, a necessary experience. It is necessary to health and, shall I say, duodenal comfort. And it's a figure of speech, telling us something of psychology. Psychologically, we have to puke up our past, retch up our love for our father and mother, if we would be free and strong, independent, going our own road in our own way. This is what we need to do if we would be men and women instead of emotional and psychological crutches for those who have already lived their lives, had their little day, walked to the end of their own particular little road."

"Ed, why do you go on like this when I want to know what happened to you today?"

"What happened to me is unimportant. What I am saying is important."

"You're afraid to tell me."

"Now, how did you guess that so correctly," he asked her, smiling in a genially sardonic manner.

"You don't care about me. You were with some other girl."

"There was another female involved in it," he said.

"And you didn't even call me up. I suppose I'll get a verse of poetry from you in the mail in the morning."

"No, no verses."

"That will be kind of you."

Ed watched her, his eyes twinkling.

"Who was she? You might as well tell me her name."

"It was a he. A fairy tried to make me."

"Disgusting! How disgusting!"

"Now, that will teach you not to be jealous of me. Now I'll really tell you about today."

"Ed, why do you play with me? When I'm anxious you beat around the bush."

"Ellen, are you losing your sense of playfulness?"

"No, I'm not. Not at all. Only I worry about you."

"Today my landlady called the cops, and I was arrested for not paying my room rent."

"How terrible! Why didn't you call me?"

"I was only allowed one call. I didn't want to subject you to humiliation. I called Mother. I told Mother to tell you where I was, but she was ashamed to. Poor Mother. Anyway, I'm out."

"Are you still in trouble?"

"No. Mother paid the bill. I was let go. They didn't book me."

"Tell me about it, Ed."

III

"Ed, how long will it take you to get settled in New York?" Ellen asked as they were strolling along Stony Island Avenue toward Sixty-third Street and she was clinging to his arm.

"Not long."

"But how long do you plan on?"

"Plan? Why should Lanson plan?"

"So that I'll know."

"The answer is simple. Not long. Not very long. Less time than you imagine."

"That's still not definite," she said.

"I can't be definite and give specific periods. I don't know. I only am sure of this. I'll be on my feet very soon, and when I am, I'll send for you. Ellen, you talk as if only you will suffer from this separation, as if it will mean nothing to me. Well, don't think that I shan't be missing you. I'll be alone. At first

I'll be alone in a dreary little room. I'll come home alone at night and find no Ellen. My only communication with her will be by mail. No, don't think that only you will suffer."

"Ed, what I can't get out of my mind is this: Why must we tear ourselves away from one another now? Isn't it foolish? Couldn't you first locate here, make good in Chicago, and then go to New York?"

"Ellen, it's my nature always to do things the hard way."

"But why?"

"I must live dangerously, and, to use a figure, on a volcano. Nothing is gained the easy way."

"If you feel that way, can't you make it hard for yourself in Chicago?"

"I need to be lonely. If I am, I will be spurred on to greater efforts. I need to walk streets alone in a strange town, not even knowing one soul."

"But will that happen? You'll get to know people in a hurry, wherever you are."

"That's not my aim nor my purpose on this trip. I plan to live like a recluse in New York. I'm going into a kind of solitude."

"Ed, maybe you think this is necessary, but, honestly, I don't see or understand why it is."

"You must take my word for it that it is."

She would take his word on almost everything. But still, she could not grasp why this proposed move of his was necessary. Suddenly she became frightened. Was it a kind of fate that was driving him on to do this? Was it an evil fate? Couldn't she save him, if this were what it was? But no, it was silly to think about some evil fate. No such thing existed in the world.

They turned the corner at Sixty-third Street and Stony Island Avenue.

Ed nodded to the group of fellows standing at the corner, and they returned the greeting, some of them tipping their hats. They strolled on down Sixty-third Street.

"Ellen, I have to conquer myself. That is the only way I can achieve self-conquest."

"Ed, I wouldn't stand in your way in anything. If it is necessary, I'll understand."

But why was it necessary? How could she show him that it wasn't necessary?

"I looked forward to the summer so much, the things we'd do this summer," she said.

"So did I," he said regretfully. "But there will be other summers, other days." He smiled. "There will be better times, pal."

Would there? Was she letting Ed slip through her fingers? Was she losing him, losing him without even putting up a fight?

"I want to go with you. Ed, darling, I do. I won't be able to stand it without you. Why can't we make this struggle together?"

"Sweet, I can't. I am tempted." He waited for an instant. "I am tempted, but no, I can't. How can I conquer myself, as I must, if you are with me?"

"After all, you are going to New York principally to make good and earn the means of our getting married, so that we can be independent—isn't that so, Ed?"

"That's correct. That is the major reason for my trip. But the other reason is . . . spiritual. I'm going to New York to be alone, to conquer myself, to harden my soul."

"Oh, Ed, why harden yourself? You're hard enough. You don't need to do that."

"But I do. And out of this loneliness, as a result of my isolation, I'll write my book."

Everything came before her. All this talk.

"Ed, you talk almost as if you thought I was bad for you."

"No, not at all. No, I don't at all imply that. Sweet, I have to go through this to earn you."

"Oh, Ed, that's not so."

"In my own mind, it is. I must act as I plan. Sweet, I must always be able to look myself in the face, and not be weak, not flinch, not say that I am ashamed of myself."

His explanations were getting much too complicated for her. All she knew was that she wanted him. He was her man, and she wanted him, but he was going into all this talk in order to explain why he had to go away, why he had to leave her.

She stared glumly ahead.

"Ed, can't we have something to drink?"

"Let's. . . . But I don't have much cash on me."

She looked into her pocketbook and pulled out a ten-dollar bill which she gave him. He took it indifferently.

IV

They sat at a table at The Palm Tree Inn. It was only half filled.

"Ed, I'm not a good girl," she said, and they both laughed.

"Oh, yes, you are," he said.

"No, I'm not. Not good. Not a good girl. A good girl, she doesn't drink, doesn't . . ."

"You're better than a good girl."

"What's that?"

"You're a superior girl."

"You just say that to flatter me."

"No, I don't."

The orchestra began playing. They stood up to dance.

"Superior? No. But I'm hard. You don't think I'm hard, do you, Ed? You think I'm soft, pliant. Well, I'm hard. Oh, yes I am. Hard. If you knew what I did to men, what I could do to them."

"Tell me."

"No, I won't."

"Why?"

"Secrets of the trade."

"What trade?"

"Woman's trade."

They shimmied.

"I don't want to go home tonight," she said.

"You don't have to."

"I'm hard."

"Are you, Sweet?"

"Don't you want me to be hard?"

"No, I want you to be soft."

"Then I'm soft . . . and I'm hard, too."

"What have you done that's hard?"

"Wound fellows around my fingers like a piece of string."

"And then what did you do?"

"Unwound them, threw the string away."

"Is that a threat?"

"Darling, no . . . no . . . no . . . no . . . no."

"You promise never to wind me around your fingers like a piece of string?" he asked.

"Promise."

"That's kind of you."

"Kiss me."

Ed kissed her.

The orchestra stopped. They stood at the edge of the floor, waiting for the music to be resumed. Ed clapped noisily.

"Why, there's Bill Northrup."

"Is he the old flame you told me about?" Ed asked.

"Yes, that's *him*," she said, pronouncing her last word with contempt.

"I don't like his looks," Ed said.

"Neither do I, Ed darling," she said, pulling Ed toward Bill. Surprised to see her, Bill drew back a pace.

"Hello," Ellen said.

"Hello," Bill said coldly.

"Bill Northrup, this is Edmond Lanson," Ellen said.

"Pleased to meet you," Ed said coldly, measuring Bill.

Bill bowed. He was with a dark, pretty girl, and he didn't introduce her to them.

"My, you're not friendly," Ellen said.

"You seem rather distant toward us," Ed said.

"I'm minding my own business. Ellen, I have to go. Excuse me."

"Bill, you've been telling lies around town about me."

"Ellen, I have not. Whoever says that is a liar."

"I say that."

"You call her a liar?" Ed asked.

"I don't know that this concerns you," Bill said to Ed.

"It doesn't?"

"Lie about you? I wouldn't even talk about a person like you," Bill said to Ellen, sneering.

"Take that back," Ed ordered him.

"This isn't any of your business," Bill said.

Ed crowded on him, punching with his left. Ellen, in her state of mild intoxication, had enjoyed the exchange of words. The excitement, the sudden flare-up of the fight, sobered her.

"Ed, stop!" she called loudly.

The girl with Bill screamed. Bill tried to defend himself, help-lessly. As people rushed around them and Chinese waiters scur-ried to the scene of action, Bill went down, his nose bleeding.

"Get up, you yellow louse!" Ed said, standing over him.

"Can't you see the guy's beat?" a big, burly dull-faced fellow yelled at Ed.

"Who solicited your opinion?" Ed asked, turning toward the fellow.

"I don't like your looks," the big fellow answered.

"Put 'em up," Ed said, advancing a step.

"Ed, Ed, let's go," Ellen called.

The big fellow rushed Ed. Ed checked him with a left jab. The big fellow rushed again, and, taking another jab, got in close and shoved Ed back. Then he tried to knee Ed, but Ed swerved a little to the side and raised his left leg, successfully protecting his groin. Ed pummelled the big fellow in the stomach with both hands and, getting an opening, shot his left to the big fellow's jaw.

The Palm Tree Inn was in a state of bedlam. Girls were screaming. Some guests watched the fight. Others threw food at the spectators and fighters. The Chinese waiters struggled to break up the fight. With the aid of several guests, they sepa-rated Ed and the big fellow.

"Ed, are you all right?" Ellen called.

She went to his side. He smiled at her. She was pale, but see-ing that he was unmarked and showed no signs of injury, she was consoled.

Several men stood between Ed and the big fellow. Heedless of them, Ed kept his eyes on the big fellow. In back of him, Ed saw Bill Northrup, bewildered, his nose still bleeding.

"You had enough?" Ed asked the big fellow.

"No, punk."

"Come on down in the alley behind this place," Ed said.

"All right."

Ed walked to his table, followed by a group.

"Ed, darling, please don't fight," Ellen pleaded.

Ed picked up the bill and paid it.

"Ed, won't you listen to me?"

"I'm all right. You wait here and I'll be right back."

"Don't go and fight him. He's bigger than you. I can't stand it," she said hysterically.

"I'll be back quickly. You wait here."

"What, are you yellow? Hiding behind your skirt?" the big fellow asked, coming to Ed's table.

"You'll see who's yellow," Ed said, walking toward the exit.

A crowd followed him. Ellen tried to catch up with him, but she couldn't until they were downstairs on the sidewalk.

"Ed, won't you—for me? Ed, please don't fight him."

"Ellen, you stay here, and I'll be right back," he told her.

"Come on, you!" the big fellow said, sneering.

Ed kissed Ellen. He turned and walked back to the alley with the big fellow. Ellen ran after him. Ed took off his coat and rolled up his sleeve. A ring of shouting persons formed around him and the big fellow.

"Come on now. And listen," Ed said, his voice very calm. "If you try any more dirty tricks, if you try to give me the knee again, I'm going to cut that face of yours to ribbons with my left. One more dirty trick in this fight and your mother won't ever recognize your face again."

The big fellow suddenly smiled conciliatingly, stepping back to be sure he was out of the range of Ed's fists.

"Listen, boy, this is all a misunderstanding. If you insist on fighting, I'll fight you. But this is a misunderstanding."

Ellen stepped forward from the crowd and stood at Ed's side.

"How is it a misunderstanding?"

"Ed, shake hands and forget it," she said. Ed didn't answer her.

Ed and the big fellow walked off a few paces. Ellen followed.

"That bozo you pasted. He isn't a friend of mine. I don't see why you and me should fight over him. Here, do you want a drink?"

The big fellow pulled out a bottle of gin. He and Ed drank.

"Ed, darling, give me a sip," Ellen said.

Ed handed Ellen the bottle. She sipped it and made a face.

"Let's go some place else," he said to Ellen.

"Mind if me and my girl join you? Our treat," the big fellow said.

"Not at all. But what's your name? Mine's Jones, and this is Miss Smith," Ed said.

Ellen was dumbfounded, but she said nothing.

"Mine's O'Toole. Duffy O'Toole."

They shook hands.

V

They sat in a booth at the Dive Inn with O'Toole and his girl, a plump, bleached blonde. The Dive Inn was a notorious tavern on South Chicago Avenue. It was crowded, and noisy drunks kept staggering past their booth.

"Jones and Smith, now who would have thought that I would meet people like you two?" Duffy O'Toole said.

"Yes, it's a card, our meeting is," Ed said, smiling cordially.

Ellen picked her glass up to drink. Ed kicked her under the table. She set down her glass. Just then the orchestra broke into raucous jazz.

"Excuse us," Ed said, standing up.

"Sure thing, pal," O'Toole said.

Ed led Ellen to the jammed dance floor.

"Sweet, don't drink any more," Ed said on the dance floor.

"Why?"

"Because I say so."

"Ed, don't go way and leave me."

They were shoved into a corner in the jam of dancers. Ellen clung to him.

"Why?" Ed asked.

"Because I say so," she said.

"Ellen, listen to me. I don't like to be challenged."

"Well, I don't either," she said.

"Listen to me! You're with strangers. You don't know them. That's why I didn't give our real names. This dumb Irishman is a big fool, but he's a bootlegger, too. I don't want him to know who you are. And I don't think either of us should get drunk with them. Pretend you're a little drunk. And don't go fighting with me. I'm taking care of you because I love you, Sweet."

"I'm not drunk."

They were shoved again by dancers.

"You will be if you drink more of his hooch. It's potent."

"Just one more."

"No more."

"And if I do have one more?" she asked.

"I'll leave. I'll walk out of the joint."

She crushed herself against him.

"I love you, darling," she said, blowing an alcoholic breath in his face.

He clutched her firmly to him.

VI

"Come on, stay a while longer," O'Toole said drunkenly.

"I'm sorry, but we have to go."

"Ah, hell with it. Stay. We're friends. Bes' friends in the world. Bes' friends."

"Shake on that," Ed said, standing up and shaking O'Toole's hand firmly.

"Here's my card. My card. Name, address, telephone number," O'Toole said, relaxing his grip on Ed's hand and giving Ed a card.

"I'll get in touch with you," Ed said.

He and Ellen said good night and left.

"What an unusual night it's been," she said outside.

"Hang around with me and something will always happen," Ed said.

They stood in front of the Dive Inn. It was a low, sprawling structure. They heard the loud music of the orchestra.

"I'm sober now. And it's good to get some air after that stifling crowd inside," she said.

"Only for me, you wouldn't be sober."

"You don't approve of me drunk. I know you don't. You talk about free spirits, and you tell me you want me to be a free spirit, but if I get a little drunk you disapprove, don't you?"

"No, not at all. I don't disapprove morally. But after all, I don't like the sight of a woman too drunk. And we were with strangers. I didn't trust them."

"But then, Ed, why did you go with him?"

"Because I didn't want him to think I was afraid to."

"You're funny, but I love you so," she said.

He hailed a taxi cab. They got in it. Ellen flung herself in his arms. He kissed and petted her.

Ed called to the driver.

"Take it easy and drive us through Jackson Park," he ordered.

Chapter Twenty-three

I

Out of a sense of duty, Ed was staying home to have supper with his parents. He had promised his mother that he would, and she was in the kitchen, cooking. His father was taking a nap before eating.

He sat alone in his room, smoking a cigarette. He had just finished writing letters to his two brothers and his sister, and he didn't feel like reading. He had come back home to live until he left for New York. Living at home had its advantages as well as its disadvantages. It pleased his mother and father, especially now that the other children were all out of town. It meant that no fat landlady would be running for the cops in order to collect the week's rent from the star boarder. But his folks now lived on the near North Side instead of around Fifty-eighth Street. He would have to take long trips every day to see Ellen. Withal, that was not such a hardship. He could read en route.

He had not failed to observe how his mother had cleaned the room for him, and how she had placed a photograph of him as a boy on the dresser. He had been in the eighth grade at Crucifixion when it had been taken. His mother appeared pathetic in doing this. To her he remained a boy, although she was too clever, too understanding, really to treat him as a child.

It was depressing to return home. Father was in a new business again, promoting an invention. His folks were just getting along. They had raised their family, and what had happened? The children were all high-spirited, filled with wanderlust, always coming and going, getting into scrapes, violating one or another rule of his father's Victorian code. And after all these years Father was still struggling to make a living, meeting with the same old ups and downs, going from one business to another. Some day he would do something big for them. But such a life was fundamentally stupid.

He thought about his father. The gaffer was a curious cuss. He was aloof, formal, dignified. When Arlette, his sister, had run off from a convent at seventeen and married a Jewish advertising man, his father had not said a word. In his presence, Arlette's marriage was never to be mentioned. This was his typical reaction. It was almost as if his father practiced a form of magic, believing that if unpleasant or disturbing incidents or actions of his children were not mentioned, they therefore had never happened. When Pierre, during the war, had run away from school and joined the navy, again his father had said nothing. He had suffered in silence, always maintaining his dignified demeanor, never allowing himself to appear ruffled. At times this trait of his father's was admirable. At times it was comic. When he and Pierre would fight at home, and his mother, in order to end the fight, would faint, his father, while efficiently and tenderly taking care of his mother, would not unbend once, not allow his worry or strain to be observable. Yes, his gaffer was curious. But underneath the surface his father was kind, loveable. Yes, he respected his father, even though he·couldn't get along with him. After all, Ed Lanson was traveling his own road in his own way. Pierre and Arlette were, too, and his younger brother, Bob, sometimes showed the same spirit.

But it was gloomy to come back home with the folks. If Bob were home, it would be more pleasant. But every one must go his own way. It was cruel to grow old, and those who grew old had to face the music. His mother and father were doing it gracefully. His father was superior to the fathers of most chaps he knew. Think of him and contrast him with Ellen's fat dumb slob of a father.

He hoped that he wouldn't get into an argument with his

father this evening. For Mother's sake he was going to be on his best behavior.

He went to his desk in the corner and looked at the letter he'd written to his older brother, addressed to Calcutta. He wanted to travel around the world, too. He would. He would accomplish every aim in life, realize every dream, actualize every wish.

He heard his mother calling him to supper.

II

"Hello, Edmond," Mr. Lanson said as Ed sat down to eat. Mr. Lanson was tall, swarthy, good-looking, with gentle eyes; Ed resembled him physically in a rather vague way.

Just as Ed had expected, the gaffer said not a word about yesterday's arrest.

"How are you, Edmond?"

"I'm well, Father, how are you?"

"Oh, satisfactory."

"How is business? Are you making any progress launching that invention?"

"Yes, I think it will go. It's promising, very promising."

Mrs. Lanson sat down after bringing in the food.

"Mother, it was sweet of you to make a cheese soufflé."

"We hadn't had one of late. Your father likes cheese soufflé as much as you do, Edmond," she said, serving them.

"Your mother tells me that you are going to bring the girl to whom you are engaged over to see us, Edmond."

"Yes, Father, I plan to."

"Fine. Your mother and I should be pleased to know her."

"I'm sure that you'll both like Ellen." He took a plate from his mother. "Thank you, Mother."

"She sounds like a very sweet girl on the telephone," Mrs. Lanson said.

"Of course, Edmond, marriage is a very serious undertaking. Marriage is something sacred," Mr. Lanson said.

"Father, I think Edmond realizes that," his mother said.

Ed listened with amused tolerance. He knew that a lecture

was coming. Yesterday's escapade was probably the cause, and this was the gaffer's way of registering disapproval.

"Coming home this afternoon, I was thinking about some general matters. Perhaps they would interest you, Edmond," Mr. Lanson said.

Ed restrained himself from smiling. His father's little tricks, habits, mannerisms, were so amusingly transparent.

"Of course, I'd be interested to hear of your reflections, Father."

"It occurred to me that the simplest virtues are, because of their simplicity, the ones least recognized and heeded. There is no novelty in them, and this is an age when novelties are appreciated. We want everything new in this day and age. We don't want to be attached to the old moorings. Our books and our lives reflect such sentiments. We are always moving, always wanting a new house, a new automobile, a new gadget, a new book. There was a time when we wanted things to be mellowed before we prized them."

Ed reflected that this was a real Babbitt-like speech. He realized how profound was the cleavage in outlook between himself and his father. Yes, two worlds sat at this supper table, looking at each other across a chasm, talking at cross purposes. Mother could partly bridge these worlds. That was her way of keeping peace when they were all home together.

"Yes, it occurred to me, we no longer place the same significance on words like *mellowed*, *mellow*. It's the spirit of the age. The old concepts, the old virtues, seem too homely for this day. One gets the feeling sometimes that no one had ever lived before this present century. Sometimes we act as if we were the first generation instead of the heirs of centuries of human wisdom. We are heedless of the truths these centuries teach us, these same simple virtues and mellow maxims about honesty, prudence, foresight, respect for authority. The more I think of these matters, the more I realize their importance. The notion that the new is so superior to the old is the product of the confidence of inexperience. Perhaps because the Bible is true in telling us that there is nothing new under the sun, perhaps because of this, many people today are so eager to find destructive novelty."

So this was the gaffer's way of telling him off. Ed was moved. There was something poignant about his father's speech, formulated in generalities when its entire meaning was direct, specific. However, he had to answer his father. He could not make admissions which would lead his father to think that he was surrendering, retreating, forced to act like the prodigal son. He was no prodigal son.

"Father, merely because something is old, that does not make it good."

Mr. Lanson reflected for a moment before answering.

"The reverse of what you say, Edmond, is also not true. So what does it mean? It means that we must practice discrimination. Discrimination is nothing more nor less than the golden mean. In some instances something new is better than something old. For instance, machinery. New machinery is better than old machinery. A new automobile runs more smoothly than an old automobile."

Listening to his father, Ed was amazed that it had taken him so long to make a relatively simple observation. In some ways he and the gaffer were alike. Making allowance for the difference in their ages, the difference in their attitudes and values, they both had the same inclinations. They liked to talk, to philosophize out loud, to hold the floor. His father seemed to lack vanity in every way. And what had happened: just as when you repressed sex it came out in other ways, on a soapbox and so on, it also happened that when you suppressed the ego, it came out in other ways. This was his father's ego gratification, his father's expression of the will-to-power.

"Of course, I did not have machinery in mind. What I had in mind is what we called wisdom. Wisdom by its very nature is not novel, new. It is tried, tested by centuries of experience. Wisdom is not concerned with choosing between a new automobile and an old automobile. It is concerned with testing new values before it substitutes them for old values. That is why wisdom is mellow, why I was remarking a moment ago that in an age like this one we no longer place the same value on words like *mellow* that we used to."

"Values and ideas become as worn out, as rusty, Father, as automobiles or typewriters. That is why it is always necessary to transvalue all values," Ed said.

"Oh, let's not have any long discussions tonight. Let's just talk. Here, J. P., pass me your plate and I'll give you the rest of this soufflé," Mrs. Lanson said.

Mr. Lanson handed her his plate.

"That's what I was doing, explaining to you and Edmond some reflections that came to my mind as I was riding home. I have to write to Pierre and Robert, and I was thinking of what I was going to write."

"When will my family be home with me again?" Mrs. Lanson asked.

Ed felt that this remark of his mother's was not merely a spontaneous outcry. It was a calculated remark which she hoped would touch him, impel him not to leave Chicago. His mother was clever.

"Edmond, what are your plans?" Mr. Lanson asked, taking his plate from his wife. "Your mother told me you intend to go to New York."

"Yes, Father. I think that I can locate there and do better than here."

"I hope that this isn't a wild goose chase."

"No, Father, it isn't. I think that there are more prospects in advertising in New York than here. I've had enough experience now to make the right kind of a connection."

Mrs. Lanson focused gently satiric eyes on her son.

"Mother, you seem skeptical?" he said, not missing her glance.

"Why do you say that, Edmond?"

"The way you were looking at me."

"I wasn't saying a word, Edmond."

"I know it. But you were looking them."

"Not at all. I did, of course, remember that I've heard the same story before. Pierre can't locate in Chicago, and so he's now on a ship bound for India. Robert is in Wisconsin. You had to go South once. Now, it's New York. Chicago is just the most frustrating city in the whole world for my children."

"The only cure for restlessness is discipline," Mr. Lanson said.

Mrs. Lanson brought in coffee and a chocolate cake she had baked.

"Mother, what a tasty-looking cake. Did you bake that?" Ed asked.

"Yes, instead of deciding this afternoon that it would be best for me if I located in Kobe, Japan, or Bombay, India, where I could go my own road in my own way, I baked a cake," she said.

"You're being ironic, Mother, and after baking such a tempting morsel as that cake."

She laughed and, cutting large slices of cake, passed them to her son and husband. She poured coffee for them and passed the cups.

"Are you going to be home this evening, Edmond?"

"I have to see Ellen."

"Well, some evening, now that the prodigal has temporarily returned, you might remain home long enough to renew old acquaintances."

"I will, Mother. Tonight, though, I must see Ellen."

"Your father likes a game of checkers now and then."

"I'll stay home tomorrow night if I can."

"I want to continue our discussion, Edmond," Mr. Lanson said.

"I have to go now. As it is, I'll be late for my date."

He rose. His mother followed him down the hall to his bedroom.

"I pinched this from your father's pocket," she said, handing him a dollar. "J.P. doesn't ever miss a dollar. But now, you be good and come home early. I'll be worried if you're out too late."

"Mother, you're wonderful. You're adorable. You're . . . Mother," he said, kissing her.

"Yes, I know. And now I'll have to worry about another son away from home, too. And your father is upset, but he doesn't show it."

"One thing you mustn't do is to worry about me. I'm always able to take care of myself under all circumstances."

"So I learned yesterday. Edmond, I wish you were as able to take care of yourself as well as Pierre. He manages to take care of himself better than you do."

He frowned.

"I'm not a child," he said.

"Now you stop being surly. Ellen won't like it."

"I have to go," he said, feigning good nature.

Some day he would make her take back what she said of him and Pierre. But that was a matter for the future. He kissed her again. Smiling although she was very sad, she watched him leave, and then went back to sit with her husband.

Chapter Twenty-four

I

Ellen paid no attention to her father at the table. Her mind was filled with the events of last night. It had been so exciting, the fight, Dive Inn, and then the taxicab ride she and Ed had taken in Jackson Park.

"Ellen, you were out late last night," Mr. Rogers said.

"What did you say, Father?"

"Yes, it was very late when you came in."

"It wasn't so late. And there isn't anything wrong with being out a little late once in a while. After all, I'm going to marry Ed."

"It doesn't look decent to see a girl coming home at all hours of the morning. And it isn't good for your health, either."

Ellen knew that he wasn't bothered about her being out late. She had been out late before and he'd never reprimanded her. It was because she had been with Ed.

"When you are engaged to a young man, you must show restraint and dignity. A young man isn't going to think too much of a girl if she lets him keep her out until the small hours of the morning."

The philosophy of love and marriage was now being expounded, Ellen thought ironically.

"Maybe it was I who wanted to stay out. Maybe I kept Ed out," she said.

Mr. Rogers was taken aback by her remark. He said nothing. She thought that her father should just know the whole story of last night, the fight, the people she had been with, the taxicab ride. And he should know that Ed had been arrested yesterday because he wasn't able to pay his landlady.

"Ellen, that isn't the way to conduct yourself. Even if you are engaged to Ed, you must maintain your dignity, your bearing, your control. You must act so that you are sure you will keep his respect. You can't do that if you keep urging him to stay out late, to keep you out that way."

"Why is it so wrong to be out late?"

"It is."

"Why?"

"It isn't right for a decent young girl of your age to be out until half past three and four in the morning."

Ellen was glad that Aunt Alice wasn't well. Aunt Alice had planned to come to Chicago just to meet Ed and pass judgment on her engagement. She even suspected that her father had written, asking Aunt Alice to come. But sometimes operations served their purpose, even if she didn't wish her aunt any unnecessary trouble. She didn't mean to entertain such cynical thoughts. And they wouldn't even occur to her if her father and aunt showed any intelligence and imagination about life.

"Ellen, do you get these new ideas of yours from him?"

"What new ideas?"

"Telling me that it's proper if you stay out as late as you please?"

"But you haven't told me what's wrong with my being out late once in a while."

"Decent people are in bed at that time."

"Then I'm not decent, is that what you mean?"

He stared at her, first in surprise, then with uneasiness.

"I don't at all like the way you talk since you met this fellow."

"Father, you are worrying yourself unnecessarily. You know I wouldn't ever do anything to cause you trouble. Haven't I always told you everything I do?"

"Yes—so far as I know."

"Then you do doubt me, and that is why you ask me questions and are talking to me the way you are tonight."

Ed should hear her now. He would approve of the way she was playing her cards and handling her father.

"Father, didn't I come home and tell you that I was engaged? Couldn't I have run off and gotten married secretly if I wanted to? But I didn't. Still you don't trust me."

"Did he want you to do that?" Mr. Rogers asked in mounting anxiety.

"No, he didn't. All I—"

"Where did you get that idea?" he asked, interrupting her.

"Anybody could get such an idea. All I meant was that if I wanted to act that way, to deceive you, then I could. But I don't want to. I wouldn't. I want to make you understand that you have no reason to distrust me. And I always wanted you to feel you trust me. After we are married, I will feel the same toward you as I do now."

He looked at her guiltily. She was moved.

She was sorry for him. He was sad, pathetic. She didn't want to deceive him, but what else could she do? If she told him the truth, he would be more hurt. She was selfish in acting the way she did. But she had to be selfish. It was her life. She had to live it. And her father was selfish. She could clearly understand what was behind his dislike of Ed. He wanted her home. Her father pretended that it was for her own good that he advised her. But it was really for his good. She had to lie to her father. Her father had to lie to her.

God—did Ed lie to her too?

"Ellen, there is no question about my trusting you. I do. You are a crackerjack of a girl. What I want to make sure about is that Ed is good enough for you."

No, Ed didn't lie to her. He loved her. He wouldn't lie to her, and he didn't have to. There was no need for their lying to each other.

"Father, I'm going to be happy with Ed," she said in answer to his last statement.

"I hope so." He added, as if it were an afterthought: "When is he going to New York?"

"He's making his plans."

"Seems to me it's a wild goose chase. If a person can't make good in one place, it isn't likely he will in another."

"Ed can make good in any place."

"Well, then, why does he have to go to New York?"

"He thinks he has a better chance there."

"Do you want him to go?"

"No, I don't," Ellen found herself saying before she realized it.

"So he's going against your wishes?"

"Not exactly that."

Mr. Rogers didn't pursue the question further. His face became that of a man relieved of a pressing worry. Ellen did not fail to observe this change. She guessed that she should resent it, but somehow she didn't. It wasn't really important to her what her father thought.

Chapter Twenty-five

I

There was a jarring clatter of dishes and noise in the Raklios Restaurant on Randolph near State Street. Ed sat in a corner with a cup of coffee before him, looking out of the window, idly watching the flow of pedestrians on the sidewalk.

He would be disturbed and annoyed by the noise here if it were not for the fact that he was sitting pretty and proud of his finesse. Finesse was the exact word. He had handled this dumb Irishman, Duffy O'Toole, just right. O'Toole had been prepared like a lamb for the slaughter. He could now turn this trick neatly. His guess was that the precise amount to get was fifty bucks. He would like to raise the ante, but he was inclined to believe that if he did, he'd scare his chump away. It was better to settle for fifty rather than scare the bird out of the bushes.

He inhaled, lifted his head, and in utter contentment let the smoke escape through his nose. He whistled a phrase of music. He reflected on how the human animal was a source of endless surprise, of ever-recurring amazement. They were fooled so easily. They were so credulous, born to be such suckers. Talk to them in the appropriate setting, with seeming conviction, and it was usually a foregone conclusion that they would believe you. Men were such fools. They were motivated not only by the will-to-power; many of them were more strongly motivated by the will-to-believe. The folly of men was one of his assets. He smiled sardonically over this reflection. But if this were so, what should he say of the folly of women?

The sight of Duffy O'Toole coming through the swinging

doors of the restaurant interrupted his meditations. He got up and waited for O'Toole, who approached him smiling genially.

"How's tricks, Jones?"

"Oh, just so-so. I lined up a new job and I'm going to be able to make more money than I've ever earned."

"Glad to hear it."

"Everything looks rosy."

"You're looking at the world through rose-colored glasses, huh?"

"Yes, everything's jake," Ed said.

"I'm damned glad to hear it, Jack."

Duffy went to the counter and returned with coffee and a hamburger sandwich. Finishing his coffee, Ed lit another cigarette.

"Well, I ain't got no complaints myself. People buy the gin I sell, and that just sets me to feeling the way I want to feel," Duffy said.

"How do you get it?"

"I buy the alcohol from a friend of mine. He runs a drug-store. I mix it myself and sell it. You know, I just sell it to people I know. I go to a couple of different places where there is a gay young crowd, and I get to know them. So I make a good living that way, much better and much easier than I used to make helping on a truck for the Continental Express Company."

"I'd say you would."

Duffy took out a bank book and waved it in front of Ed.

"I never had this when I was helpin' on an express truck. No sir, I didn't."

"That's a card."

"It's more than a card. It's a good time."

"What's the use of living if you don't have a good time, isn't that so, Duffy?"

"You said it, Jack, old pal."

"Look at the people in the city. Right now, while you and I are sitting here, they're working their pants off."

"Saps."

"Yes, that's just the word. The world is full of saps. Duffy, I'm glad I met you. We see things the same way."

"Sure thing. It was a mistake, our fighting. But if we didn't tangle that way, why then we wouldn't have met each other. Say, how's the bim?"

"Oh, she's all right."

"Neat little trick, she is."

"Yes, she's keen."

"And wild, too," Duffy said, leering.

Ed didn't answer. He studied O'Toole's stupid, ruddy face. How he would like to take a punch at it! Gross, prejudiced, dumb. Well, all the better for him. Duffy was talking about the world being full of saps.

Should he spring it yet? No, he'd wait a few minutes.

"What else is new, Duffy?"

"Nothing much. Like I said, things go along, nice and smooth for me. I'm gettin' along."

"That's because you're smart."

"Well, I ain't dumb."

"Nobody would dare call you that."

"You said it, pal."

"Sometime, just for the fun of it, Duff, you and I'll have to go out alone some night and get into a few fights. I think we could take care of such little matters and have some fun doing it."

"We sure could. Kid, you and me can go a long ways. We can knock 'em dead."

Duffy lit a cigarette and sat back in his chair, oozing conceit.

"Duffy, can you do me a little favor?"

"Sure can, pal."

"My bank is out on the North Side, and I have a check I want to cash. I have to get my mother a present. Today is her birthday."

"Sure, no trouble at all."

"I hate to bother you. But if I can't get it cashed, why, then I have to go out north and come back here to get the present. It's a lot of trouble. And I have a date."

"With the gal?"

"No, this is extra-curricular."

Duffy laughed. Ed laughed with him.

"Well, let's see—it's one-thirty. I got to step on it," Ed said.

"All right, let's go over to my bank."

They got up, and Ed did not demur when Duffy O'Toole took his check for coffee. They stepped onto Randolph Street.

"By the way, my check is for fifty bucks. Is that all right?"

"Sure. We're pals. I'm always glad to do a little favor for a pal."

Ed handed him the check. As they walked over to a bank on La Salle Street, Ed regretted that he hadn't made the amount seventy-five dollars instead of fifty.

II

She squeezed his hand.

It was late, and they sat on a bench in Jackson Park, silent, languorous as the soft warm night. A bluish gray mist hung over the park and over them. Their clothes were damp and crumpled, and her hair was mussed.

"I'll worry about you," she said.

She didn't see his frown. But she sensed that he was staring at her in disapproval.

"Ed, darling, what's the matter?" she asked.

"You must not be a weakling. Worry—don't even use the word. Don't act like one of the puny members of the multitude. My sweetheart has to be strong."

"I will—" She paused. She spoke very slowly. "I will be strong. . . . But, Ed, you must take care of yourself."

"I've done that successfully for twenty-one years. In that period I've been learning how to take care of myself. Now, darling, I'm going to achieve big things. I have an inspiration, and that is what I have always needed. You are my inspiration."

"And I have an inspiration, too. Ed, darling, you make me want to be better. And stronger. Darling, I'll be waiting for you. And we'll be so happy. We'll have so many things to do together."

"You don't know how much I'll miss you," he said.

She still didn't understand why he had to leave. If he was going to miss her, why should he go?

"I'm going forth to misery."

"But, dear, you often say that life is so short. If you know that, and know that you're going to feel miserable, why do it?"

"I must. I said that I was going. If there were no other reason motivating me, that in itself would be enough. Now I have to go."

"But, Ed, haven't you always told me that only a fool is always consistent?"

"But, Ellen, you see, I'm consistent about my inconsistency. I have to be alone, to face the unknown."

So often he said things that made sense and were true. Now she didn't agree with him; she didn't see why he had to go if these were his reasons.

But she was going to be brave. He would love her more if she were strong. She would be strong.

"You'll write to me often?" she said.

"You know that I will. But, Sweet, will you write to me— every day?"

"I'll write every day. Twice a day. I'll write you all the time."

"I'll need your letters. They will buoy up my spirits. You must think of me, alone, feeling miserable, missing you. I'll be struggling to get on, and in my thoughts I'll be living with you, and I'll be thinking hard and dangerously, struggling to put down on paper the most subtle philosophy. For now I am ready to write my book."

He kissed her tenderly.

"You will think of me, Sweet, always and all of the time?"

"Yes."

"And I will come through with flying colors. Then, for Mr. and Mrs. Lanson, the world will be our onion."

"I don't like onions."

"You'll like this onion. When we peel it, it won't cause us to shed tears. Yes, the world will be our onion, and we're going to know high times, peeling it to our hearts' content."

She rested her head on his shoulder.

"I'll think of my Ellen Rogers, of her lips, her kisses. When I have felt the pressure of her lips on mine, I have known Beauty."

She kissed him. The touch of his lips roused her.

III

There was a rustle in the bushes. Ed looked up and saw a badge caught in a gleam of moonlight.

"A cop. We got to beat it," he said, breathing hard.

He got to his feet, hastily trying to rearrange his clothing. She slid off the bench, her hair mussed, her clothes disheveled. She didn't know what to do. Ed took her hand, and they ran across the wet grass, pursued by a struggling flat-footed beefy policeman who yelled after them. They ran on. Ellen was breathless. Ed looked back. He saw that they were not being pursued. He pulled her on, and they passed through the bushes and came out on Sixty-seventh Street. She gasped for breath. He turned away from her to finish rearranging his clothes. They both burst out laughing.

"I must look a sight," she said.

"Let's get away from here. He might have gotten help," Ed said.

They crossed the street and walked on for a block along the south side of Sixty-seventh. She halted under a lamppost and hurriedly combed her hair and powdered her face. Ed then took her mirror and looked at himself. He laughed.

"I'm streaked with rouge. I'm bleeding rouge."

"Why, you are!"

Again they laughed.

"Ed, wipe it off."

"I will not. I'll leave it on, and see if somebody doesn't like it."

"Ed, you always tell me: 'Darling, your slightest wish is my command.'"

"It is."

"Well, if I want you to take the rouge off your face, will you?"

He reached for her mirror again, spat on his handkerchief, and wiped the streaks of rouge off his face. He combed his hair, straightened his tie, and cursorily brushed his suit with his hands.

IV

They strolled on aimlessly, up one street and down another, in the South Shore district. The streets were deserted. The houses were almost all darkened.

"Ed, have you enough money?"

"Yes. Mother loaned me fifty dollars today, and then Father added twenty-five more to it."

"Ed, don't be angry with me for what I'm going to say."

"I couldn't be angry with you."

"If you need money, you'll write to me, won't you?"

"I won't need it."

"If you do?"

"Yes, I will, Sweet. It's so kind, so sweet of you to say that."

They turned the corner of Seventieth and Euclid.

"Ed, you will keep out of trouble?"

"Ellen, since I have met you, I have changed. I'm going to settle down. From now on, when I live dangerously it will be here," he said, pointing to his head.

"And you are really going to write a book?"

"Do you doubt me?"

"I didn't mean it that way. You know I don't doubt you. It's merely that I'm so dumb that I can't understand how anyone can write a book."

"I need your faith in me in order to write. I'm usually confident and cocky, but about this proposition. . . . No. I'm humble. After all, I have the greatest thinker the world ever knew as a model. I keep thinking of him, Nietzsche. I have something tremendous to surpass."

"You can do anything you want to."

"Ellen, I'll carry those very words of yours away with me as if they were flowers pressed close to my heart. Say them to me again."

"You can do anything you want to."

"With your faith and love, Hellfire can't fail. You're all that he needed in his life."

"Honestly, am I?"

"More than you'll ever know."

"Ed, I'll be strong while you're away. But I'll miss you."

"And think of how much more wonderful, more beautiful it will be when we meet again."

She smiled at him, sweetly, sadly.

Why must he go? Again and again this question kept coming into her head. For a while she had refused to believe that he was going. But he was. What could she do?

They walked on. Suddenly it seemed as if there were nothing more to be said.

v

Downstairs, in front of the building, they had kissed for the last time. They had said all the words there were to be said. She had watched him saunter off gaily with a song on his lips. He had looked back and blown her a kiss, and then he had gone on, swinging his arms.

Was that the last she would ever see of him?

Ellen sank her head in the pillow and kicked her legs. She stretched out and lay in bed, tense. She wouldn't cry. She would be hard. That was what Ed had taught her. No, she wouldn't be a puny weakling. She was a woman now, and hard, too—a woman was capable of a great love because she was hard and like Ed. She would be worthy of him.

Great love? She thought of herself and Ed surprised on the park bench by the cop. It was funny.

Ellen laughed. But she was in no mood for laughter. He was leaving in the morning. Once he had called this journey his *quest*. He used words so unusually, so differently from others.

She told herself that she didn't have to think that the worst would happen. He loved her. She was certain he did. Perhaps absence would make him love her more. Two could play every game that one could play. When she wrote him she would state things in a veiled way in order to make him a little jealous. That might pull him back to her.

But she had let her man, her wonderful man, slip through her fingers. He was gone. Gone. No, he wasn't. She and Ed were really in love. And because she had not tried to keep him, because she had made no false plays for his sympathy, he would love her all the more. If she had made scenes, he would feel that he could do what he wanted with her. His affection might have been weakened. But she hadn't. He was so observant that he could not have missed noticing this. He would realize that Ellen had made no scenes. She had let him go when he said he must. This would bring him back to her arms.

But she wanted Ed. She didn't want all these games, pretenses, sparrings. She wanted her Ed. She wanted him now, in bed with her, now, and always and forever. And he had gone away.

Ellen brooded. Again and again she told herself that she would be hard and strong. She would not let herself cry.

Chapter Twenty-six

May 28, 1925
Wash., D. C.

My Sweet:

It may surprise you to receive this letter from Washington, rather than from New York. En route, I changed my mind and my plans and decided I could make a bigger splash in the national capital than I could in New York. There should be all sorts of possibilities in Washington, and I'm going to look into them. I thought that perhaps I might get myself lined up as a lobbyist.

But so much for mundane trivia. What is that compared to what I really want to write to you? And that is to tell you that I adore you. I think of you always. At the moment it is twenty minutes after two and the sun is shining. The same sun shines on you if you are outdoors now. I see the sun as a link between you and me.

I am miserable. I am without my Ellen. I am alone, and my adored and adorable is miles and miles away. Nothing compensates for that distance which separates us. Ah, my sweet, the pathos of distance.

I now have the idea for the first chapter of my book. I am going to call it the Great Beginning. But even that is mundane trivia alongside of what lies on my heart now. Ellen, her pertness, the beauty of her lips, the light that shines in her eyes. But I will fight through the pangs of loneliness. I'll come through this period of search, quest, discovery, and it will help to cement the more firmly the love of Ellen and her Hellfire. Think of me. Always. I will think of you. Always.

Farewell for the moment,
Your Adoring   Hellfire

P.S. *Hellfire is going to make a splash in Wash., D. C. that will make his adorable proud of him yet.*

II

May 30th

Darling Ed

So *many postcards and then your letter from Washington, the first letter I ever received from you. I knock on wood that it be not the last. Darling, your letter was so lovely, so beautiful. But what a surprise! So you are in Washington. I thought it was necessary for you to be in New York, and here, you turn up in Washington. Hellfire is full of no end of surprises. But for God's sake, darling, don't turn up next in Shanghai.*

You are gone only a few days, and how long it seems. Every hour is a day. But I want my Hellfire to know that Ellen has learned her lesson from him. She loves him, and he has taught her so much. She is going to be brave and hard and strong. She misses him with an ache in her heart, but she will dry her eyes and wait patiently, but bravely. She misses him. Kisses to you, kisses sent over miles of distance. And what a lovely phrase of yours—the pathos of distance. It has been ringing in my mind ever since your letter came this morning.

But now, Ed dearest for news. It seems that the Great Hellfire left Chicago in the nick of time. The day after you left some policemen came. They had a warrant for you. That cad, that coward, Bill Northrup, swore out a warrant, charging you with assault and battery. Fortunately I was home and saw the policemen without attracting any attention. If Father knew it, he would be fit to be tied. But I can handle Father. I told the policemen that you were, to my knowledge, not in town.

I have done nothing since you left. Poor Frank tries to be sweet and calls me up. But I say I am busy. How can I go out with Frank after Hellfire?

Darling, I love you—miss you. I bless you. I send you kisses across the pathos of distance. I am thinking of you. Take care

*of yourself. Your book will be lovely. Take care of yourself
and write me. I loved your letter.*

Many many many xxxxxxxxx's

Your Ellen

III

June 1st, 25

Sweet:

*At last, a letter from my adored. But I was disappointed in
the letter I received. Perhaps I was so hungry to hear from my
Sweet that my own expectations and anticipations caused me
to be disappointed. Your letter caused me concern. You say
that you are going to be brave and hard and strong. Does that
mean that you are going to forget me, here, alone, miles away
from you in a strange city? I hate to ask the question. But I
was dismayed by the tone of your letter. It did cause me concern. I received it after tramping around in the heat, and I
was dog tired. I went to the post office full of hopes, eager. I
tore your letter open, and I read it like a famished man. I was
let down. Sweet, if our love is going to become matter-of-fact,
it will be bad. Perhaps you will become so hard and strong and
brave that you can dispense with me.*

*I write this way because my heart aches for you. I think of
what you might be doing at this minute, that minute—every
minute. I try to visualize you in my mind. I think of you.*

*So far, I have spent my time looking around. I'm mapping
out plans. That is the first stage. The next will be contacts.
After I have mapped out my strategy, I'll take the next step.
I'm confident that I am going to get on to something good
here. My main idea right now is something in the line of a
lobbyist. I figure that I should be a good lobbyist, and there
is lots of money in it and the work isn't hard. After all, what
do you do but see Congressmen and Senators and give them a
sales talk. It's a good beginning. But of course, I have to look
the ground over.*

*I had a fine time last night. I read in the library until ten
o'clock, and then wandered home, strolling along, singing.*

Do you know what I sang? All Alone. I thought of you as I strolled home to my room. I'm living at the Y.M.C.A. I have a clean room. It's a card, Hellfire at the Y.M.C.A. But I met a couple of fellows there. They're atheists like me. We had a rousing time the night before last. We bought a little gin and sat in my room talking, and we gave God and Jesus a workout in my room, in the Young Men's Christian Association. Isn't that a card?

But all such mundane matters, what do they count? Why waste paper on them when there are more important things to tell you? What are these? Three trivial little words that seem so simple, that have been said so many times, but that are a world of feelings, sentiments, emotions, desires, worries . . . Sweet—I love you.

> You send me your love in a letter,
> I send you my love in a song.

But ah, ah, that I were a singer—a poet. I should like to be a poet, I would garland your name with verses. I would make Ellen a more beautiful name than Swinburne's Felise, "The sweetest name that love ever waxed weary of." But I am no poet. All I can do is send you from my heart words that are banal, simple, that are cold on paper. I love you. But don't write me in return that you are too hard and brave and strong. These words in your lovely hand stare coldly at me, like ice. Alone in a strange city, I read these words. And they caused me worry, anxiety.

Hellfire misses Ellen. I think of you, you don't know how much. I am brave and strong and hard, and yet, yet a hundred times over, I am unbearably lonely . . . without Ellen.

Always adoring my Sweet,

Your Ed.

P.S. So Bill Northrup has a warrant out for me. Assault and battery. Chalk that up on my record. Tell him to have the cops look long and carefully for me. By the time I come back to get you, perhaps he will be just recuperating from the ef-

*fects of the last meeting he had with me. And we might have
another pleasant rendezvous again.*

*P.S. I put a little x at the bottom of my letter. How pale a
symbol for a kiss on those lips of yours, lips from which beauty
is drunk like nectar.*

Au revoir

E.

IV

June 1, 1925

Ed Darling

This morning I dashed down to the mail box the minute
I got out of bed. And there was no letter. Are you all right?
Are you well? Are you in trouble? Do you need anything?
You don't begin to know how blank the day seems to me. I
don't know what to think. Ed, don't treat me this way. Write
to me, you must, every day. I wrote to you about how brave
and hard and strong I was going to make myself for you. But
I have to hear from you, and when I don't hear, I am worried,
for fear lest something has happened to you. Ed you promised
to write me every day. I need your letters. Never before has
the mail man been so important. I never thought much of the
mail man before in my whole life.

Last night I went to a movie with Gertrude Dorgan. Afterward we had hot chocolate. These days, I feel so sorry for
Gertrude. I feel so sorry for every girl in the world. Guess
why? Three guesses, but I'll penalize you if you don't guess
right the first time. Gertrude says that she saw Catherine Anne.
Catherine Anne asked her about you and me. Poor Gertrude.
It must be terrible to be lame and ugly.

In his first letter Hellfire didn't tell me very much of what
he does. Everything he does interests me. Even if he walks
down a street. I'd like to know which street it is, and what it
looks like. And he hasn't told me much about Washington.
Is it a beautiful city? Do you like it better than Chicago?
Would you and I be happier there than in Chicago?

I have so many questions to ask you. They spill out of me as *write. It seems so many years since you left. How soon will you be settled? I hope it is very soon. Ed my darling, if you only knew how much I miss you. When you were here the days were so short. Now the days are so long.*

Father asks after you. I think he admires what you did. He has to. Everybody has to admire my Hellfire. The world has to pay tribute to him because he is just that wonderful.

Ed, please write me. Don't let me go through more mornings like this morning.

x

Your Ellen

v

June 3, 1925

My dearest Ed

Your letter of June 1st just came. I have read it over three times. It was so wonderful to hear from you. But, Ed, you must not be concerned and anxious over me. When I wrote that I was going to try to be brave and strong and hard, it was for you. I meant that I was not going to wear my heart on my sleeve but that I would keep my heart inside, all closed and warm and waiting only for you. You poor thing alone in a strange city! It makes me feel sad.

And it was such a lovely letter you wrote. It was so thoughtful of you to tell me that you wished you were a poet so that you could make my name like Felise. Ed, you are a darling. And you are so subtle.

What are the atheists in the Y.M.C.A. like? And what are their names? Tell me about them. Tell me about yourself, about Washington, about your fine, wonderful, subtle thoughts. When you begin writing your book send what you do on to me. Oh, it will be grand to see you write that book. But everything you do is grand. My Hellfire has style—I am so proud of him—so proud I could sing all the time. Sure you could be a lobbyist, whatever that really is. Poor me, I know nothing about politics. But you could be a lobbyist. Ed, if I can only convince you how much promise you have in so many ways. Why, you could be anything you want to be, if you set yourself to it.

Is your room cosy? Is it comfortable? Is it too warm in Washington? If it is, don't wear yourself out tramping the streets. Are the buildings beautiful? When will you be meeting the President, and when will you be President? But my lovely, in all the excitement of Washington, don't forget your little Ellen, waiting for you, waiting with her heart kept guarded and storing up love, so much love too for just you. Just because you're you. Letters are so unsatisfactory. Ed, don't think that my letters are cold or matter-of-fact. They're not. When I sit down to write to you, oh, how I wish I could write marvelous letters the way you can. But I can't. All I can do is spill out to you that I am thinking of you, missing you more than you could ever know, waiting for you, thinking of your wonderful voice and handsome face and curly hair, and yes thinking of other things about you, too. Ed, you have made me grow up. I am a woman now. When I met you I was a little girl, yes, I was a silly little girl. But you taught me so much and I am a different person. I hope I am a better person. I am a woman waiting for letters from her beloved, and waiting for the day when I can take him in my arms and let him go to sleep on my shoulder.

I have so much faith in you, more than words can tell. I know you will make good. It is written in the stars. And make good fast for your Ellen who misses you, and pines and pines for you.

Write me Ed, gobs of letters. I never can get enough letters from you. Your

Ellen with trillions of xxxxx's.

VI

June 3

Ellen, lovelier than Felise:

I have just a minute. My Sweet, the difference in time between Chicago and Washington is one hour. At twelve o'clock on June fifth, I shall look at the moon. That will be eleven *o'clock. Chicago time. Look at the moon at that moment. I shall be looking at the silver and lucent orb and thinking of you. You look at it and think of me. Think that there are only the two of us in the world looking at the moon, and that its silvery dazzling rays are spilling out of the sky only for us.*

Don't think me silly in telling you to do this. It will be a form of communion between us.

Always and always yours

E

xxxxxxxxxx

VII

June 5, 25

Sweetest Ed

I just came in off the balcony. Wasn't the moon lovely? And it was such a poetic idea of yours for me to look at the moon, and for you to look at the moon at the same minute. I stood on the balcony. Oh, such a night as this. And just as if it were for us, the moon was so glorious—and I never realized that there were so many stars in the sky—and I saw a shooting star. I thought that's like my Ed. Sweetheart, I looked at the moon just as you asked me to. I blew it kisses, thinking those kisses would go to the moon and become rays that cross Ed's face. Oh, I miss you so.

I am happy. And I am so sad. Do hurry up and make good, for I miss you so much.

I'll write again tomorrow morning first thing. I'm running out to mail this letter now for you.

I love you always always, forevermore with kisses

Ellen

VIII

June 6, 1925

Sweet:

Did you look at the moon? It was a thrilling experience, because trusting as I am, I thought that you did, and that there was between us something that was sacred. Don't laugh at the word. It was the way I felt. Here, it was a fine night too. Cool, after a warm and almost stifling day. I was keyed up all day, waiting, waiting for the moment when by doing such a seemingly silly thing as gaze upon the moon, I would establish a feeling, a fiction of contact. There is a German book of philosophy by a man called Vaihinger, The Philosophy of As If. He talks about fictions. We really know fiction. The world is as if. I thought of this last night. I thought what a lovely fiction, the lovelist of all fictions, a fiction of love. What was it? That Hellfire at one end of the world and Ellen, miles away, could gaze upon that cold orb of ice, the moon, and that their thoughts went out in a way that deepened their love and feeling for one another, and that gave them—at least me—such consolation such gratification. Don't think me sentimental for writing you these letters.

I wish that I could invent a whole new vocabulary just to tell you how adorable you are. Words are paltry things. But accept my paltry words as tokens of love.

Ed with kisses

IX

June 8th

My love
What a lovely letter. You are so thoughtful. And you are so humble. You write me letters that are so enchanting and humbly say they are sentimental. Silly? You adorable charming lovely wonderful unexcelled—Ed. But don't say your words are fictions. Don't say that they are as if. I don't care if all the philosophers in the world write books like the one you mentioned. I don't care about books and philosophers this minute. I care about Ed.

Sweetheart tell me more about what you are doing. You write me the most wonderful letters, but I want more, more oh, so much more. I want every little scrap of information about you. Are you lonesome? Do you know any people? Are you making progress? Please, please, please pretty please make progress so that I can have my Hellfire back again. And don't get in any fights. Please don't. And how are you getting along? Oh, tell me, tell me everything my darling.

I worry about you. If you only knew how much. I was walking through Jackson Park yesterday. Guess why? Because it made me remember you. I walked and walked. I was so lonesome. I missed you so much. How can I describe how much I missed you? You say words are paltry. Yours are not. But Ed, sweet Ed, divine Ed, mine are. How can I tell you how much I missed you. Would that I could. I saw you all over the park. And you were not there. I walked and walked until I was simply exhausted just because I missed you. I tried to imagine you by my side. I thought of you walking with me and singing. Oh, Ed, when will I hear that dear voice of yours break out into song? When? Make progress. Be the greatest lobbyist in the world and do it soon, right away. You can. Because I miss you.

I have a new dress. Organdy. But I won't wear it for a while. What is a new dress when I have no Ed to look at it? What care I for anybody else looking at it?

Six fellows called me up for dates. Know what I said? No, no, no, no, no, no, no, no. I dreamed of you last night. Silly dream and silly me. I dreamed that you were President.

Ed, write me letters and letters and letters. Write me and tell me everything about yourself. Write me how you are getting along. Do you need anything? Oh write me.

I think of the silliest things. This morning when I woke up, I lay in bed and I thought, wouldn't it be wonderful if I could make a wish to see Ed and then see him? Am I foolish?

Honeychild Ed, just to think of you makes me so sad. I miss you so terribly. Kisses and you know what else.

your Ellen

X

June 10th, 1925

Ellen darling girl:

You write that you miss me. What do you think I feel? I miss you—the very sight of you—your lips—your warm and open arms. You are home, in familiar surroundings. I am alone in a strange city. What do I do? You should pose the question differently? Outside of thinking of Ellen, missing her, yes, pining for her, what do I do? I don't have time to do much else. What else do I do?—how unimportant. Oh, why bother about such meager details? Know this. You are in my mind and my heart all of the time, every minute, waking and sleeping. You fill my dreams like a song that causes pain. That's what I do.

For the rest. I read, and I survey the situation. I have a new idea. Of course it will require a little capital, and I have to find that. But for Hellfire, what is impossible? Conceit? Yes, it is conceit. But I will justify my conceit. I will justify it if Ellen trusts me, has faith in me. My idea is a clever one. I have not worked out all of the details, but I have thought about it and the general plan is there. It is much better than my idea of being a lobbyist. Here it is. Congressmen have to be re-elected every two years. They must keep in the public eye. Why can't I work out a system of getting them publicity? After all, with my fertile imagination, think of all the stunts I could contrive to pull off. It takes time to work out plans like these carefully, and I have spent a great deal of time applying my mind to this idea. The time I spent thinking out the lobbyist angle is waste in one sense, and in another it isn't, because after all, I did think about things, survey and canvass the situation, and learn something.

Sweet, there is nothing to worry about except one thing only. Not to let your love for me grow cold. That, and only that, could be a calamity. For the rest, why nothing ill could befall Hellfire. You know that. No calamity can overtake me. Why, I am one up on fate every day in the week. Now, my Sweet, worry ill befits a girl as adorable as you. Worry ill befits you for another reason. You are not one of the hoi polloi. You are not a weakling of the multitude. You are far superior to that. You and I will raise one another up. So—cease worrying.

Ah, adorable, more adorable than Felise, lovelier than Faustine, ah, my one and only incomparable Ellen, ah, that time would permit me to write even more. Adieu for the moment.

Your

Ed

123456789 times 123456789 millions of kisses to Ellen.
P.S. What happened to that warrant against me for assault and battery?

XI

June 19th, 1925

Ellen my Sweet Felise:

I received many letters from you. And if you only knew how much I treasure them. I always carry your latest letter around with me, and I constantly take it out and read it. But, Ellen, sweetest, I must ask you to have faith and trust in me. I need it badly. I have been less than diligent in writing to you, but you must, you will understand. It is very difficult to get launched here. I am fed up, but I will not quit. I have scouted around a lot, and I think that if I can hang on by my teeth a little while, I can connect in a big way. But in the meantime it has been very difficult. I have been struggling with myself. I have had my periods and my moments of let-down. At times I have not written you because I did not want to cause you worry. I was in such black moods that I feared even to put pen to paper lest I convey these moods to you. But, Ellen, Ellen so wonderful, I know that you will understand.

I cannot quit. I must go on. And I have met with temporary embarrassments. Sweet, could you send me any money? I hate to ask you, but I can think of no one in all the world to whom I should turn before turning to you. You are closer to me than any human being on this sorry, paltry little planet. That is why I turn to you. You will understand what a wrench it is to my pride. But there are things in life that are of greater significance than pride. I could appeal to others and get the wherewithal to keep me going through this first and most difficult period. But I have given the whole question much thought. I have come to this conclusion. I owe it to Ellen to write to her first. Ellen would, I have reasoned, be disappointed in me were I to write to others on this matter, rather than to her. I can hang on with this sum until something breaks.

I am full of plans. One day, I was walking down Pennsylvania Avenue—in slang parlance that's the main drag—and it occurred to me—why should Hellfire waste his talents trying to get the mug of some dumb Congressman in the paper for the booboisie back home? Why should I devote my energies to getting one set of morons to look with pleasure on another set of morons whom they elect to make dumb laws for the slaves? So I put my mind to the problems at hand and decided that what I would do would be canvass Washington with the idea of direct-by-mail advertising schemes. Washington is fertile. Now I am preparing to do this. I can succeed in my plans here, and do it much more quickly than I could with the other plans I have discarded. So that is what I am going to do. But I have to hang on.

Ellen, I am beastly disgusted with life. It is beastly hot. But I will not give up. I'll hang on. And I'll make you proud of me. And don't you worry. And don't you be jealous. What girls could take your place in my heart? Impossible even to think of such a question. Oh, my sweet, don't make it harder for your Ed.

Think of me and I will think of you, often and always.

Your

Ed

P.S. *Out of the night that covers me*
Black as the Pit from pole to pole,
I thank whatever gods may be
For my unconquerable soul.
And for my Ellen.

P.S. *It is wiser to write me General Delivery. I have changed quarters. It is a small comfortable rooming house. But I don't like nosey people looking at mail from the sweetest girl that ever lived when it is laid on the table downstairs.*

P.S. *Ah, my sweetheart how I miss you this very minute!*

Kisses in superabundance

E. Your E.

Chapter Twenty-seven

I

Not a breath of air stirring. Such heat! Such a frying pan! Such a town! How could any man with brains have any ambition in the inferno called Washington, D. C.?

Wearing his B.V.D.'s, Ed lay on the couch in his one-room-and-kitchenette apartment, reading James Branch Cabell's *The Rivet in Grandfather's Neck*. His arms and legs were tanned. The small room was in disorder. His clothes were tossed in a heap with soiled feminine underthings. But it was too hot to worry about a little disarray.

He put his book aside and picked up a towel to mop his face. The sight of the apartment filled him with sudden disgust. On a day like this the joint didn't have to be such a mess. But then there was nothing to do unless he wanted to straighten out things himself. He wouldn't mind doing it, except for the heat, and for his dignity. Hilda was bringing home the bacon for him, and he didn't want to turn himself into her chief cook and bottle-washer. So there was nothing to do but bear the mess. Elisa, Hilda's maid, hadn't shown up today. She must have gotten herself ginned up with some black buck boy in Alexandria where she lived. But then, what difference did it make? Hilda would be home soon from work and they would go to some place where they could get cool, some place along the Potomac. They ought to go back to that fish place and have supper there.

He'd received another letter from Ellen. God, why did that woman take things so seriously? One subject that old Hellfire had really gotten to know was that which concerned the feminine heart. He could pride himself on never having made a mistake in strategy or technique with a female. The slave-minded and the conventional of this world would call him a sonofabitch. From their point of view he was an S.O.B. Ah, what fools there were! The idealization of woman was pernicious, a curse—a curse particularly to a man with intelligence. Women were selfish, in their fashion. They were like leeches, and when they attached themselves to a man they sucked every bit of independence out of him. When he had strolled around Washington, observing, studying, looking, he had seen much to reinforce these conclusions. He had seen so many of the government clerks with their wives, window-shopping, staring into the store windows at furniture, dresses, rings. What a picture! What a story it told! These tight little girls, these Catherine Annes, had all gotten their men, and they were holding them captives with hooks of steel. How smug they were. And these little clerks who toiled away in the Department of Agriculture, the Department of the Interior, all the other damned departments of the government, growing old, knowing not what it means to live, no exaltations, no adventures, never in their lives enjoying the romance of their own egotism. They would grow old with a burden of installment payments on their backs; they would grow old with contented bovine little Catherine Annes who had gotten their men and were keeping their possession by hell, heaven, and high water.

He lit a cigarette and mopped his brow. Ah, the chasm that separated Washington, D. C., from Poictesme. Contrast Hilda and the women of Poictesme. But then, Hilda had her place and her function. She was inferior to Ellen, but, withal, she had her definite uses. And Ellen—ah, Ellen!

He must write her a letter that would put her heart at ease. For he really did care for her.

I have been faithful to thee, Cynara, in my fashion.

What plans should he make? Should he return to Chicago and to Ellen? No, he couldn't go back defeated. He had to catch on to something. Go on to New York, New Orleans, Galveston and go to sea? Go to New York? Well, all this could be taken care of in due time. It was too hot even to think.

In the morning when Hilda was at work he'd write a letter to Ellen. She would be home from the Department of Agriculture any minute.

Ellen had been so adorable, so pert and sweet, so lovely. But his absence from her would be good for her soul. Still, it would be fun to be on the beach with her now, to look at her body in a swimming suit, and to lie on the sand with his head in her lap, waiting for darkness to spread over the lake, and to sing to her out of sheer happiness and exaltation.

Yes, he loved Ellen in his fashion.

He had merely been fed up with Chicago. Suddenly it had occurred to him that it was time to shove off. So here he was in Washington, D. C., the capital of the nation, the home of Cal himself. However, he would give Washington its due. It did have its attractions, and these were pleasant enough in their fashion before the weather had become unbearable. Washington was a city whose main attraction was the government girls. They came from all over the nation and they were to be found in Washington in superabundant quantities. And, oh, the government should know something about the government girls.

Back home in the corn belt, the cow belt, the Bible Belt, back home in the provinces, these girls had probably been looked upon as sweet and innocent homebodies. Perhaps they were. Hilda had a reputation in Kansas City. But when these girls got to Washington. . . . He laughed. It was a card, amusing to think about. And after all was said and done, what could you expect when a lot of Congressmen were let loose?

The funniest he had ever met was the Indian, Josephine. He had never seen an Indian before, except wooden ones in front of cigar stores. But Josephine was a live, honest-to-God Indian girl. Ah, my sweet papoose. He had Josephine all doped out. She was too dumb, almost too dumb to have fallen for him.

Thank God, if such there be, that Josephine didn't work in the Department of Agriculture where Hilda did. Josephine was in the Department of the Interior. But she was so cold. She was not worth all the time and effort he gave to making her. A whole week of his life had gone into that effort.

But even Josephine had fallen for him and he'd had to move. After the night he'd made her, she had called him up every day for a week. He had moved. It wasn't any use sending her that last verse from *Félise*. She wouldn't understand it.

Ah, the little ironies, the little stories, the people you met along the waysides of life. He squashed his cigarette and lit another one.

He picked up his book again, puffed on his cigarette, and read. Why think of Indian girls and Washington, D. C., when his spirit could roam in the deliciously ironical and beautiful pages of Cabell?

II

"Hellfire."

"Hilda knows my name," Ed replied, getting up as she let herself in.

She went to him, kissed and hugged him.

"This goddamned heat is insulting. It is an unwarranted piece of cosmic insolence."

"Ed, I almost died at work today."

"Who in the hell had the idea of making Washington the national capital? In this heat. And, my God, I can't go out of the house. That convention of Odd Fellows drives me crazy. The booboisie of America has gathered here. I almost teed off on one of the Odd Fellows yesterday, crowding over the sidewalk as if he owned it. And he was dressed up in his monkey suit, too."

"Oh, Ed, they're not so bad."

He frowned. His B.V.D.'s fitted him badly, hanging around the seat in an undignified swirl.

"Hilda, have you deserted to the other camp?"

"Ed, you talk so funny."

"So the Odd Fellows aren't so bad?"

"Why get excited about them? They never did anything to me."

"They have to me."

"What? Did one of them cause you any trouble?"

"They all have. The entire organization of Odd Fellows."

"What did they do to you?"

"They exist."

"Ed, you're so funny."

"I wouldn't call that a neat choice of adjectives."

She flopped down in a chair, pushing off some soiled under-things of her own.

"I'm hot," she said.

Ed lit a cigarette and looked at Hilda. He decided that she was not up to Ellen. There was something of the thoroughbred in Ellen. In some ways she was like a fine race horse. Hilda was a pretty little thing. She was trim. Her legs were neat and thin, as good as Ellen's, and she had lovely little breasts that stood up straight, almost a virgin's breasts, although Hilda was twenty-five. She was brown-eyed, snub-nosed, and had thin little lips. And her ears. He appreciated her little ears and liked to pretend that he would bite them.

"I'm hot and I'm all tired out. You might be tired of Odd Fellows, Ed, but do you know what I'm tired of?"

"Me?"

"Oh, stop that! I'm tired of hogs, cattle, feed, fertilizer."

"We all, some day, must become fertilizer. Yes, that's the fate of all men, of all beautiful things."

"Ed, take a bath with me," she said, getting up and beginning to undress.

III

Ed leaned back in the wooden booth, puffing on a cigarette. The restaurant was crowded; there was a steady echo of talk from all the booths and tables. Sweating Negro waiters rushed about carrying plates.

"What'll we do tonight, Hilda?"

"I don't know. Anything. Oh, Ed, my darling, how did I find you?"

He smiled.

"How did I find you?" she repeated.

"Just think, I have only known you ten days, and we have only lived together a week, and it seems that we have lived forever. Together. Forever together," Hilda said.

"I often feel as if I had lived forever."

"Ed, you sometimes talk in a way that makes me think there must have been great sadness in your life."

Ed's brows knitted.

"If I can only make you forget the past," she said.

"I don't like to speak of it."

"Ed, tell me. Ed, I love you. Maybe I can make you forget."

"It's humiliating even to think of it."

"I don't care. I love you."

"Sweet, I'll tell you. Did you ever hear of Sappho, the Greek poet?"

"Who?"

"Sappho was a Lesbian. Do you know what that is?"

She smiled at him.

"I was married. She was a beautiful girl, almost as beautiful as you. I was young. I didn't know better. I was swept off my feet. I married her. Her name was Faustine. A strange name, isn't it? She was a strange girl. But I was young. I had a good job, too. I was making a lot of money, one hundred and fifty dollars a week. That's why she married me. She was looking for a chump and for some fellow to serve as a cover for her."

"She must have been awful. A terrible bitch."

Ed laughed deprecatingly.

"Forget it, it's a joke. Why, traveling salesmen tell stories about how husbands come home and find somebody else, preferably a traveling salesman, in their wives' beds. Well, it's funny, too, to come home and find a woman in bed with your wife."

"No, it isn't. It's terrible. I hate people like that."

"I was young and full of illusions. This ordeal shattered them.

I threw up everything, threw all the work I had done overboard. That's why I came to Washington. Do you know that when I met you I was on the verge of suicide?"

She looked at him with pity and reached across the table to squeeze his hand.

"Get me a cup of coffee," he ordered the passing waiter.

"It's like a nightmare. I can't begin to tell you what I went through," he said.

"God, what a bitch!"

"Well, I'm charitable. Nothing's good nor bad but thinking makes it so. I just wasn't strong enough. I always said that I was beyond good and evil. But it was a jolt. Not that I was morally shocked. It was a terrible blow to my illusions. Ah, illusions, illusions, man is full of them. They destroy our balance. But what would we have without illusions? What? Just the miserable little paltry commonplaces of life—fertilizer, pigs, cows, cattle, the seething dullness of the market place. Ah, illusions. Hilda, we will preserve our illusions."

"Yes, Ed."

The Negro waiter set another cup of coffee before Ed.

"It has taken me four years to recover from the shock. I cursed the day I ever met Faustine."

"I'm jealous of her."

"Don't say that. It's the dead and dull past. The past is a bucket of ashes." Ed laughed again, deprecatingly. "But sometimes the ashes taste bitter in your mouth."

"I hate her. I never saw her and I hate her."

"Those who live in glass houses should pull down the shades, Hilda."

"Ed, what do you mean?"

"I'm jealous, too. I'm jealous of the men you've known."

"They meant nothing to me. If I had known I was going to meet someone like you some day, I would have saved myself."

"But if you had, then you wouldn't have been you. You would have been somebody else. I'm glad you didn't. Not that I'm not jealous. I'm glad, because it's *you* I love. You would have been different if you had met me a virgin, much different.

Hilda, virtue may be its own reward, but experience teaches us—how to make love."

"You could have been my teacher."

"And you are my teacher."

"Ed, I have something to say."

"What?" he asked, puffing on a cigarette again.

"I am engaged to be married."

He frowned.

"But I'm breaking it off."

"Why didn't you tell me?"

"Ed, I was afraid to. And I didn't think."

"You deceived me."

"But, Ed, I'm telling you now."

"You deceived me, Hilda."

"Oh, Ed, I didn't think it was important."

"Perhaps it wasn't," he said.

She smiled broadly, happy. He watched her closely.

"Perhaps it wasn't important to you that you deceived me."

"Oh, Ed, please don't say such things to me."

"It isn't pleasant, Hilda. It disturbs me, distresses me."

"Ed, listen to me, honest, this is the truth. The fellow from home in Kansas City, his name is Charley White, I never let him even touch me. Honest I didn't. Isn't that enough to show you? Ed, let's get married this minute. That will prove to you, won't it, that I didn't really deceive you?"

"I'm a pauper. A pauper."

"I don't care. I don't. I love you. Oh, let the government support us. I make money. We can live."

Hilda opened her purse and got a bill. She reached across the table with her right hand cupped and slipped a five-dollar bill to Ed. He got up and signaled for the waiter peremptorily.

IV

Ed and Hilda leaned over the railing of the stone bridge, gazing at the dark, flowing water of the Potomac.

"It's so romantic."

"Ah, illusions. The water, dark and mysterious. It's just

water, merely a river. Nothing but an aggregation of the elements of hydrogen and oxygen, H_2O. Look at the way the
moon dances on it. The rays of the moon seem like creatures,
wonderful strange creatures. Illusions. Look up at the moon."

She looked at the moon; so did he. It was round, full, bluish.

"It seems like something precious. Look at it, so big, round,
full, so beautiful. Why? Because it is so far away. Up close it
is a huge, cold and uninhabited stellar body. Illusions."

"Oh, Ed, I don't care. Call it whatever you like. I love it."

"But you, Hilda, you're not an illusion. You're real. I
wouldn't trade you for the light of the moon that shimmers on
the dark waters of the Potomac. I wouldn't change you for the
moon. Look across at the darkness beyond the edge of the
bridge. There lies the whole state of Virginia. I wouldn't trade
you for that."

She kissed him passionately.

"Ed, honey, take me home."

She clung to him and again kissed him passionately.

v

The kitchenette apartment was clean, and they sat by the
table near the window with the dinner dishes before them. Ed
pushed his coffee cup aside and lit a cigarette.

"I'll tell him that I'm married to you," Hilda said.

"But that's a lie."

"But I don't want the people back home to think things about
me."

"Kansas City! Who cares about Kansas City?"

"I do."

"That's because you've not freed yourself. You're not yet
a free spirit."

"Oh, Ed, why be foolish? I don't want my friends back there
to know. After all, I want to keep my job and not get in any
trouble."

"Jobs, jobs. Nobody in Washington thinks of anything else.
Here everybody wants a job, and then a better job. Ah, I laugh.
Back home the booboisie thinks of Washington as the national

capital. Here it is the seat of government. Here the sage
wise men make laws, and here is concentrated all the dignity of
the country. Every time you turn around, a building or a monu-
ment sticks in your face. This burg is a mausoleum. All the dead
in it think of a job. Washington's a public feed trough, that's
what it is."

"What's wrong with it?"

"Oh, nothing. Why do I care if the people, the nation, is
fooled? I should worry. Hell, I'm not a humanity-savior."

"Ed, sometimes you talk so funny."

"Ah, funny! Yes, I talk funny. Funny!"

"Sometimes I can't make you out."

"What did you say his name was?"

"Charley White." She did not speak for a moment. "Ed, I'll
say I'm married. I don't want to see him. I won't see him. I
won't."

"That would be cowardly. You must face him."

"But it's so foolish. I don't love him. I don't want to see him.
Honey, I don't ever want to love anybody again but you."

"See him. Perhaps we can use him."

"But what'll I tell him?"

"Sweetheart, listen to me. I'd better take a room somewhere.
And you act as if you were still engaged to him."

"But why? Why—when I don't want to?"

"We might use him. How? I'll figure that out."

"Oh, Ed, please, let's not."

"All right. We won't," Ed said; he left the table. She watched
him. He put on his hat and coat and started to walk out of the
apartment, his face surly.

She ran to him and clutched at him from behind. He turned
around. She kissed him frantically. He was unresponsive.

"What's the matter, Ed?" she asked, an expression of horror
conquering her features.

"Nothing."

"The way you act to me."

"You refuse to take my advice. All right, you needn't."

"I will. I'll do anything you say. Only please don't act that way. Ed, I love you," she said.

He remained cold, forcing her to continue kissing him. Finally, he permitted himself to respond to her embrace.

VI

Ed sat at the desk in his room at the Y.M.C.A. He sealed the envelope of the letter he had just written to Ellen. It ought to put her a little bit at ease. He was getting fed up with Washington and perhaps he would go back to Chicago. Of course, returning was like an admission of defeat. But whose defeat was it? After all, what standard was there to apply to defeat? Was it defeat that he didn't feed at the public trough by filing papers at the Interstate Commerce Commission or doing some useless job? Defeat? How could that be defeat? Ellen wouldn't really think it was defeat. She would be so glad to have him home. He'd hinted in his letter to her, too, that he was getting fed up, but he'd also written that he had finally landed a job in the Department of Agriculture. That would allay her worries. He would go back soon and say to her that he'd given up a good job for her because he could not stand to be separated from her any longer.

He smiled.

Hilda was out with her fiancé tonight. He had insisted that she do it. He was supposed to go to her place at one o'clock and see her. Hilda was a nice girl, but she had conventional ideas. If he were fool enough to marry her, she would change. He guessed that they all did. There was a deep-seated selfishness in a woman in love and if she married, society considered her actions moral, whereas society would call his conduct immoral.

He snapped his fingers in contempt of society.

A woman would take a man's freedom and turn him into an appendage to her, dictate his life, cry, put on the martyr act— what wouldn't she do to hold and dominate her man? Love between the sexes was war.

He whistled, deciding that he'd stroll around and go to the library and read tonight. Something of Nietzsche would be a tonic. And he had to get back to thinking about that book he would write. He really intended to write it.

He carefully tied his tie, put a little powder on his face, greased and combed his curly hair, put his straw hat on at a jaunty angle, and left his room.

VII

"Ed, he tried to make me tonight," Hilda said as they lay in bed, lassitudinous.

"Yes?"

"I hated him when he did. And he got mad. He said we were going to be married. I said: 'No, we aren't.' I said that if that was how much he respected me, I was glad I learned about his real nature in time. He's so smug. He's so conventional."

"He should have been here for the Odd Fellows' convention last week."

"Oh, honey, know what?"

"I couldn't know what, unless you told me."

"Know what I adore?"

"*Je t'adore.*"

"What's that?"

"I adore you, in French."

"Do you speak French?"

"A little."

"Say something for me."

"Some other time."

He lit a cigarette.

"Hilda, I've been thinking. I have a plan."

"Yes, Ed," she said, and then she waited for him to continue.

"I'm going to locate in Washington."

"Honey, in the fall, when the heat is over, we can have so much fun here together."

"I ought to be able to get a good job here. I'm going to run back and settle all my affairs back home and see my folks, and then settle here."

She looked at him, anxious.

"Honey, you're going away?"

"Just to settle my affairs. I'll only be gone a week or ten days."

"Ed, are you telling me the truth?"

A sulky expression crossed his face.

"Ed, please, you must tell me the truth."

He sat up in bed, exposed from the waist up, his torso swarthy and perfectly modelled, his arms strong and firm, but slender. He did not speak. His expression was icy.

"You question me?" he asked, his voice melodramatic.

"Ed, you know I don't."

"You ask me to tell you the truth as if I were capable of lying to you, deceiving you."

She began to cry. Allowing her to cry, he stared coldly at the wall.

"Ed, please forgive me. But do hurry back here to me. Oh, I'll miss you. Will you write to me every day?"

"Are you sorry for what you said?"

She kissed him and nestled her head against his shoulder. He put his left arm around her.

"I'll write to my lovely pagan enamorata," he said tenderly.

She wiped away her tears with the back of her hand, streaking her face.

"How are you going to travel?"

"Freight."

"Oh, you can't. It's dangerous. I'll die of worry."

"I can't be a chooser."

"Ed, no, you can't go that way. You mustn't do that."

"It's a good idea. To leave Washington by a freight train and then to return and knock the town dead."

"Ed, honey, you wait until my next payday. I'm short because of your rent at the Y.M.C.A. and our other expenses. You wait, and you can go by train."

"You won't have enough to live on."

"Oh, I don't care. I'll get it."

"How?"

She thought a moment.

"Why don't you borrow it off this fellow, White? He has it, hasn't he?" Ed asked.

"Yes, he has. But, no, I hate to."

"Don't be so foolish. People like him exist so that they may be used by people like you and me. He'd marry you and ruin your life by making you into a meek little Mrs. Wife, never knowing adventure, robbing life of all illusions, making you into nothing but a sweet little missus. He's selfish in his way. What he would do to you would be to stamp out of you all flair, all *esprit,* all color and beauty. That's the highest form of selfishness. People like him are to be used. I have an idea."

She gaped at him, loving and full of devotion.

"You tell him that you signed a note for a girl friend, and that if you don't make it good the loan firm will garnishee your wage with the government, and that if that happens, you'll get in trouble with your boss and might even lose your job. He'll fall for that and you'll get the hundred. I can go home and come back on that without pinching you, and then, when I come back, I'll get down to the serious business of landing a job."

"But, Ed."

"Of course, I can travel on a freight train. I don't think that I'll lose a leg or that anything harmful will happen to me."

She looked at him, horror-stricken.

"Ed, when should I tell him?"

"Write him after he leaves."

She thought a minute.

"Ed, I don't like to ask him for anything."

"Look at it this way. You are using him. Why? Because that's his function—to be used. Hilda, you and I are not part of the greedy little multitude. We're different."

She kissed him passionately.

"My pagan love girl," he said, turning out the light.

Afterward, with the light on again, Hilda gazed at him.

"Ed, you're a god," she said.

VIII

Ed sat by the train window, looking out as the train raced on across open country. He slouched back in his seat and let his eyes drift to the ceiling. Well, an episode closed. Charming in some ways, amusing in others. Hilda had been sad kissing him good-bye. She would get over it. She would some day be grateful to him for giving her as much of himself as he had. He had earned what he had gotten from her. My god, she had never had a love affair like the one with him.

But he'd almost forgotten something. He took out his little book, and under Hilda's name and the money she'd spent on him he put down the name White, and after it, a hundred dollars. This one was a card.

He was glad to be going back. Ellen would be fresh and new, charming. She didn't know he was coming home either. He would surprise her, thereby making his return more delightful.

Hilda had cried as the train pulled out. Time would dry her tears. How should he handle her by mail? Send her a verse from *Félise?* Well, he'd see about that.

Good-bye Washington, Cal Coolidge, monuments, public buildings, government girls, Indians. . . . good-bye, Hilda!

He smiled again.

He closed his eyes and tried to visualize Ellen. It was difficult. She had blonde hair, blue eyes, a mobile face. But somehow he couldn't just place her face clearly in his mind. Well, he would be seeing her soon.

He opened his eyes. Come to think of it, he hadn't had one fight in Washington. Yesterday, some cluck in an automobile had almost run him down. He'd shaken his fist after the sonofabitch, and challenged him to come back, but the car had gone on.

Again, farewell, Washington, D. C. Farewell, Hilda.

He looked out at green countryside as the train raced and clattered along.

SECTION FOUR

Chapter Twenty-eight

I

Ed swung along Sixty-seventh Street at a good pace. His straw hat was slanted at a becoming angle. He whistled gaily. It was satisfying to return to Chicago. The weather was pleasanter than it had been in Washington. After his trip Chicago seemed fresh and new, exhilarating.

A block away, he saw Frank and Ellen coming toward him.

He had timed things perfectly. He continued on at the same chipper pace. Ellen saw him. She waved her arms. He did not respond. He saw that she was getting more excited, and she was calling to him. He could hear his name now, and then a passing streetcar drowned out her voice for a moment. As the noise of the car receded, he again heard her calling to him. He didn't change his pace. She was running toward him, and Frank trotted behind her, a grin on his face. Ellen came to him and flung herself into his arms.

"Ed, Ed, why didn't you telephone me? When did you get back?"

Ed smiled mysteriously.

"Ah, I apprehend you out with my best friend."

Frank grinned.

"Ed?" she said, startled, anxious.

She looked to Frank and saw his grin.

"Now I am beginning to understand," she said.

Ed smiled.

"You've grown more beautiful since I went away," he told her.

"Let me look at you."

"Well, I'm not charging people this week to look at me. But I think I'll begin to demand a fee next week."

"Darling, I can't believe my eyes," Ellen said.

"Ellen didn't know what I had in mind. I insisted that I see her, like you told me, and she was asking me what for when we were walking down the street. That was before we saw you. I kept saying that it was something important, and I'd tell her later," Frank said.

"Frank, you played your part perfectly," Ed said.

"Good old Frank Dolan," Ellen said.

"Yes, Frank, I congratulate you," Ed said.

"Ed, you never do things the way other people do," she said.

"Isn't this more exciting than the regular thing to do, telegram, meet me at the station."

"That would have been so exciting, too."

"I've got to go now, but let's all get together and have a double date soon real soon," Frank said.

"Let's, it'll be lots of fun," Ellen said.

"I'll buzz you tomorrow," Ed said.

Frank walked off.

Ed and Ellen faced each other for a moment, neither of them speaking.

"Oh, Ed, I missed you so. You're really back. You've really come back to me."

"Yes, my Sweet."

"I want to kiss you, right now in the street."

"I haven't said I'd disapprove."

She kissed him.

II

Ellen had her head nestled against Ed's shoulder. His hat lay on the park bench to his left.

"Ellen, I threw everything up for you. I had a good job, but I couldn't stand it, being without you any longer."

"If you only knew how I missed you."

"Honestly?"

"Oh, I never knew that I could miss anyone so much, that I could need a person so much."

She took his hand and kissed it, greedily. She ran her hands up and down his shoulders, held his face in her hands, kissed him passionately.

"Ed, if I had only known, if you had only told me, I could have told Father I was staying with some girl and we could have stayed together," she said.

"I can solve that," he said.

She waited.

"I'll take a room in a hotel. You come up, and we can use it, and then we'll have pancakes and coffee."

She got up from the bench. He got to his feet. They walked toward a park exit.

"But have you got money, Ed?"

"Of course I have. I got my pay and quit."

"Was it a good job?"

"My salary was a hundred a week."

"And you gave it up—for me?"

"I'd give up anything for you, Ellen."

III

"It takes time to get readjusted after one has been away. Everything is new," he said, looking at her across a table in a restaurant on Sixty-third Street.

"It's just like old times to me."

"Everything is fresh. To come back and see my Ellen, it makes me feel as if the world has just begun. It gives me the illusion that this is the first day of the world."

"I feel that it is the first day of the world, and at the same time I feel that I've known you, oh, forever."

Ed forked a large slice of pancake and ate it.

"I have new plans. I'm going to locate here. I might even go back working with John Devormer. And I'm seriously going to work on my book. I've done lots of thinking about it. But in Washington I couldn't write. Things were too unsettled for me. I missed you. I was living in a suitcase. You can't do concentrated work that way, and my book involves such extremely concentrated work."

"Oh, Ed, we're going to do everything. You're going to do everything. Let's not talk about plans right now."

"You're not interested?"

"I am interested, dearest. I am, but I'm so happy to see you that I just want to be with you."

"Ellen, aren't my plans really interesting to you? I have given up a job, a good one, after weeks of utter depression, and I come back and you aren't interested in my plans."

"Ed, I didn't mean that."

"But still, you step on me when I begin to outline my plans."

"Please don't misunderstand me. I didn't mean that. I meant, you're back, we can do everything we want to now, and this is your first night, our first meeting, and oh, just let's be like children."

"Like children." He sighed. "Long ago, I grew up. I can't be a child again. I've seen too much of life, experienced too many disillusionments. No, that is over."

"Ed, I know. I've felt the same way many times. But you make me feel like a child. Just as you said, you said you felt as if it was the first day of the world."

"It is, and it isn't."

Ellen sipped her coffee.

"Ellen?" he asked, suddenly serious again.

"What?"

"Ellen, I know you'll answer me honestly. We have always been frank and honest in our relationship, and we always will be. So I know you'll be frank with me now. Ellen, were you faithful to me when I was gone?"

"Why, of course I was. Why, I couldn't be anything else. I couldn't look at anyone else."

"I believe you. But it was necessary to ask you."

"Don't you trust me?"

"I do."

He lit a cigarette.

"It's really so exhilarating to return. You don't know how miserable I was in Washington."

"You poor thing. You know, when you wrote me that letter about money, I almost cried. I took every cent I had in the bank, and added my weekly allowance to it and sent it, and I cried. I cried because you were suffering, and because I didn't have more to send you."

"It saved my life. I was in the dumps. I was on the verge of losing faith in myself. I was disgusted, fed up. But I hung on. And then—but I am a fool. I threw up all I'd been building for, just when I had landed something. That's the way my whole life has been. But this time I'm starting right in. I learned a lot in Washington. It has been beneficial for me, miserable though it was. But I couldn't stand it any more. Had you been with me, I might have fought on. But you weren't, you were miles away. Finally, I chucked it in order to come back to you."

"My darling!"

"That's past. But I tell you, it is a disheartening experience to walk the streets of a strange town, alone, broke, feeling out of everything."

"I know. I know, Ed. It must have been. But now it's all over and we have each other. We have—so much."

"Ah, Sweet, you're such compensation. Compensation for all the damned muck of life."

"Ed, I want to be—for you."

Ed lit another cigarette.

"Ah, Washington."

"How did it happen the girls didn't try to steal my Ed from me?"

"I had serious problems on my mind. I couldn't be bothered with flirtations. But Washington is past. Bury it. Sweet, we have the future."

"I can't really believe it, dearest. You're back. You're really back."

"Yes, I'm back."

"Aren't you glad?"

"Glad is a mild word with which to describe my reaction."

"Let's walk. It's so wonderful tonight. Let's walk," she said.

Chapter Twenty-nine

I

"You say Ed is back?" Mr. Rogers said after dinner.

"Yes, he came back."

"Funny, isn't it, that he didn't let you know?"

"He did it that way to surprise me."

"What's the matter, couldn't make a go of it in Washington?"

"Father, Ed is going to make you swallow all the things you think about him. Some day you'll have to swallow every one of them."

"Now what did I say? I only asked you a question about him, how he made out in Washington."

"He was earning a hundred dollars a week in the Department of Agriculture, but he gave it up to come back here, for me."

"Oh, so you plan to settle here in Chicago when you marry him?"

"Yes, we do."

"That's sensible. No use in running off to a strange place when all your friends and your life are here."

"What's Ed going to do now?"

"He's thinking of getting a job with Mr. Devormer. He used to work for him."

"Seems to me he's flighty. Every time I see him, every time you see him, seems to me he has new plans. He can't keep himself down to one thing and stick at it. That's not a good sign."

"I wouldn't stick at anything either, not if I wasn't satisfied with it."

"You don't have to. You're a girl."

"Well, I don't think a man should either."

"How is he going to support you then?"

"I don't want to argue with you. You don't have to worry about Ed."

"Ellen, I can't understand why young folks act so short with the experience of those who know a few things. Young folks think that we older people are old fogies. Well, we know a thing or two."

"What has that got to do with it?"

"With what?"

"With Ed and me?"

Mr. Rogers looked at her, stumped.

"Experience hasn't anything to do with it? Where do you get your ideas?"

"I know why you asked me that question. You're going to say Ed is giving me false ideas, that's the next step."

"I'm only saying that young people might listen to reason. If they did they'd be better off."

Ellen looked bored.

"Oh, Father, I love you. You're even right in what you say, only it doesn't mean Ed and me. It doesn't mean Ed. Some day you'll be proud of Ed."

"Well, since he's going to be my son-in-law," Mr. Rogers spoke gloomily, "I hope so."

"You will," Ellen said.

II

"What's new?" Ed asked Ellen after kissing her and sitting down beside her on the sofa.

"Oh, nothing much. I didn't do much of anything today. The day just passed."

"I have news. I've landed a job. With my old boss, John Devormer."

"Oh, grand. I wish Father hadn't gone out, so I could tell him." Her face changed; she became apprehensive. "But will you have to travel? You told me you traveled for him before."

"At first he wanted me to. Do you know why I refused to go back on the road for him?"

"It might not be adventurous?"

"Guess again."

"You don't want to leave your mother and father?"

"Guess again."

"You like Chicago?"

"You're getting hot. Again."

"You like the sunsets in Chicago?"

"A certain kind of sun, yes. Guess again."

"The sun is. . . ." She laughed and kissed him.

"You," he said.

"You're so darling, Ed."

"Not precisely darling. I should say I was anything but darling."

"You are darling."

"Those are fighting words."

Ed jumped to his feet, balanced himself on his toes, in fighting posture.

"Come on, fight."

"I'm afraid to."

"Get up."

She obeyed him, coquettishly. They sparred, and she tapped at him girlishly. He tipped her nose with his left.

"Come on," he said, smiling.

She tapped him again, and he fell.

"Count me out. Count to ten."

She counted.

"Now I'm your slave," he said.

"An unruly and unmanageable slave, I'd say."

"No, a very meek slave."

He got up, smiling, and took her in his arms and hugged her. They sat down on the sofa again.

"Sweet, I'm selling here in the city. It's a cinch job. I get fifty dollars a week, an expense account, and commissions. I can make good money. And it isn't hard work. You know, a salesman doesn't have to work hard. He laughed gaily. "Do you think I'd take a job if it was hard work? I'll never get a strong back from hard work. Not I."

"You're too smart to have to work hard."

"At all events, I won't have to. There are only certain hours in which you can really sell. In the morning after, say, about ten-thirty until lunch time is the best. Perhaps an hour in the afternoon. I usually feel that if you pile into an office too early, the prospect is reading his mail and resents your intrusion. After three in the afternoon, it is the fag end of the day. The prospect probably feels you are harried and anxious to sell because you haven't had any success, and so you give him a feeling of failure about yourself. So why try then? Tomorrow is always another day. And I'll sell enough so that I won't have to worry about afternoons. I'll have all the time to myself that we'll need."

"Oh, that's glorious."

Ellen had an impulse to speak about marriage, but she decided not to for the present. Ed could not be pushed, and he didn't like to feel that he was being led into anything.

"I suppose this will make your old man happy."

"He thinks you're flighty and won't stick at anything."

"I'm too smart for that. Why stick to something all my life and end up a dumb cluck in an office? And, anyway, it's a hell of a lot of crust on his part. And if he sticks his nose into my business, he'll know how I feel about him."

"Please don't fight with him. It's not necessary. Nothing he says can sway me or change my mind or have any influence on me whatsoever."

"It'd better not."

"It won't."

"Well, I won't be Freudian in my analysis of him."

"What's that?"

"Psychoanalysis."

"I've heard of that, but I don't know anything about it."

"According to Freud, the basis of all action is sex."

Ellen was unconvinced.

"You don't believe that?" he asked.

"I don't know. It has a great deal to do with many things."

"It has to do with everything. The motives of all human action are the will-to-power and sex. One of the most common situations is that of repressed and sublimated love between mother and son, father and daughter."

"You mean?"

"Yes and no. I don't mean that your father wants to go to bed with you. I mean that his libido is fastened upon you, and that is why he is jealous of me."

"What's libido?"

"Love—the sex urge."

"Ed, I don't really believe that."

"What don't you believe?"

"That Father wants . . ."

"I said sublimated. That means the sex urge takes another expression. Repress sex, and it will come out indirectly in many devious and different ways."

"When we get married, and if we have children, does that mean the same thing will happen?"

"Well, let's not worry about that. I am talking about the springs of action in all human beings, including your father."

"Of course, I think what you say is true. In fact, I always sensed that he was jealous of me, afraid I would leave him. I thought it was because he would be lonesome, all alone."

"He will be lonesome. That's true. But why talk profundities now? I love you. I have a swell job."

"It's wonderful. I knew you'd land something like this. I did. I knew it all along. I know you'll be wonderful. Why, Ed, you'll sell everything in sight. Only now be fair. Don't sell Lake Michigan to somebody as a real-estate development."

"Ellen, it's all right to make jokes like that, but after all, don't be flip. I'm not a crook, you know."

"Darling, please forgive me. I'm sorry. Please!"

He smiled at her with condescension.

"I'm a young businessman," he said, grinning. "And I touched John Devormer for a twenty-five dollar advance. Let's go places tonight."

"Yes, let's celebrate."

Chapter Thirty

I

It was a warm, sunny day. The Jackson Park beach was crowded.

"This is the life," Ed said; he lay beside Ellen, his face on the sand.

"Just think, I was afraid we wouldn't be able to do all the things I wanted to do this summer. I was afraid you would not be back from Washington in time."

"And here I am."

"And here I am."

"This is Thursday. I'm finished for the week. I'll work again on Monday morning. I made fifty dollars already in commissions this week. Hell, that's enough."

Ellen thought that since Ed was making good money, he ought to save some. But it was very ticklish to give him advice. He shouldn't throw away all his money. They would need it. He didn't talk much about marriage any more. But now, with his new job, they ought to be able to get married soon. With him doing so well, she could wangle help from her Father. They ought, at least, to get a very nice apartment from him, free.

She looked off, smiling. Just think, a year ago she would have laughed if anyone had predicted that she would be entertaining thoughts like these.

"Ed?"

"This is the life."

"Ed, what are you going to do with the money you make this week?"

"Oh, there are uses to which it will be put."

"I know that. What uses?"

"I don't know. I lost a lot last week on the ponies. I think I'll recoup this week."

"Ed, I'm not trying to be bossy, but don't you think you ought to save a little?"

"I presume that I should—for a rainy day. However, I like the rain. It wrinkles up the clothing of all the smug little people, robbing them of their dignity when it takes the press and shape out of their clothing. It makes them wear rubbers, lest they catch cold. Yes, the rain—it's one of my elements."

"But, darling, I was speaking seriously—for us."

"Some day, Sweet, won't it be too Humoresque? I'll be Mr. and you'll be Mrs. I'll bring my pay check home, and you'll cash it and give me an allowance."

"Now you're being sarcastic."

"Oh, not at all. Sweet, this is the life. Why bother ourselves with such paltry considerations? I'll make as much or more commissions next week. Hell, I can sell like wildfire."

"How do you do it?"

"A line. I talk."

"I never heard anybody who could talk as convincingly as my Ed."

"Look at all the girls out here. They're so pert, so lovely. But they fade into insignificance beside you."

"Oh, that's an exaggeration."

"I'm moving, taking a place of my own on the South Side. I'm tired of this goddamned business of clutching at love in the park, in cabs, in hallways. I'm taking a nice apartment. My mother and father are disappointed, but that's too bad. I'm moving Saturday."

"I'll help you find a place."

"I found it—in the Kendale Apartments at Sixty-second and Kenwood. A new place, thirty bucks a week with maid service. I'll even cook some meals for you."

"Teach me to cook."

"No. You might soil your hands. You're a flower. You don't want to bother about cooking."

"I do wish I could cook you a meal."

"I'm not in love with a cook."

"What are you in love with?"

"You. Ellen. To say that is more than to talk in similes and metaphors."

"You say darling things."

"I'm getting a new suit, too. And a new hat."

"You bought a straw hat two weeks ago."

"I know. And I broke it. I met a chap I know. He dared me to stick my hand through it. So I did."

"Why did you do that?"

"Gesture."

"I want you, Ed, always to be like you are."

"Well, I'll try to fulfill your expectations."

But did she? It was nice to tell him that. A little white lie when she loved him so. She glanced sidewise at him. He had such a splendid body.

He sank his head in her lap. She stroked his hair, utterly contented. The sun burned on her tanned legs and shoulders; her mind wandered off, drifted away in dreams and hopes of the future.

She had used to be so nervous, once. What Ed said about Freud, it was true. What had been the real reason was sex, love; not that she hadn't had experience, but it had not been satisfactory. When she had been a little girl, love had been something so romantic. Real love was so much different. It was so much more wonderful.

She stroked Ed's curly hair. He lay inert, sleeping in the sun. He looked up at her.

"Come on, I'll teach you something more about swimming," he said.

II

"Hello, Ellen," Ed said as if there were nothing out of the ordinary.

He wore a cream-colored suit with wide trousers, a white shirt, a low white stiff collar, an orange tie, and a new straw hat with a red, white and blue band.

"I got all dolled up."

"My goodness. You sure have."

He strolled into the parlor.

"I got them at the Hub. I bought them on the installment plan—two suits. I could have paid spot cash with my salary this week, but why be a sucker?"

"Darling, why did you pick such a tie?"

"So that everybody could see it."

Ellen didn't answer. He was wonderful. But he looked like a Polack.

"Hello, Mr. Rogers," Ed said as Ellen's father came into the room.

"Hello, Ed. How's business?"

"Fine. I'm building up a lot of accounts, and I'm getting along famously. I'm going to stick to this work now. It's my line."

"As long as you stick and get along, that's the thing to do. Congratulations. . . . I see you're all dressed up."

"Oh, sort of."

"Sort of?" Ellen said with a smile.

"This is better than working for the government," Ed said.

"You're right, there," Mr. Rogers said. "There's not much future in being a bureaucrat for the government. There's too much government, even though we have a good man in the White House. The less government we have, I mean, of course, in the line of business, the better. We have to have police, and clerks to register things, but I mean in the line of business. But then, the man in the White House, Mr. Coolidge, he sees to that. But for a young fellow the real future lies in business, not in working for the government."

"I didn't actually like Washington. Chicago's a much livelier town."

"I went there once to a convention. Pretty town to look at. But dead, I guess, except for conventions that go there. Some of the fellows, of course, livened the town up. But not me, I'm not much for that sort of thing."

"Yes, there was an Odd Fellows convention when I was there."

"Ellen tells me you were working in the Department of Agriculture for a spell."

"Yes I was, Mr. Rogers."

"What were you doing?"

"It's amusing. There was not much to do."

"That's the way those fellows are. Wasting the taxpayer's money. But you surely had something to do?"

"I had to handle all sorts of reports—reports on fertilizers, pigs, cattle, you know, all sorts of reports that go out to the farmer." Speaking of Washington reminded him of Hilda.

Poor Hilda. In her letters she now threatened to come to Chicago after him. There were millions of people in Chicago, and the only address she had was General Delivery. Poor Hilda. Perhaps she would be well off if she married White.

"Prospects are looking up for you, huh, Ed?"

"Yes. And they'll be better in the fall."

"Yes, it was a wise move, leaving Washington and coming back here and really getting your teeth into something."

"I think it was. Of course, Mr. Rogers, there is no teacher like experience."

"You said something there."

"Whatever I have learned, I've learned that way," Ed said.

Ed took out a cigarette.

"May I smoke, Ellen?" Ed asked.

"Of course."

Mr. Rogers observed Ed's politeness.

Ed lit his cigarette.

Mr. Rogers rose.

"I have to go now. See you again."

Ellen got up and kissed him good-bye. He shook hands with Ed and left the room.

"What'll we do?" Ellen asked.

"I don't care. Want to go some place? How about a movie? Or dancing?"

"I want to go to your apartment—for asterisks."

"All right," Ed said, not enthusiastically.

"Ed, don't you want to?"

"Of course I do," he answered with forced gaiety.

"Oh, let's," she said.

III

Wearing his trousers but not his shirt, Ed sat with Ellen in his apartment. She was dressed. It was a one-room apartment with kitchenette, furnished with cheap, showy pieces. In one corner there was a bulgy sofa covered with bright red leather. In another corner there was a desk, and on it were four empty gin bottles. Neither of them had spoken for a period.

"Excuse me for a moment," Ed said, rising and going to the bathroom.

Alone in the room, Ellen idly wandered about. She glanced for a moment at a water color of a river which hung framed over the low studio bed. Interested in nothing in particular, she turned from the picture and crossed over to the desk. She looked at the gin bottles, mildly amused. Her eyes roved about and idly returned to the desk. The first page of a letter lay before her.

Oh, my darling Ed

You are gone so long and you have not written. Why don't I hear from you? Is something wrong? Are you tired of me? What is the matter? I must know, need to know. I cannot go on like this. I cannot stand your silence. If you don't—

"What are you doing?"

Ellen turned around. He strode angrily across the room, snatched the letter from the desk, and stuck it in his pocket.

"Ed, how could you?"

"What?"

"How could you lie to me?"

"Can I help it if a crazy woman thinks she's in love with me? Can I help it if she has delusions of grandeur? She worked in the Department of Argiculture. I never mentioned her to you because what's the use? She writes me these crazy letters and I tear them up."

"Yes?"

"Don't you believe me?"

Ellen said nothing. She was spiritless. She was unable to realize the full import of the words she had just read in the handwriting of this strange girl. She was hurt. Her emotion changed from one of shock and surprise to sadness. Slowly, it occurred to her that he had probably said the same tender things to this girl that he had said to her; he had probably made love to this girl as he had to her. She wanted to cry. Pale, looking almost like a wounded animal, she faced Ed.

"Ellen, this is no way to act."

She did not answer.

"Ellen, are you listening?"

"Yes, I'm listening," she said lifelessly.

"Do you believe me?"

"Please, I'll scream if you talk to me that way."

Ed began to pace back and forth histrionically. He dropped onto the studio bed and sulked. Ellen sat by the table, gazing at the wall. Bewildered, she still struggled to grasp what this meant. She was crushed. All love, all sentiment had been drained out of her. She felt as if she had died inside.

"Well?" Ed asked.

Ellen did not answer.

"You don't want any explanations? You don't want to hear my side of the story?"

"Ed, please don't lie to me."

"So I'm a liar," he said, leaping to his feet.

"You fooled me terribly."

"You accuse me falsely," he said melodramatically. "I can't help it, can I, if some crazy girl falls in love with me?"

"How many times have you said to me that we must never lie to each other?"

"That's it, just like a female, recriminations! Recriminations! A female won't let a man call his soul his own."

"Ed, if you had told me, if you had only told me, I would have forgiven anything."

"Forgiven? So you are a Christian. Forgiveness! I suppose next it will be faith, hope, and charity. Forgiveness! Bless me, Ellen, for I have sinned. I confess my sin. Please give me absolution."

She looked at him, her expression pleading for him to stop.

He turned his back on her and stood posing for a moment, his head lowered. He began to move about the room restlessly, dragging his feet. He stopped by the desk and drummed his fingers upon it. He swung back and fixed his eyes on Ellen. Her head was lowered. She was fighting with herself not to cry.

"Perhaps I was mistaken in you," he said in tones of infinite regret. "I was deluded. Illusions! Delusions!" He moved slowly across the room. "I thought that you were superior, a soaring person, above the conventions of the multitude, beyond good and evil."

He turned an agonized expression on her.

"Ed," she said, speaking slowly, forming her words carefully, as if she were having difficulty in choosing them. "Ed, can't you understand how I feel? Can't you realize what a shock this is to me?"

"How do you think I feel?"

"I don't know how you feel. I know that I have received a terrible shock."

"Ellen, are we boy and girl—or are we adults?"

"Ed, what has that question got to do with it?"

He lit a cigarette.

"Please answer my question. I ask you to."

"What question?" she asked.

"Are we a boy and a girl, or a man and a woman?"

"I don't know. Which do you think we are?"

"I thought we were the latter. Now I'm not so sure. If I am talking to a girl, I'll have to talk one way. To a woman, another."

Ellen stood up.

"Don't you want to sit down and thrash this out?"

"I'm going home."

"Wait a minute. Let me take you home."

"No, please, Ed."

"Ellen," he said, his voice insistent.

Ignoring him, she put on her hat. She walked slowly to the door, like one in a trance.

"Ellen!" Ed commanded.

She left, closing the door gently. Ed stood in the center of the room, looking at the door she had just closed.

IV

She had tossed and cried, unable to sleep all night. And on top of it, what a terrible day she had spent, unable to interest herself in anything, moping, mooning about the house, waiting for Ed to telephone. And he hadn't called.

Now the day was over. She sat on her bed waiting for supper.

She was not certain that her conduct with Ed yesterday had been the wisest. But this was something that was beyond being wise or unwise, good or bad, right or wrong. Last night, when she had left his apartment, she had not acted as the result of thought and premeditation. She had acted automatically, getting up and leaving. When she had gotten downstairs, she had suddenly realized that she was no longer in his apartment. She had had an impulse to go back to him. But she hadn't been able to make herself do that. She had walked home slowly, wanting to feel nothing. It had only been after she had gotten home that she had felt the full force of what she had learned. Home, alone in her bed, she had given way to grief. She had never been so unhappy in her life as she had been last night, alone in her bed.

And she knew one thing, one thing above all else—she loved Ed.

She was called to supper and went into the dining room to join her father, reluctant, having no appetite. She didn't want to talk. She didn't want him to know. She had to act, pretend.

"Well, here's my girl."

"Hello, Father."

"How are you tonight, Ellen?"

"I'm all right."

"Say, I've been thinking. Now, I don't say yes and I don't say no about this. I say just maybe. What I mean is, maybe I might have been wrong on Ed. Not really wrong. Because all I said, after all, was I wanted to see. Well, if he sticks to what he has, he ought to go a long way."

"He will, Father."

And would it mean anything to her if he did or if he didn't? Of course it would, because she loved him. But was everything over between them?

"Yes, he made a good impression on me last night."

She must not break down. She must not.

"I'm so glad," she said.

She went on eating.

"Say, Ellen, what's the matter? You don't seem to be acting yourself tonight? Anything happen?"

"No, I just don't feel well. I'm not feeling well."

Her father seemed embarrassed. Ellen guessed why he was embarrassed and she was glad that she had said this. It would be an excuse.

They said scarcely anything else to each other during their meal.

v

Alone in her room, Ellen sat in a rocking chair, lifeless and dull.

"Ellen, a young man to see you," her father called.

She got up and went to the front of the apartment.

"Hello, Ellen," Frank Dolan said as she entered the parlor.

"Oh, how are you, Frank?"

"Oh, all right. Ellen, Ed sent me to ask you to come out and meet him. He said that he wants to see you. You must come."

Ellen felt that Ed must love her, after all. She suddenly changed. Now, since he had sent for her, she must be sure to handle him right. She couldn't give in to him too easily.

"I'm so sorry, Frank. Tell him that I can't come tonight, but ask him to call me up tomorrow."

"But he said he wanted you to come without fail."

"I know. But you tell him I'm sorry."

"Well!" Frank exclaimed, shrugging his shoulders and rising.

Ellen saw him to the door. She went to her room, closed the door, flung herself on the bed, and cried.

VI

Three days had passed. No further word from Ed. Oh, what a fool she had been. She should have accepted Ed on any terms. She was such a fool. Why did human beings have to do such terrible things to one another?

Ellen paced back and forth about her room, smoking a cigarette, nervous. Her old restlessness had come back.

Better to have loved and lost than never to have loved at all. Was it? How many times during the last three days had she not told herself that it was all over, and that she and Ed were finished? What a cold, terrible fact to face! It was the same, almost, as if she were to have to tell herself that Ed was dead.

She flung her cigarette out of the window. She lit another.

How could anyone else interest her now?

The doorbell rang.

Ellen answered it herself.

"Oh, hello, Frank," she said, suddenly gay.

He had come from Ed.

She had won.

"Can I come in, Ellen?"

"Of course."

She led him to the parlor.

"Ellen, I just came from Ed. He gave me this to give you. You got to go see him right away. He's feeling lousy."

Ellen tore open the sealed envelope and read eagerly.

Dear Ellen
I am not responsible for what I do. I forgive you. E.

Horror and agony swept through Ellen, distorting her face, so that when she turned toward Frank, he was shocked.

"Where is he?"

"At his apartment. Ellen, I don't know what's the matter, but he looks in a heck of a shape. You better go and see him."

"Telephone for a taxicab," Ellen said.

"I have my car downstairs."

Ellen rushed to her bedroom, saying as she moved:

"I'll be right downstairs. Go down and get the engine going and I'll be right after you."

Chapter Thirty-one

I

"Come in," Ed said in a husky, spiritless voice after Frank had rapped on the door of his apartment.

Ellen was suddenly relieved. He was still alive. Absurd fears had raced through her mind all the way down, and she had urged Frank repeatedly to make more speed.

Frank pushed the door open. They entered.

Ed sat at a table, unshaven. His hair was unkempt and unruly. He wore a dirty shirt, with the collar open at the neck. When they entered, he looked at Frank, then at Ellen, dully.

"Ed?" Ellen said.

He did not answer. She paused in the center of the room, staring at him. He gazed past her at the wall.

"Sit down. Let's talk," he said.

"Ed, perhaps I better leave you and Ellen alone," Frank said.

"No, stay," Ed ordered.

Frank and Ellen sat down.

"I want to talk. I want to talk with Frank. And I want to talk with you, Ellen."

Ellen sat anxiously on the edge of her chair.

"Frank, do you think life is worth living?"

"Ed, what's the matter? I never heard you talk that way."

"Frank, you're my friend. I wish that you would answer my question."

"But, Ed . . ."

"Frank, as my friend, will you answer my question—do you think life is worth living?"

"Sure I do. Don't you?"

"We'll come to that in a moment."

"Ellen, do you think that life is worth living?"

"Ed, please tell me, please tell us, what's the matter?" she replied.

"I will in a moment. Everything will unfold. But let us deal with first things first. Do you think that life is worth living?"

"Yes, I do."

"Well, I don't."

"Ed, what's gotten into you? I never heard you talk that way before. A fellow like you talking this way when you have everything in the world before you, and when you can get whatever you want by reaching out and taking it," Frank said.

"Listen," Ed said; he recited mournfully:

Even the weariest river winds somewhere safe to sea.

Ed laughed affectedly.

"Ed, what's the matter?" Ellen asked.

"A straight line, a goal, and then go to it. The shortest distance between two points is a straight line. The shortest distance between living and not living, between entity and non-entity, what is it? A little pill. A little leap headfirst out the window. A slash of the razor. Did you ever think of that, Ellen?"

She was puzzled and frightened. Without her will functioning, she seemed to tell herself that Ed wouldn't do it. But he might. Had she brought him to this state? What should she do?

"Did you ever think of that, Ellen?"

"Yes, often."

"Perhaps you want to commit suicide with me."

"Ed, what are you saying?" Frank asked.

"Do you?" Ed asked, looking at her in an effort to pierce and impress her with his gaze.

"If you mean am I afraid to—no. If you mean do I want to—the answer is I do not. Ed, why don't you listen to reason?"

"Ah, listen to reason. My reason is pretty good. Why should I live? Who can answer that question?"

Ellen wanted to say—you should live for me, Ed. She faced him, with a serious expression, but she said nothing.

"For three days I have not slept. I have not eaten. As you see, I have not even shaved myself. What have I thought about? Ellen. I have thought about Ellen. And what else have I thought about? Life. When I say that life is not worth living, I speak after deep probing into the very bowels of my spirit."

"Ed, please tell me, what is the matter?" she asked.

"Why don't you forget this? Ed, you're not serious. You're spoofing me," Frank interjected.

Ed turned to Frank. He walked slowly toward the bathroom door.

Frank followed. Ellen rose.

"Go back!" Ed commanded, swinging around on Frank.

Ed returned to the room, carrying a razor.

"Now what did you say? I'm afraid to do it? I'm not serious? I'm bluffing?"

He looked from one to the other. They were all tense. Ellen thought that he might do it.

"Please don't, Ed! I love you!" she screamed and ran toward him.

He held her off with his left hand, fixing a stern and disapproving glance on her.

"Sit down, Ellen!" he ordered, raising his voice.

Limp, she turned, obeyed, sinking helplessly and hopelessly into her chair.

"Let us proceed," Ed said, smiling in a forced, strained way, putting the razor on the table beside him. He said, "Have a drink."

They both shook their heads. Ed poured himself a drink, guzzled it, sat down on his chair, leaned forward, elbows resting on knees, chin in hands, and faced Ellen, who stood rigid.

"Do you know what my major problem is?" he asked.

"What?" Ellen asked, timid, tense, almost breathless.

"How to commit suicide."

"Ed, do you know what you're saying? For God's sake, Ed," Frank shouted.

Ellen kept her eyes on Ed, pleadingly, pityingly. She wished, oh, she wished that she could believe in a God, and that she could get down on her knees and pray to Him, pray to Him to stop Ed.

"Is it immoral to commit suicide?"

"Of course it is," Frank said.

"Ed, don't you see what you're doing to me? Please, Ed, please, I beg you, stop it! Stop it! Stop it!" Ellen cried out.

"Ellen, please don't," Frank said helplessly.

Ed started to pace about the room. He turned unexpectedly and held them with a piercing gaze.

II

"Let us consider the question. I want to thrash this out with both of you. Now, what does it mean to say it's wrong to commit suicide?"

"It means you do something hideous to those you leave behind," Ellen answered.

"They can come with me, Ellen."

"Ed, I never knew you had ideas like this," Frank said.

"To be wrong implies there must be some standard given as the basis for judging right and wrong. If there is some standard of right and wrong, that means that there is someone to give us the standard. It can't be man. Man is fallible. It must be God. But God is a figment of man's imagination. Therefore, it isn't wrong. Now, is it wise?"

Ellen clenched her fists. She began to cry.

"Am I going to go out of this beautiful world, Ellen, with my last image of you one in which you are in tears?" Ed asked.

"Ed, please. Oh, let's get out of here. It's a wonderful night." Ellen replied, wiping away her tears.

"A wonderful night. When Hellfire accepted the destiny of oblivion, it was a wonderful night. The moon was shining, all silver. Lovers walked arm-in-arm, trusting one another. Thinking the world was new. Lovers walked arm-in-arm, not yet disillusioned. And Hellfire sputtered out like a dying can-dle and was no more. Yes, it was a balmy summer evening when Hellfire sputtered out of existence—into non-existence."

"Ed, do you really mean this?" Frank asked.

"What did you say?" Ed asked, calmly picking up his razor.

"Ed, I'm all mixed up. Listen, this is a terrible thing to do," Frank said.

Ed sat down.

"Well, let's continue our discussion."

"Ed, I love you. Ed, I forgive everything," Ellen said hys-terically.

"I ask not forgiveness. Forgiveness is a Christian virtue; t is unmanning," Ed announced, taking another drink.

"Ed, for me, please," Ellen begged.

"Ah, but Ellen, you deserted me in my hour of need. I sent Frank for you, humiliating myself, and you did not come."

"Ed, I'm sorry."

Ed lowered his head reflectively.

"How fragile are our emotions, our affections. Suppose I should live? We will grow old together. A day will come when we will have to separate. Yes, the candle will go out. Ah, the ultimate bravery is not to wait for the candle to go out. Squash t in the fullness of life."

Ellen took several steps back and forth.

"Don't be nervous, Ellen. This will soon be over. And time, time healeth everything, all wounds, everything."

"Ed, what must I do? Tell me. Please don't subject me to this. Please don't go on. Forgive me. I'll do anything for you."

"Ed, can't you see—Ellen loves you?" Frank said.

"I prefer to continue with what I have to say. Of course, f you do not want to listen. . . ." He looked directly at Ellen. "Do you prefer to listen to me?"

She shook her head affirmatively. She sat now like one in a trance.

"You, Frank—do you want to hear me go on?"

"Yes, Ed, but listen, man, my God . . ."

"Ellen, you were the last enchantment of my life. But you did not trust me."

"Ed, I love you. Tell me what to do. Tell me how to prove it to you."

Ed put up his hand. He strolled to the window.

"Eight stories. A dive, a few seconds through the air, squash and smash." He turned around. "You know, it ought to be thrilling to dive out the window headfirst. Those last seconds when you crash down toward the sidewalk in obedience to the laws of gravity, those should really be thrilling. What do you think?"

They both rushed to him.

"Step back!" Ed commanded.

They halted in their tracks.

"Slitting my wrist would mean a slower demise. I would gradually get weak, with the blood gushing out of my severed vein. I might do it like a Roman in my bathtub. Or I might get a gat and do it that way."

Ellen held out her hands to him.

Ed strolled about the room, ignoring them, sunk in his own thoughts.

III

Ellen remembered how she had played with boys, how she had frightened Bill Northrup by threatening to jump off her own front porch. Bill must have felt a little the way she did now. God, the worm had certainly turned on her! Would he do it? Was he bluffing? She hadn't been bluffing. Ed was strong, terribly strong. He would do it. He was going to. He was going to do it. Oh, why hadn't she come the other night? What if he had slept with another girl? What did anything matter, if only, only Ed would come to his senses.

"Perhaps I ought to write farewell notes, explaining why I did this. But that would mean that I was trying to justify my act. Why should I justify my act?" Ed soliloquized, still moving about the room.

He faced Ellen.

"Ellen, I loved you. Were it possible for me to think and remember after I am gone, I should remember you as the most beautiful person in my life. But now the time has come. I dare not kiss you good-bye. Better make the break clean and sharp.

. . . Yet each man kills the thing he loves . . .

Ed seemed resolute. He turned and slowly walked toward the window.

Ellen ran to him, screaming and flung her arms around his neck. She clung to him. He turned. She kissed him feverishly.

"Ed, don't, don't, don't . . . don't."

He responded to her kisses.

"You do love me?"

"Oh, Ed, I do! I do!"

"You trust me?"

"Ed, please, yes, yes!"

"You believe me?"

In answer, she kissed him frantically.

"I believe you. For your sake I shall refrain from taking the action which I had just contemplated."

Frank dropped into a chair, relieved. He mopped his brow. Ed walked to him.

"Frank, you have been a friend to me, a friend as no other one, save Ellen, has ever been."

"I'm glad to be a friend to you. Ed, I am your friend."

They shook hands.

Ellen looked at Frank, embarrassed.

"Well, I guess I better run along. I have a date with a fellow at nine o'clock. Trying to sell him a Ford."

Frank left.

Ellen looked at Ed. Now she wondered had he been playing with her? She had to dismiss such thoughts, such questions from her mind. And yet, the question persisted.

Ed took her in his arms.

SECTION FIVE

"Ed, it's been a grand summer, and we won't have many more nights like this." Ellen clung to his arm as they strolled southward along Stony Island Avenue. "I'm sorry to see the summer end—but the fall can be lovely, too."

"Things look good for me this fall. Maybe we can soon make plans. I'll start saving money. I've been foolish, pouring money down the drainage system since I started working for John Devormer. But do I regret it? No. Why have vain regrets?" Ed asked, and he laughed gaily.

"Yes, why?"

"A great deal has happened, hasn't it, Ellen, since we met?"

"Yes."

"At all events, you can't say that I have made it dull for you."

"No, I certainly can't say that, Ed."

"Yes, in our way we've lived fully. We'll go on. But the future is going to be comparatively easy in many respects. After all, the way things are looking up, why, goddamn it, Ellen, I'm bound to become a Babbitt; I'm on my way to Babbittry."

"You never could be a Babbitt, Ed—never."

"Your father thinks so. He acts as if he were beginning to like me."

"Yes, he's changing about you."

"Mother is pleased with me, too. I think she's reconciled to my getting married. Father is proud of me. I, the rebel, seem on my way to Babbittry. I am satisfying my father. I seem to be pleasing your father, eliciting words of laudation from my boss, John Devormer, getting a name for myself as a live wire in the advertising business—say, what the hell is happening to me?"

"Ed, you're still Hellfire, no matter what happens."

"Yes, I suppose so. But it just dawned on me. I'll have to do something."

"Oh, Ed, you're not going to throw over the chance you have, are you?"

"No, Sweet. I'm going to be a wolf in the sheep's clothing of a Babbitt."

She put her arm inside of his.

"Ed, should I go to school?"

"Don't ask me."

"Father says if I get married or not, he doesn't see why I don't get more education, and my aunt in Indianapolis is writing again, prodding him about my going to school."

"Education is something that I can't talk about. You see, I'm not educated."

"Now, now, stop that. You know you are better educated than most college graduates."

"Are you trying to woo me with flattery?"

"Yes."

"Well, try flattering me this way. Say to me, you no-good, impolite, immoral, goddamned bastardly sonofabitch of a tramp. Now, that's flattery. But also, when you do flatter me with all those kind words, sort of say it with a smile."

"Ed, you're in good form tonight."

"Not particularly. As a matter of fact, I feel cantankerous. I had to work four hours today. What the hell is the world coming to, Ellen, when I am forced to work four hours a day? It's disgusting."

"Poor, poor Ed. Yes, it's very sad. You have all my sympathy."

"I need it."

They laughed and strolled on.

II

"Ed, you don't seem yourself. What's the matter?" Ellen asked, sitting down with him in a little restaurant on North Michigan Boulevard.

"I'm fed up."

"Ed, tell me. What's the trouble?"

"Ellen, don't ever be a salesman."

"But, Ed, you've been so successful."

He beamed. Quickly he changed his expression to a frown. The waitress came and they ordered lunch.

"I had to try and sell an old duffer today who belongs in the horse-and-buggy days."

"Oh, Ed, don't let one or two discouragements have such an effect on you. It isn't worth it."

"It's humiliating to me to have to kowtow to damned old fools, to cater to them in order to get their goddamned names on a dotted line."

He was in a nasty mood, and she wondered what she should do to bring him out of it? Sometimes there was nothing to do with Ed except to let him come out of it himself. Sometimes she was afraid of him, particularly because of the night when he'd threatened to commit suicide.

"This fellow's name is Mr. Smithson. The weazened old fool is head of a hardware company. I had to try and convince him that he should let us conduct a direct-by-mail campaign for him. I had all sorts of arguments, appeals, specifications. And the damned fool still lives in the age when there were unpaved streets in the Loop and Chicago was nothing but mud. But why should I bore you with such stuff?"

"I want to hear about your work."

"It's sweet of you to say so, but, no, I shall not bore you. Do you know what a fundamental law of all human intercourse is? It's this: don't be a bore. Well, I won't."

"Ed, you couldn't be a bore. Even if you tried."

"What are you doing this afternoon?" he asked.

"I didn't have any definite plans."

"I'm not going to do any more work. I have some appointments, but I'm not going to keep them. I'll change them to another day."

Ellen wanted to tell him to keep the appointments and that she would wait for him some place. But she didn't. He was in one of his moods when he had better not be crossed. She was ashamed of herself at the same time, but she thought she'd better not cross him. After all, he wasn't the only person in the world who had spirit. But she loved him so much she wouldn't risk losing him. Love did such strange things to a person, wrought such changes in their character. It had in hers. And it was continuing to change her.

"Yes, I'll be damned if I'm going to go and see any more Babbitts today."

Ellen nodded, waiting for him to go on.

"They give me a pain in my rump. With their goddamn talk about quotas and sales and their notion that all human worth is summed up in a goddamned balance sheet."

She wanted to tell him to save his anger, to save it for something that was important.

"I suppose you don't approve of me feeling this way."

"Ed, did I say I disapproved?"

"I didn't say you said so. I wanted to know how you felt."

"Oh, Ed, please, let's drop it. It's over with."

"Drop it? Drop indignities cast upon one? Let one's soul be covered with a mass of indignities and humiliations?"

The waitress came and took their dishes away. They ordered dessert.

"Sometimes even you act as if you sided with the Babbitts against me," Ed said.

"Ed, tell me, what's the matter? I'm not going to fight with you over something for which I am utterly irresponsible. What have I got to do with this old man?"

"Did I say you had?"

"No, but you acted as if I did."

"I certainly did not."

"Oh, let's drop it."

"I see that I must be boring you."

"Oh, come on, Ed, let's forget it and go to a movie. Let's do something."

"A movie. Entertainment for morons and imbeciles."

"Let's just walk."

"And what do we see—people, the human race, idiots, morons, human mud dressed up in fine clothes! They sicken me."

Ed was worse today than he had been that day when they had been in the park last spring and he had disapproved of the wind. She grew nostalgic for that day. It had been a fine day, and they'd had a wonderful time, too.

The waitress brought the dessert and coffee.

Ed dug his fork into his lemon cream pie.

"And I saw John Devormer today. He's so goddamned pompous, I have to restrain myself or I'll bust out laughing when I look at him."

"Hellfire is in form today, isn't he?"

"Ellen, I'm not kidding. I'm serious. I'm fed up with a lot of damned things."

He leaned back in his chair, glowering.

Chapter Thirty-three

I

Ellen was wearing her new plaid dress, and she was waiting for Ed. He was late, and she was alone in the house. She puffed nervously on a cigarette and wished he would come.

Ed had been acting queerly, fretting, getting irritable, inclining more and more to brooding fits and moods these last few days, and she was apprehensive. She wasn't sure how she should handle him. Sometimes he would speak angrily to her, accuse her, treat her as if she were against him and causing him trouble.

She had hoped all day that he would be his old self tonight, and she was dressed up for him. She wanted him to be proud of her, to like her in her new dress. It was so becoming. She did hope so much that tonight wouldn't be like that day last week when she had gone downtown to meet him for lunch. He had been impossible all afternoon, and since then he had not been his usual charming self. What could she do to bring him out of his funk? She wanted him to be resilient, boyish, gay again, and she wanted him to keep his job. It was amazing, how successful he was with it, but now he was losing interest in his work.

Being with Ed was trying when he acted the way he had been acting all week. And you couldn't fool Ed easily the way you could fool so many others. Ed sensed too many things. Sometimes he sensed your moods. And it was worse when he didn't. Then he made wild interpretations.

Maybe if she talked about his book, that would interest him. Perhaps they might go to the library and read during the next

312

few nights. It was a bore sometimes to spend the whole evening in the library, but it was better to be bored doing that than to let Ed go on in his present mood and throw up his job. What she feared was that he was going to get some whim, throw up his job, and perhaps leave town again. She couldn't stand that. And with the memory of his Washington trip, and with the little she had learned of that girl Hilda, she'd go crazy if she were alone again, with him away in some other city.

He was often late. She was used to it. She convinced herself that there was no need for worrying. But somehow she was uneasy. He always showed up. Why should she be uneasy? Ed had never failed to show up.

Last night Ed had one ridiculous flare-up of temper and had been jealous. He had accused her of making eyes at some fellow at the next table when they were out dancing at Fraternity Row. That had been unpleasant, but at the same time it had been a good sign. If he had fits of jealousy, he must love her. You are not jealous about someone if you don't love him.

But she did wish he would come. She refrained from looking at the clock. If she was unaware of minutes, perhaps the time would pass faster. She squashed her cigarette in an ash tray and stretched out on the sofa.

Of course, Ed had acted peculiarly before this. But now he was acting strangely over a period of time. Before when he had had his moods, they would come and go quickly.

Before she knew Ed, she had never imagined that love could cause so much worry, anxiety, agony. That time seemed so long ago now, and it was less than a year. It was strange to look back on the time before she knew him. It was so different. Yes, then she had thought that love was a fraud and a lot of fakery, falderal, tinfoil, confetti, used to mask sleeping together, and that sleeping together, too, was not half of what it was supposed to be. How quickly such notions had vanished after she had met him. Those first days after she and Ed had fallen in love had been something heavenly. But now she saw more into what love was. It was sad, too. When you were in

love you could be so happy, and you could be so unhappy.
Little things that you once did not notice assumed such great
importance and had such influence in making you fantastically
happy, or terribly miserable.

She turned over and lay on her back.

Why didn't Ed come?

She could imagine Ed coming tonight, jaunty, gay, happy,
his ugly mood over with, entirely forgotten.

She should really not feel so uneasy. If he were never late,
then she could worry. But he was so often late. Still, something
might have happened. He might have gotten into a fight and
he might be in a hospital. In the mood Ed had been in all week,
she could scarcely understand how it had happened that he had
not gotten into a fight. He usually came out of his fights un-
injured. But it could happen, couldn't it, that he would be
injured. He had once been thrown off a freight car.

But it hadn't happened. He was just taking his own sweet
time as he always did.

Ellen thought, as she had many times in recent weeks, that
she was not handling Ed right. She should get the upper hand
with him and keep it. She should be the one who was always
late. She should be the one who got angry. She knew, and she
knew profoundly, that she should keep the upper hand over
him. Hadn't she intended to do this many times? Hadn't she
planned to do it? And then, she couldn't. She knew that she
should act differently than she acted, and she just couldn't.
Yes, she was in love with him, and her very love might cause
her to lose him unless she were careful.

He ought to be here now. What was he doing?

Was he with some girl?

He had lied to her, hadn't he, about the time he was in
Washington? Might he not lie a second time? Why, he might
be with some girl now in his apartment, the two of them together, naked. Oh, God!

She jumped to her feet and rushed to the phone.

II

Ellen returned to the parlor as much relieved as she was disappointed. He was not in. That probably meant that he was on his way to see her. It didn't take long to get here from his apartment, either. He would arrive soon, very soon.

If he wasn't in, at least that meant that he wasn't in his apartment with some girl.

She went to the kitchen and looked at the clock. It was a quarter after nine. He was only forty-five minutes late.

Didn't Ed realize that it was terrible to make her suffer this way? Then why did he do it?

Ed was selfish.

She didn't care what he was. She loved him.

Why didn't he come?

Ellen sat down on the sofa and waited.

What would they do tonight?

She had often kept others waiting for her. Had they felt this way? Of course, it had not been love as it was between her and Ed. There was not the same closeness. Still, they must have felt something of what she felt.

The bell? No, it wasn't. She had imagined herself into thinking it was the bell.

He must be hurt. Otherwise, he would have called up. Ed was often so considerate. He often telephoned when he was late. Other times he was late and he didn't. She couldn't tell from his not calling. It might be nothing. He might have met some fellow and stood talking on a corner. If he did, it was selfish. But Ed didn't mean to be selfish.

She paced back and forth across the parlor.

III

Ed had no right to do this to her. Here it was ten-thirty and she had not heard from him.

She was nervous, restless, exhausted. Still, she found it difficult to concentrate on anything, even to sit still for any period of time.

Ed was doing a terrible thing to her. She remembered a line he had quoted to her a number of times.

. . . Yet each man kills the thing he loves.

Did Ed love her, and was he, in a sense, killing her? Was it necessary that this always happen? Did it have to happen with her and Ed?

Why couldn't he telephone her? It wasn't fair. It wasn't decent. You shouldn't treat another person the way Ed was treating her. It was all right if he couldn't come, if only he would let her know so that she wouldn't worry, with all kinds of fears about him coming into her mind, sending her almost half out of her head.

She nervously slapped her hands together and looked at herself in the parlor mirror. She had so carefully fixed herself up this evening. Now her hair was mussed. Her face was anxious. Oh, what the hell!

She swung around on her high heels, away from the mirror.

She was not going to stand for such treatment. If she did, she would be a fool. Only a fool would be willing to take this. What did Ed think he was? Who did Ed think she was—Catherine Anne? If he thought that he could treat her the way he treated girls like Catherine Anne, he was mighty mistaken, and the sooner she taught him that he was mistaken, the better off he would be.

My God, who did he think he was? Always talking about using people, was he? Well, it was just about time that he should be used. Ah, she had made a grave mistake last summer when she had accidentally learned of that girl in Washington. A grave mistake. She had let him off too easy.

Ellen sat down in a chair, limp, worn out.

What should she do?

Was anything worth while? What would she do if Ed gave her the gate? A nice way of putting it, wasn't it? What should she do? She hated to think of this possibility. Yet it forced itself into her consciousness and remained there, challenging her. In a way, this thought was like the thought of death. Losing Ed, that would be worse than death. Just as Ed had said so often, death was a sleep, a sleep forever and forever. Yes, forever and forever. That was not so bad, not half so bad to think of, as it was to think of going on living, day after day, hour after hour, minute after minute, without Ed.

Suppose something had happened to Ed? Perhaps she was unfair. How would she feel if she were to learn that he was injured, in a critical condition?

But no, no, that hadn't happened. It couldn't happen.

She paced the floor again.

Ed led a charmed life. Nothing terrible would ever happen to him. To her, yes, something terrible would happen. She had always felt so. She had always felt, without really expressing it clearly even to herself, that something tragic would happen to her some day. Perhaps this would come about through Ed.

Why did Ed do this to her?

She heard a key in the lock and ran to her bedroom. She didn't want to speak to her father or see him.

In her dark bedroom she undressed and went to bed, but she couldn't sleep. Thoughts, fears, worries, turned and turned like a wheel in her head.

She lay in the dark, and she still hoped that he would at least telephone her.

Chapter Thirty-four

I

Ed signaled to the tall, homely waitress.

"More black coffee for me." He turned to Ellen, and she again noticed the bruise and discoloration on his right cheek. "Will you have some coffee?" he asked her.

"Yes, please—with cream."

His left hand lay on the table. The knuckles were stained with iodine.

"Ed, why did you do it?" she asked.

"Ellen, I'm in no mood to hear recriminations. I tell you, I had to let off steam. It was necessary, psychologically necessary. I was fed up, so goddamned fed up that I had to do something. I did—I got drunk and got into a fight."

"You might have been hurt. Something serious might have happened to you."

"The answer is that it didn't."

The waitress returned with their coffee.

"I feel better for having let off steam. As for the marks and and bruises, well, I was in a fight. I won, and the other fellow is in worse shape than I am. I sprained a knuckle, but his face is adequately decorated this morning."

"You don't seem to think of what you did to me."

"Ellen, must you rake over ashes?"

"It's raking over ashes, is it, when I waited and waited? I felt like a fool."

"Ellen, you understand me. Why do I love you? Because you are capable of understanding so much. The world is full of pretty faces. Yes, the world is full of pretty faces and lovely

318

bodies. I need more than that. That is why I love you. I know you'll understand."

"Yes, Ed," she said, flattered, grateful to him for what he had just said.

When Ed talked to her, he was so convincing. She watched his eyes. He seemed so sincere. She believed him. Immediately, she remembered about that girl in Washington. Yes, he seemed so sincere, but he had appeared equally so when he had lied to her then. She regretted having ever learned of his infidelity. Now she silenced her doubts.

"I really meant to call you, Sweet, but I was drunk."

It could have happened. And perhaps his drunk would have a beneficial effect on her relationship with him. Now he might settle down to work again, and she might not be subjected to his moods and outbursts.

He's lying to you. He's lying to you. The words popped into her mind against her will. She tried to convince herself that it wasn't so.

"What did you do, darling?" she asked.

For the briefest moment there was a strange expression on his face, one which puzzled her.

"You don't believe me?" he asked.

"You know I do."

"Ellen, I was in a strange mood. I wanted to think. I should say commune with myself, if it didn't sound a little melodramatic. I drank. I sang melancholy songs to myself. I wandered around, singing songs. I gave the world a free concert. Do you know what song I sang most often?"

"What?"

"*All Alone*. I kept thinking that I had to call you up, and I would say I need one more drink before I do. Well, I drank too much. Somehow I wandered back to our old neighborhood around Fifty-eighth Street, and I was staggering along South Park Avenue, singing at the top of my voice. Some snotty chap made a crack. I called him, and we went across the street to Washington Park, and without spectators we fought it out. He gave me a fight, but I crowned him. Then I wandered around, all by myself, blue, lonesome, killing the bottle of gin I'd bought. That is all I did."

Yes, when she was with him all doubts were stifled and she believed him.

He gulped down his coffee and motioned for more.

"But, Ed, why didn't you call me up?"

"I meant to. Ellen, I had every intention in the world of calling you up, but I was drunk."

"But you remember now that you didn't call me."

"Oh, for God's sake, I feel rotten. I got drunk, and I'm sorry. But don't act like a monitor."

"I'm not. Only, Ed, I waited and worried all night. It wasn't any fun for me."

"Frequently, life is no fun. Is it fun for me to have to deal with Babbitts all week, working in order to fulfill our plans?"

The waitress brought coffee. Ed put sugar in it and gulped it down.

"Ed, let's go back to the apartment. I'll put you to bed."

"I'd like nothing better, but I can't. I have a business appointment."

"Are you going to be able to keep it, Ed?"

"I have to. Business must go on," he said ironically.

"Are you coming to see me tonight?"

"Of course. I'll call for you, Sweet, at eight-thirty sharp."

"Ed, I'll worry waiting, not knowing if something has happened to you. You should not treat me that way."

"Sometimes I'm just no good. Useless and no damned good."

"Don't say that."

"It's true. But I have to get going. Sweet, I'll see you at eight-thirty."

Ed paid the bill and they left the restaurant. Outside, Ed kissed her and walked off. She watched him. He glanced back, blowing her a kiss.

Ellen strolled slowly toward Stony Island Avenue. She didn't feel like going home. It was around eleven o'clock, and it would be a long time until eight-thirty tonight.

It occurred to her that Ed's conduct this morning had been

peculiar. In retrospect, he had seemed casual and off-hand when he'd said he had to keep a business appointment. He broke business appointments so often, and for unimportant and whimsical reasons. Feeling as he said he had, looking as he did this morning, it didn't seem like Ed to keep a business engagement this morning.

Ellen changed her course and walked westward along Sixty-third Street. She didn't want to be suspicious and jealous. Suspicion like this could be a poison ruining her love for Ed. She felt so miserable. She should believe him. She wanted so much to trust him. She walked slowly on, full of suspicion and jealousy. She had definite reasons, too, for feeling this way. This morning he had not acted like himself. Sitting with him in the restaurant, she had been able to quiet her doubts; she had believed him. And yet, at that very time, these suspicions of hers had been planted in her mind. They had been planted before this morning, in fact. Now they were flowering. She felt so miserable.

Walking on, she observed nothing. She passed stores. Men and women walked past her. Automobiles and trucks shot by. Streetcars passed. Elevated trains rumbled overhead. And these objects, sounds, sights were less substantial to her, less real, than were the questions, recollections, memories, which all grew together in her mind to form one suspicion. Ed was not faithful to her any more because he did not love her. And if she carried out her impulse to go right to his apartment she would confirm this suspicion by obtaining real evidence.

II

Ellen let herself out of the self-starting elevator and walked quietly, slowly, along the corridor. It was dim. The carpet was red, with blue patterns, circles, flowers, and a blue border at either side. She knocked on Ed's door. She waited. There was no answer. She thought she heard a footstep. But there was no answer. She knocked again. No answer. She bent down and tried to look through the cracks of the door. It was impossible. And there was no keyhole. Disappointed, she turned away and went back to the elevator. She hurried out of the apartment hotel. Outside, in the air, she was joyous. Ed had not deceived her. Ed had told her the truth. She had had no need to be suspicious.

She walked slowly back to Sixty-third Street. She should be ashamed of herself. Going to Ed's apartment, knocking at the door, listening as she had done! Eavesdropping. It was disgusting. It was humiliating. She should have had more pride. A girl like her should be too proud to run after any man, even after Ed. And, also, it wasn't even necessary to think of these things. Hadn't she distrusted Ed and tried to check up on him? And hadn't she failed to confirm her suspicion?

She walked more briskly. It was a cold autumn day. A good walk would be a tonic. Then she would go home, sit in a warm tub, and after that, take a nap. She had not slept all night.

She would be fresh and make herself look beautiful for Ed tonight in her new plaid dress.

Chapter Thirty-five

I

Ed had acted on a hunch when he had not answered the knock on his door. He had suspected it was Ellen. When he heard departing footsteps, he was certain it was she.

His apartment was upset, showing the earmarks of a debauch of the previous night. Gin glasses, bottles, cigarette butts, female clothing were scattered about.

He turned toward the girl in his bed. She was blonde, with bobbed hair; she wasn't particularly pretty. Just a Polack, chunky, not bright, common. Her name was Mary. When he'd gone out to meet Ellen this morning, he'd left her here in his bed.

"Well, Papa, was that the mama?" she asked.

"That's irrelevant," he answered.

"Say, you use big words. Boy!"

"Aw, crap on it, Mary. How do you feel?"

"Pretty good, considering what I drank. But, say, it's sure funny, the way we met."

"Are you sorry?"

"Huh?"

Ed sat on the side of the bed.

"I'll bet you don't really know who the fellow you beat up last night really is."

"You said you go with him."

"He's my husband."

"This is a nice kettle of fish," Ed said.

"I'm not sorry none. I'm fed up with him. He ain't a man."

Ed watched her. Why had he ever picked up with her? If he

hadn't been drinking, would he have done so? He had just been
fed up, and so he'd stopped at a speakeasy and had thought he'd
have a shot or two. And so it all had happened. He had gotten
into a fight with Mary's bloke of a husband and he had ended
up in his own apartment with Mary and a bottle of gin, and
he'd never gotten to see Ellen.

But why be repentant? It wasn't worth the price. It was
weakness to feel repentance. He looked at her again. She had a
wart on her nose.

The problem was to get rid of Mary.

"You feel all right?" he asked.

"Uh huh! I don't know how my old man feels. Say, you sure
can fight. I thought my old man, the bastard, was pretty good,
but when you smacked him—say, you can fight, can't you?"

"I'll tell you a little fact about myself."

"What?"

"I'm a prize fighter."

"You are? Well, that don't surprise me none. I kind of
thought you must be something like that. Except sometimes
you use big words for a fighter."

"I broke training last night."

"You sure did."

He saw some gin left in a bottle and he took a drink.

"Want a drink, Mary?"

"Don't care if I do."

He handed her the bottle. She drank it, some of the gin
trickling down her chin.

Not aesthetic. He liked all the little flourishes, sentiments,
additions to love and sex. God, think how many Marys there
were in the world. To them, sentiment, romance, poetry, was
all so much apcray, and in a way it was.

He smiled. This constituted another adventure. He owed it
to the world to write a book about himself some day. An auto-
biography. All these adventures would fit into it nicely.

"What you smiling about, Papa?"

"You."

"Am I funny?"

"Not at all. I'd tell you you were adorable, but you wouldn't like that."

"I might."

"What does your husband do?"

"He works in the steel mills. But, I'm sick of him. What the hell, he don't make enough money. I want something better than the things he gives me. Say, you make good dough, don't you?"

"Yes."

"Let's team up. I like you. I can give you all the loving you want. I'm pretty good in a bed, ain't I?"

"And you're not bashful, are you?"

"Let's team up."

"I have a wife who's looking for me."

"That broad who came looking for you, was she your wife?"

"No, she's a society girl."

"She any good?"

"What do you mean?"

"Come on, you wasn't born yesterday."

"I have to get ready now to go."

"Where?"

"Milwaukee. I have to go into training. I have a fight booked there."

"Take me with you."

"I can't do that. I got to live a clean life now and get in condition."

"I'll be clean. I can wait. For you, I could wait a long time."

"I couldn't keep in condition if you were with me. That's how much I go for you."

"Say, are you telling me the truth?"

"Why shouldn't I tell you the truth?"

"I could go for you in a big way."

He smiled.

"How can I find you when I come back?" Ed asked.

"I don't know. I can't go back to my old man. He'd kick my pants off. I done something like this before on him, and he socked me. But this time, no, I won't go back."

"What are you going to do?"

"I got a girl friend. He knows her, and he'll come there. But I'll tell him to jump into the lake."

Ed took out his wallet and pulled out all the money he had. He handed her twenty dollars.

"Say, listen, I'm not in business, you know."

"I didn't say you were," Ed answered, enjoying his gesture.

"I can get a job, I'm a waitress. But will you come back to me?"

"You can bet on that, Mary."

"You know, even though you use big words sometimes, you're my style. You're not for society girls. They ought to make any guy like you puke."

"Them's my sentiments."

Ed took another drink.

"And now, Mary, you got to go. I have to get fixed up and clear out."

Mary yawned. She got out of bed reluctantly. She was naked. Ed decided that, well, she wasn't a bad episode. She dressed slowly. After she had gone, he piled into bed and fell asleep instantly.

Chapter Thirty-six

I

Meeting Ed at the front door, Ellen felt that it was the old Ed once again. Gay, smiling, he kissed her tenderly. She decided that perhaps getting drunk last night had been good for him. She was glad he'd done it, and she regretted her jealousy and suspicion, the distrust which had even caused her to go spying and knocking on his apartment door. This morning, outside his door, she had for a moment imagined that she had heard sounds in his apartment. Now she was sure she had gotten that impression only because of her own state of mind.

She led him into the parlor by the hand, and they sat side by side on the sofa.

"I made a big sale today," he announced.

"Good. I'm so glad."

"The damned fool prospect asked me about my face. I told him a cock-and-bull story about a fight I was in."

"Ed, you get in so many fights. Aren't you ever afraid?"

"What?"

"Afraid?"

"Why should I be afraid?"

"I don't know. People often are."

"I'm not people."

"I'm sure of that."

"I've never been afraid in my life."

"Honestly, haven't you?"

"What does it feel like to be afraid?" he asked.

"I don't know. Of course, I've been afraid for you."

"I consign fear to other people. It isn't worth the effort to have fear."

"What'll we do tonight?"

"I would like to take you out and have a big spree, but unfortunately I'm broke. I wasn't able to get in to see John Devormer and draw anything. So we'll have to content ourselves with ourselves."

"That isn't hard."

"Ellen, fall has come, and tonight is a wild autumn night. I love it. Let's just walk. We'll stick out our chins and stick our teeth in the face of the wind."

"All right, let's."

II

The night was dark and moonless. A strong wind crashed off Lake Michigan, slashing the trees and shrubbery in Jackson Park.

"Witches are bowling in the sky. Listen to them howl," he said, walking briskly with Ellen on his arm.

Ellen didn't answer. She was happy tonight. He was in rare form. She loved him so much. She didn't care about that Washington girl. It wasn't important, no more important than were the men she had slept with before she'd met Ed. Oh, he was so wonderful.

"Look at the trees—they bend like silent philosophers in the wind," Ed said.

"It's nice."

"The trees stand, year after year, like stoics, and the seasons pass, and the trees stoically munch their own eternal thoughts, calm to death and love and the rude violences of the wind."

"Ed, since I met you, since we became *us*, things like trees, skies, the wind, everything means more than it ever did before."

He laughed in self-deprecation.

"It's so," she insisted.

"I wasn't laughing at you, Sweet. I was laughing with you. But listen to the wind. The old witches in the sky have knocked down more pins."

Ed laughed.

"And now we'll go on and we'll defy the witches. In fact, we'll defy the world."

"We will, Ed, darling."

"We'll go on defying the damned world. Sweet, our walk tonight is symbolic, symbolic of our free and young spirits, hurling a challenge to the entire world."

She clung to his arm. They continued briskly along the dark and shadowed path.

"You think I'm silly?"

"Oh, Ed, no, not at all."

"Well, then you should."

"No I shouldn't."

"It is silly, talking about witches in the sky, defying illusionary witches who play illusory bowling games in the sky, and calling that challenging the world. It is silly. But I shall persist in being silly."

"And I'll love you for it."

"Does that mean that the more silly I become, the more you'll love me?"

"I'm afraid of a trap here," she said.

Ed stopped and tried to light a cigarette. After some difficulty, he succeeded.

"Now I'll sing."

He cleared his throat and sang:

Oh, one grasshopper jumped upon another grasshopper's back.

III

At eleven o'clock, Ellen idled over the breakfast table, a glow of contentment on her face. She was happy, satisfied with the world. The pleasures of last night seemed to have persisted in her sleep, to be continuing now after her breakfast. Last night, when she was with Ed, walking in the park with him, kissing him, loving him, listening to him, she had been too happy to think about it. Now she thought about her happiness.

She had never loved him more than last night. His hands touching her, his lips, his voice—she adored him. She loved

his body and she loved his soul. Even taking a walk in the park
with him was an adventure. To be in love with him, something
was always happening. The littlest things of life weren't just
trivial. They were thrilling, exciting.

The realization that she and Ed had to grow old came upon
her poignantly. Some day they both would have to die. One of
them would perhaps go first. How terrible it would be to live
longer than Ed. But why should she be having such gloomy
thoughts? Weren't they both so young? When you were young
and in love, life seemed so long and you seemed to have such a
future ahead of you. But no matter how long the future was,
it had to end, and some day Ed would die. So would she. She
would rather die first than have to live after Ed.

The ringing telephone interrupted her thoughts and she
rushed to it.

IV

Ellen put down the receiver, disappointed. Ed wouldn't be
able to see her this afternoon because of business appointments.
She consoled herself with the thought that he was serious and
settling down, and since this was the case, she had to sacrifice
seeing him during the time he must work.

She wandered into the parlor. His voice had sounded so wonderful over the telephone—such a full, deep, resonant voice.
Yes, his voice was like an organ, and so many strains could be
played on it. He could talk so gently, so low, so softly, or he
could speak in such angry tones, so sharply, so powerfully. But
she didn't love him merely because of his voice, or because of
any one characteristic or quality. She loved him for everything
about him.

Over the phone just now, she had wanted to talk with him,
just talk. No one she knew could talk just the way he could, and
be interesting about anything or about nothing. But he had
said he was terribly rushed. He was working for her.

Ellen went to her room, took a picture of Ed from the dresser,
and sat studying it.

V

The day had just passed, as if in a dream. She thought of the day as like a white cloud that floated across the sky, moving very slowly, constantly in your eye as it moved, until suddenly it was gone. The day had gone by like a cloud. She had done nothing much. She had talked with Mary about the food for supper. She had taken a bath. She had read some poems of Swinburne that Ed had stolen for her from the Public Library. Ed could have bought her the book, but he had said it was more of a gesture to steal it. The poems did not interest her very much when she read them alone. When Ed read them, he did so with rhythm and expression. He added so much to the poems. Then they became so beautiful. And she had pottered around, washed her hair, played a few victrola records. And so the day had passed, and every minute she had looked forward to the moment when she would see him. Ed had just called up again, to tell her that he must call off seeing her tonight because of business. He had said that he had to have supper with John Devormer and spend the evening with him on business matters. She was glad to make such a little sacrifice again. But she was so used to seeing him every day that missing him for one day was a real wrench in her habits.

The fall day began to darken. As the sun went down it looked cold outside in Jackson Park. Not a figure was to be seen on the golf course. She could hear the wind in the trees. Oh, as long as she lived, she'd love the wind. She would always remember it as last night's wind. Ellen stood at the window for a long time, listening to the soughing wind, looking at the bare trees.

She turned from the window and moved about the house, nervous, restless. Now she must wait until tomorrow. Time had become so slow.

Chapter Thirty-seven

I

"Ed, what's the matter?" Ellen asked.

"Nothing. Why do you ask?"

"Oh, I don't know. You don't act like yourself."

"Myself? I—myself—isn't something fixed."

"Well, you aren't as talkative as you used to be. You don't say much."

Ed stared past Ellen at the green wall of the restaurant. She watched him, fearful but anxious to mask her feelings. Ed was moody. His lips were clamped together, curled slightly in an unpleasant expression. This was a new Ed, not the same Ed who disapproved of the wind and railed at the cosmos. This kind of moodiness in him was different.

"Myself. What a changing thing myself is."

"Darling, what do you mean? You are the same Ed to me. You always will be."

"None of us is always the same. We all change."

"You mean that you are changing?"

"Every seven years the cells in our bodies change completely. All life changes, and then, finally, there is so much change that it comes back to the same thing. Remember my argument with that one-cylinder philosopher, that fool from the University who tried to refute eternal recurrence with such puerile arguments?"

"Could I ever forget that day?"

"Myself? Not myself? What is myself?"

She didn't speak lest she reveal to him how concerned she was, and for fear her words would cause misunderstanding.

He sneered.

"Ed, give me a cigarette," she said, merely to be talking and to have something to do.

He lackadaisically handed her a package of Lucky Strikes. She took a cigarette. He made no effort to light it for her. While she lit her own cigarette, he again allowed his eyes to drift to the green wall. Ellen glanced outside. Such a sunny day. She waited for him to speak. He remained silent.

Ed laughed, sardonically.

"Myself. Know thyself? If you do, what do you know?"

She grinned at him.

"Ellen, what would you say if I told you that I am a no-good louse?"

"I wouldn't believe you."

"Well, that's what I am—a no-good louse."

"Oh, Ed, tell me what's the matter? Tell me, please."

"Ellen, what do you see in a person like me? Why should you love me?"

"Ed, such a question! Why do you ask it? Tell me, Ed, has business been going badly with you?"

"Business? The market place? I can triumph in the market place as I wish. Business? If businessmen were as smart as they think they are, I'd have to work hard for a living."

Ellen waited for him to go on.

"Yes, why should a girl like you love a damned S.O.B. like me?"

"Ed, I can't stand hearing you say such things."

"Ellen, it displeases me to hear you say you can't stand something. After knowing me, knowing my philosophy, you ought not use a phrase like 'I can't stand.' "

"Ed, I didn't mean it just that way. What I meant was that I don't like to hear you say such things, that it isn't necessary to say them."

"Necessary? Necessity? The idea of necessity revolts me. Yes, there is necessity in this damned world. But it revolts me. I don't believe in free will. But I'd like to. I'd like to in this sense. I'd like to be free of all necessity. Man? Little bits of clay called men, made by unfeeling gods. It's more poetic to believe in God than not to believe in God, even though it is weak and childish to hold to such a belief. I like to indulge my fancy by imagining that God does exist. I visualize Him not as a graybeard, not as suffering Christ, not as three-in-one, like shoe polish. I visualize Him as some super cynic, holding man like potter's clay in His hand. Making little bits of clayey substances called men, who fret and strut and dream and make a mess of every damned thing. Yes, I like to visualize God as a cynic, as a great ironist."

Ed was talking like his old self now. But still, she was anxious. She felt that he was hinting at something she didn't want to hear. She smiled sweetly at him. She had to act out a part as if she were not so concerned.

"And, yes, I am one of those clayey substances too. I'm just a louse like the rest of the human race."

"Oh, Ed, I won't let you run yourself down like that."

"Am I moral? No. Am I decent? No. Am I honest? There are whole blocks in this great city that I have to avoid because of bad debts. There are hotels I dare not walk by because I left without attending to the little item of a bill. What am I? A louse. Just a louse."

"Ed, we all have done things sometimes. And what's so important about a bad debt? Who cares about some hotel? I don't."

"Ellen, what do you see in me?"

"Ed, what are you driving at?"

Ellen squashed out her cigarette.

"I'm serious. What do you see in me?" he asked.

She faced him, bewildered.

"I'd really like to know. Ellen, tell me, what do you see in me?"

"Why, Ed, such a question! I see everything."

"Everything is a big word. Specifically, what do you see in me?"

He lit a cigarette and slouched back in his chair, his long arms hanging loosely. Ellen noticed that a curl fell down over his forehead. He looked so attractive, and he looked, yes, like

a boy, a charming boy with that curl falling over his forehead.
He brushed it back carelessly.

"That's a big order. You're so intelligent."

"Ellen, now you know in your heart that a woman does not
fall in love with a man because he's intelligent. That's usually
a handicap in matters of the heart."

"I don't see why. And you are so brave, so unafraid of anything."

"Bravery is folly."

"I don't think so. I think it's wonderful to see a man who's
brave, afraid of nothing."

"Live dangerously," he said, laughing deprecatingly.

"I want to. Ed, you taught me to. Before I met you I felt
that way, but I never expressed it, it never occurred to me to
explain it that way. But think how wonderful it is, Ed, to
live dangerously."

"It's merely a paltry protest of the spirit against life. That's
all. It's tilting at the windmills of the cosmos. Riding on Rosi-
nante, with a little spear in your hand, and having the world
laugh at you because of the folly of bravery and the ineptitude
of illusions."

"Well, the world does admire it. And . . . Ed, a girl admires it. A girl admires bravery."

"But assume that you love me."

"I do love you."

"You just don't admire bravery."

"It's one of your qualities. You are brave."

"What else?"

Ellen pouted for a moment.

"Ellen, don't lead me to believe that you have to think up
reasons now to tell me what you see in me."

He leaned forward and looked at her with critical eyes.

She adored him in this posture, but he made her feel uncomfortable. She felt as if he could see inside of her, as if he were
able to gauge and grasp her feelings, her thoughts, her fears
and anxieties.

"Ed, it's not that. I want to find the right words. Ed, you're dashing. You're so attractive, so attractive in so many ways. I feel as if I had been waiting for you all my life. Oh, Ed, it's you. I love you."

"Now, from that statement, it might be deduced that I am perfect."

"You are."

"Don't try to flatter me."

"I don't want you more perfect than you are."

"Yes, yes, we all have illusions. I'm your illusion." Ed smiled and slouched back in his chair again. "It sounds like a song, doesn't it—I'm your illusion."

Ellen grinned sadly. She felt that Ed was slipping from her grip and that she had to hold onto him.

"Ed, don't you love me any more?"

"Ellen, why do you ask me that question?"

"You act so strange of late."

"I hope that question is not a symptom."

"A symptom? Of what?"

"Perhaps you don't care for me?"

"Darling, please don't say that. You know I love you."

She looked at him, devoted, adoring.

"I always feared that this might happen. That you might weary of me.

One love grows green when one turns gray."

"Ed, don't talk to me like that. Ed, it isn't true. Ed, please don't let such thoughts get into your head. It's not true. Ed, oh, Ed!"

"Of course, if you did weary of me, I would understand it. Possibly I'm really not worth you, not worthy of you."

Ellen clenched her fists under the table, fearing that she might cry, and she forced herself to smile.

"Ed, I love you. I'll always love you."

"I hope you always will."

"I will."

He took her hand, squeezed it.

"Ellen, do you know that among the many lovely features

and qualities and characteristics you have, do you know one of the loveliest? It's your hands."

He held her left hand in the palm of his two hands.

"Yes, look at it. Soft, as if made by an artist. The blind forces of this godless world turned artist when they made you."

He continued to gaze at her hand, and she repaid him with a look of profound gratitude.

"Your fingers. Thin, tapering. The formation of your hand. The gestures of your hands. Your hands are wonderful. Ah, that I were a Swinburne, to write a sensuous poem about your hand."

Ellen did not speak. She was ready to swoon. She was so moved that tears came to her eyes.

Ed dropped her hand on the table and slumped back in his chair.

"But why should tears stain those blue eyes?" he asked.

"I can't help it. I can't. I love you, Ed."

She took out a handkerchief and wiped her eyes, striving and struggling to regain her self-control. She felt that it had been wrong for her to cry. But she hadn't been able to help herself.

"Ellen, you mustn't cry," Ed said.

She held her handkerchief to her eyes. She suddenly straightened up, blew her nose, and wiped her eyes. She noticed an expression of disapproval on his face.

"Ed, please forgive me. I'm sorry. Don't think badly of me because I cried."

"Dismiss such thoughts from your mind, Ellen."

She got a mirror out of her purse and looked at herself. Her eyes were red.

"Excuse me a minute, Ed," she said, getting up and going to the ladies' room.

II

Ellen returned meek and shy. Ed was still slouched in his chair.

"Ed, let's walk in the park," she suggested.

"No, let's stay here."

She took another cigarette from his pack which lay on the table. Ed also lit a cigarette. They both puffed on their cigarettes, and neither spoke for a while.

Ellen laid her left hand on the table and looked at her engagement ring.

"What are you looking at?"

"That," she answered, pointing to her ring.

"Oh!"

"Remember the day you bought it for me? It seems so long ago, and it seems as if it were only yesterday."

"Yes, time flies, as they say."

"I like my engagement ring."

"So do I. But then I guess I should. After all, I picked it out."

"Ed?" She waited a moment. "Are you sorry you became engaged to me?"

"Ellen, why do you ask such a question?"

"To get an answer."

"And for what other reason?"

"None—except to get an answer."

"Why should I be sorry?"

"You never mention it much any more."

"I do. But you don't remember."

"No, not very often."

"Are you accusing me?"

"No, Ed, of course not. I just made a statement."

"I'll have to make a note to speak more frequently of our engagement."

Ellen's face changed. She was sad, afraid that she would cry again.

"Now what's the matter, Ellen?"

"Nothing. Nothing. Nothing's the matter," she answered, a tense feeling gripping her as she again struggled in order not to cry.

"Ellen, this is no way for us to act together."

"Ed, if you don't love me any more—if you don't want to marry me—tell me. I'll be brave. Tell me!"

Ed fixed a wounded look on her.

"Why, Ellen, how can you say that to me?"

"Just tell me, Ed. Ed, don't beat around the bush with me."

"Ellen, I adore you."

"Ed, please, don't say it unless you mean it."

"I mean it."

She smiled at him. She reached across the table, grasped his hand, and squeezed it. Their knees met under the table.

"Shall we go to your apartment?" she asked.

"Let's take a walk in the park."

"You didn't want to a minute ago."

"And I do now. You know how whimsical I am."

He got up and put on his topcoat. She put on her coat. They left the restaurant.

"Know what I'd like to do?" he said, standing with her outside of the restaurant.

"What?"

"Let's go to the library."

III

Ed entered the library with Ellen. Sitting at a table in the same place he had met her last spring, he saw Betsy. He turned and walked out hurriedly before Betsy saw him. Ellen followed him, bewildered.

"What's the matter?"

"I changed my mind. Why should I sit in a library and read today? I am with you. We are young. Why should we read? Is that the best we can do?"

Ellen was too bewildered to speak.

He took her arm and led her back to Sixty-third Street.

"I suppose you think I'm crazy?"

"Ed, you know I don't."

"I wouldn't blame you if you did. I have whims like this, and I set out to gratify them, and then I have counter whims."

"Ed, I like your whims."

"Will you like my present whim?"

"What is it?"

"Let's go to my apartment."

She took his arm obediently.

Chapter Thirty-eight

I

Ed lay on his bed, pleasantly idle, smoking, glad that he had been able to send Ellen home.

Why didn't women let him alone?

He laughed. Why should he ask that question? What he really meant was why should women think until death do us part?

This afternoon's experience convinced him that it was not going to be easy to get rid of Ellen. He feared that he wouldn't be able to manage it without some pyrotechnics. But why should he want to get rid of her? Ellen was pert, adorable, charming, cute, lovely, sweet, coy, attractive, alluring, desirable, divine, and, above all else, she was his. So why should he want to dump her? For what?

If he knew himself, he would be possessed of amazing wisdom. The greatest piece of advice ever given to the human race was—*Know thyself.*

But why bother? It was too damned much trouble. He had had enough of Ellen. My God, having to be here with her today, it had been just boring. He had brought her here because he had not thought fast enough when he had seen that little girl, Betsy, in the library. He'd have to remember that she was often to be found in the library. She might be amusing in her way.

He thought of Hilda. She could have been his excuse for dropping Ellen last summer. But he had not been ready then. He remembered how he had put on such a fine suicide act at that time. He was ashamed of himself for having done this.

He promptly allowed his memory of it to fade from his mind. Yes, there was Hilda. She had kept pestering him with letters until it had become unspeakably dreary. So he had gone to the library and copied out a Greek sentence from Aristotle and mailed it to her. He wondered what the sentence meant. He'd never know that one. But it had been a neat gesture, and it seemed finally to have stopped Hilda from sending any additional pounds of mail.

He squashed his cigarette out on the floor. He lay with his hands under his head, his eyes cast upon the ceiling.

Ellen had wanted to stay longer, and he had had to get rid of her. She didn't know when she wasn't wanted. That happened to so many women. Ellen was worried about his love. Well, she could be worried. But she was probably suffering from the mistaken notion that some other girl had cut in on her. He was getting fed up with women now. They required so much time. Because of Ellen he wasn't getting any reading done now. Ah, the library was a much finer sweetheart than a female—for a while at least.

Was he being unfair to Ellen by dumping her as he planned? She was a woman. That settled the question. Many experiences had taught him that women were inferior creatures. And they had no dignity. That's why they played the clinging vine act with men who didn't want them. Ellen was going to do that. She was a distinct disappointment to him. She had deceived him by saying that she shared his ideas. Now that he was bored with her, she wasn't gentleman enough to call it quits. Even Ellen, in whom he had invested so many dreams and illusions, was turning out to be just a female.

His relation with Ellen had produced an amusing paradox. He was bored with her. But he wasn't bored by the memory of her in the days when they had first known each other. He loved his memory of her, and he was wearied by the presence of the girl whose flesh furnished the basis for that memory. What did this paradox prove? It proved that man was a paradoxical animal. And, sad to admit, but true—he was a man. What strange emotions men could have. He would always treasure his memories of the girl to whom he would now tie the familiar tin can.

The time was rapidly approaching when Ellen Rogers would be of the past. What would he say of her!

An' I learned about women from 'er!

Yes, he would. But this line of Kipling made him think of Catherine Anne. She had taught him that poem one windy fall night. Catherine Anne—had he learned about women from her, too? Yes, he had. What was she doing now? He had an inclination to see her. He felt a genuine platonic friendship for Catherine Anne. She could always be relied on to do the sound and sensible thing. Perhaps that was why he was so attracted to her. Unlikes often attract one another more than do likes.

The girls he had known—all like the snows of yesteryear. As far as he was concerned, Ellen soon would be with the snows of yesteryear.

He lit another cigarette. It was so pleasant to be idle, as he now was. What had Nietzsche said? Something like this: *Idleness is the parent of all psychology? What? Is psychology then—a vice?* To lie on one's back and psychologize, to be idle and just think—what was more gratifying?

There were more contradictions in men than the psychologists could ever probe for. Man was more a paradoxical animal than he was a rational animal. Yes, here he was in love with a memory, and at the same time he was getting fed up with the real, physical, breathing, sensuous, actual person who formed the basis of that memory. This was an attractive contradiction to dwell upon. Here was a peculiar state of mind, too, for a realist like himself to have. What could be done with a memory? He could savour it in his mind—but that was all. He couldn't sleep with it. Yet sleeping with women was often overrated. A fight was more thrilling. Often he preferred to deliver a left hook to the jaw to going to bed with a woman. Half of the women he'd slept with hadn't really stirred strong desires in him. Pride, power, his yen for conquests, these now seemed to him to have been as important as any urge down there in his apparatus. He enjoyed this usage of the word—apparatus. He'd have to spring it on an appropriate occasion.

And in the meantime Ellen remained a problem. Today he had tried to convince her that she didn't love him, but that tactic hadn't really worked. He had devoted a great deal of time to working out how he would apply this tactic, and still it hadn't worked. He smiled up at the ceiling. This couldn't actually be chalked up as a failure. He hadn't been confident in this tactic anyway, and he'd merely tried it like a shot in the dark.

Tomorrow was another day. He had to see a hotel manager. This was a new role for him to play with a hotel manager. Usually he was the sworn enemy of hotel managers, and there was no reconciliation between him and them. Now he had to see a hotel manager and go into a thorough analysis of how to improve his business, how and where to advertise. He was getting new accounts every day for John Devormer. But it was getting boring, talking to paint men, hotel managers, hardware dealers, refrigerator makers, talking to all of the men who thought they owned the goddamned world because they made paint, or tennis rackets, or sold you a room to sleep in for the night, or were in the drug business. You saw them and made a contact. You had to be friendly. You didn't try to sell them right off. Just a chat. Mr. Blimpus, I noticed that your account with us is inactive. I just thought I'd drop around and say hello and ask how things were going. I hope business is good. And you talk about women, and their kids, and automobiles, and sundry other boring topics, and maybe the third time you saw them you sold them, and then you collected a commission, and the goddamned money went in gin, pork chops, ponies, some girl, and then you saw another goddamned Mr. Blimpus and sold him.

What the hell was the use of it? It went around and around in a circle. However, he'd stick it out until spring. Might just as well, because it would be a good idea to get a little stake and then travel to some place in style.

Ellen, Hilda, Polack Mary, Catherine Anne, and all the other girls he had ever known—oh, where, oh, where are the snows of yesteryear? It occurred to him that it would have been more amusing and attractive to have lived in Villon's time than in the twentieth century. He could fancy himself as a boon companion of Villon, rather than as an advertising salesman.

Now the real problem on the agenda was Ellen. She was worried lest he ditch her. Did she have cause for worry? She did. How should he dump her? He would settle that question. And then Ellen Rogers would be enshrouded in the pathos of distance. The telephone rang. He went to answer it.

"Hello?"

"Hello, Ed. I just called you up."

"How are you, Ellen?"

"I'm much the same. I came home and I was thinking of you, so I just called you up."

"It was very sweet and thoughtful of you to do it."

"I thought about you all the way home."

"Yes, but what thoughts? Would they make me blush?"

"What would make you blush?"

"Well, assuming I blushed easily, would they?"

"I don't know. They were very, shall I say—flattering?"

"Just a minute, Ellen."

Ed set down the phone and went to the couch for a cigarette. He took his time lighting one, and then he returned to the phone.

"I wanted to light a cigarette."

"What were you doing?"

"I was busy."

"Busy?"

"Yes, with work. I have to see a hotel manager tomorrow, and I was preparing what I had to discuss with him."

"Did I interrupt you, Ed?"

"Did you interrupt me? Yes. Am I pleased? Yes."

"Maybe I had better hang up."

"No, please don't."

"But if you're working?"

"Oh, that can wait."

"I don't want to be interrupting you, of course."

"Of course, but you do, because you don't want to, and it charms me."

"You're going to be busy tomorrow?"

"Yes, I am."

"I'm going downtown. I thought if you weren't going to be busy at lunch time, we could, perhaps, have lunch in the Loop."

"I'd like nothing better if I weren't going to be tied up. But I let myself in for this, and in a way, it's rather important."

"I understand."

"What else is new?"

"Nothing. I just saw you."

"And nothing is new here, except one—well, perhaps one little thing."

She waited for him to continue.

"Well, aren't you going to ask me what it is?" he asked.

"What is it, Ed?"

"I love you even more than ever."

"Darling, you are always able to say such charming things."

He flung his cigarette on the rug and crushed it with the heel of his slipper.

He sat down at his desk to work, but he was soon bored. Wondering what he should do, he decided that he'd go and see his mother and father. He hadn't seen them in some time.

Chapter Thirty-nine

I

"Did you get a lot done last night?" Ellen asked.

Ed spread out his legs, leaned back on the sofa in Ellen's parlor, and, smiling, nodded an affirmative answer to her question. Her expression changed instantly. She faced him with a hard and suspicious countenance. Something was up here, he realized.

"I'm glad to hear that good news," she said ironically.

After he'd left last night to go over and see his father and mother, she must have telephoned and discovered that he was out.

Ed thought that here was a storm signal. Now she was going to spy on him, try to put an alarm clock around his neck. This was a real warning that the time had come. And she was giving him an excuse, an opening. Such scenes as the one he must now contrive were usually unpleasant. But they were all in the lifetime of a Lanson.

He thought how disgusting it was to spy on another person. She had been distrustful, too, on the very evening when he had been virtuous and had gone to see his parents. That strengthened his position. Virtue and truth were now on his side.

"Yes, I'm glad to know that you worked last night," she repeated.

"I suspect a note of irony in your voice."

"No, no, not at all. I'm just glad to know that you worked last night."

"It's considerate of you to be glad, Ellen."

"You're the one who's ironical."

"Not at all. But I can be ironical. However, when I am ironical, I'm not ironical in a paltry sense."

"Of course not."

Ed lit a cigarette.

"You don't seem to believe that I worked last night. You probably are entertaining dark suspicions."

"Why do you say that?"

"Well, you are. You probably checked up on me."

She looked at him, shocked, hurt.

"What do you mean, checked up? I did call you and you weren't in, but that wasn't to check up on you at all. I just called you to ask you to telephone me today before I went downtown, that's all."

"And I wasn't in."

"No, you weren't."

"And in consequence, your mind has been full of dire suspicions, dire forebodings, dire thoughts of what I might be doing. You were jealous. You harbored mean and unkindly thoughts about me."

"No, I didn't! I didn't."

"Don't fool me, Ellen. I know."

"Of course, Ed, it isn't quite consistent with what you said to me about having to work."

"Suppose I did work?"

"I'm not saying anything, except that it isn't consistent."

"So what do you think I was doing?"

"Ed, why do you talk to me so sharply?"

"Sharply? I'll change my tone. I'll be saccharine," he answered, changing his tone of voice to one of obviously false gentleness.

"That's mean. Ed, why do you do that to me?"

"Why do you have such little faith in me?"

"I didn't say that I had little faith in you."

"Actions, intonations, gestures, expressions, little mannerisms—all these speak louder than words."

"You act as if you were on the defensive, Ed."

"I do, do I?"

She nodded her head.

"Now, to let the truth come out, I'll tell you what I did last night. And further, I'll prove it, if you want me to. I visited Mother and Father. And I took my work with me. As a matter of fact, I didn't even sleep in my apartment last night. I slept in my old room at home."

Ellen said nothing. She seemed pained.

"Now do you believe me? Or shall I prove it? I'll phone mother and let you test me to your own satisfaction."

"Ed, I believe you."

"But you didn't."

"Ed, I love you. Perhaps I worry a lot about you."

"That's an insult to me, to worry about me. What do you think I am, a child?"

Ellen was terribly unhappy, and she could not conceal her unhappiness. She did not speak.

"You suspected me. You did not trust me. You did not believe in me," he said to her, cruelly and histrionically.

"Ed, I'm sorry. Let's not quarrel."

Ed stared grimly at his image in the low mirror directly opposite where he sat. He was pleased with the face he was making; perhaps he should be an actor.

"Ed, please!"

"Most assuredly we won't fight," he said, continuing to look dour.

"Ed, forgive me."

"Ellen, I forgive you."

"But the way you say that, the way you look, it means you don't really mean what you say."

"It isn't a case of our not quarreling. It isn't a case of forgiveness. Ellen, love between a man and a woman is a very tender plant. It is exceedingly frail. Ill winds of doubt, hesitation, suspicion, can blow it over, leave it lying on the ground, kill it."

"Ed, really, all this isn't so important between us, is it?"

"Ellen, I am terribly sorry."

She smiled at him now.

"I am terribly sorry for what you have done."

"Oh, Ed, what have I done?" she asked, again troubled, anxious.

"Ah, you don't even realize what you have done."

He slumped further on the sofa. She took his hand. He held it limp. He looked utterly unresponsive.

"Oh, Ed, for God's sake, don't treat me like this. I can't stand it. I can't stand it. I love you."

"Don't get hysterical, Ellen."

"I can't help it. Tell me, what's the matter?"

"Nothing is the matter. At least, nothing was the matter until jealousy and suspicion began to cloud our relationship. It disturbs me. As I remarked, love between a man and a woman is a tender plant, very tender, very sensitive, sensitive to so many things, so many influences and factors. Ellen, do you realize how you have risked drying up, destroying, the tender, delicate, sensitive, and, yes, beautiful, or at least, once beautiful plant of our love?"

She whimpered.

"Don't cry. Is that the lesson you learned from me? Don't cry, Ellen."

"Oh, I can't help it."

She flung her head in his lap and sobbed without restraint. Ed sat, his hands idle at his side. He looked down at her blonde head. A woman in tears was disconcerting. The sight of Ellen touched him. He was sorry for her. Because she moved him, he was resentful. He sneered and warned himself that he would now be lost if he gave in to her. And it would be better for her, kinder to her, if he didn't. The kindest thing he could do would be to use a hatchet.

> . . . *Yet each man kills the thing he loves.*

What a disgusting spectacle! Why should she turn on the tears? And was she sincere? Sincerity could be selfish. If a woman loved a man *with sincerity*, did that make her love pure, devoted, unselfish? Not in the slightest. Ah, what a fraud love was! Ah, what a fraud life was! He was ashamed of the human race. And he was human.

Ellen gazed up at him, her agonized face stained by tears. She did not look beautiful now. Her eyes were red. Her unhappy frame of mind caused her to twist and distort her lips. Her cheeks were smeared, and much of her make-up was washed off.

"Ed, you're so cold. You don't love me any more."

"Did I say that?"

"You just said that actions speak louder than words," she said in a breaking voice.

She seemed suddenly like a very unhappy little girl.

"My actions do not necessarily mean that I do not love you. But I have a high conception of love. I have looked upon our love as something extraordinary, something so different, so much finer than the loves of all the Bill Northrups, Frank Dolans, and others, than the loves of all the greasy, greedy little Babbitts, the grasping little ciphers of the multitude whose trousers and dresses cannot mask them from being ciphers. I had a high conception of our love."

"Ed, don't say those things to me."

When thou goest to a woman bring thy whip. He didn't want to, but he could forecast the future. This was his chance. Yes, a hammer and a hatchet. What was a dead love worth? That love should die, was that his fault? Was love his fault? Was life his doing?

"I regret it if my words disturb you, Ellen."

He rose to his feet and paced back and forth across the room. She followed him with her eyes as if she were in a spell, fascinated, mesmerized, hypnotized by him. He continued to pace the floor. Then, he dropped back on the sofa and sat in a slumped position.

"Ellen, do you think I'm happy?"

She patted his hand. She ran her hands through his hair. She smothered him with passionate kisses. He held her gently, but failed to respond to her caresses. She dropped back beside him, limp, breathless.

"Ed, you don't love me any more?"

"Ellen, I don't know what I think. I don't know how I feel. It isn't my doing."

"Oh, Ed, forgive me. If I have done anything, forgive me. I'll never do it again. I'm sorry."

"Oh, if it were just easy, merely so easy as to forgive, then, un-Christian as I am, I should forgive. But we have now entered a region that is outside the boundaries where forgiveness has meaning and solves a problem."

"Ed, what shall I do? . . . What can we do?"

"Ellen, I must think. I must settle this question in my own heart. I must be alone, alone with myself."

"I don't understand you."

"Ellen, this hurts me, distresses me, makes me as unhappy as it can possibly make you."

He looked aside and saw his gloomy visage in the mirror. He approved of his facial expressions.

Ed stood up and gazed down at her. She raised her head. With her face, she implored him.

"Ellen, I must be alone to think. I must mull this over alone in my own heart. I will not see you for a couple of days. I must have time, time by myself."

She sobbed. He drew her to her feet, took out his handkerchief, wiped her eyes, kissed her tenderly, as if she were a little child.

"Ellen, you must not act like this. You must be brave and strong."

"But, Ed, why, why can't we talk and settle this? Why this waiting, suspense? Ed, tell me, tell me outright if you don't love me. I just want to know. If you don't love me, tell me."

"Ellen, did I say that I didn't love you?"

"Please, Ed, tell me."

"Ellen, I must be alone with my thoughts, I must look into the mirror of my heart. Now, you must be brave. By being brave, you will help me. I'm very unhappy, Ellen."

"Ed, why should we let ourselves get into this kind of state?"

"Sometimes, emotions are beyond one's choosing."

"But why should this be?"

"Ah, that I could know the answer to such questions! Were I to know them, I would have at my command the keys that unlock the door to the deep-seated secrets of the human heart."

"Ed, please don't leave me."

"Ellen, I must. I will telephone you in three days. We must both examine our hearts."

He kissed her forehead and walked slowly out of the parlor. Ellen heard the front door close. She emitted a sigh. She rushed to her bedroom, flung herself on the bed, and cried without restraint.

Chapter Forty

I

"Ellen, what the devil did that fellow do to you?" Mr. Rogers asked her.

Ellen did not answer him. She looked at her plate and pecked away, eating little bits of chicken without interest.

"Ellen?" her father called to her, raising his voice, but not in anger.

"What, Father?"

"Ellen, what's the matter?"

"Nothing."

"I know something's wrong. I can tell from the way you act, from the way you look. Why, you have no appetite. You've got circles under your eyes. Ellen, tell me, tell me what's the matter, what's happened, so that I can help you."

Help her? Who could help her? Ed. Tomorrow the three days would be up.

"Ellen, what has happened?"

"I tell you, nothing. I'm just not feeling well."

"No one is worth losing one's health for. No one is worth that much. Has there been a serious quarrel between you and Ed?"

"No, there hasn't."

"You didn't see him last night?"

"He's busy."

"Ellen, I'm not trying to pry or be nosey. I'm asking you to tell me if anything is wrong so I can help you. Maybe I could take you away on a little trip, if that would be good for you. If I only knew what was the matter, perhaps I could help you."

"Please don't ask me any questions."

"But, Ellen . . ."

"Father, I'm asking you to do me that favor. Please."

Mr. Rogers looked at his daughter, shaking his head in bewilderment. Ellen scarcely ate any supper, and they both sat in gloomy silence.

II

Ellen wished that she had someone to talk to. But whom? If she talked to some girls, it would get all over town. Then she would not be acting like the proud, haughty Ellen Rogers so many persons knew. She couldn't talk. She couldn't do it. And she had only to wait until tomorrow. Oh, she missed Ed so. She wanted him so much. She needed him.

She lay on her bed. She imagined seeing him tomorrow. He would take her in his arms and kiss her, and he would call her Sweet, and he would tell her that he loved her. He would be his old self. Her Ed. She would no longer be unhappy. If that happened, then what she had gone through yesterday and today would not have been in vain. Then how wonderful it would be to see her Ed again, to make up with him, to be loved by him, to lie in his arms.

But suppose this didn't happen? But it would. Underneath everything in the world, she was sure that Ed loved her. He was a whimsical person. He had moods. He was just in one of his moods. It would end, and he would be his old self again. And then they would love each other even more than they had ever loved each other in the past.

She could see him in her mind's eye, with his hair, his hazel eyes, soft lovely eyes, his lips, his boyish smile, walking toward her.

What could she do, what would she do, if Ed was through with her? She couldn't stand it.

If Ed only knew how she was suffering, what this all meant to her!

What should she do to bring him back? Should she pray? Should she hope?

Why had she allowed herself to get into this state, to become

so dependent on him? But she had, and against her own realization that she shouldn't. She had been drawn, magnetized,
dragged into this state, and she couldn't help herself. She had
to pull herself together. She twisted her lips in an ironical little
smile.

Hadn't she told this to herself again and again for the last
forty-eight hours? And what good had it done? She couldn't
think herself into a condition where she wouldn't be so upset.
When you loved someone as she loved Ed, then you were unable
to control yourself. Then will power was meaningless.

She turned over and stared vacantly at the ceiling. Suddenly her face softened, seemed to lose its careworn, haggard,
worried character. What dress would she wear tomorrow? She
should have thought to go downtown and get a new dress just
for this occasion. She might wear her black tailored suit. Ed
liked her in that. In the morning she would get a permanent.
She needed one. And she wanted to look so wonderful for Ed.
She wanted to be dressed up smartly and then to let Ed muss
her all up.

But wouldn't it be sad if Ed didn't call her or if he told her
that he no longer loved her and that everything was broken
up?

She couldn't bear that. It would be worse than death. She
would talk to him, talk to him until he did love her. She
wouldn't let him go. She couldn't. He and she were part of each
other. Letting him go was like losing part of yourself, part of
yourself more valuable than an arm or a leg. No, she couldn't
lose him. How could she lose something that was a part of herself? It was too ridiculous for words.

Ed had just been in one of his moody fits. He had these
moods every now and then. He was more sensitive, more profound than other boys. That was why he had these moods.

But didn't he know what he was doing to her? He was selfish. She had to change him. Once they were married, she would
change him, but not for the worse. But he shouldn't have moods
like this and cause her to undergo such—torture.

She rolled over and lay on her stomach. She kicked off her high-heeled shoes, and they dropped noisily onto the floor.

Just tonight to go through. What time tomorrow would he call her? It should be in the morning. What was he doing this minute? Had he been unhappy these last two days? He couldn't have been as unhappy as she had been. No one ever suffered more from love than she had these last two days. She had found love so wonderful, and suddenly it was something terrible, yes, terrible. She couldn't eat. She couldn't sleep. She couldn't think of anything, she couldn't do anything except think of Ed and wait until the time their separation would be over. When Ed had been in Washington, she had been so miserable. But it had been nothing to what she had been suffering yesterday and today.

Why did this have to be? Why did such situations have to arise between lovers? Had she ever made anyone suffer the way she was now suffering? She couldn't. No man could suffer as much as she was suffering.

What would she say to Ed when he took her in his arms tomorrow? Would she have to say anything? Would words be necessary? She wished he would call her in the morning and that they would spend the whole day together, doing things, walking, being in each other's company, talking. Oh, if that could happen—it was so sweet to make up after a quarrel. Tomorrow could be so sweet a day.

Was she only dreaming? Maybe she had better prepare for the worst? What had really happened to cause Ed to do this, to insist on this separation? She had really done nothing to warrant it. If there was such a crisis it was because of some other reason, and that reason would have to be because Ed wanted it. Why should he be tired of her? Could any other girl satisfy him more fully? It wouldn't seem that way. Oh, to have him sleeping, tired and worn out, his head resting on her shoulder, just like a little boy. Oh, if that could happen tomorrow, wouldn't it be—sweet. And just to look at him while he would be sleeping on her shoulder.

Not ever to have this pleasure again? She wouldn't think

of this as possible. It wasn't. Ed loved her. Ed needed her. Ed wouldn't find a girl more suited to him than she was.

Suddenly she laid taut and tense.

Yes, suppose he told her it was all over?

Her face became twisted, distorted. She gazed at the wall behind the head of the bed. No, no, no, she couldn't believe it was possible. It wasn't possible.

If it were only tomorrow and Ed were with her. If this were only over.

Ed! Ed! Ed!

Oh Ed!

III

Mary, the maid, brought a letter in to Ellen. She had just had breakfast in bed and she lay there, waiting, just waiting to pass the time. She observed that the letter was in Ed's handwriting. Ed had such a distinctive handwriting. She stared at it. Her hand trembled. Good news? Bad news? She felt it was bad news. But, no, it must be good news. It must be. She tore open the letter.

Dear Ellen

Don't think badly of me. I am taking the necessary course. We have beautiful memories in common. We owe much to one another. But if we do not break it off now, we will destroy these memories. Believe me, Ellen, I am doing the necessary thing, taking the only possible course for you, as well as for myself. I have taught you to be brave. You have taught me the poetry of love. Our life together has been like a candle flame. "To burn always with this hard, gemlike flame, to maintain this ecstasy, is success in life." Pater. Our love has burned hard like a gemlike flame. But all flames die. Before our flame has turned to bitter ash, let us bravely snuff it out. This is necessary. It is more necessary for you than for me, if you will only realize it. I have pondered deeply, Ellen, about our problem. I have thought long. I have suffered agonies of doubt. And I know best. Ellen don't blame me. Blame life. Life has been good to us. And now life, grinning like a super-ironist, takes back the gifts, snatches out of our hearts the dying flame —snuffs it out. Life is careless that way. But, Ellen, let us leave pure and beautiful those memories we have had together. Good-bye, Ellen.

As a farewell, please accept these lines of poetry from Swinburne. Accept them as a rose of yesterday, one of those flowers that are crushed in books and always kept there as a memento of what once was, and of what can be no more. For such is life.

> *Let this be said between us here,*
> *One love grows green when one turns gray;*
> *This year knows nothing of last year:*
> *Tomorrow has no more to say*
> *To yesterday,*

> *Live and let live, as I will do,*
> *Love and let love, and so will I.*
> *But, sweet, for me no more with you:*
> *Not while I live, not though I die.*
> *Good night, good-bye.*

Au revoir, Ellen. You have been good to me. I have tried to be good to you. Life is sad. Love is sad. But we must brace ourselves and ever hold our heads high in pride. We must bravely part like two free spirits who laugh at the gods of life, the gods of life who make us pay such prices to appease their super cynicism and their super irony. Farewell, au revoir, Ellen.

Ed.

Ellen's eyes were vacant. She held the letter in her hand. Suddenly, she said aloud, speaking as one in a trance:

> *Tomorrow has no more to say*
> *To yesterday.*

The letter fell from her hand. She repeated aloud:

> *Tomorrow has no more to say*
> *To yesterday.*

Ellen remained too stunned to think, to cry, to suffer. She felt numb, vacant; it seemed as if everything inside of her had been sucked out, and she were empty, a shell, a doll, a mere hollow form. She sat rigid, seeing nothing, repeating the two lines of poetry, saying them dully, without emphasis or rhythm.

Chapter Forty-one

I

Her eyes were red. She had sobbed loudly, without restraint. She was haggard from anxiety and lack of sleep. Barefoot, she went to the telephone in her hall and called up Ed.

"Apartment 4 E?"

She waited, trembling, while the operator rang. She didn't know what she would say to him. She had to hear his voice. She had to speak to him. She had to see him once again. If he would see her, tell her to her face, then she would do nothing. But this much he could grant her.

There was no answer.

"Oh, pardon me. Was it Mr. Lanson you wanted?"

"Yes."

"One moment, please."

She waited. How long a second could be! But it must mean that she would get Ed on the phone. He would see her.

"Mr. Lanson left here this morning."

"When will he be back? Did he leave a message?"

"You misunderstood me. He is no longer living here. He left early this morning."

"What address did he leave?"

"Just a moment, please."

Ellen waited.

"He left a forwarding address."

"Could I have it, please?"

"Yes. General Delivery. New York City."

Ellen hung up. She sat by the phone.

II

"Hello, is this the Devormer Advertising Agency?"

"Yes."

"Mr. Edmond Lanson."

"I'm sorry, Mr. Lanson is not in."

"When do you expect him?"

"I don't know. He telephones in every morning. Is there any message, please?"

"Yes. Ask him to phone Miss Rogers at her home, immediately."

"I have your message, Miss Rogers. It will be delivered to Mr. Lanson."

"What time do you expect to hear from him?"

"I just said that I do not know," the girl on the other end of the wire stated in an impatient voice.

"But he is still working with your firm?"

"Yes, Mr. Lanson is. I will deliver your message to him."

Ellen heard the click of the receiver at the other end of the connection.

III

How could he refuse to call her up? But she had waited an hour, and there was no call. Had he received the message? Had he already gone to New York?

Ellen went back to the telephone and called the Devormer Agency again.

"Mr. Lanson, please."

"He's not in."

"This is Miss Rogers. Did you give him the message I left for him about an hour ago?"

"Yes, Miss Rogers, I delivered your message."

"Did he leave any message for me?"

"No, Miss Rogers."

"What time do you expect him in your office?"

"I can't say," the girl said, her tone one of vexation.

"Do you think he will be in this morning?"

"I delivered your message, Miss Rogers," the girl said, her tone like ice.

Hopelessly, Ellen hung up. She sat by the phone.

He had not called her. He had the message. Why didn't he call? Didn't he know what she was suffering? Didn't he care? He didn't. Ed didn't care for her. Ed didn't love her. Ed was through with her. It was not a dream. It was true. No more Ed. No marriage. Ed had told her he was through with her.

Who did he think he was that he could get away with this with her? Well, if he thought that he could treat her like a door mat, he was mistaken. She was never going to be any man's door mat, not even Ed Lanson's, with all his fine-spun talk. Ever since she had known him, he had been writing a book. Where was it? He talked about himself as if he were a god or something. She had to laugh. And so this was the end of it all between them, the end of all this talk about their souls flying over the mountains where only eagles could fly.

Who was the other girl?

Ellen paced the parlor nervously. Had he found another girl? What kind of a girl was she? What was wrong with her herself that Ed should throw her overboard for another girl? What was wrong with her?

The trouble with Ed was that he didn't know his own interest. He didn't really know that she was best for him.

Would he come back? If he didn't, might he not ruin both their lives? They were young, very young yet, and they had their lives ahead of them. How could she go through life without him? How? And why? Why had it had to happen?

She sat on the sofa. What had she really done? What was the defect in her? What did some other girl have that she didn't have? What?

Ellen jumped to her feet. She thought she heard the telephone.

God! Was she going out of her head? Hearing sounds where there were none.

Was Ed in New York? That was the cruelest touch of all.

To go away like this. But he hadn't gone. His office said that he had phoned in this morning. He hadn't quit his work.

She jumped to her feet. Ed Lanson thought that he knew her? Well, he didn't. If he really knew her, he would have known that she was not the kind of a person to take this lying down and not do anything. She wasn't a Catherine Anne. Ed Lanson didn't know her.

Should she tell him that she was pregnant? Should she do to him what she'd done to Bill Northrup? But if she did, could she get away with it with Ed? She wasn't dealing with the same kind of person as Bill. What could she do?

She slumped in a chair. Oh, she loved Ed. She wanted Ed. She wanted Ed, and nothing else in the world. She wanted him on any terms just so long as he was hers, all hers.

She sobbed hysterically.

IV

Dear Ed

I have waited an hour to hear from you after leaving a message with the telephone girl at your office. I hope that I have heard from you and seen you before this letter arrives. You left as your address General Delivery, New York, but you are still in Chicago. Ed, why did you lie to me? Ed, even if you don't love me any more, after all there has been between us can't you see me? Even if we have to part, can't we part as friends? Must you sneak away from me like this?

All I ask is that you see me. I must speak to you. Oh, Ed, I will not do anything to hold you if you don't love me any more, but I must see you. I must see you once more and talk to you and know why this has happened. You write to me and say it has happened but you don't say why except that you quote poems. But the poems don't tell me why. Ed won't you please see me and tell me why. I will not do one thing to hold you if you will only tell me why. I want to know, Ed. I want to see you. Ed, don't go away and not even see me. You owe me that much. After all we have been through, it is the least that can be done. We ought to see each other. We have hardly talked anything over. The other night you said you had to think. I have thought, too. I want to talk to you and tell you what I have thought and I must know why you have come to this decision. Ed, when you receive this letter telephone me immediately because I must see you.

Ellen

V

Ellen hurried out to mail the letter. It was a sharp, clear autumn morning and the air smelled of fall. She heard the wind in the trees and shrubbery of Jackson Park. The wind made her sad. Life made her sad. She was sad, and it was autumn, and Ed was leaving her. The winter was ahead. If he would just see her.

After she had dropped the letter in the box, she walked home slowly. She had sent the letter special delivery to him, care of his office. But when would he get it? This afternoon? Tomorrow?

Perhaps when he had received her message to telephone her, he had been busy. He might be free now, and he might telephone while she was out. Ellen walked faster. She ran along Sixty-seventh Street, developing a pain in her side. She was out of breath. She walked holding her side, and then she ran again. She hurried upstairs, panting. She let herself in the front door.

"Any telephone calls for me?" she called, out of breath.

"No, Miss Ellen."

VI

Ellen didn't know how she had gotten through the last four hours, but here it was already three-thirty. She gazed out the window. The sky was heavy and sunless. A pall seemed to hang over Jackson Park; the trees almost bare, the wind riding through them so that, behind her closed window, she could hear it. Ellen felt herself a prisoner, a prisoner in her home, a prisoner in the world that lay miserably under a miserable sky. There was no place to go, nothing to do under this sky, no place to go except wherever Ed was, nothing to do unless it

were to be done with Ed. And he had not called her up. Ed
meant what he had said in his letter. He had not telephoned.
She feared that he wouldn't. He might go to New York. He
might never come back to her. She would live under the sky
which hung so low and so heavily over Jackson Park, she would
live under that sky for days, and weeks, and years, and she
might never again see Ed.

She stood by the window. No one was to be seen in Jackson
Park. How many times had she looked out on Jackson Park
from this same window? How many times had she glanced out
of this window with Ed in her thoughts, and with the confidence of his love in her whole being? And now she was looking
out at the almost deserted golf course, the bare shrubbery, the
naked trees, the hardening earth, and thought that Ed did not
love her. Oh, what was the use? What could she do? What
should she do?

Don't give him up!

The voice seemed to beat in her mind. Excited, nervous, she
was aware of her heart palpitating, and with each palpitation
she felt as if a voice were telling her not to give him up.

But was that any good? If she couldn't find him, what did
it mean to tell herself not to give him up?

Ed had said to her that there was no God. There was no life
after death. And in this life, the only one that she had ever
known, that she would ever know, there was only one human
being whom she had ever loved. And Ed had written her a letter
saying that it was all over, saying that tomorrow has no more to
say to yesterday. Yesterday was in her heart, and tomorrow was
what she had to face. What was the use? What was the sense?
She had felt, she still felt, that her entire life was a preparation
for her meeting with Ed. And now the act was over. The curtain
had come down. Everybody was walking out of the theater. She
felt like one who sat alone in a silent theater after a play. There
were ghosts around her. No, there were not even ghosts. There
was nothing. Before she had met Ed, she had felt that there
was nothing much to life. And Ed had filled her life. Then it
had been gay and romantic to say that there was nothing.

Now, without Ed, it was so different; it had such a different meaning. Yes, she was sitting alone now in a theater, and the performance was over. That was just about her position.

Was she afraid?

Afraid of what?

Ed had told her that he was afraid of nothing.

Well, she was afraid of nothing. If she could not have Ed, she would want nothing, and she would be afraid of nothing.

But she wanted Ed. Oh, why did this have to happen? Why? Why? Why?

Suddenly she felt as if there were wheels in her head, spinning, and they spun out this question of why, why, why, why, why—why?

She turned away from the window.

Chapter Forty-two

I

Why should she humiliate herself in this way?

Ellen knew that it was irrelevant to ask herself such a question. What she was doing these days was beyond pride, will-power, questions of self-control.

She stood near the entrance to a tall office building on South Dearborn, restlessly looking up and down the street, watching the pedestrians come and go. It was a cold, gloomy morning, and the very state of the weather seemed to make more emphatic her feeling of hopelessness. Upstairs in this building was the Devormer office. Sooner or later Ed had to come in to it. She was confident that if she waited here long enough she would see him.

A streetcar passed. Two young girls struggled by on preposterously high heels. They looked like floosies. Had either of them ever lost the man she loved? Even if she had, it wouldn't have been as much of a loss as hers. How could there be others like Ed?

But what a thought to be having. Thinking that Ed was the most perfect specimen in the world when he was treating her this way.

"Hello, sister," a middle-aged man said, approaching her.

Ellen didn't answer.

"You look lonesome, sister."

She gazed at him coldly.

"Yeh, you look lonesome. And you might catch cold here. It isn't right to be cold in this world. There are ways of not being cold, you know."

Ellen cut him with her frigid look.

"You been standing here a long time, haven't you, sister? I've been watching you."

"I don't know you. Will you please stop annoying me? If you don't, my husband, who'll be along here any minute, might have something to say to you."

"I've noticed you standing here a long time."

Ellen turned her back on the masher. He shrugged his shoulders and went off. She walked slowly up and down the sidewalk, watching and peering nervously in one direction, then in another. It was ten-fifteen. He ought to be in soon. She had telephoned about twenty minutes ago and had been told that he wasn't in, and that the office didn't know whether or not he would be in today. The girl in the office was getting sick of her voice. That Ed should have forced her to put herself in such a position! She turned around and paced slowly back and forth in front of the entrance to the building. There was a steady procession of people going along the sidewalk in either direction. Ellen kept looking among them for Ed. She stopped by the side of the building entrance.

The wind was getting stiffer. Her feet and legs were cold. She waited inside the entrance for a few minutes, but then she went outside again and walked slowly back and forth in front of the building. Perhaps she was waiting in vain and he wouldn't be in this morning.

On a sudden impulse Ellen rushed into the building, took an elevator to the eighth floor, and entered the offices of the Devormer Advertising Agency. She timidly approached a plain girl who sat at a desk.

"Is Mr. Lanson in?" Ellen asked.

"No, he isn't," the girl answered, her manner almost contemptuous.

"Do you expect him in this morning?" Ellen asked.

"I don't know."

Ellen didn't know what to say. She felt humiliated.

"Can I write a note for him."

"Yes."

"Could you let me have pen and ink?"

The girl reluctantly took out a piece of paper, an envelope, and pushed them across to Ellen. She pointed to a pen lying on the desk.

Standing up, Ellen hastily scribbled a note.

Dear Ed

Why do you refuse to telephone me? You left a New York address and you are still here. Ed, I must see you. It is important. I have to see you because something has happened. I promise you if you don't care for me I won't bother you. But I must see you once. Telephone me as soon as you read this note. If I am not home, leave a message where I can see you.

Ellen

She wrote Ed's name on the envelope, inserted her note, and sealed the envelope.

"Here it is. Will you please give it to him as soon as he comes in?"

The girl nodded without interest.

"You don't know when he'll come in?"

"I just told you I didn't know."

Ellen stood there, her pride outraged.

"Thank you," she said, embarrassed.

The girl at the desk didn't answer. Ellen slunk out of the office.

II

When the doorbell rang, Ellen was certain that it was Frank Dolan, but when she answered it promptly, she hoped and imagined it would be Ed. She had telephoned Frank and asked him to come and see her. He plodded upstairs. She greeted him, took his hat and coat, hung them up, and led him into the parlor.

"How are you, Ellen?" Frank asked self-consciously.

"Have you seen Ed since we talked on the telephone this afternoon?"

Frank shook his head no. She was skeptical. She wondered whether or not Ed had seen Frank and coached him about what to say to her.

"Frank. Ed loves me. I know he does," she said.

"I always thought so."

"I don't know what's the matter with him. Frank, please don't lie to me. Tell me honestly—did you tell me the truth on the phone this afternoon when you said you hadn't seen him?"

"I haven't seen him, Ellen, honestly."

"Are you telling me the truth?"

"Why shouldn't I, Ellen?"

Silent for a moment, Ellen noticed that Frank avoided meeting her eyes.

"Couldn't you find out where he is—where he lives now?"

Frank did not enjoy being asked such questions. Well, she didn't care.

"Ellen, I don't know where Ed is."

"He isn't living at home with his folks?"

"I don't know."

"Frank, will you see Ed for me?"

He gave no sign of assent or dissent. He waited for her to go on.

"You're a close friend of his. If you telephone his office and leave a message for him, he'll call you back. You can reach him. Will you see him and tell him I have to see him once more? Tell him that I won't cause him any trouble if that's what he's afraid of. But I have to talk with him."

"Ellen, I'm sorry to hear this, but, honestly, I don't know what to say. I don't know what I can do. I can't interfere in a matter like this and do any good."

"Is it interfering merely to deliver a message for me?"

If this were the way he really felt, why had he agreed to come and see her? Once, he himself had hoped to make love to her. Did he still? Was he loyal to his friend Ed Lanson?

"Frank, all I'm asking you to do is to tell him that I must see him once. Tell him that I have to because something has happened. I have to talk with him. I'm asking you merely to deliver such a message to him."

Frank looked away.

She was definitely inclined to believe that Ed knew Frank was here seeing her and was waiting for Frank's report.

"Do you remember the time you came to get me when Ed was feeling so desperate? I went to him—didn't I?"

Frank nodded.

"Remind him of that for me. Tell him that that night I stood by him. Say that I said that the least he owes me is to see me, not to go on ignoring me the way he has."

Frank was silent.

She forced him to meet her eyes and she presented the picture of one who was infinitely sad, deeply, profoundly hurt.

"You used to say you were a friend of mine," she said in tones of recrimination and accusation.

"I am your friend, Ellen."

"Then is it asking too much of you to do such a little thing for me?"

"I'm going to do it. I didn't say I wouldn't. I was just thinking, thinking that it is too bad when things happen this way."

"Tell Ed that I won't cause him any trouble. If he's afraid of scenes, he needn't worry. He knows that I am not that type of a person. But I have to see him. I must talk to him."

"I'll tell him, if I can get in touch with him."

"And telephone me tomorrow—at one o'clock."

Ed was forcing her to be dependent on this ninny, to ask him to do her such favors. She had never imagined that this would happen to her. What a trick for Ed to play on her! But she felt helpless. It was as if tops and wheels were spinning in her head. Until she saw Ed, nothing else mattered.

"Frank, do you think it's a decent way for Ed to treat me?"

"Ellen, I don't know anything about it. I don't know what to say."

"Did Ed ever talk about me to you?"

"He always praised you. I never heard him say a word against you." Frank paused a moment, and then continued unconvincingly, "Ellen, this comes as a big surprise to me."

"Did he ever let on or hint to you that he and I might break up this way?"

"Why, no, never."

"Frank, are you telling me the truth?"

"What reason would I have for lying to you? Ellen, after all, we're friends, aren't we?"

"What do you think of Ed?"

"Ed's my friend, too. I think a lot of Ed."

"Do you think you could bring him around to his senses?"

"What do you mean, Ellen?"

"He's making a mistake. I wonder—do you think any one might be influencing him?"

"Gee, I don't know."

"Did he ever talk to you about that girl in Washington?"

"No, he never did," Frank said.

He got up.

"You don't have to go. Stay a while and talk to me."

"I'd like to very much, Ellen, but I got a date. I have to leave now. I'm late as it is."

"Can't you stay just a little while?" she asked in an almost pleading tone.

"I wish I could, Ellen, but I have to keep this date. I'll buzz you on the phone tomorrow."

She accompanied him to the door.

"Now buck up," he said, patting her shoulder.

His voice sounded so hollow.

III

Ellen grabbed a hat and coat and hurried downstairs immediately after Frank. She peered along the street in both directions, but she couldn't see him. She realized that he usually went about in a Ford. She couldn't follow him.

She remained in front of the building, utterly depressed. What was the use of anything? She began walking along Sixty-seventh Street, slowly, aimlessly. What was the use of anything, she asked herself despondently.

Oh, everything was a fraud. What was the use? Could she go on, after knowing Ed, go on without him? She walked on, still aimless. Whenever any trouble came to someone, the world would say to that person that time would heal it. How could time heal her wounds?

Had she acted right in talking to Frank? If Ed wouldn't see her after she sent notes and messages to him, what effect would Frank have on him? Hadn't Ed often said that Frank was a chump? She had laughed and been amused when Ed had called Frank his chump. But hadn't Ed treated her as a worse chump than he had ever treated Frank Dolan?

An automobile stopped at the curb, and a man in the car opened the door.

"You lonesome?"

Ellen didn't hear him. She continued on slowly.

The man in the automobile blared his horn. She turned, surprised, shocked, even frightened.

"Hey, lonesome, it's a cold night to be out walking alone."

Ellen turned her back on the man and walked on. The car pulled up ahead of her and stopped. Again the man opened the door. Ellen turned and walked in the opposite direction. She didn't want to be picked up by any stranger. In the past, hadn't affairs now and then made her forget for a few moments at least? But she didn't want to be picked up.

She heard footsteps behind her.

"Listen, girlie, you look lonesome."

Ellen swung around to face a pudgy, middle-aged man.

"Come on, let's go for a little ride. Saves shoe leather, you know."

Ellen brushed past him and walked on toward Stony Island Avenue. The man returned to his automobile. It drew ahead of her at the curb. The man opened the door a third time.

"This is no way to treat a fellow who wants to be friendly."

"If you don't stop pestering me, I'm going to scream until the entire neighborhood is looking at you out of every window on this street."

"Oh, that won't be nice."

"If you bother me again, I'll scream," she said, her voice tremulous, full of suppressed hysteria.

The man slammed the door shut and drove off.

She walked on. It would have been revenge on Ed to be picked up by someone like that and to sleep with him. But would it be revenge on Ed? What would Ed care?

What should she do? Walk the streets like this? For what?

In front of the drugstore there was a group of fellows, and, heedless of their stares, she crossed over Stony Island Avenue. She drifted on toward Sixty-third Street.

She had walked along this path with Ed many times. Across the street was Jackson Park, her park, her park and Ed's park. It would always be her park and Ed's park.

She looked ahead. That man walking. No one in the world but Ed walked that way. It was Ed in front of her. She quickened her steps. About a half a block away there was a man swinging along, walking in that jaunty way that Ed walked. It must be him. She caught herself in time just as she was going to yell. She ran and, stumbling, almost tripped because of her high heels. She regained her balance just in time.

It was Ed.

She was cutting down the distance between them.

And he was alone.

Ed.

She felt a pain in her side. She hurried in spite of it.

"Ed!" she called, breathless, when she was about ten feet behind the man.

He turned around.

It wasn't Ed.

She was too embarrassed to speak. There was little resemblance between Ed and this fellow.

"Oh, hello!"

"I'm sorry. I thought you were someone else," she said.

"Well, can I substitute for this Ed?"

"I'm sorry. I thought you were my brother. You look like him."

"Perhaps it is a bit of luck that I'm not your brother."

"Excuse me."

"That's easy to do."

"I'm sorry," she said, walking on.

The fellow looked at her, perplexed.

"I say!" he called after her.

How easy it was to be picked up. How easy it was to get men. A particular man wasn't the only pebble on the beach. The beach was full of them. And Ed was only one of the pebbles on the beach. But she didn't want any other pebble.

She walked on, not knowing what to do with herself. Sad, dreamy, she went along Sixty-third Street and strolled back and forth in front of the Kendale Apartment Hotel where Ed used to live. This building, the stones of this building, the canopy in front of it, the red furniture in the lobby, were all so precious to her. The light inside was so warm. A particle of Ed remained in that light. Something of Ed was in the stones, the glass, the wood, the very color of this building. She walked back and forth in front of it. Two couples came out of the apartment hotel and walked away from her. She heard one of the girls laugh happily. She had gone out with Ed and laughed that way.

Where was Ed now? What was he doing?

She walked away from the hotel.

Not knowing what to do with herself, she went to a moving picture show. She paid no attention to the picture. She sat in the darkened theater like a person in a trance.

Chapter Forty-three

I

The sun outside the quiet little tea room was warm. What a glorious Indian summer day! To spend a day like this with Ed, doing nothing, wandering around, talking, listening to him talk, contentedly forgetting oneself so completely that all sense of time passing was lost, to spend a day like this with Ed, aware of nothing in the world except herself and him. And Ed did not love her any longer.

Ellen turned from the window where she had seen the sun shining on the grayish stone pavement.

"Why did he say he couldn't see me?" she asked Frank with an insistent note in her voice.

"Ellen, Ed said that it is no use. He said that you would understand, that everything had been explained to you."

It was clear to her that Frank was not enjoying the role that had been forced upon him. She didn't care. Frank wanted to get away. She wouldn't let him. Frank was a contact with Ed.

"He explained everything? He did, did he? He explained everything? He quoted some poems to me. What do I care about the poetry he recites to me. It doesn't explain anything."

"He said I should tell you that if you and he went on, you would both hate each other and destroy all the beauty of what had once been."

"Why?"

Frank didn't answer. Uneasy under her sharp eyes, he lit a cigarette.

"Where does Ed live?"

"I don't know."

"Didn't you ask him? I want to know where he lives."

"He wouldn't tell me."

She laughed at him sarcastically. Disquieted, he looked away so as not to meet her eyes.

"I had always thought that you were my friend, Frank, but I was wrong."

"I wouldn't say that, Ellen."

"Why not? Ed is your friend, and you don't even know his address. He wouldn't tell you his address because he's afraid you'd tell me. Frank, you think you are his friend, don't you?"

"Yes. Ellen, I feel badly about what has happened. If I could do anything, you know I would."

"Frank, do you know what he told me about you?"

He was blank-faced.

"He told me you were his chump."

Frank's face remained expressionless.

"I suppose you don't believe me."

"Ellen, I don't know what you mean."

"I mean just what I said. Frank, Ed isn't your friend. He always used to tell me that he was playing you for a chump."

"I wouldn't say that."

"You wouldn't? Well, if you want to let him treat you that way, it's none of my business. I'm just letting you know."

"Ellen, perhaps you're nervous. What you tell me doesn't at all sound like Ed."

"Oh, it doesn't? It doesn't? All right, you go ahead and do what you want to. Let him play you for a chump. If you do, it's your affair."

Frank was perplexed.

"You don't believe me? All right, but you'll learn some day."

"Ellen, I want you to know that I'd do anything I could to help you."

"Ed's afraid to see me. He turns you into his messenger boy. How do you like that—being Ed Lanson's messenger boy?"

"I'm not a messenger boy. I'm a friend of both of you."

"Yes, and he thinks your friendship for him is so staunch that you'll give me his address."

"Ellen, don't be sarcastic. That only makes everything worse."

"Makes what worse?"

"The situation between you and Ed."

"Frank, I'll tell you why I want to see him. Do you think it's for love? Love? Not at all. Do you think I could love anyone who acts the way he does to me? What do you think I am?"

"Ellen, of course, if something like this breaks up, the only thing to do is to look at it philosophically."

"Ed Lanson owes me money. I want my money back. That's why I want to see him. Frank, have you ever borrowed money from a girl?"

"No. I have a pretty good job and I'm doing well."

"Would you borrow money of a girl—her last cent?"

"Ellen, you know me. You know I wouldn't."

"Of course you wouldn't. You're a different kind of a person than Ed Lanson. Well, he borrowed a hundred dollars from me. Would you do that?"

"Ellen, I don't know anything about these matters. And I'm sure Ed will pay you back."

"Yes, he's breaking his arm paying me."

He looked at his watch.

"Frank, will you tell Ed that I want my money back?"

"Ellen, this is . . . embarrassing for me. I don't want to have either of you get sore at me."

"How can that happen? You're our friend. All I want you to do is to ask him to give me my money back."

"Ellen, I wouldn't take this so hard if I were you. It doesn't do any good to take it so hard."

"I'm not taking it hard. But if Ed Lanson thinks he can walk all over me, he has guessed wrong."

"I don't believe he thinks that."

"Oh, Frank, your loyalty is going to lead you into making a fool out of yourself."

"I don't think anyone is going to make a fool out of me."

"Well, I've warned you."

"I wish I could stay. But I have to meet a prospect and give

a demonstration. I'm late now," Frank said, picking up the
check and rising.

"Can't you call this prospect up? Stay, I want to talk to you,
Frank."

"I wish I could. He's waiting for me on a corner, so I can't."

Ellen got to her feet and glumly followed him out of the
tea room.

"Ellen, I'd like to take you wherever you're going, but I
have to hurry and meet this prospect."

"Frank, did Ed say anything about Catherine Anne?"

"Why, no, he didn't mention any girl's name?"

"Frank, will you telephone me tonight?"

"I have a date. Of course, I can telephone you. But I won't
see Ed."

"Telephone me."

"All right, I will. And, Ellen, I want you to know I'm your
friend."

He said good-bye to her, and she watched him get into his
Ford. He waved and was off. She laughed sarcastically.

She had undoubtedly made everything worse. Oh, she didn't
care. She didn't care what happened.

Frank was probably going to meet Ed now and would tell
him everything she had said.

It was such a glorious day. What good was the weather? Oh,
to be with Ed on days like this! No, she hated Ed. She just
wanted to get even with him. She wanted to teach him a lesson.
She wanted to pay him back in his own coin. And she wanted
to get her money back.

She knew that she was trying to fool herself. She loved Ed
and she wanted him.

II

Ellen returned to the parlor after speaking with Frank on
the telephone. Frank had kept his promise and called her, but
he'd given her a pep talk. He'd denied having seen Ed after
leaving her today. Had he told her the truth? And she was
afraid, too, that Frank would tell Ed what she'd said this after-

noon in the tea room. That might make everything worse. But she was justified in what she'd said and done. It was all over between them. She knew it was, and yet she couldn't give up hope.

She sat down with Gertrude.

"That was Frank," she said.

"Did he have anything to say?"

"Nothing."

They sat, looking away from one another. God, for years, she had thought always of—poor Gertrude. Was Gertrude now thinking—poor Ellen?

"Ellen," Gertrude said to break the silence. "Ellen, I never would have expected it to happen. Why, you and Ed seemed to be so suited to each other. Why, when you told me about it just now, you could have knocked me over with a feather."

Ellen thought that if she could truly in her heart look on herself as an object of pity, wallow in self-pity, it might be better for her. But she couldn't. Then why was she carrying on as she had been? She couldn't control what she did.

"I didn't expect it. Gertrude, have you seen Catherine Anne lately?"

"No, I haven't. I've been staying home. I haven't been seeing much of anybody. Mother hasn't been well."

"I wonder if Ed has gone back to her. If he has, that's the cream of the jest."

"I guess that men are all alike," Gertrude said with a sigh. Ellen didn't respond to this comment.

"Ellen, you have to be brave now."

"Gertrude, I wouldn't take Ed Lanson back if he came crawling to me on his knees. What concerns me is not to get him back. After what he's done to me, I don't want him."

Gertrude leaned forward in her chair, waiting for Ellen to go on.

"Ed likes to say that he's not a Christian," Ellen said.

"How sinful! I was always worried about that. He talks that way—well, almost sacrilegious. Why, he doesn't believe in God! Ellen, I think it's all for the best. Why, it would be dreadful to be married to an atheist. I think it's good it has happened."

Now, wasn't that a comforting thought?

"Ed used to say he's no Christian. He doesn't believe in forgiveness. Well, let me say that he will wish he did believe in forgiveness before I get through with him," Ellen said, moving about as she spoke.

"Ellen, I'd ignore him. Don't give him the satisfaction of knowing that you even give him a thought." Gertrude paused. "Men!" she added philosophically.

"Gertrude, I have a plan. I need your help."

"What is it?"

"I can't tell you right now."

Ellen noticed that Gertrude was disappointed.

"I want you to do me a favor. I want you to go to see Catherine Anne. Act as if it were just a visit, you know, for old time's sake. Try and find out if she is seeing Ed. And let me know what she says."

Gertrude didn't answer immediately.

"Well, all right, if you won't," Ellen said, shrugging her shoulders.

"I didn't say I wouldn't. It's . . ."

Gertrude stammered, not knowing what to say.

"All right, don't, then."

"Ellen, don't be angry with me."

"I'm not angry. But I did think you were my friend."

"I am. Honest I am. I just was thinking how I would do it. But I'm certain Catherine Anne will be close-mouthed."

"That's to be discovered. If she's seeing him, she'll give herself away in a hundred little ways. She'll be happy. She'll feel vindicated, justified. She'll let you know. Be sure of that. You can do it, and it won't be any trouble. You know that what you tell me is never going to go beyond us. And it's necessary for me to know about this for my plan."

"Ellen, can't you tell me your plan?"

"Gertrude, I would if I could. I can't—just now. But you'll be helping me, more, much more, than you think you are."

Why was she going on this way? She didn't have any plan. And she didn't need Gertrude's help. Except that she was eaten up with curiosity. She wanted to know if Ed had thrown her overboard for Catherine Anne. If he had!

Would Ed talk about her to Catherine Anne the same way he'd talked about Catherine Anne to her? If he did!

"Ellen, don't take it so hard. It isn't worth the candle," Gertrude said, seeing how Ellen was absorbed and wanting to be comforting and sympathetic.

"I'm not. I was thinking about my plan."

"I'm dying to know about it," Gertrude said eagerly.

"Trust me when I say that I can't tell you yet. If I could, I would."

"Ellen, you mustn't let it affect you. Show him by acting as if you were above him."

Ellen thought what silliness Gertrude was talking, what childishness.

"That's not the point. If he acted in a decent way, I would feel differently. You know me, Gertrude. I'm not the kind of a person who hangs onto a man's coat tails. I should have been perfectly willing to say that it was quits with a smile and wishes of good luck if he had only acted decently. But the way he sneaked off. Well, I'll make him pay for that."

Suddenly Ellen began to cry. Gertrude limped over to her and futilely patted her head.

"Ellen, don't cry. Ellen, you mustn't cry," Gertrude said, helpless, her words seeming to ring hollow.

"It's not that I'm crying over him. I'm just . . . oh, I hate him so!" Ellen said.

Ellen sobbed, and Gertrude sought to comfort her in vain.

III

Ellen was ashamed of herself. That she should have allowed herself to break down and cry before Gertrude Dorgan last night. What had she been doing these last days? Going to Gertrude, going to Frank Dolan, tramping the streets, trying to waylay Ed in front of the building where he worked, going to the Devormer offices, making a holy show of herself. If Ed knew all these things, he would have contempt for her. He knew some of them? What was he thinking?

Ellen pushed aside the eggs that had been placed before her. She drank only coffee. She had no appetite these days. She was losing weight. She was sleeping badly. Ed, the need to see him, filled her whole being. No matter what she tried to do, no matter how she tried to distract herself, she always came back to thinking of him. Would she go on like this for the rest of her life?

Why had this happened to her? This is what continued to puzzle and bewilder her. *Puzzle* and *bewilder*—what mild words! But why? God, why? What had she done? What did she lack? If she only knew. If only she could see him and really find out what had caused him to do this to her. If she could find out if it was another girl. If she could talk to him. See him!

She drank her coffee and left the table.

Another day! Another day of this same misery. She couldn't stand it. She couldn't go on. What was the use?

Chapter Forty-four

I

Ellen wandered about the Loop, dazed and sad. Once again she had waited in front of the building, hoping to see him, and once again she had failed. The noon hour crowd poured over the sidewalk, and the sight of so many people only made her feel the more lonesome. She felt that she was all alone in a world full of millions of people. All of these people went about their business, lived their lives, and here she was, passing them on the sidewalk, and they were not aware of what was eating into her heart. She saw laughing girls and became only the more sad, only the more lonesome. She had felt that she ought to eat, and she had gone into a restaurant and then, after ordering lunch, she had scarcely touched it. She walked over to Randolph and Michigan, and turned around and walked back toward State Street. A streetcar swung around from the little side street by the library and proceeded toward Wabash. What should she do? Oh, if Ed only knew what he had done to her? But Ed didn't know. Ed didn't care.

Ed didn't care!

She repeated these words to herself.

Even when he didn't know about it, even when it apparently did not concern him in the least, she was throwing herself away on him. Oh, was the game worth the candle?

No, no, a thousand times no.

Walking on, she didn't heed where she was going, or why. Without realizing it, she had returned to take up her post in front of the building.

II

"I must see Mr. Devormer. I'll only speak with him a minute."

"I'll inquire if he can see you," the girl at the desk said.

The girl went into an inner office. Ellen waited, hoping that Ed would walk in while she was here.

The girl came out of the inner office.

"In there," she said curtly, pointing.

Ellen walked meekly into Mr. Devormer's office. A pudgy, flashily dressed man in his thirties rose as she entered.

"Miss Rogers?"

"How do you do?" she said demurely. "I hope that you won't resent my coming to see you this way, Mr. Devormer."

"Not at all. Not at all. Please sit down."

Ellen sat down beside him, striving to look sweet, innocent, sad.

"Mr. Devormer, where is Ed Lanson?" she asked.

Instead of answering immediately, he observed her closely.

"Why, he's in the city."

"Is he still working for you?"

"Yes, of course."

"Does he come in often? I have to see him."

"No, he hasn't been coming to the office lately."

"Do you know about me?"

"No, I don't, Miss Rogers."

"Hasn't he ever told you? I was engaged to him."

"Of course. Yes, he did speak of you now and then. He spoke quite fondly of you."

"Mr. Devormer, I have to see him. He won't see me, and he won't answer. my messages."

Mr. Devormer glanced aside and out the window at an office building across the street. He turned back to Ellen and studied her.

"I don't know what to say to that, Miss Rogers. Of course, Ed works for me, but I have nothing to do with his personal affairs."

"I know you don't. I came to see you to ask you to help me. Oh, I must get help. I have to see him. I'm not trying to get him back if he doesn't want to come back to me. But I have to see him. I have to know why he acts this way, what has happened. If he will only tell me, that is all I ask."

"I don't know what to say, Miss Rogers. I don't know what I can do."

"Please help me, Mr. Devormer. Please."

"I should be delighted to help you, if I knew how. But what I can do in such a situation as this—I don't know. After all, I have no right to interfere in Ed's personal affairs. It's none of my business."

"I understand. But I must have help. Mr. Devormer, I am not chasing Ed. But he owes me money."

John Devormer didn't answer.

"I want my money."

"Of course, if you had a regular court order to garnishee his wages, I would be held. But otherwise I cannot do anything there."

"I don't want you to. I want you to help me. I must see Ed. What is his address?"

"He said he moved. I didn't get his new address. We don't have it here."

"You don't? And he works for you! Suppose you want to see him?"

"He calls us every day."

"Has he called you today?"

"Yes . . . yes."

"I suppose you think that I'm a nuisance. Oh, please don't, Mr. Devormer. If you knew how I felt, you wouldn't."

"Not at all. I am just sorry that I cannot help you. But in such personal situations a third party can do nothing."

"What can I do?" she asked him, simulating utter helplessness.

"Miss Rogers, I wish I could answer that question. Perhaps, if I knew you better, I could say something." He noticed that her legs were crossed and unobtrusively glanced at them. He looked back at her. "Yes, I wish I could help you. But what can I do?"

The telephone rang. Ellen smiled sweetly and sat while he

spoke to someone about an appointment for the next day. She wondered if it were Ed. Mr. Devormer didn't give any sign that it was. He hung up.

"That was a business call," he said, taking out a silver cigarette case.

He extended the case, and she took a cigarette. He took one. Leaning forward to light her cigarette, their eyes met and they both smiled. He leaned back in his chair.

"I suppose I am bothering you, keeping you from important business."

"Oh, no, no, not at all. Don't think of it, Miss Rogers."

"Just seeing you, Mr. Devormer, makes me feel better. Ed talked of you a lot. He always said nice things about you."

Devormer smiled again.

"Does he ever talk about me now?" Ellen asked.

"He doesn't talk to me much at all about his personal affairs. My relationship with him is purely a business one."

"I suppose I will get over feeling the way I do."

"Of course you will. You are a young and attractive girl, too attractive to allow such matters to cause you deep concern."

"I'm not really concerned any more. It was the shock of it. But I'm getting over it."

"Good. You should realize that you are young, attractive, and that you have the future ahead of you."

"I will. I was nervous when I came in here. I'm not nervous now. You have helped me more than you realize," she said, puffing at her cigarette.

"Well, I have done very little. If it has helped you, I am pleased."

"Oh, Mr. Devormer, you have."

"I feel like a drink. Miss Rogers, do you drink?" he asked, eyeing her.

"Not often. But I need one now. It would do me good."

Devormer got up, went to a corner, and pressed a button. A small bar swung into view. He got behind it.

"How cute!"

"I fixed this up here. Like it?"

"It's fetching."

"I just got in some real Scotch, from Canada."

"I'd love one."

He mixed the drinks, and he even had the ice to put in them.

He handed her a glass.

"Miss Rogers, I drink to . . . you."

"Thank you."

She tipped her glass to his.

They sat down again.

"Yes, I'm proud of my little bar there."

Ellen thought that he and Ed must have sat like this many times and drunk. Oh, would Ed come in? She wished he would walk right in.

She took a sip.

"Like it?"

She shook her head.

"Miss Rogers, of course it is none of my business, but I would like to say this to you. You are too charming a girl to worry."

"I won't. I was . . . it was a surprise. I didn't know why it happened. Ed just quit me out of a clear sky. The surprise is what bothered me."

"I know. These affairs cause a little concern at first. But they pass."

Ellen took another drink.

Suddenly she burst into tears, and Devormer went to her.

"Now, come, come!"

He patted her on the shoulders.

"I just can't help it. I'm not hurt. I don't know what it is."

Gently, he drew her out of her chair. He held her by the shoulders, looked at her, smiled.

"Now, with a face as pretty as yours, you mustn't spoil it with tears."

She gave him a weary smile.

"No, you mustn't."

She smiled again.

"I didn't mean to cry. And it isn't because I have lost Ed. I am glad to be free of him. It's . . . it's just the release of the tension I feel. Do you understand, Mr. Devormer?"

He nodded, still holding her by the shoulders. He gently embraced her. Ellen did not resist him. She felt that it was a kind of revenge on Ed. And she wanted only to forget. She let herself be drawn into his arms.

The door opened.

"Ed!" Ellen screamed.

"Excuse me. I didn't mean to intrude," Ed said; he turned and walked out.

Mr. Devormer was embarrassed. Ellen was stunned for a moment. She had seen Ed. He was outside. Why was she standing here? She hurried out of the room. The outer office was empty.

"Ed!" she called.

She turned.

"Where did he go?" she called to Mr. Devormer.

"I don't know," Devormer answered, ill at ease.

She ran out into the hallway.

"Ed! Ed!"

He wasn't in sight.

She pushed a button for the elevator. Waiting, she kept looking up and down the corridor nervously.

"Ed!"

The elevator stopped.

"Did a tall, handsome man, young, in a brown suit, just go down here—Mr. Lanson?" she asked.

"Can't prove it by me, girlie," the uniformed elevator man answered.

She stood motionless.

"Going down? I can't wait all day."

She stepped into the elevator, dazed.

She got out at the first floor and looked in the lobby. He wasn't there. She looked up and down the street. He wasn't there. She returned to go upstairs.

Now she had ruined her chances. If she saw him, she could explain.

She went up again. The girl wasn't in the outer office, and the door to Mr. Devormer's office was closed. She opened it, walked in, and found him drinking his Scotch.

"Did he come back?"

"No, he didn't."

"He didn't go down in the elevators. Where could he have gone?"

"I don't know. But sit down a moment."

"I must see him," she said. She ran out of the office.

"Ed! Ed!" she called in the corridor.

Where could she look?

She pushed the button for the elevator and waited for it anxiously. When it stopped, she got in.

Ed came out of the men's room near the Devormer offices. He hurried in to see John Devormer.

III

Ellen returned to the offices and found the girl back at her desk.

"I just went outside a minute. I have to see Mr. Devormer again."

Without answering her, the girl went inside. Ellen's hands shook as she waited. Her heart was palpitating.

The girl returned.

"Go ahead," she said curtly.

"Did you just see Mr. Lanson?" Ellen asked.

"No."

"He was here."

"I had to go away for a minute. I didn't see him," the girl said, contemptuous of Ellen.

Ellen went back to see Devormer.

"Did he come back?"

"No, he didn't."

"Where could he have gone?"

"I don't know. I was as surprised as you, Ellen."

Facing him, she now felt foolish.

"Ellen, I have to leave now on business. I would like to see you again. I want to talk to you."

She glanced around the office suspiciously. There was a door on the left which she hadn't noticed before.

"Where does that lead to?"

"It's a closet for my safe and some files."

"Is he in there?"

"He couldn't be. There's no room. Ellen, I have to go now to keep a business appointment. I'd like to see you again. And if you are going anywhere in my direction, I can drop you off in my cab."

"He didn't come back?" she asked.

"No. Don't you believe me?"

"Yes . . . yes. It was just . . . the surprise of his appearing just when he did."

They both smiled.

Devormer put on his hat and topcoat. He took Ellen by the arm and led her toward the outer door. She glanced back at the other door, but allowed him to take her out of the office.

IV

Ellen reread the letter she had received from Ed.

Dear Miss Rogers:

I am regretful that I so rudely interrupted your pastime this afternoon at my employer's office. Had I known that I would intrude in such a delicate situation, I naturally should have refrained from it. At all events, please excuse my gaucheness. It was accidental. I have of late received messages and notes from you, pleading with me to see you. I cannot believe in your pleas. I have evidence now that your sorrow is skin-deep, and that you fare well in life's game of hearts. You avow that you love me. But you do not find your love of me incompatible with falling into the arms of others. I draw the proper conclusions. You vow you love me. But you talk against me to my friends. I assume that greater love hath no woman. You find it not dishonorable to claim that I owe you money. I spent money on you, much money, more than the sum that you loaned me when you wanted me back from Washington. To come back to see you I sacrificed a job where I could have earned much more than the sum you loaned me. I shall repay that loan in due time when my circumstances permit. In the meantime, since you have decided to place our former relationship on the scales of utilitarianism and to measure it by the values of the cash register, so will I. You have set that precedent for me. I repeat—I have spent more money on you than you have on me. I gave you a ring when I did not have a job or any source of income. If you want to measure things by dollars and cents, so will I. You want back the money you loaned me. I want back my ring.

I have learned the measure of you these last days. My action was a test of you. I loved you once. I might have still loved you. But you did not meet the test. You showed your true character when I tested you. You find it easy to go from one man's arms to those of another. You slander me to my friends. You try to spoil my friendship with others. You bite like a snake. Don't tell me by letters that you love me. Please don't make me laugh. Had you loved me, you would have acted differently. You have torn away the last shred of illusion I had concerning you. I hope that you are satisfied.

You will get your filthy money.

Farewell. Good-bye, illusions turned to ashes.

E. Lanson.

She put the letter in a dresser drawer. Pale and shaken, she looked at herself in the mirror. Her eyes were red from crying.

She sat down at a little desk in her room to write to Ed. She wrote and rewrote and tore up sheet after sheet of paper. She sat there, pen in hand, her eyes blank. She went to the dresser and got out his letter. She reread it.

She wept.

Chapter Forty-five

I

"You say you could learn nothing from Catherine Anne?"

Gertrude nodded her head negatively.

"Was she happy? What about the way she acted, the way she seemed? If Ed had come back to her and was seeing her, she would probably be so happy that you couldn't mistake a change in her."

"I couldn't say."

Ellen reflected a moment. Had she let herself get into the position where Gertrude might be hiding information from her? Oh, God, why had she done all this? Why, when she had received the first letter from him, ending everything, why hadn't she been strong and hard, crushed the love within her, not said a word to anyone, met the world with a face of stone? Why hadn't she been able to do it? Now it was too late. What was being said about Ellen Rogers among the people she knew? There were so many, too, who had wanted to see her ride to a fall. They must be gloating.

"Are you telling me the truth, Gertrude?"

"Honest, Ellen, you know I wouldn't lie to you," Gertrude said with an injured look.

"What's the difference who he's seen. Why should I care? I'm through with him and I don't care. I'm blotting him out of my mind forever."

"Ellen, that's what you should do."

"I've done it."

"Does your father know?"

"Yes, he senses something. I haven't told him much."

"I'll bet he'd like to get his hands on Ed."

Ellen shrugged her shoulders.

She wanted to get rid of Gertrude. She disliked Gertrude now. Why had she talked to her as she had, asked her to go spying on Catherine Anne? What good did it do? Look at the girl, ugly as sin, doting on gossip, living by gossiping about the love and the unhappiness of other girls. She hated this lame girl.

"Listen, Gertrude, I have to go out. I have a date."

Gertrude got up, meek and apologetic.

"Of course, I won't keep you. I'm glad you have a date, Ellen. That's what you ought to do—show him that you aren't sitting home and pining away to a shadow."

"I'll call you," Ellen said.

She followed Gertrude to the door.

"Ellen, now don't you pine over that Ed. You go out and have a good time."

Ellen closed the door after Gertrude and returned to the parlor.

She wished she could undo everything she had done since Ed had sent her his first terrible letter. It wasn't enough that she should suffer and feel so miserable. She had to wear her heart on her sleeve. She had had to do things which resulted in everybody knowing.

What was the matter with her that she should have let herself get into the position she was in? Why, oh, why couldn't things be done differently? Once you did something, there was no erasing it. And she so wanted to take an eraser to her life, so that she could start fresh. There was one eraser you could always take. Then, after you did take it, the blackboard was really black. Was she afraid? Afraid? Afraid of what?

Suppose there were a Hell, and she would go there and burn in fire, would that be any worse, would that be any more miserable than the life she had led the last few weeks? Could it be? And suppose there were no Hell, there were nothing but sleep. She would go to sleep. Ed had sometimes talked about death as if it were a sleep without dreams.

She would be doing this for love.

Love!

She laughed to herself ironically, a laugh full of suppressed hysteria.

Yes, she would wipe the mess away clean. But what about her father? He would do anything in the world for her. If she did this, he would be broken. He would be more than unhappy. But could she sacrifice herself for Father even though this would be so terrible for him to bear? Could she go on with this misery gripping her? At times since Ed had left her, she had feared that she was going crazy. Last night, after finally falling asleep, she had awakened in utter terror, alone, with her heart pounding. She had been having some terrible dream. She could not even remember the dream now. And she had tossed in bed for what seemed like hours. Was this going to go on night after night? Should she go on like this just because of Father?

How would Ed take the news? Would it phase him? What would he think? Would he be sorry?

What would others say? The nuns at Saint Paul's? Gertrude? Catherine Anne? Would everyone she knew say something about poor Ellen Rogers?

She didn't want anyone to say—*poor Ellen Rogers.*

She wasn't poor Ellen Rogers.

No, she wasn't.

How many people would really guess or learn why she had done it?

Oh, then, what would anything matter, anything at all? She would be sleeping in peace, forever.

She had been happy. But she had let happiness slip through her fingers.

The telephone rang. She rushed to it.

II

Ellen dressed hurriedly but carefully. She knew why John Devormer had just called her and asked her if she were doing anything. She felt that she would regret what she was doing. But now, what did it matter? What was one more regret? For a few minutes she might forget. She might feel as if all of herself was going out of herself in a few moments. She would ease, drive away, defeat these thoughts that turned and twisted inside of her.

Would he tell Ed? What difference did it make? Ed wouldn't be jealous. Or would he? Was Ed just like other men? Would Ed and John Devormer compare notes about her? Oh, God, God, she wanted to stop this!

An eraser.

She slipped into her new navy blue woolen dress and sat down before her dresser to comb her hair and make up.

He would be here soon. She would be dressed up. She would look very attractive. She would forget. Tomorrow? Oh, the hell with tomorrow! All that she wanted to do was to forget. For tonight she would forget.

When the bell rang she was ready.

III

It was late, and the night was cold. Ellen heard the wind soughing across the street in the shrubbery. John Devormer followed her out of the car into the hallway. They were languid, and both of them yawned. Ellen turned mechanically to him and waited for him to embrace her and kiss her good night.

"Now what do we say?" Ellen said.

"Ellen, you are a wonderful girl. Ellen, forget it all. You have your life to live."

"Yes, I've started living it."

He hugged her again.

"Good night, John," she said spiritlessly.

"You don't feel blue now, do you?"

"How could I? After all, I'm tired. Aren't you?"

His smile quickly turned into a yawn.

"Well, good night."

"Good night," she said.

"I'll telephone you."

"You know the number."

She watched him get into his automobile. She heard the motor sputter. She saw him wave. The car was gone.

She trudged upstairs. Her forgetfulness was gone. She had lain in his arms and tried to forget. She had closed her eyes in his arms and she had tried to think that it was not John Devormer, but that it was Ed.

She let herself in quietly and tiptoed to her room. Automatically, she undressed, put on a nightgown, went to bed, lay there, hoping now to sleep. She was so tired that she couldn't sleep. She had gone to his apartment. How had he felt? Were men constructed so differently from women that it didn't matter if it were one woman or another woman? This man didn't love her. She didn't love this man.

She had talked with him about Ed, too. He had been guarded, but he didn't really like Ed. He had said that Ed was a crackerjack salesman and making money for him. He'd told her that Ed was not stable. He'd advised her to forget Ed, not to allow him to ruin her life. Ruin what?

Alone in the darkness, she smiled. Ruin her life?

Many nights she had lain in this bed and wept. She couldn't cry now. She had scarcely the emotional energy to feel sad. She felt empty, depleted.

Should she go on doing what she had done tonight? Why? It did not make her really forget.

This man had not treated her badly. But she felt nothing, nothing as far as he was concerned. She had gone to him, she imagined, just as some people perhaps go to narcotics. Being with him was a substitute for sleep. It was an eraser used for a few moments.

She had thought that she was taking a kind of revenge on Ed. What revenge was it?

She just felt dreary, terribly dreary. After it was all over, she had been disgusted. She was disgusted now, but too tired to feel her disgust strongly.

She turned over on her side.

John Devormer had told her what a beautiful body she had. For a moment she had been pleased. For what was her beautiful body? Why had she been given it? Was she any happier with her beautiful body than Gertrude Dorgan was with an ugly body?

Now she wanted that body that men told her was beautiful, she wanted that body to feel nothing, to sleep. She just wanted whatever it was inside of that body that made her herself, she just wanted that to sleep, to sleep without even dreaming.

Ed appeared in her mind, smiling, but not saying a word. He grew vague, as if he were fading from her mind. She drowsed into sleep, and the wind flapped the curtain of her bedroom window.

SECTION SIX

Chapter Forty-six

I

"Catherine Anne, you must think that I'm a rotter."

"Edmond, please don't talk that way. Don't run yourself down. You know I don't think that. How could I?" Catherine Anne said, smiling sweetly and understandingly.

Ed and Catherine Anne sat in her living room, a large and pleasant one on the ground floor of a two-story house at Forty-eighth and Kimbark which her parents owned. Tea things were spread before them on a small table. Outside, it was slowly beginning to grow dark.

"I did treat you shabbily. You must forgive me. I don't usually ask forgiveness."

"Please don't." She smiled. "It doesn't befit . . . Hellfire."

"What happened to me is explicable. I was infatuated."

Catherine Anne poured more tea for herself and Ed. She put sugar and a slice of lemon in his cup and handed it to him. He stirred the tea.

"Yes, I was infatuated."

"Ellen Rogers is a very attractive girl."

"I have nothing against her. She doesn't know that I am doing her a favor."

"Maybe she cares for you, Edmond."

"It's more complicated than that. I think I have reason to believe that she doesn't care quite as much as she lets on. She has been going out with my boss. She has found means of reconciling how much she cares for me with being able to care for other men."

Catherine Anne showed uneasiness.

"Edmond, I don't know what to say about these matters."

"Ellen couldn't bring me that element which I most need in my life—stability."

Ed watched Catherine Anne closely. She was poised. Her expression was tender, the expression which he had often seen on the face of girls when he talked to them in a way which pleased and flattered them, promised them something. What was that promise? Need he ask himself that question? It was himself.

"I need stability."

"Edmond, you are a romantic."

He frowned.

"You're not angry because I say that?" she asked.

"I was thinking of a book I just read in the library. I don't know how I happened to read it, but I was fed up the other day with selling, talking about direct-by-mail, newspapers, billboards, the way to increase the sale of paints, the number of guests in hotels, the best way to add to the volume of the sale of tacks, brushes, shoes, guns, mittens, and stationery, and all that. I dropped up at the Crerar Library and just looked through the B files. I saw the name Babbitt and drew out a book, *Rousseau and Romanticism,* by Irving Babbitt."

"Oh, one of my history profs told us to read that book. I started it. It was dry."

"Well, I'm not a romantic, not precisely that."

"Edmond, you are a romantic. That is what is so charming about you."

"Babbitt says that a realist is a romantic on all fours. He doesn't understand realism. I'm a realist."

Catherine Anne took a sip of tea.

"Yes, I am a realist. Why do I do certain things which seem romantic? I'm so realistic that I have a measure of the realities of the world. I snap my fingers at most of them."

"Edmond, but what's the use?"

"What's the use of what?" Ed asked, lighting a cigarette.

"Oh, of hitting your head against stone walls."

"When I do, the stone walls break." He smiled charmingly. "That's conceited of me."

It was warm and pleasant in the room. She poured herself more tea.

"You've known Ellen a long time?" Ed asked.

"Yes, but not well. She never seemed to like me."

"I don't think she likes any other girls."

"Well, of course, she is so beautiful. She always was rather lofty. Even in second-year high school she was kind of wild and reckless. She was smart in school when she wanted to be. She got things quickly if she took the trouble. But she didn't like to take the trouble. But, oh, then we were all kids. I didn't see her much after we graduated. I don't think I have seen her since last spring that day, you know."

Ed smiled.

"When I discussed Nietzsche with your philosopher friend."

"John is a smart boy, Ed."

"He's a philosopher," Ed said contemptuously.

"He is intelligent and earnest."

"You say that Ellen was always reckless?"

"Yes. I guess she and I are different types."

Ed smiled knowingly.

"Do you know what I have been doing of late? I've been reading as much as I can in the library. I've been so happy and contented spending night after night in the library. I've read a great deal and I've been happy. You must come with me some nights to the library and we'll read."

"I'd love to."

"Books stabilize me. I need stabilizing influences. And Ellen couldn't give me that. Actually, it's her vanity, her pride more than anything else that is causing her to chase me the way she does. Had she been the one who used the hatchet instead of me, she would feel differently."

"Ellen used to be very proud. Gertrude Dorgan came to see me and Gertrude told me Ellen is very upset."

"Gertrude Dorgan! That! She sent her to spy on you."

"Poor Gertrude hasn't anything else to do in life. Poor thing, she lives on such tidbits of other people's lives."

"Make a female ugly and she is a social jackal."

"She's a drab thing. I was sure that she would carry anything I said back to Ellen. And I don't want to have any trouble with Ellen."

"Spying on me indirectly, disgusting!"

During a pause in their conversation, Ed lit another cigarette.

"When this all happened, she taught me what she is, going to my office, haunting the building. The elevator men tell me about her. They have gotten to know her."

"Maybe if you saw her?"

"I won't. I shan't give her the satisfaction. What's the use? She will weep on my shoulder. She will play the martyr. I don't like to see people play the martyr."

Catherine Anne's lips traced a very thin, apologetic smile.

"I haven't been unfair to her. What does she want of me? My soul?"

Catherine Anne quickly erased an unhappy expression from her face.

"You believe in a soul. You still go to mass."

"Edmond, let's not argue about religion. I have faith."

"All right, we'll call a truce. But remember, it's a truce."

"Maybe I am weak. But I'm me."

"I wouldn't want you to be anything else but 'me.' "

He slouched in his chair and drained his cup of tea.

"Edmond, do you want more tea?"

"No, thanks. I'm not a strong tea drinker."

They laughed.

"It's awfully pleasant here, Catherine Anne."

"Is it?"

"It's too pleasant. I couldn't bear it to be so pleasant."

"Why?"

"It can be stifling. Mother and Father make it as pleasant as they can for me at home. That's when I live home. But it stifles me."

"Maybe it's a stabilizing influence."

"You're too smart. You shouldn't trip me up that way."

"Edmond, I think that a stabilizing influence is good. Don't think I'm trying to give you . . . advice. I know you don't like to be advised. But, after all, don't we need stability to do anything?"

"Yes. But then we have to have an aim. Stability for what? To do what? My motto is a yea, a nay, a straight line, and a goal." He smiled. "The whole question is the goal. Of course, I am going to write my book now."

"I think you could be a wonderful writer."

"That flatters me, but I can't. I need concentration, stability, and then, what is there for me to say?"

"Edmond, you always have so much to say. You talk so interestingly."

"I can't be satisfied with just anything. If I write my book, it has to be original. I wouldn't write a book unless it could be profound."

"Well, you can try."

"I won't try anything unless I am certain I can do it. I won't be licked in anything. I would rather be Caesar in a village than second fiddler in Rome." He smiled condescendingly. "But I don't think I'll stop with being Caesar in a little village."

"Neither do I, Edmond. I have faith in you."

"Catherine Anne, you're an angel." He paused, seemingly embarrassed. "And I want to mention something. I'm going to pay you back that money."

"It's not important."

"I was so infatuated. Well, we live and learn. But what a platitude that is. Is Lanson reduced to platitudes?" He squashed his cigarette. "I don't know what to do. I feel the old wanderlust. That's why I say I need a stabilizing influence. Is the wanderlust good for me?"

"Edmond, you're not going to give up this job you have?"

"My life has been a matter of giving up jobs."

"But, Edmond, don't be foolish."

"Folly to the world is often the highest wisdom."

"Yes, you always say things like that. But then you tell me

how lonesome it is being alone in a strange town, hungry, making the fight all over again to get a fresh start."

"What are obstacles? That which must be surmounted. Ellen is making the job more unpalatable for me than even the businessmen are. I am fed up with her haunting my place of business. Now, to cap the climax, she takes up with John Devormer."

"Is it serious?"

"Nothing could really be serious with him except those red and black figures in his books. He feels a little guilty now when he sees me because of Ellen. Well, hell hath no fury . . ."

"Edmond, honestly, don't you think that maybe she does care for you, and maybe if you saw her . . . ?"

"That won't do any good." He looked out the window and exclaimed emphatically, "My God!"

Catherine Anne was startled.

"There she is. Don't let her in."

"Maybe it's better to see her. She'll come back if I don't, and it will make her suspicious. You go in the back if you don't want to see her."

They snatched up the tea things and a filled ash tray and hurried to the kitchen with these.

"Edmond, you stay in the dining room and close the folding doors, please."

"I will. But bring my hat and coat out from the hall before you let her in."

The bell rang. Catherine Anne got Ed's coat and hat and brought them to the rear of the house. She answered the door bell.

II

"I suppose you are surprised to see me, Catherine Anne."

"Well, we haven't seen much of each other, Ellen, since graduation."

"I know it. It's a shame that things happen this way. I meant to see you, and, oh, you know how it is."

"I've been busy, too, at school."

"I'm thinking of going to the University for the next term. How is it?"

"I like it. It's a good school."

"Father is after me to go. I didn't feel as if I wanted any more of school after Saint Paul's. But maybe I might try it now."

"Why don't you?"

"Do you think I'd like it at the University?" Ellen asked.

"I think so. Some of the courses are pretty stiff, and naturally it's harder than it was at Saint Paul's. But I think you'd like it."

"I can't make up my mind. But perhaps I'll go."

"And besides the studies, you can have a good time there."

"I wouldn't go to school just to have a good time. Catherine Anne, you haven't seen me often and we haven't had any serious talks since Saint Paul's. I'm a different person now from what I used to be."

"I suppose we've all changed. We're all older."

"I am. The experiences I've had since I was at Saint Paul's have caused me to do a great deal of thinking. I'm a different person now. That is why I am asking you about the University. I'm thinking of studying seriously. Of course, I wasn't very serious at Saint Paul's."

"I don't think any of us were very serious then. We were just kids."

"We were children then. Well, I'm not a child any more."

Catherine Anne toyed with a bracelet she was wearing.

"Would you like some tea or something, Ellen? I can make some for you."

"No, no, thanks. I just came to see you, hoping that I'd find you in. I wanted to talk. We never did happen to get to be friends in school. We didn't quite move in exactly the same set."

"I can make you some tea if you would like it, Ellen."

"No, no, please don't. Catherine Anne, did you hear about Ed and me?"

"No, what do you mean?"

"We broke up."

"Is it serious?"

"Yes. It's final. All bridges are burned."

"I'm sorry to hear that."

Was Catherine Anne lying to her?

"You hadn't heard of it?"

Ellen remembered that Gertrude had told her she'd told Catherine Anne.

"What am I thinking about? I did hear about it. From someone. I didn't hear much about it, though."

"You haven't seen Ed?"

"No, not in some time."

"It's for the best. Of course, such things are a surprise. But it's for the best."

"I don't know what to say. No third person can say much about such things."

"You know Ed. It was an experience to know him."

Catherine Anne nodded, her face noncommittal.

"It's a costly experience, but it's worth the cost."

"Edmond's intelligent."

"Yes, remember the discussion he had with your friend last spring?"

"With John Delafield. It was interesting."

"It was a bit over my head."

"Mine, too, because I haven't taken many courses in philosophy, and in the ones I did take, I only got C's."

"I'm seriously thinking of taking courses in philosophy at the University. I learned a lot about philosophy from Ed."

Neither girl spoke for a minute.

"Catherine Anne, what do you think of Ed?"

"He's intelligent. I think he will go a long way in the world."

"Yes, he will. He needs someone to inspire him, though. He's so changeable. One minute he is so happy. The next minute he changes."

"We're all a little bit like that."

"He's difficult. You know, he gets into fights and changes

his mind all the time. I like him. I'm fond of him, but he's trying."

Catherine Anne didn't respond when Ellen paused. She would not allow Ellen to draw her out.

"I'm glad it's over. I couldn't have made a go of it with him. I would be walking in the park with him, and suddenly he would curse the wind and tell me he didn't approve of the wind. I never heard anybody talk like that. He's very trying. It was an experience to know him. I learned a lot. But I'm just as pleased that it's over. I would rather go with another kind of boy. And marry him? Well, he wanted to marry me. He did all of the rushing. If we had gotten married, it would have been a mistake, at least, it would have been a mistake on my part."

"Of course, if you feel that way . . ."

"I do. Decidedly. Catherine Anne, you know I met Ed when he was out with you. I do hope you didn't feel angry with me. I didn't take him away from you. He rushed me. I must admit that I was almost swept off my feet, but those things happen to one, and one gets over them. But I have been meaning to see you and talk to you for a long time. I didn't want you to think that I had designed anything."

"Why, Ellen! I never thought that. I used to go out with Edmond sometimes, but it wasn't . . . well, exactly serious."

"You know, Catherine Anne, when a situation of that kind arises, some girls become frightfully jealous. They think another girl is designing. Well, I wasn't designing. I wanted you to know it. Ed Lanson rushed me."

Ellen waited for Catherine Anne to speak. Catherine Anne said nothing.

"He's too fickle. If I were a different kind of a girl, I should have felt differently at some of the things he did. He had a girl while he was in Washington. I found that out. And when I did, I realized that he was not a person to take seriously. He was awfully upset. I wouldn't tell this to anyone else. But since you know him, I'll tell you."

"I don't like to hear secrets like that."

"It's not exactly a secret. After I found out, I thought that I shouldn't take my engagement to him seriously. So when he telephoned me, I was busy and wouldn't see him. He carried on foolishly, very melodramatically. Do you know, except for me, for my rushing down to see him one night, he would have committed suicide?"

Catherine Anne was surprised and speechless.

"Ellen, I'd rather not talk about it. It's none of my business, you know."

"I just thought that I'd tell you. Yes, he's too trying for a girl with any sense. I suppose you didn't know him well enough to meet with that side of his character."

"I'm sorry I can't ask you to stay longer, but I have to go out myself. I have a date, Ellen."

"I have also. I just thought . . ."

Ed quietly stepped into the parlor. Catherine Anne saw him and she became transfixed, rigidly staring at him like one who has been hypnotized. Seeing the change in Catherine Anne, Ellen turned. She saw Ed standing with arms folded, lips curled in a supreme attempt at a Mephistophelean, sardonic sneer.

"Ed! Ed!"

"Don't call me by my first name."

Ellen rose excitedly and turned accusingly to Catherine Anne.

"You had him here listening to me through the keyhole."

"Shut up!" Ed commanded.

"Ellen, this is my home. Will you please leave it?"

"I'll leave when I am ready."

Ellen swung around toward Ed.

"You heard what I said."

"It doesn't surprise me to hear you lie."

"Lie! Lie! I lied? I suppose I didn't save you from jumping out of a window. I suppose you didn't take a razor to cut your throat. If I had any sense, I'd have let you do it. Ed Lanson, when I saved you from ridding the world of your presence— that was the greatest mistake of my life."

"I don't discuss such matters with persons like you. It's beneath me."

"Ed Lanson, after the way you've treated me, nothing is beneath you."

"Ellen, please leave."

"I shall."

Catherine Anne was very pale.

"Catherine Anne, I regret that this creature has subjected you to this scene. If she weren't a woman, I'd throw her out for you."

"You don't hit women. You just fleece them. And what did you use to say to me about Catherine Anne? You called her a martyr. You said you couldn't stand martyrdom. Well, I'll be no martyr for you, Ed Lanson. There's your martyr. Go back to her." She turned to Catherine Anne. "And there's your intelligent Edmond. I hope he costs you less than he did me."

"Goddam you!" Ed shouted.

"Why don't you hit me? Tee off on me, now. Tell me to freeze my teeth and give my tongue a sleigh ride. Oh, Ed Lanson, you thought you were going to make a door mat out of me. Well, this time you called the wrong number. There's the type to be your door mat, your adoring Félise. Why don't you quote a poem for both of us? A poem about love. Swinburne."

Catherine Anne twitched nervously.

Ed stepped forward and grabbed Ellen. She flung her head back in a proud and defiant challenge and firmly held her eyes upon him.

Ed released her. He relaxed his clenched fists.

"I wouldn't soil my hands."

Ellen laughed.

"And now, I am going. You may have your Romeo, Catherine Anne. I give him to you. On a platter," Ellen said; she marched out of the room.

Ed followed her. As she was putting her coat on, he made as if to spit at her.

"That's a brave gesture," she said.

"You bitch, you'll pay for this. You scurvy alley cat."

"Oh, what beautiful poetry. Write a poem with those words and call it *Félise*. The sweetest name."

Ellen pinned him with her eyes for a moment. She turned her back on him and quietly left.

III

Ellen shook and trembled. What had she done? Why had she done it?

Darkness was rapidly covering Kimbark Avenue. Ellen remained out of sight of Catherine Anne's parlor window. What was Ed saying? What was Ed saying about her to Catherine Anne? Now there was no hope. She had thrown away her last chance. She had gone to Catherine Anne's in order to pump her. Talking to Catherine Anne, her tongue had run away with her. And then, when Ed had appeared, she had lost all control.

It had been good for him after the shameless way he had treated her. She hated that man.

She hated him, and here she was, waiting for him to come out of Catherine Anne's house.

Why didn't she go home? Do something. Go sleep with John Devormer, anybody. Drink. Forget. Get away from him. She had won a victory over him, and here she was, destroying the fruits of her victory.

I can't help myself. I can't help myself. I can't help myself.

She took out her handkerchief and dried her eyes. A passing woman gaped at her.

Ed would never forgive her. She was afraid of what he would do. No, she wasn't. Let him do what he wanted.

She walked a few paces and then stopped in order not to pass before Catherine Anne's window.

What was the use of seeing him now? Could she ever win him back after this scene?

Why should she want him back? She had turned the tables on him. Now, she could say that she was the victor over Ed

Lanson. Could any other girl say that? She had paid him back in full for all that he had done to her these past few weeks.

Ellen took off her glove and looked at her engagement ring. She cried again.

"What's the matter, Miss?"

With a tear-stained face, she looked up at a middle-aged man.

"Nothing."

"Has something happened to you? Can I help you, Miss?"

"No, you can't help me."

The man walked on. She paced back and forth over a small area of sidewalk, ignoring passing strangers who glanced at her with curiosity.

Catherine Anne's parlor was still lit. Ed was still there. Well, he would have to use all of his charm now to explain to Catherine Anne. Catherine Anne must hate her. Oh, what Ed had said about Catherine Anne was so true. She was a martyr. Well, he could never tell Catherine Anne or any other girl that Ellen Rogers was a martyr.

Oh, why had all this had to happen?

Oh, what a dreadful victory she had won!

Now, at last, she had come to understand what love was. Now she knew all she needed to know of love. The world told one only lies about love.

She became suddenly alert and dismissed her reflections. Catherine Anne's parlor light had gone out.

She saw Ed coming down the steps. She ran forward.

"Ed, Ed, I've got to talk to you."

Ed turned to her, surprised.

"You did all the talking you will ever do to me," he said.

"Ed, please, I have to talk to you."

He sneered at her. He turned his back and walked away.

"Ed! Ed!" she called after him.

She caught up to him.

"You've got to talk to me. I'm having a baby."

"If John Devormer doesn't know about that, the neighborhood does. For all I know, the marine corps might be the father of your bastard."

"Ed, you owe it to me."

"Hire a lawyer and sue me."

"I'll scream and make a holy show of you if you don't come with me."

"Scream, for all I care. My ears aren't sensitive. I was around you too long to have sensitive ears."

He strode on.

"Ed Lanson!" she called loudly.

Ed started to run. Ellen pursued him. She fell on the sidewalk. He disappeared around the corner. Getting up, her knees stung. She didn't bother about them. She hurried around the corner. He was not in sight. She ran breathlessly down Forty-eighth Street, but he had disappeared. She halted, out of breath. She looked at her knees. Her stockings were torn, and her knees were bleeding and smarted.

She walked on slowly, crying, heedless of all who stared at her.

She kept asking herself what could she do, what could she do?

Chapter Forty-seven

I

"I see you had your hair fixed up today."

"Yes, Father, I just had it washed and set," Ellen answered lifelessly.

"Ellen, are you all right?"

"Yes, Father," she said mechanically.

Her home had never seemed more gloomy than it did at this moment while she and her father were eating supper.

A long silence pulsed between them.

"How are you feeling?" he asked.

"I'm all right."

"You and Ed, you are really busted up, for good?"

"Father, I don't want to talk about it."

"He's no good. I always felt that he wasn't any good. I never trusted him."

Ellen was impassive.

"Ellen, why don't you start at the University next term?"

"I'll think about it."

The entire universe became like a stream which poured only misery, gloom, unhappiness, frustration, into this dining room.

"He wasn't your type, Ellen."

She continued to eat automatically.

"Ellen, you haven't been acting . . . like yourself."

"I'm all right."

"Ellen, I want you always to know that you can come to me. If anything is wrong, you know you can come to me."

She smiled at him sadly.

"Ellen, don't take it so hard. It's all for the best. You were too good for him. He's not stable. Always going off on some

new thing, never settling down to one thing. A young fellow
like that can never amount to anything in this man's world."

"What difference does it make?"

"Well, it does make a difference."

The room seemed stifling, oppressed with such gloom.

"Ellen, the worst tragedy that can happen in this life is to
marry the wrong person. That's why it's for the best."

"Father, that doesn't affect me now. It's all over."

"Yes, it's for the best. You just want to forget, dance, see
your girl friends, have a good time. I'm terribly busy right now,
but when things slacken a bit, we'll go away together. I need
a vacation. We could go South. We could spend the holidays
this year in Florida."

Ellen shook her head up and down, and gave him a strained
smile.

"Ellen, I never told you this. I didn't want you to know it.
But now you are old enough to know." He was embarrassed
and talked haltingly, with uneven emphasis. "Ellen, your
mother made me unhappy. She was not always a good wife . . .
you know what I mean. . . . I never left her, because of you.
I was very unhappy. Ellen, I know what I'm talking about.
It's best for these things to break up in the beginning. Not
later."

"I know that. I know."

"I feel that I had to tell you this—about your mother. You
know what I mean. She didn't act like a wife to me. I made a
mistake in marrying her. Ellen, it's an awful thing to make a
mistake in marrying the wrong person, marrying anyone who
isn't good enough for you. You mustn't feel bad about that
fellow. He showed you his true colors. You should be happy
you learned in time."

She shook her head in mechanical affirmation.

"Ellen, there's nothing the matter with you? Nothing
wrong? You're all right. You aren't in any . . . trouble?" he
asked in alarm.

"No, I'm not a child. I'm all right."

The father listlessly went on eating.

"Ellen, did that fellow—"

"Oh, please let's drop it. I'm all right," she quickly interrupted.

"If I was sure he did anything to you . . ." He clenched his fists. "I'd kill him."

"You don't have to worry."

"Something ought to be done about fellows like that. They're no good."

She shrugged her shoulders.

"Ellen, you used to have lots of parties and have your friends over. Why don't you have some parties? They were all fine young people. You never have them to the house any more."

"I will."

They finished supper.

"Come and sit on my lap."

She obeyed, listless.

"Whose girl are you?"

"Father's."

"Whose girl will you always be?"

"Yours."

She kissed his forehead and slipped off his lap.

"What are you going to do tonight?"

She was walking away from him and didn't hear what he had said.

"Let's you and I go to a movie."

"I have to see a girl friend. Gertrude Dorgan. I'm going over to her house."

He was disappointed.

"Well, be home early. You need sleep."

"I'll get sleep."

She left the dining room. He sat at the table, a bewildered old man.

II

She looked radiant. She wore her new black velvet dress, and it covered her sleekly, emphasizing every curve and line of her slender figure. She had used rouge, face powder, mascara. She

had penciled her eyebrows. She had sat at her dresser and prepared herself as if for a rite, or as if she were going out with
someone whom she wanted to think of her as very beautiful.

Now she walked through Jackson Park alone. It was a dark
night. Shadows slept peacefully on the dead grass and the gravel
path around the golf course which she took. The wind drummed
in the bare trees. The wind in the park was something that
belonged in her life. For years, she had heard it, in summer,
autumn, winter, spring. It was full of her own moods, and
her own moods were in the winds that blew off Lake Michigan
and through the trees and shrubbery of Jackson Park. It was
part of her life, this wind. It had laughed when she was happy:
it had moaned and shrieked when she was sad. It was part of
her memory of Ed. He had railed and shaken his fist at it on
that glorious day last spring. It had been their wind then. It was
now her wind. And it was singing a funeral song for her.

She was all alone now, isolated from the entire world. But
her gait was resolute. She puffed on a cigarette. For two days
she had thought about what she was going to do. Two days
ago she had seen Ed at Catherine Anne's. She had done one
more foolish thing. She had gone to see Ed's mother. Mrs. Lanson was a lovely woman. But what had it accomplished? Nothing. She had talked to John Devormer on the telephone. Ed
had quit his job and gone away. Gone away. Ed had gone away.

Tonight there had been moments when she felt sorry for
her father. He was old. He would not live an awful long time,
anyway. Poor Father! But he didn't understand. At supper he
had told her about her Mother. Had her Mother been like her?
Did she take after her Mother? She had seen pictures of Mother.
Mother had been beautiful. Mother was looking down at her.
No, Mother was no more. Ed was no more. He was alive. He
was living somewhere at this moment. But he was alive no
more for her.

Ellen got gravel in her shoes. But she did not bother to sit
down on a bench, remove her shoes, and empty the gravel.
What difference did it make?

Just quietly, without any fuss, she was going to settle everything. She was not going to do it with a splash. No sensationalism and no notes left behind.

Was she afraid?

She puffed at her cigarette.

Silly question.

The time for thinking was over. The time for feeling sorry was over. She didn't want anything more now.

Ed?

She couldn't have Ed. If she had gotten him back, it would only have been for a little while. She was not angry with him. She did not hate Ed. She loved him. She had loved him. Now there was no love in her. No, no love.

She lit another cigarette.

There was no love in the wind, was there? There was no love in Lake Michigan. Was there love in a stone? Was there love in her?

She laughed hysterically.

People would ask all kinds of questions. They would be sorry. They would say that she was so young, such a beautiful girl, with everything to look forward to.

She walked on in an even, steady gait, swinging her arms, puffing on her cigarette.

Yes, the time for thinking was over.

She and Ed had strolled along this same path. They had made love on some of these benches. They had listened to this wind in some of its changing moods.

Tonight, Father had told her that she needed sleep. She did. She needed sleep. She was going to take what she needed. Sleep. Sleep. She was going to sleep now.

Ellen's feet sank in the damp sand as she walked down to the shore line at a portion of the lake front immediately north of the fence enclosing the Jackson Park Bathing Beach.

It was a lonely, deserted spot. The waves beat on the shore. No human being was in sight. Before her, the moaning waters were dark. In the encompassing blackness, she saw the white caps break and foam in a thousand angers. Far out over these black waters was the wind which traveled shoreward, screamed past to drive across Jackson Park, the wind that she had heard so many times, in so many moods ever since she had been a little girl. She would go out and meet that wind. Funny thought. The wind felt nothing. Nothing in the world could feel, really feel, except human beings. But sometimes they felt too much. She had felt too much these last weeks. Now she would feel nothing. It would make no difference then.

She stumbled. She regained her balance.

She moved on steadily. She stood a moment just beyond where the waters stopped and receded. No one was in sight. The water was black. Far out she could see nothing. Across this stretch of dark and mad water, the world ended in empty blackness. She continued to stand by the water's edge.

Should she not do it? Should she pray? What about her father?

Her pocketbook slipped from her hand. She did not trouble to pick it up.

She stepped back and sat down on the sand. She took her shoes off. She dropped her coat beside them. She got up. She walked forward. It was very lonely, and the icy water shocked and numbed her. She was cold, and the waves slapped against her legs and thighs, wetting her, toying with her black velvet dress. She felt soggy. Her clothes were weighted, heavy with wetness. She pushed slowly forward, shivering, half numb.

Just quietly, alone, without tears, she would push on.

The waves rolled by her, splashing her face. She stumbled, but regained her slippery balance. It was difficult moving out against the waves. Her clothing was heavy and dragged on her like lead weights. She was weary. She could scarcely take a step forward. She stood, between waves, and in water up to her breasts.

She should stop, go back before it was too late.

A towering wave knocked her down. She got to her feet slowly, coughing with water in her nose and ears. Her eyes smarted. She sneezed. Now, she was neither cold nor numbed. She would not cry. Let all the waters of this lake be her tears. Let the moaning wind be her cries of unhappiness. She pushed on against the beating waves, on out. She was up to her neck, and the waves buffeted her, swept over her head.

She tried to swim out against the waves. Impeded by her clothing, she went under. Suddenly a blind and powerful instinct to save herself gripped her. Choking and frantic, she fought against the waves. She tried to turn around and swim in. Again she was dragged under. She rose to the surface. A powerful wave enveloped her. Vainly she struggled a short distance out in the lonely lake. It was too late.

Chapter Forty-eight

I

Ed Lanson turned his eyes from the window as the train pulled through the dreary, sooty, industrial district outside Chicago.

He was en route to Cleveland. Why? Oh, he had decided to go somewhere, and the first city that had come to his mind was Cleveland. So he would go there. Just another whim.

He set down the book he had stolen from the Chicago Public Library to read on the train, *The Breaking Point* by Artzy-bashef, a suicide symphony. In fact, there were so many suicides in the novel that he considered it ridiculous.

But it would be a long trip, and he would have time enough for reading. He stretched his feet out on the seat opposite him and reflected that another chapter of his life was closed. What would the next chapter be like? He was curious about it. He hoped that it would not just introduce another female. He wanted a little period of quiet, rest, isolation from the female of the species.

He was traveling the wrong way. It was a kind of blemish on his escutcheon that he should leave on a train with sixty-five dollars in his pocket. This gave him a stake with which to crack a new town. If he had something to go on, he didn't have to use his ingenuity. Well, so be it. He had not felt like bumming his way this time. He had been too impatient Everything had conspired to make him fed up.

Ellen!

He wondered how she was. God, what a mess she had turned out to be! But he was not angry with her. As a matter of fact, he would have to devise a scheme of repayment to her for what

424

she had done to him at Catherine Anne's two days ago. But he would not do it out of motives of revenge. Rather, he would do it out of a realization of the necessity for retribution. She must be taught with one final and conclusive gesture that she could not win the last battle. But as a matter of fact, he felt sorry for her.

What did she want of him when he had made it clear to her that for him, no more of her. Of course, he had never really been in the position where he was torn apart with wanting a female. He had always gotten the female he had wanted, and then he had discovered the feet of clay. Ellen had feet of clay, too.

Yes, he had loved Ellen in his fashion. The rub was that his fashion and her fashion came into conflict, developed contradictions.

He could remember Ellen when he loved her. Yes, he had loved. He had loved her sincerely while it lasted. But *tempus fugit*. Should he send her a note saying only—*tempus fugit*. If he knew Latin, he could send her an excellent letter in Latin. He remembered her, pert and charming, alive and gay, yes, adorable, pretty, her lovely body, her happy laugh, the way she had nestled her arm under his, and the way the two of them would swing along the street. But Ellen was not the sum and substance of life. She was a chapter, a good chapter, too, until she got bitchy at the end. Well, she would get over it. He had a knowledge of the heart of the female of the species. Vanity, pride, habit, possessiveness, many factors came into play in the love of a female. But these would fade away in Ellen. She would change. Perhaps his love affair with her would have taught her something, made her grow up into a woman, and then she would be happy with some other man, and that man would not even know that Ed Lanson had been that fellow's unknown benefactor.

He should be resentful of Ellen because of the names she had called him in Catherine Anne's presence. Catherine Anne had been very upset, and he had had to talk convincingly and very sympathetically to quiet her after Ellen had left. He had

gone to see Catherine Anne thinking that he would go around
with her again, but after the scene with Ellen, that plan was
out of the window. If he returned to Chicago, would he some
day make Catherine Anne? Probably not. It would amuse him
more to retain Catherine Anne. She was a kind of stable and
fixed star in his life. He enjoyed coming back to her every so
often. But something had been left out of Catherine Anne. She
was conventional and afraid. She would not, dare not, break
with her family and her *milieu*. She hung onto her virginity because she feared experience. And he preferred to permit her
to retain that virginity.

He closed his eyes, smiled with gratification, and thought of
Ellen and Catherine Anne. In many ways Ellen was the better
person, the more courageous spirit. But then, he had given the
best of himself to Ellen, and what more did she want?

But now his girls in Chicago belonged to the past. He was
embarked on a new journey. He would move in new scenes
and see new faces. He planned, for a while at least, to settle
down and live an isolated life. He would find a job selling advertising which would not take up too much time, and he would
read a great deal and probably do some writing. The winter
would pass idyllically, and when spring came he might try to
get on the lake boats. Or else he'd go South and get on a ship
for Europe or the East. He had to go to sea; if for no other
reason than that he must surpass his older brother, Pierre.

He did not know a soul in Cleveland, and he anticipated how
he would enjoy his isolation. This time there would be no episodes like that with Hilda in Washington. As a matter of fact,
he was going to be a pure young man and would even stay
at the Y.M.C.A.

Mother? He would write her from Cleveland. He had wanted
to avoid the discussion, the reasoning, the explanations. But
Mother was used to him, used to his popping up here or there.
Mother must have been a wonderful girl when she was young.
Even now she was gay and full of spirit, intelligent, sensitive,
and she had imagination. None of the girls he had known could
touch his mother. She was an exception to all rules. Poor Mother.

He gave her hard going. He didn't like to have her worrying about him. And why should she? He was more than competent to take care of himself. But all his little scrapes, shifts, these worried poor Mother. And Father? Father was a Babbitt, but a Babbitt with qualities. Father respected him. He would some day do something big for Mother and Father. But to Mother he was still her little boy who came home and had jam in the kitchen. It was inevitable. So much was inevitable in the course of human emotions.

Ah, yes, life was droll.

He would go and eat soon.

He wondered what Ellen was doing? What Catherine Anne was doing? And John Devormer? That bag of . . . But why think of John Devormer? John had not wanted to see him go because he made money for John. All John's apcray about a future. And it was amusing, the way John was sensitive because he had played around with Ellen.

Ellen had said she was knocked up. He didn't believe her. That game had been pulled on him before. Women were so unoriginal.

Woman?

Man thinks woman profound—Why? Because he can never fathom her depths. Woman is not even shallow.

This winter he would definitely sit himself down and write his book, a book consisting mainly of epigrams, one after the other. Epigrams and maxims and little paragraphs. And he would read omnivorously. He hoped that Cleveland had a good library. This new life would be an excellent and beneficial change. He would live all alone in a little world of his own thoughts, his own dreams, his own doings. It would even be an interesting experiment to see how long he could remain celibate. Well, they had cold showers at the Y.M.C.A.

The trip was already dragging. He could go on reading. But it was pleasant to sit here, to let his thoughts wander at random, to review experiences in his mind.

He wondered about his chump, Frank Dolan. Frank had

tried to argue him into going back to Ellen. He, however, had tried to make it a clean, swift break, the best kind of break. And he was not to blame if she had made such a mess of it.

He saw the lake, dull greenish gray, dirty and brackish-looking from the moving train window. He loved water. He enjoyed the lake at night, the music of the waves, the moonlight that danced upon it. Now Lake Michigan was wavy, wild, its surface alive with angry white caps. He told himself that the white caps were demons snarling on the wrinkled quilt of Father Neptune. They were small devils dancing madly on the breasts of their mother. The waves were gestures of the powerful lake telling man that he was mortal, and that the immortal lake looked upon him with the amusement of a god who saw men come and go and continued ever to roll its waves in gesture after gesture onto the shore line where man stood in . . . awe. And in fear. The lake was too powerful to be vain, to possess man's little emotions, foibles, peccadilloes. He was proud of his figures of speech about the lake.

But he was hungry now, and he would sit himself down in the dining car and while away the time eating a good meal.

II

The sky was low, leaden. Through the dining-car window, Ed could see the flat fields of Indiana speed away from him. Not interesting scenery; in fact, it was distinctly dull. The landscape of feminine pulchritude seated opposite to him at the table was more alluring to the eye, more comforting to the soul, more relaxing to the mind than was that of the entire state of Indiana. Such being the case, he must neglect the Hoosier state and dedicate his eye to that which was more beautiful.

The girl opposite him was eating a salad, acting as if she were unaware that his eyes were on her. Yes, she was distinctly appealing. She didn't give him the impression that she was overloaded with brains, but then, why should anyone with such lovely red lips need brains. He flashed a charming smile upon her. She gave it no heed.

"I'm very sorry there isn't an open window that I might close for you," Ed said, smiling.

She looked up at him, perplexed.

"I don't understand you."

"The accustomed procedure for a man to meet a woman on a train is for him to perform the service of opening or closing a window for her. At least, isn't that the way it happens in stories?"

"I don't travel much. I don't know."

"I have always understood that such was the procedure. Are you going to Cleveland?"

"Yes."

"Tell me about Cleveland," Ed said.

"I've never been there before. I can't."

"I have never been to Cleveland, either. So let me tell you all about it," Ed said, again smiling graciously.

He won a smile from her.

"What I like best about Cleveland is the way the girls smile."

"How do they smile?"

"Like you do."

She smiled at him again. He decided that he was going to have a very pleasant trip.